JOURNEY'S
ARCANE

JOURNEY'S ARCANE

EDA SCOTT

atmosphere press

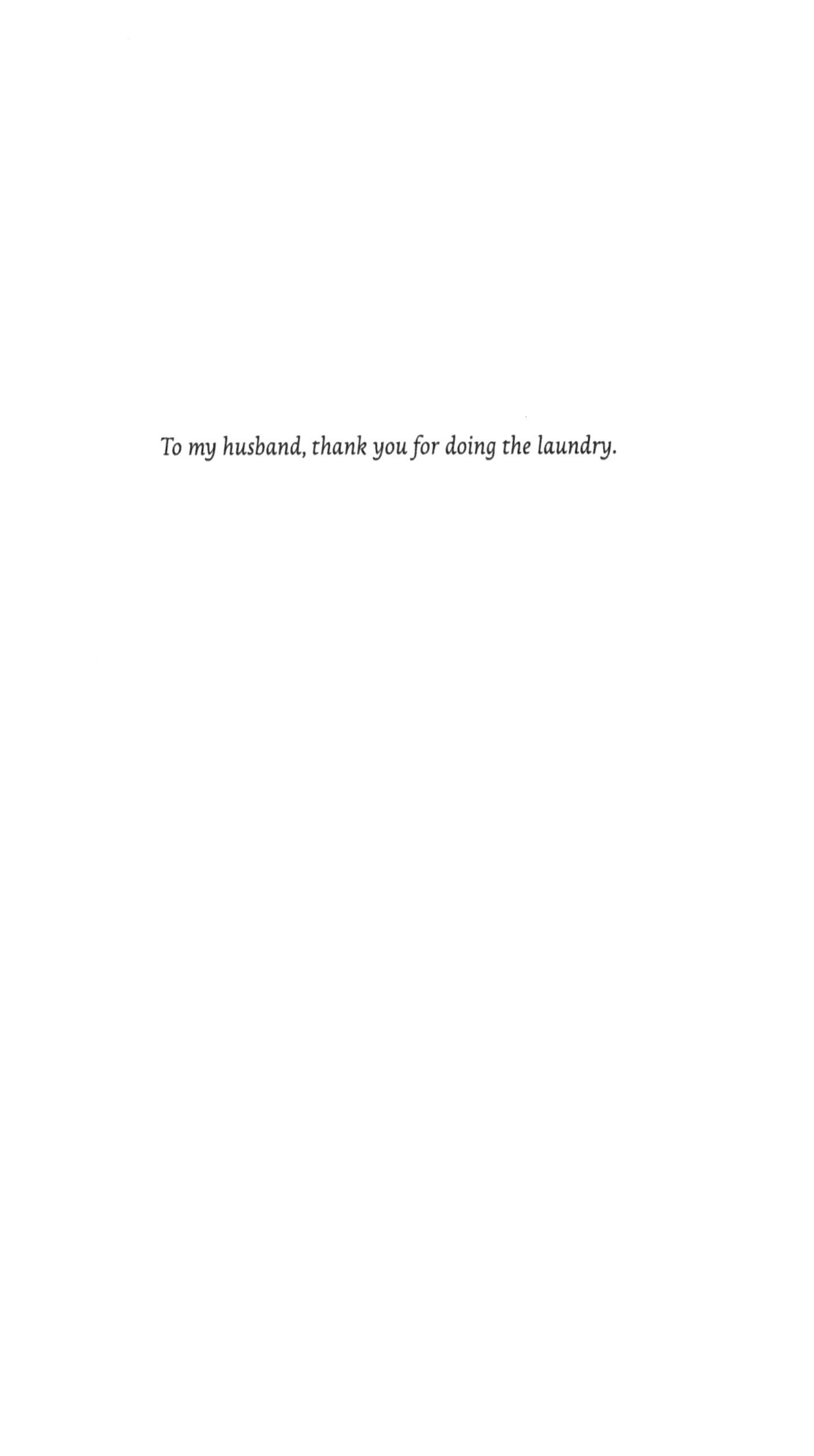

To my husband, thank you for doing the laundry.

CHAPTER 1

It was a little after five when I pulled onto the main street of this small town, the enchantment of which I had fallen in love with years ago. One would not have felt this right now by all the closing signs popping up left and right in the little shops as I traveled farther down Journey's main street. No one could fault them; it was after five on a Thursday evening, and they all had their own lives to get to. I had intended to get here earlier in the day. It should have been an eight-hour drive from my hometown, Puth, North Dakota, but today's trip was not. I couldn't just blame it on traffic, either—there wasn't much traffic on that old two-lane highway to Journey, Manitoba. For most of my trip up, I was accompanied by trucks pulling campers or boats. It was my own doing: when I crossed the USA-Canadian border I stopped at the first town that had a dealership. I underestimated the time required to trade in a vehicle and ended up being off by an hour and a half.

After sitting behind the windshield for the last six hours, there was going to be only one place left that could possibly be an option to be around people again—the local bar. Such as the one at the end of the street that looked as if someone placed a medieval castle upon a little black, boxy tavern. It wasn't a cheesy medieval-themed castle type; it was more authentic. The upper half of the building was tannish and brown brick, or possibly it was all tannish, but the weather and moss had aged a few of the bricks to a browner shade. Besides the coloring of the bricks that gave the building its aged feeling, the castle's appearance came from its shape as there were random brick pop-outs along the wall of the building that looked like mini tower walls. In all truth, this building resembled a castle more than a bar. The bar aspect was more like someone cut out a rectangle on the bottom of the castle and shoehorned in a modern black with gold lettering and trim facade. It was interesting and unexpected for current times to see a building designed such as this one. Generally, the building would have been completely remodeled to one design. I appreciated that the architect hadn't completely remodeled it that way. The originality of the medieval top filled you with a sense of fantasy, while the sleekness of the modern bottom gave you a different sense of romance.

Except for the old, dusty white boxed delivery truck with broken reflective tape that should have spanned the side of the box blocking all the main front parking spots. With it being a delivery truck, I wanted to avoid blocking any access to this truck, so instead I pulled up along the side of the building next to a white stripe sandwiched between two blue stripes that matched the sky above—an old pickup. By the coloring, I'm guessing it was a truck from the 70s—granted, vehicles were not my thing at all.

With the blue truck and the delivery truck only ones there, perhaps the tavern wasn't open yet. This wasn't looking good for me wanting to spend time around people. To make the best of my time while I waited for the bar to open, I was going to park next to the blue truck, then take a walk down Main Street to stretch a little.

I made it to the back of the delivery truck when there was a movement from the box that caught my eye. There was an old fella stacking cardboard boxes. He looked as if he had been at this for the last forty years; his hair was thinning and white, and his lower eyelids dropped down a touch, making him resemble a basset hound. He had to know if the bar was open.

Knocking on the side of the delivery truck's box, I peered in. "Excuse me, sir?"

The fella stopped in his tracks, then jumped out of the truck before me as the corner of his sun-aged lips moved up. "What can I do for you, my dear?"

"Do you know if the bar is open?"

"Oh yes, it is." He chuckled and wiped his brow with the back of his hand. "Now it is me that's running late. I better get a move on it soon; this place is going to be hopping with young lads any minute, and I am blocking the best parking spots." In an animated way, his jaw swung to the side as his left eye closed quickly.

There was that spark in his eyes; I knew he was going to be entertaining. And since I wanted company, he was going to be the best candidate right now. "Maybe I can help you get caught up; I wouldn't mind giving you a hand."

His hands moved to his tan belt against his faded blue work slacks as he examined me. He nodded up at me. "How much can you carry?"

With his mannerisms, there was no hiding my Duchenne smile. "Let's find out."

"That's the spirit, sweetie!"

He gave me one box—it must have been fountain syrups as it made a sloshing sound when I lowered my left hand.

"Good?"

"Good." It must have been about thirty pounds. I could handle more. "Add another."

He placed two more boxes on top. "Good?"

Since they were similar in shape and weight, I assumed they were syrup boxes as well. "Yes, sir."

It was a touch of a struggle now, though I wasn't going to let him know this; it was better I take them than make him carry them. "I'll take another one, please."

He added one more, and my hands sunk a touch. I was just barely up to my neck in boxes. Even being fit, I was probably going to regret this later; I could feel tension running up my neck.

"All right, one more," he cheerfully replied. "It's as light as a feather, but awkwardly large. Are you ready?"

"Yes." I chuckled at his enthusiasm as he placed the last box on the stack, blocking my view.

"Okay, head into the bar and turn left right away. Or just yell for the bartender to come help you."

"Got it."

I struggled a touch with the boxes. Looking down at the street, I tried to gauge where the curb was since my view was blocked by the box that was a foot above my head. This was about to get interesting—I might have overestimated my strength and now I was starting to question the strength of the syrup bag in the event that I made a tumble and the boxes exploded all over the sidewalk. If this happened, in my defense I was walking sideways so I could see my way.

The air went from being filled with the smell of cardboard and warehouse dust to being overpowered by the smell of pine. It was as if there was a real Christmas tree at the entrance of the bar, the scent was so dominating. For being a bar, it was oddly comforting and relaxing, allowing my mind to drift back to what was hidden in the boreal forest that brought me back here in the first place. The comfort reassured me that what I was doing here was justified.

As I was backing into the swinging door of the back room, a gentleman yelled out to me, "Hank..." He grumbled a touch. "I don't know why you do this to yourself. Let me know that you are here, and I will come help you."

I ignored him as I continued into the brightly lit back room. Taking a few steps away from the door, I rested my head against the box blocking my view. Hank had to be a few steps behind me and would vouch for me if Mr. Bartender didn't approve of a stranger in his back room. I hoped that he was—I overestimated my strength with these boxes and didn't know where I could set them down.

Footsteps neared, then the cardboard box before me budged. Without a second thought, I straightened as I watched the box move as if it was a garage door, revealing a gentleman in his mid-twenties with his lips curled up in surprise.

"Oh," his voice softened as his head leaned to the side ever so, "you're not Hank."

"Nope." The boxes were becoming too much for me now; however, I didn't want him to know this. Trying to add a little humor so he didn't realize, I curved the right side of my upper lip up and playfully widened my eyes. "Thanks for taking the lightest box off my stack."

Mr. Bartender didn't move outside of the thumbprint pattern, appearing just below the bill of his cap with the rising of his eyebrows. It was too much for me. I could feel my lips curling as I tried to hold back my giggles. His expression was worth standing here, stretching out my arms with the enormous weight of the fountain syrup boxes.

Wheels from a dolly squeaked past us.

"She's got you there," Hank chuckled as the squeak of the wheels moved away from us.

Mr. Bartender's eyes, hidden behind ill-fitting brown contacts, remained fixed on me as he spoke to Hank. "Well, it's about time they got you some help."

"Help," Hank gasped, "oh no, no, no...I found her on the street."

Mr. Bartender's bushy check-mark eyebrows rose as I bounced mine at him. I knew how he was taking that comment—however, I liked Hank's spitfire personality and was going to play along with him.

"I think I'm going to keep her. What do you think Peggy will say if I bring her home with me tonight?"

I pinched my lips into an O and slowly moved my head side to side. There was a feeling that Mrs. Peggy wouldn't appreciate Hank bringing me home with him, even if she found out I didn't have a proper place to stay tonight. My original plan was to camp out in my new SUV for the night since I only planned on being here a couple hours tomorrow before moving on. The nearest hotel was two hours away from this little town.

"On second thought," Hank paused as he glanced around the back room, "maybe I could just keep her here."

With the shenanigans back on, I moved my head to the side so I could see around the speechless Mr. Bartender as he continued to peer in my direction. With him still watching me, I examined the back room with my lips pressed together. Then I peered around the other side of him with a shrug of my shoulders. It was a standard back room: boxes stacked up, dishes organized on wire shelves by size, a large cooler, and a mop sink in the back corner. I wasn't expecting much more than that, nor was I expecting Mr. Bartender's comical expressions. Hank and I's shenanigans were worth every wrinkle that appeared on Mr. Bartender's forehead from his perplexed expression.

Hank came over and patted Mr. Bartender's shoulder. "I trust that you will take good care of her and not leave her standing here with the heaviest boxes in her arms all night."

I couldn't blame him for standing here baffled; he was caught off guard, and to add to that, I was making silly faces at him. I had to look like a complete dork, but his curved eyebrows and thumbprint forehead were fueling my desire to continue.

My bottom lip pushed out as I gazed up into his contact-covered eyes, mustering my best puppy-eyes sorrow. I hoped he was going to catch on that he needed to take these boxes away before I dropped them on our feet.

"Oh, right." Swiftly Mr. Bartender's hands grazed mine as he reached under to lift the boxes from my hands.

For that split second, I could feel how cold his hands were. I guess that could be expected from handling cold beverages all evening. It must get tiring, constantly trying to warm his hands up between mug after mug of cold beer. It had to be the worst in the winter, for sure—everything was more difficult when you couldn't get rid of the winter nip.

"All right, sweet cheeks." Hank came over and gave me a hug. He drew back a touch. "You play nice with him. I see the ornery twinkling in your eyes."

This was why I loved this town; the people up here were always the best to be around. They treated you as if you had known them forever. I glanced over to Mr. Bartender stacking the boxes on a stainless-steel table. He must have had about four inches on me and a proud chest that stayed in perfect position as he moved about. Outside of his shape, there wasn't much more I could examine of him at this angle. Besides the obvious, he was wearing khakis, with a black button-up shirt and a black baseball cap.

Before it got weird, I turned back to Hank and pinched my index finger and thumb together, almost touching, with my bottom lip out a touch. "Just a little?"

"Of course, sweetheart. How could I say no to you?" He walked over to Mr. Bartender and patted his shoulder. "She's all yours. Be good to her—it's not every day I find one like her on the street."

Mr. Bartender glanced over to Hank, then back to me, mouthing "what" as I gave him a Pan Am smile and two thumbs up.

With Hank gone now, here was the tricky part—do I continue with Hank's mischief, or do I just go sit in the bar and be a normal customer? This poor guy had no clue that we were just messing with him. On top of that, by his pale skin and his hands, perhaps he wasn't feeling well.

"I'm not a street walker." I leaned back with my hips resting on the stainless-steel table and crossed my arms against my chest. "In all seriousness, is there something I can help you with?"

His head rolled over to me, and with a soft closed-lips grin, he said, "Thanks for helping Hank." His eyes moved up from my lips. "But I got it from here."

There was something about how he delivered that look that stopped my heart for a second, then restarted it with a new skip to its beat. I gazed up at him, returning his soft grin, then looked down to the side, trying to hide my ever-growing flirtatious smile. I needed to walk away before I made this more awkward for him.

"Okay." I stood and walked out of the back room to find the restroom.

Before me was my answer to the strong pine smell; there were wooden arch beams throughout the main floor and all along the ceiling. The floor was constructed of flat cream and grey stones in various sizes up to the bar then to the dance floor. The dance floor was a dark pine, almost briarsmoke, that matched the bar's main counter. I let my hand glide against the smoothness of the back of the chair as I continued to the restroom. It almost appeared as if all the chairs were hand-made, with each chair having a different knotting engraving on the top rail and back. Behind the main counter was a mirror in the middle of the wall with a flashing neon light. There were four different beer taps, or perhaps one was a fountain. In today's standards, this would be a themed bar, but despite that fact, everything in here felt genuine and aged. Perhaps it was only the facade that was modern, and the rest of this building was still true to its original days.

Mr. Bartender was behind the bar when I returned from freshening up. There were a few more customers present, sitting at the tables. Just as in the back room, I still didn't want things to get awkward between us with Hank gone, so I sat on the stool at the bar in the far corner, somewhat trying to avoid him and somewhat not wanting to tie up a table if the bar filled up quickly since it was now after-hours and there were only a handful of tables.

On the other side of things, with only being here for the night, I wasn't sure what type of social interactions I should be having with the locals. I wanted to be around people since it was my birthday, and I didn't want to spend it alone. On the other hand, I couldn't get rooted here; I was on a mission. But this was my favorite town I had ever visited. The people here were the best, and the country was beautiful. And now there was that last look Mr. Bartender gave me in the back room—it almost felt as if it kindled something new within me.

"What will it be today?" Mr. Bartender's calm, collected, slightly smoky voice stopped me from drawing my book out of my purse on my lap. Glancing up, he slowly leaned on the counter, resting his arms against it so he was at my level. He was intriguing with his pale features.

Mirroring his stance, I leaned forward. "A double warm green tea in a tall mug and a glass of water, please."

That got me a raised eyebrow. "Umm...okay."

He headed to the back room while I returned my attention to my book. I knew exactly what I was doing, and it had nothing to do with being mischievous with him—quite the opposite.

A tall white mug as large as the water glass next to it drew my attention from Queen Nefertiti arguing with King Akhenaten again in the latest chapter. "Thanks." Glancing up, I handed him the hundred-dollar bill I was using as a bookmark. "Don't worry about the exchange rate. I don't want any change back."

He held the bill up in his left hand. "Are you sure? This is a hundred dollars."

"I know, and I am sure."

There was a subtle snort before he gave me a soft grin. "Thanks."

I watched him add the bill to his till, then he squatted down with one knee up as if checking the inventory of something under the counter.

Leaning back, I scanned the bar swiftly to make sure that this next interaction between Mr. Bartender and me was going to remain just between us. With no one else appearing as if they were going to approach the bar and a deep breath of confidence, I held up the mug by the handle.

"Mr. Bartender," I cleared my throat as he stood up, "will you please take this for me?"

That got his attention; he promptly rushed over to me. "Is there something wrong with your tea?" he asked, grasping the mug in his left hand and inspecting its contents.

"Oh, not at all," I tittered. "In the back, when you were lifting the boxes from my arms, your hands felt cold when they touched mine. I figured"—maybe this was a dumb idea; he was going to think I was crazy—"it would feel nice to hold something warm for once instead of another mug of cold beer. So, the tea is for you." I gave him my best affirmative grin, trying to drive my point home while praying in my head that he didn't think I was crazy. "I hope you like green tea."

The manner with which he held the mug in both hands while the right corner of his lips curled up made it seem as if I had warmed more than just his hands. His thumbs rubbed the handle while his pinkie moved from the underside of the mug up. The way he let out a little snort from his nose and the way his cheeks moved, this was worth every penny. It may have warmed his hands, but his reaction was warming me.

There was something particular about him, perhaps because it was nice to see this reaction. Men in my family did not show emotion unless it was anger, frustration, or any of the other negative reactions. There was more than a softness about him; Mr. Bartender felt familiar. Which was odd—even being here before, I had never met him.

On the other side of the bar, a man in a navy T-shirt and blue jeans sat down.

"I have to help him." Mr. Bartender glanced back at the tea, then one more time at me. "I'll be right back."

Two chapters down, I glanced up, watching a young couple swing about the dance floor. They were a younger couple than I had expected. I had forgotten that the drinking age up here was eighteen; at the tender age of twenty-two, I was now the old dame here. I mean twenty-three as of today, though it didn't feel like my birthday since I was sent up here to handle some business for my sister. Or I was just that old and forgetful now—perhaps I could get a senior discount at the bar like they do at the grocery store.

I watched as the man spun the girl through his legs, then brought her back up to him as she giggled. I wasn't the only one watching them. Glancing down the bar, someone else was leaning against the back counter with his arms crossed against his chest, watching the young couple. Perhaps one of them was his younger sibling and he taught them how to dance. With that endearing thought, I dropped my gaze to my book again.

"What brought you to town?" Mr. Bartender must have caught me grinning to myself as once more he leaned against the wall on the other side of the counter before me.

"If we are going to go down this road," I chortled, "I need to introduce myself first." I held out my hand. "You are less likely to call me crazy if you have a name to call me. I am Nora Carter."

He curved a hook and fist-bumped my open palm. My head dropped to the side and my brows lowered as I glared at him. If I held my hand out to someone, I expected a handshake, not knuckles to my palm. I hated this trend of fist bumping.

"All right." His shoulders bounced with his chuckles and a newfound dorkiness. "I'm sorry." He leaned toward me, grasping my hand, and turned it so he could kiss the top of it. That wasn't dorkiness; that was old-fashioned chivalry. It was sweet and unexpected.

Mr. Bartender straightened a touch, so we were once again at the same level. His cold hand remained under my hand as his pixelated brown contact lenses peered into my eyes. He didn't move, almost as if he was allowing me to study his features.

Moving my gaze from the awful contact lenses, I saw his

skin was copy-paper white, while his eyelashes, eyebrows, and the curls peeking out from his black baseball cap were almost translucent.

"You're albino." The words softly slipped from my lips when I realized he had no pigment anywhere. This had to be the reason for the awful contacts—he wanted a common eye color.

This wasn't the first time I had met a person with albinism. Up until last Tuesday, when I was forced to resign to handle my sister's wedding, I worked as an optical technician. I started working there in my sophomore year in high school. My first year working there, a family came in with their little six-year-old daughter. She was a beautiful mixture of her father and mother, though she was missing their alluring darker skin. Her name was Pearl; she was this colorful, spunky little girl. She was extra special, and no matter what, I hoped it would lead her to having a beautiful life.

"Not quite," Mr. Bartender grumbled, dropping my hand.

"I'm sorry." I clenched my fist and drew it up to my chest. That was so inappropriate. "I didn't mean anything negative by it. I was excited and it slipped out. A few years ago, I met this little girl who was albino. Her colorful personality filled you with the rainbow. All you could do was smile when she came bouncing into the optical." With a deep breath, this was reality. I wasn't going to see her or any of my customers anymore. "Those days are gone, and I'm off to a new adventure." My lip curled as I gave him a wistful grin. "Please accept my apology—I am sorry."

"Hey, Leo." The holler came from a man of average height who appeared to be around the same age as Mr. Bartender. His hair was dirty blond. He brushed off his khaki pants before resting his elbow on the counter, holding his hand out to Mr. Bartender while he flexed his biceps. His thick bottom lip pushed the corner of his mouth up as he gave me a sly grin, his ocean blue eyes bouncing around my body.

And this was why I was sitting in the corner, reading.

I rolled my head toward Mr. Bartender, whom I was now assuming to be Leo, and rolled my eyes, then ducked my head back into my book. The only positive from this new situation was it was a distraction from me offending Leo any further.

"Well, anyways," Mr. Muscles snickered, "Leo, can you come out to the farm later? It was either a coyote or a fox that got into our chickens again."

Peeking over my book, I watched as Leo took his hand. It appeared like he was pretending to struggle to let Mr. Muscles win. That was the only thing Mr. Muscles was going to win in this bar tonight—I was only going to be in town for the night. I would finish my business first thing in the morning, then move on. A one-night stand with a random fellow from the bar didn't interest me in the slightest.

"I'll come out after work," Leo grunted as his hand slammed against the bar. "Tell your parents so I don't end up startling them again."

This made me chuckle a touch to myself. Mr. Muscles still lived with his parents. Not that he ever had a chance, but now for sure I wasn't going home with him. And we were not going to test out the shocks on my new SUV.

"Great." Mr. Muscles stood, patting my shoulder with a call-me-baby wink.

I was going to have a little fun with him. I gave him a large, awkward, open-mouth wink back.

Leo must have been watching. His head rested on his closed fist as he stared at me, baffled.

"What?" I tittered. "I've learned from past experiences that the more awkward you are with a guy, the more likely he is to leave you alone." I picked up my glass, holding it to my lips. "Well, it seems to work on my sister's fiancé when he's..."

"When he is what?"

How did he hear that? I had whispered it into my glass. I didn't even think I said all the words, either. "It's nothing." I glanced up to him. "So, you have an exciting night planned out. Are you going to set a trap or sit out there and wait for the fox?"

"Sit out there." His voice was getting heavier. "What does your sister's fiancé do?"

"How are you going to stay awake? After working in the bar all night, I would be passed out over the mop bucket or in the hen house with the chickens." As much as I didn't want to be hit on right now, I didn't feel like talking about it either. "Do you think chickens are good cuddlers?"

"Nora, please."

I had another way around this. I smiled up at him. "Mr. Bartender, I have introduced myself to you, but I still don't know your name."

"Leon..."

I didn't listen to his last name. I should have, but just hearing that name sparked my excitement. I set my book on the bar and rested my crossed arms on the counter, leaning closer to him. The whole bar didn't need to hear my master plan. "So, Leon the Great."

That stopped him in his tracks for a second from drying the mug in his hand. Possibly no one had ever called him that before. Leon the Great was my favorite Leon in all of history. Mr. Bartender should be taking it as a compliment.

I continued, "The reason I am here is because tomorrow I am heading over to the county office to meet with the county recorder so I can find the owner of a particular property. Then"—this was going to get awkward—"I'm going to pay the owner of the property a hefty amount to say no to me."

He set the clear glass beer mug down, his head tilted to the side a touch. "You are going to pay someone to say no to you?"

"Yes," I squealed as my head bobbed up and down. "It's going to be worth every penny."

His nose crinkled as if I was losing it. "Why?"

After my next statement, he was going to believe that I

was losing it, but at least he would know that I wasn't interested in him. "To show my twelve-year-old self that no matter who you were born to or how you were raised, as long as you believe in love, it will always win."

"Forget the fox tonight," he chortled, rubbing his eyebrows. "I'm going to be here all night trying to unravel understanding you."

"Yeah, sorry." I had no reason not to be honest with him; I was never going to come back to this place after the arrangement was made. I pointed to Mr. Muscles, who was leaning against the jukebox. "Maybe just tell Mr. Muscles over there that you are going to be late, but I'll start talking fast."

Leon pulled a stool over to his side of the bar and set it opposite from mine. "There's no need to talk fast."

"As Leonora Marigold Carter," I held my hand over the bar to him again, "you have my word that I will sweep and mop the bar for you if I get long-winded or if I have you so confused it takes forever to unravel you."

Leon took my hand again, although, before he could talk, another fellow walked up, leaned over, and was resting his shoulder against mine. With his face right next to mine, it was clear that he had a little too much garlic for dinner. There were also the remnants of what must have been a breadstick between his teeth.

"Hey there, babe." His head leaned closer to mine. "You'll want to buy me a drink after I teach you some new moves on the dance floor."

"Oooh, new dance moves." I rested my elbow on the bar with my head on my closed fist. "Like ones that the state record holder doesn't know after thirteen years of dancing?" I didn't let him answer. "Or do you mean horizontal dancing, because I might need a few more days before my antibiotics start working and I'm not contagious anymore."

I watched as he got up without saying a word and walked into the men's room. Leon just stared at me wide-eyed.

"Yeah." I straightened out and shrugged my shoulders. "I know it was cold, but I'm not a one-night stand type of gal. I don't want to lead anyone on. I'm only going to be here until I can get the owner to agree to say no to me."

"Then what happens?"

"Then I get to go be me: no more Snora, no more Marigold, and no more Lee."

Leon's brows lowered. "I might add washing dishes to your list if you keep talking like that. And I need to check your ID."

"It's a deal to washing your dishes." I raised my voice a touch for playful dramatics. "Do you not believe that my name is Leonora?"

"You have rattled off what is now ten names to me." He held his hand out to me, palm up.

"Fine." I slapped my driver's license into his palm. "My older sister, who is getting married, calls me Snora, because I'm boring. To her, everything about me is boring. However, the one thing that drives her crazy is that I held onto the words of that old lady and I follow it to this day."

"Here's your license back and," he leaned over, reaching for his dish towel, "here's a towel."

"This isn't my first trip up here. Ten years ago, when I was twelve, my father thought it would be a good idea—or, more likely, he was pressured into taking my mother, sister, and me on one of his fishing trips. We ended up at the lake just north of here. Sometimes, he would let me go fishing with him, in spite of that fact since his guy friends were up here with their sons, I wasn't allowed to go. Which wasn't shocking; the only time he would let me go fishing with him was when all his friends were busy. I don't know why he would never let me go with him when his friends went with him. To this day he treats me like I'm more of his son than daughter, hence where the name Lee comes into play. Stephanie is his precious, and I was supposed to be his replacement son for the twin boys they lost prematurely."

I held up my index finger as I took a drink of my water. I

was going to have to tell him the real reason my mother called me Marigold before going into the rest of this rat's nest. This poor man had no clue what he was getting himself into.

"I'm just going to get it over with, then I will get back to the story. My mother calls me Marigold because I'm a dime a dozen beauty and I stink. Physically, of course, when I came home after fishing with my father. How do you not smell like fish after handling them all day, then cleaning them? I guess, whatever, this and along with other things, she likes to say it more often than anyone should say to their young child that isn't true, but still is hurtful."

"That's awful." He leaned forward for a second, resting his chilled cheek against mine, before slowly sitting back just enough to gaze into my eyes.

I think he just smelled me, yet I couldn't get past his contacts to comprehend why.

"This isn't fair—you can read my eyes, but your eyes are hidden behind those poorly fitted color contacts. I wish you would take them off."

"Leo," a voice boomed across the bar.

Leon moved to the side of me; it almost appeared as if he was giving someone a wide sneer, exposing his long white teeth. "Okay," he swiftly snapped.

This was odd; it was the first time I had seen his teeth. His smiles were always a closed grin. Which didn't make sense— his teeth appeared to be straight and white, nothing to be ashamed of. They were fitting for his longer face shape and I bet could light up this old dim bar with just a smile.

"Hey, Leo." That oddly deep voice now came from the gentleman towering over me as he took the stool beside me. He was the opposite of Mr. Muscles, with real body-building muscles. For sure, his build was impressive; I felt as if I was two inches tall sitting next to a brick wall. Normally I would have better manners, but I couldn't help it as I studied his features. His extremely short hair was the only thing short on him. Long black lashes framed his narrow, wide-set dark eyes.

Following his just-as-narrow bridge down to his nose was a thinner upper lip and a thick, pouting bottom lip. That was as far as my examination could make it, as my eyes kept being drawn to his massive arm beside me. There was a new desire to poke his upper arm to see if the muscle remained as rock-hard as it appeared or if was softer when relaxed.

"Hey, Sean." Leon gave him a handshake after he stood up. "What do you want to drink?"

"Nah, I'm good." Sean leaned closer to Leon. "The guys and I were talking—" He stopped, glancing over to me. I was busted.

With the heat rising in my cheeks swiftly, I hid behind my book. I wasn't checking him out for my pleasure; I was impressed by the massive work he must have dedicated to his body to be built in that statue. Not only that, but he reminded me of that actor that played in *Armageddon*, *The Whole Nine Yards*, and I think he was best known for his role in *The Green Mile*. I wished I could think of his name, but I was too amazed by the similarities between them.

The desire to drop my book and ask him what he did for a profession was burning within me, mostly to see if his build was necessary for his job. Thankfully, I had more sense than to showcase to these gentlemen that I grew up sheltered. Instead, I kept my nose in my book so he would continue his conversation, hoping to hear if maybe the answer would come out.

"So, the guys and I were throwing around lighting a bonfire and staying out there. After you close, you should come join us."

"I have a fox to handle for Trevor."

And there it was: Mr. Muscles was Trevor. Yet more intriguing was this bonfire. I could never pass one up. Besides that fact, I had no intention of wasting money on a hotel room for one night. My plan was to sleep in the tailgate of my new vehicle but laying around a fire under the stars sounded much more appealing than the top down in a tailgate by myself on my birthday.

"Come on, man, you tell the best stories."

Ooh...there were going to be stories; this was going to be so much better. Slowly I lowered my book just enough to conceal my smile.

"Nora," Leon's attention drew back to me, "is there something I can help you with?"

"Umm, no, but thanks for checking." I turned more toward Sean. "May I join your bonfire? I mean, I was planning on sleeping in my SUV with the top down already for the night, but at least this way the fire will keep the bugs away."

"Who is she?" Sean pointed at me with his hand resting on the bar.

"There are bears out here, Nora. It's not safe for you to be sleeping out in the open by yourself. Why didn't you get a room or something before you got to town?"

"Money, Leon." I dropped my book. "Money. I'm not wasting money on a sketchy hotel for a night when I have a brand-new SUV with a huge tailgate and the stars above me."

His shoulders dropped and his eyes closed for a second. "You bought me a drink with a hundred-dollar bill and told me to keep the change. And aren't you paying someone to say no to you tomorrow?"

"Well, yeah...I have money for things like that. I just prefer not to waste money on dumb things that can potentially give me bedbugs."

"She's doing what?" Sean turned toward Leon. "Who is she?"

"I have no clue," Leon chuckled. "I've been trying to get it out of her for what feels like forever." He leaned on the counter closer to me. "But I do know she has a huge problem with my contacts." He leaned even closer. "Show me who you really are physically."

I sat up as my shoulders moved back—did he just challenge me? And I thought poking Sean's arm would have been inappropriate; essentially, he just asked me to prove to him what was real on my body. My eyes narrowed as I peered into those awful contacts as the right corner of my mouth curled up. Oh, this was going to be easy. He was under the impression that my face was painted on, and my hair was fake.

Reaching up, I was going to start from the top down. I began pulling out bobby pins from my hair. "My hair is my own. It has," I dropped another bobby pin and slid down the hair tie, "never been dyed or will it ever be." Big onyx pop-can curls created from being in a bun all day bounced like bungee cords down my shoulders and chest. Running my fingernails against my scalp, I fluffed my hair. Every time I let my hair down, it was a relaxing feeling to run my nails against my scalp.

I wasn't done yet. I glanced at my glass of water, possibly only a third of a cup full at this point. Again, I leaned right in Leon's face for a second, narrowing my eyes, then swiftly turned to the side of him, grabbing his towel. He was going to need to get a new one.

Sitting back, I held the towel under my chin. "I may be a dime a dozen..." With my other hand, I poured my glass of water down my widow's peak. Setting the glass aside, I gasped from the cold water, then took the towel and wiped my face. Throwing the towel at Leon's head, I said, "But I am not painted like the rest of them."

My shoulder curled in as I lowered to Leon, my lips almost grazing his. "My eyes are my own." And they were—my eyes were my favorite feature of my whole body. Sure, I was of average height at five-foot-seven and thin from running every day, but it was my thick black eyelashes that gave my eyes the appearance I was wearing liner. That wasn't my unique factor, either; it was that my eyes were emerald-green. Only about two percent of the population had true green eyes, and I was lucky enough to be one of them.

There was one place left that women were notorious for enhancing. Glancing between Sean and Leon, I breathed in a little courage. This was going to be embarrassing—granted, he did ask for it. I shifted my shoulder while crossing my arms against the bar, then rested my breasts on my arms, raising them up a touch. My confidence was rushing through me—it was needed, or this was going to be awkward. I slid forward so I was closer to Leon without breaking my gaze from him. "They are real; you are just going to have to trust me on that one." Without control, my left eye gave Leon a sly wink while the right side of my lips remained in a seductive grin.

Wow, my confidence needed to tone it down on the whole sex factor; that wasn't what I was in town for.

I felt Sean's eyes on me, and it wasn't pleasant. By Mr. Bartender's expression, I think if he could blush, he would be blushing.

"I... I... Excuse me," Leon rambled for a second.

He was about to walk away. If I wanted my chance to hang out with these guys tonight so I wasn't alone, I was going to need to convince Leon to let me join them. By the scowl Mr. Brick Wall was giving me, there was nothing I was going to be able to do to change his mind.

Gently I rested my hand on top of Leon's, curling my fingers into his palm before he had a chance to take a step away. "Please, may I join you?"

His gaze was fixed on our hands. With his head down, there was no way to read his expression now. Possibly this was offensive to him; people didn't like people in their bubbles. Swiftly, I drew my hand back and hid both in my lap. Maybe I just needed to approach this differently to get my way.

"As was Leonidas I and Leon the Great, I believe the Leon before me is a man of his people." I leaned to the side and, with a stern look, glared into Sean's eyes. "Who will be deciding if I may join in tonight."

Sean's eyes widened, then stiffly he turned toward Leon. I wasn't going to let Sean's input ruin this—it was time to plead my case to Leon.

"I know how to handle Mr. Muscles and Mr. Casanova over there. When I'm not being a dork, I am quite pleasant to be around. I have no intentions of any shenanigans; I simply wish to be around people while I sit and read my book."

"Leon," Sean muttered with a cock of his head.

I needed to drive this home; I didn't want it to come to this, but not tonight, not on my birthday did I want to be alone. It didn't matter how cool I thought glamping in my SUV was going to be; I just wanted to be around people. My bottom lip pushed out a touch. "If I start flipping chairs, then start sweeping, may I please join you guys after I finish mopping?" That wasn't some line I was feeding them to get my way—I was more than willing to help to make Leon's evening easier. Especially if he wasn't feeling well.

Trevor—Mr. Muscles—sat on the other side of Sean, instantly drawing Sean's attention to him. This was a good thing for Sean and me. It felt as if the more I talked, the less Sean liked me. I don't know why, unless Mr. Casanova shared his first experience with me—in that case it was fair. At some point that was bound to come back and bite me.

"Do you really have no place to stay tonight?" Leon sat back down on his stool on the other side of the bar.

"I do." My head tilted to the side a touch giving him a soft grin. He didn't need to worry about that. "I have my new SUV; it's more that I want to be around people a little longer tonight. I guess after my meeting tomorrow, my next quest will be finding a new place to call home. Between these two countries, there are a lot of miles to cover, so I feel like I'm going to be spending a lot of lonely time behind the windshield." As much as I loved this little town, this wasn't going to be it. I had my reasons why I couldn't stay here and had my sights set on further north to Alaska.

Leon tittered, "That is not a place to stay; it's a form of transportation."

"For the next few weeks or so, it will be both for me. I've got it all planned out." I had already made a fool of myself by telling him why my mother called me Marigold. I didn't want to disgust him with the thought that I was an unhygienic person. "I have an app on my phone showing me all the comfort stations along any of my routes."

He rested his cool cheek against my cheek once more as his breath gently danced into my ear. "She was wrong—you don't stink; you smell as beautiful as lilacs on a spring morning after a rain."

CHAPTER 2

Leon didn't get an explanation as to why I was paying some-one to say no to me and I didn't get to help clean the bar after it closed. Instead, Trevor had me follow his oversized hunter-green F-350 truck out to the countryside. I was expecting the bonfire to be along the shoreline of the lake; however, it was along the outer edge of the forest where the lights didn't pollute the sky and the insects provided the score to set the mood, peaceful and calm. Well, that is, until a group of rowdy guys showed up blasting their music. Laying in the tall grass admiring the stars wasn't going to happen tonight. Just like most bonfires back in the States, I ended up on one side of the fire with all the local girls, chatting. The guys were either gathered around the bed of one of their trucks or on the other side of the fire. Once in a while, a boyfriend or another guy would stumble over to us, though the girls would swiftly usher them back to his own side before picking up where they left off in their story.

As I listened to one of the girls talking about her third year of college in the States, I peered through the flames of the fire to see that Mr. Bartender had finished closing the bar and was now seated next to Sean on the log across the fire from us. He must have come straight from the bar as he was still in his khakis with the black button-up shirt and black baseball cap. By the lowering of his eyes, it didn't seem as if he was interested in what Sean was saying. From my view, it almost appeared as if he was zoning out into the fire. This would be justified; he had worked all evening at the bar by himself. Despite that fact, his lip pressing in the corner, causing a deep crease above them, would give him away. Thankfully, I would be pulled back into the girls' conversation before our gaze meeting over the flames became that weird awkwardness.

That didn't stop me from glancing back across the fire on occasion. Once in a while, our eyes would meet. The last unfortunate time, I was met with narrowed, scowling eyes and thick, pinched lips. I didn't know what I did to Sean in our first ten seconds of meeting each other, but it felt like he didn't like me in the slightest. Back in the bar, he was incredibly vocal that I shouldn't be invited to this fire. To sum up his words: I was stranger danger, basically. With a few girls standing behind me, Sean was outnumbered, and I was invited out.

As the night carried on, more and more people left the fire. It had to be nearing around two when it was only Leon, Sean, Trevor, and me remaining. More than anything, I just wanted to lay down and go to sleep. The best I could do for now was rest against the log that I had been sitting on all night as a pillow and snuggle into my half-grey, half-pink hooded sweatshirt.

I watched as Leon walked away from Sean and Trevor, only to stop before me. He began to kneel before he fell onto his butt in the dirt, then kicked his legs out straight toward the fire. Once situated, he gave me another one of his soft grins. With him beside me now, I was able to breathe in more of his enticement over the fire scent. One would not have known it from our silly grins to each other all night through the fire, but this was the first time we were near each other out here tonight.

"Are you going to finish your story from the bar? I would like to hear your reason for paying someone to say no to you."

"Seriously, are you going to pay someone to say no to you?" Baffled, Sean moved to my other side. "How much are you going to pay this person to say no to you?"

"What?" Trevor tittered as he joined us on the other side of Sean.

I drew my hands into my sleeves, then hid them by crossing my arms against my chest as I softly spoke. "Fifty thousand dollars, but they'll have to sign a contract saying they will refuse any offer from anyone else. I hope they are honorable—after this, I won't have the funds for a legal team to go after them if they take both offers."

"Hold up, fifty thousand to say no!?" Sean started cackling. "You are a crazy American, throwing your money around to get your way." He nudged my shoulder with his as his voice smoothed out. "I already said no to you. Where is my fifty thousand?"

It didn't matter anymore that Sean disliked me; he was off-putting with his attitude.

"You're right." I leaned forward as I glared back at Sean and sneered. "But here you are, sitting right next to me. And I know that you have this image of me in your head, but it's all wrong. I am only here to save a historical site in your hometown from being desecrated and turned into a roadside attraction by my family." I gestured toward the fire. "Call me whatever you want, misjudge me all you want; I don't care as long as it's from the other side of the fire."

Leon's arm rested on my shoulder as he drew me back, so I was somewhat resting on the side of his chest. He must have wanted his answers, and he was going to pin me here until he got them. Fairly, for sure—I was being unjust to him. In my mind it was as if he was watching a show with commercial break after commercial break. Utterly frustrating when all you wanted to do was see how it was going to end. If I was going to get through this, I needed to stop focusing on distractions and just get it out already.

I fixed my gaze on the fire, watching it dance for the heavens. "My sister is getting married, and she wants the wedding at one of the properties up here. I wish it was that simple, but it's not. For the exterior, so far, she wants the property painted matte black with white skull spotlights projecting on it. She wants an eight-foot moat dug around the property with the water dyed blood-red. In the interior, she wants any remaining original pictures of the king repainted to include blood dripping from his mouth as he holds a severed head. For any other pictures, she wants blood painted dripping from their eyes." I closed my eyes; this was animal cruelty at its finest. "And the worst one is she wants live bats hanging upside down from the chandeliers. She doesn't care if they have to be glued to it—she wants it."

Leon, Sean, and Trevor all looked as if they had seen a ghost with their wide eyes and mouths dropped a touch.

I snorted. "I know, right, we just got out of a pandemic caused by people mishandling bats and now she wants this."

Trevor reached over the log. "What is wrong with your sister that she would ever want a wedding like that?" He pulled over a clear bottle with golden liquid in it. After taking a swig, he passed it to Sean.

"I didn't grow up watching cartoons like my friends. My mother and sister would have horror movie marathons. Dracula, Frankenstein's monster, mummies, zombies, other monsters, demons, and every type of killer, I have seen them all. They love them so much that this is the type of wedding that she wants to have. And if you are Stephanie, you get everything you want. She's your spoiled, rich American."

"There's no way your father could agree to this." Sean handed me the bottle after he took a drink. "Is he around?"

This was different—he was now offering me a drink. I couldn't help smiling as I accepted the bottle. "Thanks. It's easier to just say yes to his precious than have to deal with her and my mother against him." The liquid swirled around as in my head I tried to figure out if this was rum or another amber-colored liquor. "My father is never around. We may come from old oil money, but he's either working or fishing. And that is all you will get out of him; however, he does give nasty glares for free."

When my father was around, he lived in front of the television. Outside of his fishing trips, there was no point in traveling the world when he could watch it all from his television. There was no point in being present in your family either when you could just join a fake one on the latest top hit sitcom.

"Don't drink that," Leon whispered into my ear, trying to reach around me for the bottle. "You're going to regret it in the morning."

His hand pressed into my chest, his thumb just barely between my breasts as I leaned forward so he couldn't reach the bottle with his other hand. A bartender was telling me not to drink something while the other two already had. Forget the expert, I was interested.

But then again, I wasn't one to go against the grain—or, should I say, without approval first. I leaned back, only turning my head in his direction. "Please can I just try a little?" I peered up through my eyebrows with my bottom lip pushed out just a touch. "Just a little?"

His shoulders dropped—it worked. I was going to get my way. I didn't see the harm in it if the other two had just taken a drink. Why couldn't I? I was way over the legal drinking age and not driving anywhere. In no way was I going to regret one drink in the morning; I had a stronger tolerance than that, even with not drinking often.

"I own the bar." Leon leaned past me, defeated, toward Sean and Trevor. "There's no reason for busting out that stuff anymore."

"It's your recipe." Sean's left brow dropped as he examined me. "And it's a tradition."

Forget Sean's look—that's all I needed to hear; now I was curious. I pulled the cork out, and the bottle welcomed me with a *pop*. How cool was it going to be to drink from a bottle that had a cork, like a pirate? Perhaps it had been aged since the pirate times. That thought only excited me more.

My nose hairs singed as I took a sniff of the open bottle. On second thought, maybe I should have listened to Mr. Bartender. I watched from the opening of the bottle as the liquid swirled around—when would I ever have the chance to drink pirate whiskey? This was going to happen. I held the smooth glass so it barely touched my lips and poured it into my mouth. Instantly it burned the coughs right out of me as it hit the back of my throat. I was going to be three sheets to the wind if I took another drink of that. Leaning forward, trying to contain my coughing, I held the bottle behind me for the next brave soul to try.

A chilly hand rubbed against my upper back. "I should have warned you about the burn." It was Leon. "If you were to drink more, it'll get better."

I fell sideways onto Leon's legs. "I just drank amber-colored rubbing alcohol. I mean, I am planning on starting a new life, I just didn't think it was going to start six feet below the ground and the rest of me above here."

Slowly Leon moved forward until he was blocking my view of the starry night. His eyebrows pinched, giving him abstract wave patterns on his forehead. Minus his horrendous contacts, his expressions were priceless, and this one was right up there, giving me the giggles.

"Nora, what do you mean by that?"

I couldn't tell you what he just said; I was again distracted by his expression. Blowing it off, I was going to explain myself to him so he didn't think I was a lightweight. I shook my index finger toward Leon's face. "Hank told me I needed to play nice with you." I examined his raised cheek. "But if you keep giving me these looks, I can't keep my side of that anymore."

Biting my lower lip, I tried to hide my Duchenne smile

from growing, but the way his right brow dropped, I couldn't. "This might be the weirdest compliment I have ever given, but here it goes." I inhaled courage, hoping he didn't find this offensive. Exhaling, I decided I would blame the moonshine if he did. "By far you have the best perplexed expressions; from the first one to this one, I just…" I wanted to say I loved them, but I wasn't sure if I should be using that word with him.

"What?" Leon tittered, interrupting me.

He heard me. His head lowered and his lips duck-billed out, moving closer to his nose as his eyes widened. The widening eyes was the creepy factor, but for all that, his lips made up for it. I giggled as his lips lowered. Playfully, I squeezed his cheeks. His head lowered further, and I released his cheeks just enough for his lips to relax. My eyes moved from his lips to his eyes. More than anything I wished he would remove those contacts. I could play out in my head what was going to happen. Granted, I wanted to get lost in his eyes before it did. I wanted to see his desire projecting from his eyes, not just his movements.

"Dude." Sean's chuckle stopped Leon in his tracks, then Leon sat up. "That was weird. It had to be a backhanded compliment."

"Wrong," I growled as I sat up, now facing all of them, mixed with annoyance and panic. "I think they are cute, and I love it when he does it. In no way was that meant to be an insult." Nor did it seem that he took it as an insult. Maybe if Sean had given us a moment longer, he would have seen the truth.

"Nora," Leon moved back to his original position, "come back and finish your story about paying someone to tell you no."

Now here was the thing—should I sit up to him again or beside him? A moment longer with him before Sean interrupted us would have been the deciding factor. Perhaps I was reading him wrong and nothing was going to happen.

"Right here." Leon's index finger tapped his left pec. "Come keep me warm."

Sean and Trevor's mirrored each other as their heads simultaneously turned toward Leon. "Leo, I thought..."

Leon waved his left arm at Trevor, almost as if muting him.

This man wanted his answers, and I wanted to be next to him, not really giving him his answers. He was going to think I was crazy after he got them. I think it was going to be hard for people to understand my actions going forward or to believe my past unless they had lived in a situation as I had. We may have appeared to be that *all-American family*, but behind closed doors we were far from it. When I crossed that border this morning, I promised myself I was going to free myself from my family in every way possible.

Trevor held out his hand for the bottle. "So, your family is a real piece of work, but how does that tie in with her getting married up here?"

"Or we should be asking are you truly protecting this place or," Sean tossed the bottle to Trevor, "just trying to be spiteful toward your family for revenge? Because it sounds like there is favoritism and it's not you."

"Oh, there is favoritism, although this isn't about me." I shifted my shoulders more up against Leon. Even with the fire, it was getting cool out here. "My first thought when she told me that she wanted to get married up here was about how disrespectful it was towards Leon the Great. I get that he died hundreds of years ago, but that story the sweet old lady at the campgrounds told me ten years ago cemented within me."

My heart dropped as the image of her sweet face—with dimples and a nose that was almost a heart—was being replaced with the realization that if you threw a wig on Sean, rounded and softened his features, he could pass as her. My heart thumped a little harder as I stared at Sean. They were from the same family tree; she must have been a great-aunt or grand-mother to him. Out of all the people here tonight, the one that wasn't keen on me was a relative to the one lady I wanted to track down while I was here. This was somewhat problematic;

I had a couple things to give to her. Possibly, if Sean was willing, he could help me track her down if they were related. I didn't have much to go on, except her description and where she worked at one point. As much as she guided me through life, the regret of never getting her name was heavy. To me, she was the sweet old lady from the campgrounds with magic in her heart.

"Can I help you?" Sean sneered at me, making me realize I was still staring at him.

"Oops," I tittered as I picked up Leon's hand and locked my fingers into his. Without looking up, I continued, "Sorry about that. I was just picturing that sweet old lady again, and a few of your features resemble her. In fact, your nose—I remember her nose was the same, but smaller than yours." This wasn't helping; Sean's eyes were narrowed as if he was putting up the defense with me again. "I'm sorry. Do you have a female relative that worked at the campground just north of here ten years ago?"

Trevor handed me the bottle, his expression dropping. Now this wasn't good either; he was mourning someone or getting me ready for Sean to unleash on me for staring at him.

Leon curled his arm, taking my arm and hand with him. "No more for the night. This isn't good for you, and I would like to hear the reasoning for paying someone to say no to you."

"My grandmother did." Sean softly spoke. "For many years she watched over this area." His eyes met mine, glistening with new shorelines. "She passed away two years ago."

My heart ached as it dropped. I just wanted a chance to pay my respects to her, though not in this manner. There was no hiding the disappointment from my cheeks; I needed to tell her thank you. I needed her to tell me that she was proud of me after all these years of holding on. I released Leon's hand. I didn't care if Sean was cross with me—I think we both needed each other at this moment.

Swiftly I wrapped my arms around Sean and rested his

head on my shoulder. "I met her only once—in spite of that, she was such a beautiful lady inside and out. She gave me so much guidance." I rested my head against his and softly whispered to him, "Sometimes the person that we least expect will impact our lives forever. Gosh, your grandmother saved me that day in so many ways."

Sean didn't move as I drew back, wiping my tears off his head. This was too much. I needed to step away. I didn't know these men, and I was being emotional in front of them. This couldn't have been comfortable for them, and there was only so much left in that bottle. I held up my index finger to the guys, then walked away. I wasn't just walking away—I had written her a letter, thanking her for her time that day, then I had added something a little extra to the envelope. The envelope was in my glove box, and since she was no longer with us, the best course of action was to give it to Sean.

Hanging half in and half out of the passenger-side door, I checked myself one more time in the visor mirror to make sure I wasn't a snotty mess. With a deep breath and the envelope in hand, I composed myself before heading back. I didn't want them to think I was leaving after drinking their pirate whiskey. Nor did I want to make them uncomfortable with the thought that I was having some breakdown.

The yelps, croaks, buzzes, clicks, and rustling of the leaves from the forest returned as I gazed above, walking back to the bonfire. Allowing my mind to drift away from the last ten minutes, I couldn't figure out why they didn't have a bonfire down at the lake. The sky reflecting into the water would have been alluring. Although, with the stars above breathtaking, there was no reason to admire their reflections.

"Are you all right?"

"Aaaaah!" I shrieked. Folding myself forward, I giggled at my overly dramatic reaction. I had been so in my head and with my eyes toward the heavens that I didn't realize Leon had met up with me.

Standing back up, I said, "Of course," then stretched up to kiss his smooth cheek. "I have something for Sean. On second thought, I'll meet you back at the fire." Before he could say anything, I turned around to head back to my SUV. I knew exactly what Leon needed—as he said earlier, I was supposed to keep him warm. So far, this man had a chill like no other; I needed reinforcements to get the job done.

Back at the fire, I knelt before Sean and handed him the envelope. "This was for your grandmother. Please use it to do something in her memory."

Leon had his arm resting against the top of the log. That was all the invitation I needed. I sat in his open arm, up against his chest. Then I unrolled my gold-and-white flannel blanket, covering our legs and part of my torso.

Trevor took a drink as he weaved over, handing me the bottle. "This will help with the cool night air."

Even sloshed, he was still being sweet. "Thanks, buddy. Do you need a hand back down?"

"Nope," he wobbled back to his original spot, "I'm still good."

As much as this was the best position to be in right now, there was still that lump in my throat that I had missed my chance of ever seeing her again by just two years. I took a larger swig from the bottle before Leon could object. I wanted the alcohol to burn away that lump of pain in the back of my throat from disappointment. I didn't need sorrow looming around with these guys. I just needed the alcohol to wash it away for tonight.

"Holy Nora," Sean yelped. "There's over seventy thousand dollars in here!" His head slowly turned toward me as his eyes became inverted moons. "Are you dying or something?"

"She is going to be if she takes another drink of that." Leon held out his hand as the blankets fell down on us. "Can I have the bottle back, please?"

"Nope." I grinned softly up at him, admiring his features from this angle. He possibly had the cutest nose for a man.

There was this slight indent at his supratip, giving it more character. His nostrils seemed like they arched up a touch, but from the side, it was because his nose pointed up. And not in a pig nose or snobby way, only ever so slightly to give him a button tip.

"There has to be more to this." Trevor's glossy eyes moved from the envelope to Sean. "There's no way all your grandmother did was tell her the story of King Leon."

From glossy eyes to a snarl again, Sean's brows lowered. "What story did she tell you about him?"

I stretched my legs out, making sure not to uncover Leon and myself any further. "He was an honorable king, a man of his people; without second thought he was always there to help anyone in need." Of course, my conversation with Sean's grandma contained more than that; I just wasn't ready to share. "That's why he is also known as Leon the Great."

"Have you ever," Leon's words tickled my ear, "seen a picture of Leon the Great or looked him up?"

"Nope." That was an easy answer. Fear stopped me from looking him up. Love stopped my imagination from filling in what I thought of him. I told myself growing up that the man I married would fill in the image of Leon the Great. Could I tell three guys this? Nope. I didn't need them thinking I got here on the crazy train.

"What?" Trevor had to be getting lightheaded. His head jostled toward me and he pointed his index finger at me. "The story changed your life, but you have had no interest in seeing what your king looked like?"

"First of all," I sat up, turning to him, "he's not my king." I sat back into Leon and lowered my head against his chest as my voice lowered as well. "Fear is why I cannot look him up."

"Nora," Leon lifted my chin so I would look at him, "why?"

First stop on the crazy train—Leon was going to get the real reason I was fearful of Leon the Great's image. "What happened was I was banned from swimming, so I dragged my sister along with me to go explore. I was trying to do anything to get away from the campgrounds. See, there was this situation growing, and I didn't feel comfortable being alone there. Anyways, we ended up finding this castle. As two excited little girls, we rushed back to the office of the campgrounds to find any local to tell us more about the castle. On the porch were two ladies, Sean's grandmother and another. Well, his grandmother tells my sister and I all about Leon the Great. Her voice was amazing; it painted pictures in my head of back in that time. Then she stops, but the other lady fills in her own ending."

"I would like to see that seventy-thousand-dollar painting that my grandmother painted in your head."

This late or this early in the morning, all Sean was going to get was the discounted knockoff because the seventy thousand dollars had nothing to do with the king. I didn't feel like going around with him at this hour. "According to your grandmother, this king wasn't a womanizer; he was waiting to find the one that he truly loved. Kings across the world would bring their beautiful daughters here for King Leon. Their beauty didn't matter; he would send them off. It was never right in his heart; he wasn't going to settle until he found the right one, royal or not." I swung my index finger at Sean and Trevor. "That is why I am paying someone fifty thousand dollars to say no to me. King Leon believed in love. What my sister and Ivan have is far from love—plus, they are going to destroy King Leon's legacy with all their obscene demands."

"Give her another drink." Trevor tossed the bottle down. "That was far from a seventy-thousand-dollar painting."

"The money has nothing to do with Leon the Great and everything to do with... Forget it. The fifty thousand is to stop what the other lady told us from coming to life."

"What could that other..." Trevor leaned away from us for a second, then moved right back to an upright position, "lady have possibly said that they would want to glue bats to the lights?"

There was no way Trevor was going to last much longer with the way he was starting to sway. Sean, on the other hand, seemed like he was using it as fuel to fire off more and more questions at me. Leon, who I hadn't seen take one drink, stayed quiet behind me. His presence was only known because he would tighten his arms around me after failing to grasp the bottle from my hands.

"According to the other lady, one of the fathers became enraged at the thought of someone refusing his daughter. I don't remember if it was a curse or had him bitten, but anyways, Leon the Great became a vampire."

"Good god," Sean rolled his head toward me, "that was Thelma. It had to be Thelma; she was the only crazy goat that ever talked about things like that."

"I hate that whole scare factor horror movie crap." I clenched my fists. "I hate it. And for how much I hate it, I do not believe in it either. But Thelma's words that day scared me more than any horror movie I have ever watched. I would like to add that I was forced to watch every black-and-white or colored crazed creature, evil person—but for whatever reason, her description put an ounce of realism in me. Laugh at me all you want, but to this day I will not look him up. For fear that it will give life to her words. And he will haunt my dreams, until I have no more."

"I might have some silver bullets in my truck," Trevor tittered. "You'll be safe if he is what she says he is and shows up."

"That's werewolves..."

Sean cut me off. "I'm up for a good campfire scare. Tell me what that crazy goat told you."

The fret in my chest was growing—what was I doing? I was in the middle of nowhere with three guys that I didn't know, about to tell them dreadful things about someone who showed me men were born with the same love I had in my heart. It was wrong. "For respect for the deceased, no more needs to be said about him."

"Maybe he's not dead," Trevor's voice lowered, "but in the trees over there, listening and just waiting for the right time to strike."

I tipped my index finger away from my forehead toward Trevor. "Good luck to you and it was nice to meet you."

"What?" he chuckled. "Why am I going to die?"

With his silver bullet comment, I shouldn't have been surprised that he didn't understand why he would be axed first. "If you truly believe in this crap, whores die first, and virgins survive." I shrugged my shoulders and gave Trevor a grin. "Mr. Muscles, I feel like you're not so pure by your game with the other girls tonight."

Sean leaned over to Trevor, looking up at him. He snatched the bottle from him. "In case you couldn't figure it out, she just called you a man-whore, like the one that you are."

For whatever reason, that struck something within Sean, and he fell over into Trevor, laughing. The lighthearted glares and endearing banter reminded me of sitting around the fire with my friends back home in Puth. These three here must have grown up together for this behavior with each other. Leon wasn't bantering with them as much, but I could see him being there, giving the other two just as much grief.

And with that, Leon had to be exhausted from working all night, then sitting out here. Maybe if I took the first step, the other two would follow so Leon could go to bed.

I watched the other two go back and forth about whatever as I leaned against Leon's chest. "With the drive up here, I've hit my peak. It's going to be all downhill from here if I don't get to bed soon." I tried to gaze past those awful contacts. "Thank you for sharing your friends and bonfire with me." I couldn't do it—they were too much—and my eyes moved down to his lips. His Cupid's bow was more of a soothing wave, not so sharp and defined, more of the calm morning wave washing against the shoreline with two wide ripples. "I appreciate your kindness."

It was no joke that I had hit my peak; I must have zoned out in his lips. I didn't realize the tip of his thumb and index finger moved my head up until those contacts were back in my view again.

"Don't leave." He spoke softly, as if he didn't want the other guys to hear him. "I would like to hear the rest of your story. If you leave now, I may never get to."

"Aren't you tired from working at the bar all night?"

His arm moved down from my shoulders to my back and tightened against my torso. "It's worth it to have your warmth against me on this cool night."

It was a good thing that the fire was giving everything an orangish-red glow; all my warmth was resting on my cheeks. Perhaps we could just skip the story for the night, snuggle in a little more, and then continue in the morning light. Nevertheless, I was going to need a way to suggest that to him. If I wasn't able to sleep in my car because of bears, I had no idea how I was going to sell this new idea to him.

"Tell me what Thelma said," he whispered to me.

He had no game. We just went from a hopelessly endearing moment to wanting to meet the guard at the gates of Hell.

My nose crinkled and I whined, "Please tell me that you are not a horror fan." That would be my luck; he was an attractive, enchanting gentleman with a freakish love of horror that stemmed from growing up with the urban legend of Leon the Great. I would need to note this going forward if that was the case: make sure not to settle down in a town with an urban legend.

"I'm not. Nonetheless, if her words could give you such a fright, I'm interested in what they are."

That was a relief—however, he was still expecting his answers. "You are going to regret this." I dropped my head into his chest. "His hair was black as the haunted night sky; his ears were long and narrow. There were thick black hairs protruding from them, giving them the appearance of tarantula legs creeping out. His neck was twice as long, yet you would never know it; he carried himself hunched over until he lunged at you. His eyes were slit like snake eyes, but with blood-red irises. When you looked into his eyes, you knew death was coming. His nose was sunken in, almost as if it had been cut off. If you were to get a look into his nose, your eyes would be met with the eyes of the spider from his ears. His lips had four gaps or slits for his four canines that were three times larger to be exposed. For the rest of his teeth, it was as if someone took a file to each one to turn them into daggers."

Squinting my eyes closed wasn't enough for this next part. I pressed my fingers into the corners of my eyes until I saw loud black and white geometrical shapes as I tightened my other arm around Leon's torso. "His tongue slithered as if it were two snakes, each in control of itself, because his tongue was sliced down the middle. He enjoyed taunting his victims—he would stick one part in their ear, while the other half rubbed down the exterior of their ear. When he had enough of the squirming with fear, he would bite their ear off. When the blood would run down their arm, onto their hand, then fingers, he liked to wrap his tongue around their fingers to squeegee the blood off. And speaking of fingers, his nails were black points, again like daggers, with one side serrated. He used the serrated side to slice the throats of his victims so their blood would flow out of them from the arteries showering him. The only warmth that he could feel was that of human blood—it was his warm shower."

Leon shifted a touch as if he was getting uncomfortable sitting on the dirt. Or he was getting uncomfortable with me, which would be understandable; I was this new little thing in his bubble and currently squeezing his torso to comfort me as I recited those words I never wanted to speak. In my defense, for whatever reason, I was drawn to him. Even with that, I didn't want to make him uncomfortable.

"Would you like me to move?"

He pinched his lips over his teeth and slowly moved his head side to side. He must not have enjoyed horror or didn't believe me that it was going to be that awful.

"I'm sorry," I sighed, "there's more. To wrap it up, he was a shapeshifter. He would transform into a bat and taunt his next victim, whispering into their ears that they were going to die. Or he would tell them how it was going to be painful and messy." I shrugged my shoulders. "Her account was more detailed than the one I just gave you. I'm sure that I missed something because I had never been more scared in my life. I could feel the color drain from my face and be released in one constant stream down my left cheek."

"Holy shit," Sean mumbled. "Where's the bottle?"

For the first time in the last hour, Trevor's arm moved straight out, without the slightest weave, as he handed the bottle past Sean to Leon instead. He must have been a good friend of Leon to know that he didn't enjoy the horror genre. Or he was able to read him to see that he was stressed from my story. It wasn't that I wanted to stress anyone; they were the ones asking to hear what was said.

"What was said next?" Leon put his hand up to refuse the bottle, then tucked it back under the blanket against me.

"I don't know if anything else was said, my ears were ringing with fear. I stood there paralyzed. Sean's grandmother picked me up and tossed me over her shoulder. She walked us away from I'm assuming my sister asking Thelma a thousand questions to a small semi-enclosed bay. She sat me down in waist-high, calm water. I remember there was a bloop in the water and her telling me to look below the surface. I asked her if she needed help finding something, and she told me that she did, but first I was supposed to tell her," I tapped Leon's head, "what I thought in there happened to King Leon. My response was it was possible that a father did have him off like the mob does. Her head bobbed slightly as if she was process- ing it in her mind. Then she tapped my chest, asking me to tell her," I tapped his sternum, "what I thought happened to him, but it must come from in there."

Moving my hand back down, I locked my fingers into Leon's, then rested his hand against the palm of my open right hand. "I didn't say anything. I kept my head down, watching my hand on the rocks below the water. She told me it was okay for me to take my time, she had nowhere to be but right here with me. For whatever reason, her telling me that gave me a sense of comfort. I sat there for a moment longer, watching two little juvenile fish trying to eat my painted pinkie nail. Without looking up, I went on to tell her that King Leon knew other countries were overthrowing the monarch. Never did he think that his people would do that to him, but he also knew that they would never agree to letting him step down. His people were his family in his heart; he wanted to give them their freedom. Slowly he started teaching his counsel about items he only knew. When he felt they were ready, he called his two loyal knights forward. They were his brothers; it would be wrong for him to just walk out of their life without telling them goodbye. The knights begged and pleaded for him not to go, but he told them it was best for the country, and they should become governor and lieutenant governor. He promised them that he would return when the time was right, and he would become their equal."

Leon curled his fingers into my open hand and rubbed the side of my right hand with his thumb. There was still a chill about them. The cool air out here couldn't be helping, as the temperature felt as if it was dropping. I needed to wrap this up before it cooled down any more. Snuggling by the fire all night was, in all likelihood, off the table.

"I continued to tell her that he took off in the middle of the night on his shire, heading south. This was important, because the rising sun reminded him of the one knight and the setting sun reminded him of the other knight—at all times he wanted his knights beside him. Traveling after a few days, his shire became spooked and bucked the king off. It knocked him unconscious, and his leg was injured. Fortunately, there was a young lady, about his age, gathering flowers nearby. She came across the king and his shire on her way home. Thankfully, she was able to get him on her horse, then she walked both horses to her home. The king stayed unconscious for a few days while she tended to his injuries. He woke up not knowing where he was, so he remained still with his eyes closed, learning about his surroundings. People would come into the house, asking the lady for help with various issues. The king assumed she was a healer of the people. Still under the notion that he was unconscious, she would softly sing to him when she was changing his bandages and, in the evenings, pray for his recovery. Her voice was so beautiful, and her touch was that of petals of a flower. He was falling in love with her without ever seeing her. The next morning, he was awoken to pressure on his chest and something licking him. The king remembered hearing people telling her that she needed to eat her goat before his injury spoiled his meat. Her response to them was it wasn't his time, he needed to live his life longer. With that he realized it was the goat on his chest. He finally opened his eyes, laughing and petting the goat. He could have just knocked the goat off his chest; despite that, he awoke with compassion for her mischievous little goat. Her heart told her that if he could wake up with so much compassion after being asleep for so long and not knowing what was going on, his heart had to be pure."

Sean tapped my knee to get my attention. "What did my grandma say to that?"

"She probably melted her like butter in that moment," Trevor snickered, "with Grandma Gemma Ann's big heart."

I released Leon's hands and leaned over Sean to Trevor. "May I have a drink?"

Trevor handed me the bottle with one brow down, as if he was unsure if he should let me drink since I was asking for it.

I tittered as I opened the bottle. "The next part you are going to hear the reason why a rich American girl is leaving her rich, comfortable life to pay someone to say no to her with the last of her money. And then I am going to continue to drink until I can't remember that I told you guys this."

I swirled the amber liquid around once before taking an extra-size swig. The crystallized caramel taste didn't burn as much this time. Despite that, before I could take another one, Sean confiscated the bottle from me.

"Right." I needed to get back to this or it was going to be daylight soon. "Miss Gemma Ann, who has a beautiful name, didn't say anything right away after I told her that story. Which sent me into a panicked, sobbing mess. I begged and pleaded with Miss Gemma Ann not to tell my mother what I had just said, because I would be in so much trouble. My mother repeatedly told me that fairy tales were just lies they told girls to make them feel better for marrying poor. It may be something so small, but I knew what happened if I went against her beliefs."

"Ouch," Sean snapped, handing Trevor the bottle again.

If there was a person that needed to be cut off, it was Trevor. That man was a rollercoaster of buzzing and being tipsy. I hope he didn't have cattle to care for tomorrow, because I couldn't imagine that smell mixed with a hangover was going to end well. I also hoped he had understanding parents and a few extra siblings to pick up his slack tomorrow.

"According to my mother, there is only one way to make a man love you and that's going to come out soon, but first to Miss Gemma Ann. Oh, but I need to stress I was twelve at this time. Miss Gemma Ann was trying to calm me down by getting me to talk about why I would be in trouble over a fable. She was soothing, and for whatever reason the words and the truth would flow out of me to her. I ended up calming down enough to tell her that earlier in the day I had gone to my mother because one of the boys—he wasn't even a boy, he was eighteen—kept rubbing his roll of quarters in his pocket against me while he told me we should go play with his joystick. I despised video games and told him no. He wouldn't drop it; each time he asked me again, he was more aggressive. A couple times he cornered me; once, he slammed me against the wall with his body. I don't have brothers or close male cousins to know if this was normal. All I knew was he was scaring me, so I went to my mother because I didn't know what else to do. I told Miss Gemma Ann when I went to my mother for help, my mother started laughing and told me to just go along with what he wants. He's going to show me his love for me. Just to think of it as a dance, but don't be alarmed; it's going to hurt at first, but put on your best competition face, and pretend to enjoy it."

"Oh, fuck," one of the guys whined—I think it was Trevor.

"Again, I'm twelve and I have no clue what's going on. I'm sobbing to your grandmother that my mother is already mad at me because I am refusing to go dance with Ivan after she had just explained to me how guys love. Your grandmother was white. I was freaked out about being in more trouble that I started spilling everything to her that happened on that trip, thinking that it might stop her from saying anything to my mother because there has been enough punishment so far this trip. Which included my father reaming me for my swimsuit being inappropriate. My mother bought and packed a new swimsuit for me, a white tube top with matching bikini bottoms. I'm going to note that I was flat-chested at that point, so the tube top didn't bother me, I was just excited to go play in the lake. One of my father's friend's wives made a comment to my father about my suit being see-through when wet. My father walked into the water and pulled me out of the lake while laying into me for being inappropriate in front of all his friends. I tried telling him my mother bought the suit, I didn't pick it out, but he wouldn't hear of it. On the other hand, my mother did, so once my father left, it was her turn.

She screamed at me for throwing her under the bus—all she was trying to do was make sure I would have a comfortable future like she has. If I couldn't get it through my thick head, I was going to end up poor if I didn't start trying to attract male attention."

Now there was silence.

"Your poor grandmother wasn't expecting this. She lunged forward, wrapping me in her arms. She was crying; I could feel the tears rolling down my neck. I apologized up and down to her for my behavior. I told her not that it was right, but I was scared. After years of dancing, never had a dance been painful. I was scared of Ivan because if my mother knew he was going to hurt me, he had to have known as well."

"Dear god." Sean rubbed his eyebrows with his index finger and his thumb. "What are we listening to?"

"It's going to get worse." I glanced back at Sean. "I don't think I have mentioned it, but that eighteen-year-old boy that was harassing me is my sister's fiancé."

"Wait," Trevor snapped, pulling me to his attention, "Ivan is the man that is going to marry your sister up here, and he's the same eighteen-year-old that wanted to dance with you?"

"Yep, and he has not changed a bit since that summer. Ivan likes to come stay with us when my father leaves for his fishing trips," I puffed out my chest and deepened my voice, "so there's a man of the house to protect us girls."

"Let's go back to talking about vampires," Trevor whined. "I have a feeling I know where this is going to go."

"No," Leon growled from behind me, "I want to hear this— let her continue."

He wasn't going to want to hear this; I was going to get vulgar.

"When my sister passes out from the booze and my mother passes out from the pills, Ivan likes to sneak into my bedroom. It may not seem like it here and now, but I don't drink often. I've never touched drugs or narcotics, so he knows I will be conscious. He will sit backwards on my desk chair and wheel it over to the bed. Then he will lecture me on the importance of family and how I have an important role in this family to keep each member of it happy. Since my sister is wearing his ring, he is family." I watched the fire dancing. "I'm disappointing the family because I have not given him a warm welcome yet. It shouldn't be that way, because I'm going to enjoy him as much as my sister and mother do."

"I want to contribute to your stopping this wedding fund." Sean handed the envelope back to me. "Pardon my language, but your family is fucked up."

"No," I shook my head. "I can't accept that money; that money is revenge." I paused, realizing that sounded cruel. "Excuse me: that envelope is kindness, love, justice, and thanks owed to Miss Gemma Ann."

"Has he ever..." Leon leaned forward, seeming to want to look into my eyes to see the truth from them as much as my words.

I wasn't going to make him uncomfortable by finishing his sentence. "No," I interrupted. "Ivan's parents bought his grades all the way through his university studies—he's not bright and incredibly gullible. When I was younger, to get him out of my room I used to tell him an exaggerated graphic version of my menstrual cycle. Once I got to the part about blood clots looking like prunes, he would get up and walk out. Since I've used that so much and he's around more, he finally caught on. I moved on to telling him I had a herpes outbreak. For the most part that worked, until last month he told me that he had one too, so it would be okay. At that moment I threw out that I had gonorrhea and went into detail about the discharge. And since my father is currently on a six-week-long fishing trip in another country, my gonorrhea is going to last just as long."

There needed to be a moment for damage control. It wasn't that I was trying to get with any of these guys here, but despite that, I didn't want them carrying the stigma that I had an STI.

Well, Trevor was in and out of it, and Sean had already formed his opinion of me—this was more for Leon. Even just sitting here, I didn't want it to make him uncomfortable. I didn't want him to think lower of me. I may not be staying much longer, but I was enjoying whatever we had going on this evening. I wasn't going to object to one more day of it, either.

"I'm sorry for being gross—those are just tall tales that I tell Ivan to get him to back down. Miss Gemma Ann opened my eyes to the truth, saving me from becoming my mother and sister."

"I don't believe that you are like them." Leon's hand wavered a little before he rested it on my cheek.

I let my head fall a touch into his hand and placed my hand over the top of his. His hand still felt cold to the touch. His temperature felt as if it didn't change even when being against something warm. I was now starting to wonder if it was a medical condition.

Leon gave me a wistful grin, drawing me back out of my new investigation. "We all miss Grandma Gemma Ann's words of wisdom. Would you mind sharing what she said to you?"

This next part was going to be easy to talk about; it wasn't disgusting, scary, or even childish. "When she was hugging me, she told me we are born with love. If a person couldn't believe in a fairy tale or a love story, they have never allowed real love in. It's silly to deny it. Love is something that is beautiful, magical, and worth every second, minute, hour, day, week, month, and year waiting for. There is only one part of you that can dance to create love, and that is your heart."

Leon's thumb glided across my cheek. "I would have to agree with her."

"She released me," my hand dropped from his hand, "and told me that she feared for my heart. She feared that, growing up in that environment, I was going to lose it. Her hand waved just below the water, as if she was creating something below the surface. She stops and tells me to look down. Doing as told, I looked down to see, resting among the black, grey, and red stones in the water, a translucent agate."

Leaning forward, I began to undo my bun. It wasn't to show Leon my hair as mine, it was to show him my heart. Now with a loose bun, I held out my heart to Leon. This heart was special; it was a heart-shaped with burnt brown and white translucent agate. There were random pits throughout the stone, but she taught me no matter how many hits it took, it would remain a heart.

"I held up the agate to her and asked if this was what she lost earlier. She told me no, child, this was to protect me when times were difficult, to remind me that my heart was strong and, like this stone, would never lose its shape. Even with all the beatings and awful words spewed at it, it was strong enough to remain in its true form. I had a realistic head and a pure heart—for that, no one should ever be able to tell me how to give or how to accept love." I held the heart out as the fire made it glow orange. "I'm not superstitious, although I feel like I'm carrying her words and love with me every day. Part of me wanted to come back here just to hear her tell me that she was proud that I overcame my environment."

I kissed the warm stone, then handed it over to Sean with a wistful grin. "With her passing, this should go back to your family so you can feel her love again."

With the rock in his palm, Sean closed his hand and held it up to his chest. It was as if he knew of the rock to have that reaction. Past him, Trevor was passed out with his legs stretched out and his arms crossed against his chest. That would explain why he was being so quiet. And that was my cue—it was time to call it a night and say my goodbyes.

Leon had shown me nothing but kindness, even through all my silly shenanigans and my uncalled-for rudeness about his contacts. I didn't want to leave him with rudeness or light-hearted silliness. I wanted to leave an imprint on him that I was kind.

Turning, I straddled his legs, but before I could say anything, his hand rose.

"What else do you have hiding in that nest?" Gently, he slid my hair tie from my hair, allowing it to bounce down as it had before at the bar.

I watched him softly grin to himself as he watched my hair, then his head moved to be parallel with mine. He was starting to make this goodbye more difficult. I was just going to apologize to him and give him a hug, but now I was starting to second guess my original plan.

"I have nothing else up there, my heart is gone now."

"I don't know about that." He leaned forward with his cheek against mine, moving all my hair over to my left shoulder and let his fingers glide through my hair as he sat back. "See, your hair is still protecting your heart."

His softness was endearing; he wasn't supposed to be like this with me. I'd been nothing but up in his face and almost forcing my way into his guy time. The other two didn't have girls curled up to them—it was just the four of us out here. And out of the three of them, he was the one that should have been more standoffish with me, since he had worked all night. I would have been exhausted. For sure, I wouldn't have wanted to listen to crazed stories from someone that followed me here. Despite that, he was the opposite. Even with the awful contacts, there was softness behind them. When I would catch him looking at me, his head would tilt ever so slightly to the left as the right side of his lips moved up gently. There was more than that—he kept me close. It was as if he was protecting me, as if he wanted me close to him as much as I just wanted to be close to him. For tonight, I didn't want to let him go. I wanted to live in this sweet illusion that this was what love felt like.

My eyes moved back to his as my head blocked the light of the fire from his face. "You shouldn't be like this with me; it's only making it harder to say goodbye."

His arms moved up my back, drawing me closer to his chest. "Don't say it."

I didn't—instead, I showed him how much I didn't want to leave him yet. Swiftly, I wrapped my arms behind his neck and lowered my head to his. My lips moved to just below his ear on his jawline, showing their objection to my next line. "I can't stay here," I whispered softly into his ear.

"I don't think..." He kept his voice lower so the others couldn't hear him. "That is what you really want. I will make sure that you have a safe place to stay tonight." His lips were in agreement with mine as they moved just before my ear. "For now, stay."

This was going to get harder if we stayed on this path. I was going to end up surrendering to him if the atmosphere between us didn't change.

"I"—quickly I pecked his left cheek—"have"—I pecked his forehead—"to"—I pecked his right cheek—"go."

All of this was new to me. Yes, I had been in his personal space, but in spite of that I would have never kissed him even if just in a silly manner. But now my lips were dishing out kisses as if they were free samples at a grocery store.

Sitting back on his legs, I said, "I'm sorry, my family is under the impression that I'm up here to organize my sister's wedding. After I secure my no, I'm canceling my cell phone and disappearing. Which means I can't stay here; my family knows I'm here."

"Disappearing?"

"Yeah, I don't want to be a Carter anymore. In order to escape them, I have to walk away from that life and everyone else." I leaned forward so Sean couldn't hear us. "This is not a good reason to drink, but I'm scared."

Leon secured his arms around me and ran his hand through my hair. "I believe everything is going to work out for you."

Resting my head on his shoulder, he was peaceful to be against. Mediterranean scents mixed with aquatic ones danced in my nose, lowering my eyes. There was no fighting it; he was mysterious and magical, but mostly I felt comforted as if I was home in my own bed.

Movements below me woke me up a touch. Leon must have been inching down to straighten out, because it felt as if I was more parallel with his body. My shirt decided it was going to stay put and rolled up underneath my breasts. It was going to stay this way—even with the shifting around, I was still comfortable and wasn't going to move.

The blanket was drawn up, then Leon's chilly hands slithered under it. Gently he corrected my shirt, then rested his hands on the middle of my back. And his hands remained on my back; they didn't sneak into my waistband or rest on my butt. All his movements were respectful and courteous toward my body.

Sean must have been dozing off and on as there were moments of silence between their conversation. I wasn't fully awake either. It was more of that state when you knew your surroundings but felt as if you were sleeping. Leon must have been right there with Sean, dozing off. His head slowly lowered more and more until his lips were almost resting against the middle of my nose.

We had been at that moment so many times tonight. With Trevor passed out and Sean's snorts, I wanted to know if we were back there. Gently I slid up, resting my hand on his chest. His head lowered toward mine, then stopped. It wasn't a stop of regret; it felt more like a stop because he was a gentleman. My eyes closed as the image of his eyes blurred, my lips moving to his just long enough to feel their silkiness.

His eyes opened with disappointment that I had stopped. His hand moved up my back into my hair, gently drawing me back to him as if his lips were longing for more. There were no objections from me. Without parting from his lips, I moved up to straddle his waist as his lips told mine how much he wanted this since the first time I caught him staring at my lips. It wasn't only his lips; the rest of him wanted me as well. His left hand moved down the side of my head to rest on the side of my neck with his right arm tight around my back, drawing me into his chest more. My warmth overtook the coolness of the night against his body, while his lips told my lips good night in his own melody.

CHAPTER 3

The sweat dripped down my chest. I was roasting. Throwing the blankets from me as I sat up, half-awake, I took my hoodie off and tossed it to the side. This wasn't enough; I pulled up my shirt, only exposing my stomach. I wasn't comfortable taking it off. Last night when I fell asleep somewhat, I heard Leon and Sean talking about sleeping arrangements. Leon was going to take Trevor home and handle his fox problem, while Sean was going to take me to his parents' house. For how hot this room was, I understood why Leon told him to open the window. It was brutal in here.

It was interesting that we didn't just stay out there and camp around the fire as originally planned, yet Leon was being weird about the bears. He made a comment that he was going to return this morning to check on me and speak to Sean's father about opening bear hunting again. The weird part was, he made a comment that there were too many and he couldn't handle it himself anymore. It was odd; it almost seemed as if they were using Leon as the exterminator. Possibly Leon was a taxidermist. He could be using the bear mounts to display his work at sporting stores. Or he worked under Sean's father in the game and fish department and Leon oversaw the predator animal division. He could have been the only one allowed to hunt the predators so he could keep an accurate count on the herds, flocks, or whatever the group of predators were called. I was going to stick with this theory until I knew the truth;

animal mounts freaked me out enough that I would not go near them.

Moving on from that, I continued to analyze their conversation. His next comment seized everything within me, including the throbbing in my head. Leon had said he felt his forever was coming to an end sooner rather than later. Events in this conversation were not lining up, yet at another point I could recall Sean asking questions about Leon's illness. It almost sounded like Leon had some type of autoimmune disease. He had made a comment that he couldn't feel temperatures, but there was excitement in his voice when he was telling Sean that he could feel the warmth from my hands and the warmth of my drool on his shoulder. Not the most glamorous moment for myself, but at least he was excited about it.

Rolling to my side, I drew the sheet up, covering my eyes. Even with my eyes closed, the room was bright from the sunshine penetrating the window. Perhaps Leon was wrong; his end wasn't coming, but the autoimmune disease within him was leaving his body. Either way, going forward I needed to treat him for him, not punishing him for what his body was doing to him. I needed to apologize for being crude about his contacts.

My head was punishing me for drinking. I needed to go get some aspirin out of my SUV. Once more, I rolled over to slowly open my eyes to the white wainscoting on the lower part of the wall. Squinting my eyes closed for a second, I opened them again to see the soft yellow wall above the wainscoting adorned with white shelves that had ceramic geese with light blue bows around the middle of their necks. This room was homey, even under my current conditions, and cheerful. This was a way better place to wake up than the back of my SUV, covered in mosquito bites. For this I was going to have to track down Leon and thank him. Maybe I could talk him into going on a picnic with me. Since he worked at the bar and I already had plans for the day, I could stay one more day to thank him.

For now, I needed to get going with my day, so I slowly pushed myself up, only for a sharp pain in my head to cause me to fall back into the bed. I suffocated myself in the sweet floral-scented plush pillow. Closing my eyes, I remained still with my face hidden in the pillow.

"Oh, you poor thing." A chilly hand moved across my back, moving my hair to the side.

Slowly rolling to my side, more than anything I was thankful that he was in here. Why he was in here, I had no idea. It didn't matter; I wanted him to be. Oddly enough, he was comfort to me. Which was strange—I had never had this inclination to be up in a guy's personal space as much as I did with Leon. I would like to say that it had started out as playfulness, but when he lifted that box off the stack, it felt as if my prize was revealed to me. We just needed to replace Hank's faded blue delivery uniform with a black suit and give him a pencil-thin microphone instead of a dolly, and he would be my game show host. Hank would have made the perfect game show host, quick and witty. And not that people are possessions, but for whatever reason, Leon was the perfect prize. That feeling of falling asleep against him was like no other I had ever felt watching fairy tales or reading romance novels.

I opened my eyes to see Leon with his head down, sitting on the floor next to the bed. There was no baseball cap today; his thick, true white hair was wild and free, with waves and slight curls covering the upper portion of his ear. Slowly I moved my hand over to his head. Hungover, I was far from steady, but I did my best trying not to hit him.

Successfully, I ran my fingers through his hair. "Good morning."

His head remained down. "Good morning."

My head throbbed again, the lightness of the room making it worse. "I don't feel well."

Bit by bit, I inched back in the bed until I was in the middle of it. There was a chance that he was still tired from his long night. I angled toward the edge of the bed closer to him. "Will you lay with me, please?"

Turning, he rested his arms on the bed with his chin atop them. "I had a feeling this morning was going to be rough for you, so I wanted to check on you first thing."

His eyes remained closed, not fluttering, not peeking, his eyelashes intertwined. Perhaps he thought I wasn't dressed or I wasn't comfortable with him in here since we had just met yesterday.

I wasn't uncomfortable with him, though. "I'm fully dressed."

"I know." His eyes remained closed.

Maybe it was the other way around. "Are you uncomfortable being in here with me?"

"Far from it."

"Are you sure? I was up in your space last night. Normally when guys are like that with me, it makes me uncomfortable. I'm sorry for being in your space, but I like it there." What was I saying to him? That I liked being in his space after apologizing for being in his space. That had to be the worst apology—that was an Ivan apology. *Hey, I'm sorry for making you uncomfortable, but I enjoy it.* I was lame, and now I had no liquid courage to blame it on.

Leon's lips curled up, his head falling to the side. "I like it as well."

Even with that sweetness, his eyes remained closed. Cute, but an odd delivery of that statement. I needed a manual on how to read men right about now. This was baffling that he wouldn't open his eyes. I was dressed and he already said he knew that I was. Which meant that at some point, his eyes were open—they had to have been open when he entered the room.

I studied his facial features until it hit me like another sharp pain, this time in my chest. I had been so incredibly crude to him about his contacts. Since he wasn't opening his eyes and last night he told Sean he could feel my warmth, I was going to give him some warmth with my apology.

I rested my hand on his cheek with my fingers itching the hair behind his ear. "I am sorry for my comments about your contacts yesterday. Not saying what I said was right; although I had worked in an optical for years, and I've learned that people's eyes say more than their words or movements. There was something about our interactions yesterday that gave me solace, as if we have known each other for years. Yeah, I'm a friendly, social person that will dispense hugs, but that's it. I'm a little more guarded when it comes to dispensing other forms of affection or being in other people's bubbles, except with you. I guess with new sides of me appearing, I wanted to see all of you, but with your blinds on I couldn't."

He was listening; however, I noticed his head was leaning into my fingers. In my crazed rant, he must have enjoyed having my nails itch his head. Releasing his cheek, I moved my hand up the back of his neck. He was enjoying this—his chin tucked in and his forehead rested on his crossed arms now.

"Never have I ever fallen asleep on anyone before, never held hands, never snuggled, and for sure never asked anyone to join me in a bed. I'm going to be honest, so I am sorry if it makes you more uncomfortable with me. As ridiculous as this is, I know that was all me, not the alcohol. And it seems like the more I am around you, the worse it gets. Which I don't understand. For years I took Miss Gemma Ann's words to heart. But now, I don't know if it's this town, the stress in my life, or your aura."

His head rolled to the left a touch. "Maybe it's because you know that you are freeing yourself from your family's toxicity that the real you is coming forward."

In all likelihood, he was right; my heart was getting ready to start pumping out through my eyes how it truly felt. This wasn't what I wanted to hear from him; I wanted to hear that he felt the same way. I wanted this to be that grand love that only writers truly knew about. I wanted him to potentially be my King Leon in the love story I grew up daydreaming about, not that I was free now to be my horny self.

I rolled onto my back. With both my palms on my forehead, I squeezed them together—it was time to play damage control in my mind. What was I expecting? He worked in a bar; he was handsome, kind, caring, and compassionate. Girls probably threw themselves at him all the time; I was just the one he picked yesterday. Stephanie loved to bring bartenders home for the night—this wasn't anything new. Not to mention he knew I was leaving. Why would he invest anything outside of a friendship with me?

It didn't matter, it still hurt. I rolled to the other side of the bed, facing the opposite wall from him. "Yeah... You are probably right. I'm sorry." Still on my side, I brought my knees up to my chest and hugged my pillow.

"Nora," the bed lowered, "are you all right?"

This was easy to answer—I had a coverup. "No, I'm hungover. I just need an hour or maybe two, and I will be fine. But hey, I'll stop by the bar after my meeting to let you know how it went."

No more staying an extra night for a picnic; we were on different pages from each other. His thank-you was downgraded to some treats from the store and a card.

The bed rose again, there were footsteps, then it lowered a touch like when he had his arms crossed on the other side.

"Will you open your eyes for me, please?"

"No." Again, this wasn't a full lie. "The room is too bright, and it's adding more throbbing in my head. If you wouldn't mind pulling the curtains before you leave, I would appreciate it." I hid my face back into the pillow, adding a physical cue that it was time for him to leave.

"Please?"

Why was it so important for me to open my eyes to him? Unlike his, he had seen my real eyes yesterday. "Yeah, I wasn't wearing contacts," I grumbled into the pillow. "Those were my real eyes. The light hurts..."

Leon cut me off. "Your back is to the window," he said. "Please?"

This was such a weird thing to be going around with him about. Giving in, I opened my eyes to see he was right before me. His head was tilted slightly as he gazed into my eyes. What the... I sat up a touch to be at his height and angled my head to mirror his. His irises were pinkish-orange. They weren't albino red or deathly white; they were unimaginably unique and oddly alluring.

I could feel my left brow lower. "Fuck" slipped from my lips. "There's my answer." I rolled to the middle of the bed and placed my hands over my eyes so I would see loud geometrical images instead. "You're Adonis," I moaned softly to the morning air.

This wasn't some fable fairy tale; Leon could have been the mortal lover of Aphrodite. Generally, I was more familiar with Egyptian mythology, but with his pale complexion, it wasn't fitting. Leon's snowy skin, enchanting eyes, adorable nose, and natural build were that of something Aphrodite would have wanted for herself. In another world, Leon would have rivaled Adonis and would have become Aphrodite's main lover.

"Come again?" The bed shifted.

"Oh no," I tittered, "I'm not repeating that one. It wasn't meant to be said aloud—it slipped out."

"Well, since you swore at me," he made his tone sound as if he was offended, yet I could feel the silkiness of his bottom lip and breath on my own, "I think you owe it to me to open your eyes and tell me what you said."

His lips didn't move any further from gently grazing my bottom lip. I lifted my chin until my lips hugged his lower lip, drawing his head down closer to me. "Is this how you get your way?"

It was how I was going to get my way. I just wanted to lay

here with him until the throbbing in my head disappeared. Well...and a little beyond that. But I couldn't fault myself; I had gotten a little sample last night, and now I wanted more.

"No, I'm trying something new." His lips moved back to mine for a second before I felt the bed shift and his presence was above me again.

Ugh, nooo. I wanted to feel him against me. I thought that was apparent as I had pulled him down by his bottom lip.

After another stabbing pain in my head, my mind cleared for a second. Maybe I was wrong; with my actions and my mouth, perhaps I did truly offend him and the kiss could have made it worse. All of this wasn't what I wanted at all. I was going to have to cave to him and face the facts.

I opened my eyes to see the Duchenne smile he had been hiding. There wasn't a thing wrong with his smile; his teeth were straight, white, and beautiful. The two top ones were ever so longer than the rest, but it gave his smile more character. For sure, Aphrodite would have been jealous of me right now.

"I'm sorry for swearing." Slowly my view moved up to his eyes. "But I didn't swear at you. It was just a general statement, or more toward me."

With my lips together, a lift of my eyebrow, and my chin tucked a touch, I studied his eyes again with my best flirtatious smile. I was going to charm my way out of this. Perhaps that would get him to move down a little closer to me.

"I must still be drunk."

I needed a filter. Telling him I was drunk could send him down that slope that he may be uncomfortable to make any move with me since I may not be coherent enough to reject.

"Lies." His head shook from side to side. "As I recall, a moment ago you said none of that was alcohol-induced."

"And you said"—the fun was going to be slipping away after my next comment—"that it was just me being freed. Perhaps I am more like my sister than I thought, just a whore that has a thing for bartenders."

Good gosh, every other thing out of my mouth was decreasing my chance. There had to be something with this hangover; I was new to all of this, but I never imagined my game would suck as much as it did right now.

He didn't take that comment well, either; all his weight rested on my torso for a second as he tightened his arms around me. There wasn't enough time to secure my arms around him before he thrust us over until I was on his chest. His right arm remained tightened around me while his left glided up and down my back.

I let my head rest against his as I tightened my arms around his neck. It took a little while, but everything between us could pause now. This was all I wanted this morning: to lay here with him until my headache disappeared.

"I know that you don't believe that," Leon softly whispered in my ear before kissing my cheek.

His words triggered something within me, something I didn't want to be dealing with right now, but it was planted and growing. I didn't want to believe I was like anyone in my family, but I was constantly being defined by other people. There was still a part of me that I felt, since they were all saying it, they may be right. On the other side of it, people were to love their children unconditionally, not make them out to be the next villain as soon as they were five.

I pushed myself up out of his embrace until I straddled his waist with my arms crossed against my chest. "What do you believe?" I wanted to ask him who he believed I was; however, I wasn't prepared to hear if his definition of me matched my views of my mother or sister.

With a jostle of his hips, I fell forward, only catching myself with my hands on either side of his head. His actions felt as if he was aligning with how I felt about him—despite that, there was something that felt off at the same time. Miss Gemma Ann said love would be worth it. She must have forgotten to tell me that men were complicated creatures. Maybe once I was able to decipher them, then it would all be worth it.

"I know that I was wrong earlier." He moved the strand of hair covering my left eye behind my ear. "Freedom was the easy answer. The answer that I hoped for was me. I couldn't tell you that because I had a guard up. I was petrified to show you my eyes. They are repulsive, and when people see the true color, it freaks them out. They can't handle it."

Perhaps an ex had played off his insecurities. Maybe he was teased about his eyes growing up because they were unique. It didn't matter who said it or teased him; I wanted to undo their foul ways.

"First of all, you need to get rid of this notion that your eyes are repulsive—they're not. What is repulsive is the way people use words as weapons when they are jealous or upset."

"There's no way you would want anything to do with me if you couldn't handle looking into my eyes. Especially for how adamant you are against my contacts."

"I have some weird fears." I squinted as I studied his left eye. "Nope," I kissed his eyebrow, "not fearful of your left eye." I moved over to his right eye, squinting as I studied it for a second. "Nope," I kissed his right eyebrow, "neither eye has been added to my fear list."

His eyes weren't the only thing that he was hiding from me yesterday. From seeing it today, I couldn't figure out why he would hide his smile either. I was going to nip this one right away; I wanted to see the real version of him, not the hidden one. He was already showing me his Duchenne smile as he chuckled to himself. This was going to be a little more difficult with that wide smile shining up at me.

"Nope." Placing my hands on either cheek, I squished my hands together until his lips puckered. Quickly I stole a peck, then sat back up, crossing my arms against my chest, shaking my head slowly. "In no way am I fearful of your amazing smile. It's just the opposite."

His expression curved and turned. I was in for the motherload since he wasn't wearing a cap today. His brows moved in, creating a volcano silhouette with lines for lava.

My lips pinched—I was trying to encourage him about his features, but now I was going to lose it over his expression. A counter was needed. Slowly I kissed his jawline to just under his ear.

"Where did you come from?" he purred as his head rolled to the side, giving me more access.

"Hank's," my lips moved down to just beside his Adam's apple, "truck." I may have felt like crap and had some weird nerves right now, but that wasn't going to stop me from being a little playful with him. I moved back above him with my head cocked. "Didn't you order me with all the boxes of syrups?" Trying to convince myself it was for a little more dramatic effect, I gazed at him, biting my bottom lip.

By the way he was returning my look, though, we both knew it wasn't an act.

"What?" Leon tittered, tapping his fingertips against his chest.

"Maybe," I crossed my arms and moved one hand up, pinching my chin, "I was a promotional gift, like order six boxes of syrup and get a free American."

"I think I am going to return you to Hank," he winked at me, "if you don't come down here."

"Hank is fun and all, but despite that, please don't." Swiftly I bowed my head to the side. More than anything, I was starting to regret not listening to Leon last night about drinking. I gasped as my head thumped again, then I straightened back before him. "I can't imagine Peggy would like to hear how Hank picked me up off the street. I don't know her, but I feel as if she is not going to go for that."

I felt as if I was scraped off the side of the road. I bowed my head so my forehead was resting on his chest. As much as I was trying to enjoy this time with Leon, my head was fully punishing me for not listening to him.

This was the worst and the best all at once. Leon's chilly

hands moved up to the side of my head as he rubbed my temples, then moved down the back of my neck. The man could make moonshine and knew the tricks to help cure the aftermath.

With the throbbing decreasing, I moved back above him once more. "In all seriousness, I just want to see you for you—your eyes," I kissed his left eyebrow, then his right eyebrow, "your nose," I kissed the tip of his nose, then let my lips graze his lips, "your smile—are all extra bonuses to the man that my heart sees."

His hands moved to either side of my cheeks before I could spiral around that last statement. "If I am your Adonis, you are my Aphrodite. There's never been anyone that I wanted peering into my eyes so I can peer into hers as well until now."

His hands lowered my head to his, allowing my lips to feel the rush of his lips. I could taste the spark of his tongue. The sharpness flicked something on within my head; my mind filled with images as if the television was turned on. In my mind I saw Leon, but it wasn't quite my Leon before me. His hair was dark chestnut-brown, short on the sides with about an inch of length on the top. This Leon wore a white, long-sleeved shirt with the sleeves rolled up above his elbows. This was another difference between my Leon and this one; his skin was golden, as if he had been working all day in the summer sun. Physically, in every way they were the same shape; his lips matched his, his nose was the same, and it seemed as if they were the same height.

Leon looked back at the main door to the stable as if he had heard a noise, then his deep brown, almost black eyes returned to the massive midnight-black muzzle of the cool grey horse. He continued to pet the horse's muzzle as the horse hung its head outside the wooden stall door. The horse was unbelievably majestic; its muzzle had to be the same length as Leon's torso. His eyes were just as black as Leon's. A beautiful creature such as this had to be dreamt up; never had I ever seen a horse this massive in my life.

The horse's head moved above as there was another noise. It had to be from the reddish-gold dog with the black muzzle and black on her paws as if she was wearing boots as she moved along Leon. I watched as he knelt to pet her, reassuring her that it was nothing to fear.

"Don't be so sure." A hefty, round man adorned in grey and white furs moved before Leon. His heavy crown leaned to the right as his eyes narrowed into slits. "How dare you think that you are better than my daughter."

Leon petted his dog one more time before pushing up from his knee. "It has nothing to do with arrogance. Your daughter is lovely—nonetheless, we are not right for each other." His voice was strong and calm, mirroring my Leon's voice.

"It is you that is not right for her," the man growled. "You are going to pay for her tears. No one will ever want you, and you are going to crave everyone."

Before Leon could say anything, the king nodded his head, turned around, and walked out, leaving Leon transfixed on his image as it disappeared into the night.

The echoes of the horse's hooves hitting the stable floor filled the air along with his whines and snorts. It didn't matter if the horse was made up in my mind; without a doubt, this horse was spooked. Before Leon could turn to calm the horse down, his neck was embraced in a hand that had pointed nails with serrated edges cutting into his neck. It felt as if my heart stopped as I watched the iniquitous man digging his nails deeper into Leon's neck, paralyzing him.

Leon's dog charged the thin leg of the iniquitous man, her fangs showing. The man, with Leon's bleeding neck in his left hand, leaned down and snatched up the dog by her neck with his right hand. He dug his nails into her neck tighter until red streaks streamed down her coat, then he threw her against the hanging pitchforks against the wall. She yelped as the tines pierced her torso, then her body thumped against the stone floor. Her chest raised up and down, yet she didn't get up or make a sound.

It felt as if Thelma's account of King Leon was coming to life now that I had my own image of the King Leon of my dreams. I couldn't watch this anymore, but I couldn't move from it either. I still felt Leon's lips against my own, but I couldn't move from this scene in my mind. This had to be a bad hangover from drinking moonshine last night. The alcohol had to have been spoiled or laced with something for this to be happening. Never had anyone told me that this happened to them when they made out. That had to be it; that's why Leon was so adamant about me not drinking last night.

With his hand still around Leon's neck, the man ran his tongue down the outer part of Leon's ear. He turned Leon's head to the side, exposing more of his neck. "I heard that no princess has been good enough for you." He chortled. "Tish tish, you should have just settled for the last one. After I'm finished with you, no one will ever want you." He let his upper fangs pierce Leon's neck. The color retracted from Leon's hair, then his golden skin turned white. The iniquitous man's tongue moved side to side, lapping up the blood dripping from the bite. He paused. "You are going to spend eternity alone— no one will ever love a monster," he said, then he forced his bottom fangs into Leon's neck. The color drained from Leon's paralyzed eyes, leaving them an orangey-blush color.

Regaining control over myself, I gasped and drew myself away from Leon. I could feel the color drain from my face as a single stream of tears flowed from just my left eye. My hands felt cold with a slight tremble. What the hell just happened? Did I just have some weird off-the-wall panic attack while making out with Leon? Was that even possible?

Right now, it didn't matter. Leon couldn't see me like this; he was going to read it wrong. I lowered my head beside his, tightly closing my eyes. I just wanted him to hold me tight and tell me it was all right. That was the worst horror I had ever seen in my life. All I could do was pray that horror was never going to play out in my head again.

His hand moved up and down my back. "Nora," he whispered, "are you all right? I'm sorry if I..."

And there it was. "No—" I cut him off; he didn't need to be apologizing for my craziness. "I'm sorry. My head is throbbing, and I think having it in that position just made it worse. I'm so sorry; I just need a minute."

"I warned you about drinking that stuff," he tittered.

I needed a way to get around this. Making things light-hearted might help distract him until the color returned to my face. "I wanted to try your pirate whiskey. I just didn't know that it was made from burnt sugar and ninety-one-percent rubbing alcohol."

"Pirate whiskey..." His thumb and index finger stroked the back of my neck. "Rubbing alcohol?"

"Yeah, you know that it's not meant for human consumption, right?" More than ever did I believe that statement now. Never had I ever drank anything that gave me hallucinations the next day. Drinking it wasn't enjoyable, and this was horrendous. I should have just listened to him last night.

"I guess not," he chuckled, "but that means I should be the one taking care of you since I poisoned you by accident."

Just at the start of his jaw, before his ear, I let my lips seal the deal. "Yes," I softly purred, "I think that's what I need right now."

CHAPTER 4

"What is this?!"

A strong female voice shrieking throughout the house woke me up a touch, but not enough for my eyes to open. Earlier, Leon had turned to his side and drew me up to his chest in a tight embrace. At some point he must have rolled to his back, taking me with him, as my head was resting on his chest. He was holding my right hand, and my leg was wrapped over his. His hangover cure was effective; my head wasn't hurting anymore. Most of all, my heart was warm again after that horrendous nightmare.

His knuckles softly glided down my back and up. "I think the house is up." He kissed the top of my head. "If Ruby catches us in bed together, it's not going to be pretty."

All I could do was chuckle at the image of a female Sean, which would be Miss Gemma Ann, stomping up the stairs and pulling Leon out of the bed by the ear while reciting quotes from the Bible about sinning and the importance of celibacy.

I rested my arms on his chest with my chin atop them, peering up at Leon. "Are you afraid of her?"

"Yes," he said as I jostled slightly with his titters, "and if you don't move, you will see why soon."

I pushed my bottom lip out; I was comfortable on him and didn't want to move. In reality, I couldn't imagine that she was going to just walk into the room knowing there was a stranger inside. There would be a knock giving us time to reposition ourselves before the door opened.

My head dropped back to his chest as I held up the peace sign to him. "Two more minutes."

More like two seconds—someone stomped up the staircase, which must have been near for how loud it was. Then there was a second set of steps rushing near the first stomping set.

"Maaa," rang out overly loud, as if Sean was warning us—*we better be presentable, she's in no mood for shenanigans*—"she's probably sleeping. We stayed out there late last night; let her come down when she is ready."

"She can get up." Her voice was still stern; without a doubt she was a lady of authority. "Your grandma prayed every day for that little girl, and now she's in our house. I want to meet her."

If she had the same beliefs as Miss Gemma Ann, she would be disappointed to find Leon and me in bed together, even if it was innocent. That heaviness outweighed the desire to be part of Leon's space in this manner. Swiftly I bounced off Leon, grabbing my hoodie. I put it back on as I moved over to the rocking chair by the window. Nervousness was replacing that moment of zen I had been in; there was a chance that Sean's mother knew the parts of my story that I had left out last night. Even being on opposite sides of the room, this interaction may be cumbersome.

Leon chuckled as he sat up on his elbows, watching me. "What changed your mind?"

"Not everyone falls in love with me instantly" slipped out of my lips as I admired his gaze upon me.

Darn it... What was I doing dropping that L-bomb right now? Yes, we confessed our growing feelings toward each other, but that word should be avoided at all costs. I needed to get a better hold on myself now that I couldn't blame a hangover or headache anymore.

Although who could fault me? There was something about the way his eyes moved about my body, then back to my eyes.

His tense gaze raised the right side of his lips; I knew what he wanted, and it wasn't me sitting across the room from him. It was what I wanted; to be up against him again, breathing in his enchantment while my head rested on his chest. Or, better yet, allowing our lips to join again in that breathtaking dance, hopefully this time without the hallucination since I was feeling better. I could feel myself slipping away from the noise outside the door, my upper front teeth piercing my bottom lip as I admired him just the same. Oh yes, I was feeling better.

His index and middle finger curled toward his chest, then just his middle finger tapped his pec. The heater must have kicked on in the room because I was regretting putting my hoodie back on. I needed to snap out of it, as I realized there was no lock on the door, and before the desire to remove a layer of clothing was in full bloom.

Breathing deeply—gosh, what was I getting myself into this morning?—and ignoring him, I exhaled to move on. "To be honest, there were more events that happened that day than I shared. She may not think so highly of me." Judging by her tone, that was going to be the case.

The door swung open, and a lady took one step into the room, her rounded eyes scanning. She must have been about five-foot-five with a plumper body hidden underneath a navy sundress patterned with white daisies. Her lips were pinched together straight, the bottom one more pink than the upper one, which was more tan.

I couldn't help but grin to myself, as it was warming to see she was a younger version of her mother. More than anything, I just wanted to live in the fantasy that she was Miss Gemma Ann. To be able to give her a hug while telling her about myself to see if I did her proud all these years. At this point in my life it would have been my greatest achievement to date just to hear Miss Gemma Ann tell me that she was proud of me.

"Leo," she placed her hands on her hips, "why are you

sitting on the bed and she's in the rocking chair? Sean just told me that she spent the night and you went home to your apartment."

With that, my fantasy disappeared; in no way would Miss Gemma Ann approve of a boy being in bed with me last night. Even if he didn't stay the night. I didn't know how I was going to explain why he was in my room before the rest of the house was up.

"Ruby, relax." Leon sat up, drawing his left knee to his chest. "I went back to my place alone. I wanted to check on her this morning. We had a few drinks at the bonfire."

"Why did you bust that crap out?" Ruby glared at Sean, then her gaze fell back on me. "The poor thing must feel awful."

"Ruby," Leon chuckled at Ruby's changing tone, "you have had your fair share of nights out there drinking that stuff. And that is why you should understand why I wanted to check on her first thing this morning."

Her left hand gestured upward. "Get off the bed and trade spots with her. I want to speak to her."

Standing up, I pulled down my hoodie to straighten it out, then walked over to her. "Thank you, ma'am, for letting me stay here last night." Swiftly I glanced over to Leon. "Someone in this room is against me camping out in my SUV for the night. But thank you again." I held out my hand to her. "I'm Leonora Carter, although you are welcome to call me Nora."

Sean leaned past his mother. "Leonora...Carter?"

"Yep, but only for this next week. Once I find a new town to call home, I'm going to legally change my last name and possibly my middle name as well."

Now distracted by Leon, Sean's eyes widened. "Leo." He blinked at him swiftly a few times then left his eyes wide open. He had to have been trying to warn him that he had forgotten to put his contacts in this morning.

"Sean," I took a step closer to him, "do you have something in your eyes? Don't rub them; maybe go try to flush them out with some water."

"No." His hand rose to stomach-level. "I'm fine."

I was going to mess with him; maybe he was one of those who had an issue with the color of Leon's eyes. "Are you sure? Maybe it is a hair. Without fail I get fibers tangled in my lashes if I use cotton pads with my face wash. Would you like me to take a look? I'm good at finding the needle in the haystack. I guess in this case, the fiber among the lashes."

"No, really, I'm okay."

"But a moment ago," I widened my eyes, "your eyes were tripping out."

He had enough and knew I was messing with him—his head dropped to the side as he glared down at me.

Unsure how Sean's mother was going to take this since she just found us in a bedroom together, I whispered sternly through my teeth, "I like him how he is; I think his eyes are engaging and don't need to be hidden from anyone."

She heard me; her head tilted the same as Sean's had, yet she wasn't glaring at me—she was studying me. It wasn't a checking-me-out type of study, more like where-did-this-little-thing-come-from? Still trying to hold on to the hope that I didn't have a tarnished relationship with her, I gave her a wistful grin and shrugged my shoulders. I was who I was, and it wasn't a lie.

She turned around and handed Sean the envelope that was tucked in her armpit, then stepped forward, engulfing me in her arms. My nose was overcome with warm florals mixed with a touch of orange and vanilla. My body was instantly taken back to that bay with Miss Gemma Ann's arms around me. That was the last time someone hugged me this deeply in this manner.

I rested my head on her shoulder—parents should have to pass this hug test before they are allowed to take their new baby home. No child should ever grow up not knowing what this hug felt like. I closed my eyes, and the words just flowed from my mouth as my tears did.

"I know that you're not Miss Gemma Ann, but I am so sorry for everything that happened that day. She should never have stepped in front of my father; I know how to turn so the backhand doesn't hurt as much. I was prepared, she wasn't, and his wedding ring caught her lip." The tears were streaming down my cheeks onto her sundress. "I'm so sorry. I told him I didn't care if he beat me to death or never looked at me again, he had to go back and apologize to her for hitting her. I should have yelled at him for talking to her the way he did, but I didn't know what the words he was saying meant. It was the first time I had ever heard them before. They were so wrong; she was so kind and didn't deserve anything that happened that day. I'm so sorry, I couldn't protect her the way she was protecting me. I tried but it was too late, it was all after the fact. I screamed at him so much he grabbed me by the neck and held me up against the refrigerator. When that didn't stop me, he threw me in a taxi and sent me home."

"Oh, my child." Her hand stroked my hair. "Never once did she ever hold that day against you. She carried you in her heart and prayed every day for your happiness and safety."

Drawing back, I wiped my face off with the cuff of my sleeve. After pouring all that out, even in front of the guys, I was at peace. That massive word vomit a moment ago was everything that had been pitted within me since that day. Though Ruby wasn't her mother, it still gave me closure being able to apologize for the events that day.

"I brought her heart back home for her. I wanted to tell her thank you and that I have always followed her words. I wanted to tell her I didn't grow into my environment."

I looked down at the carpet. You never know who will shape your life the most until you find yourself. Family and friends tend to be the biggest influence in people's lives. Mine did influence my life in positive and negative ways. The thing is, if it wasn't for Miss Gemma Ann's words, I would never have known the person I was. I was so wrapped up in pleasing my narcissistic parents that I was drowning myself for their approval. I didn't know this could be different until Miss Gemma Ann. From that point forward, I wasn't fighting to gain Miss Gemma Ann's approval—I was fighting to be true to myself. So when the day came, I could stand proud before her and tell her who I was. And...to hear the words that she was proud of me would be the icing on the cake.

"I wanted to hear her tell me that she was proud of me for being me," I mumbled into Ruby's shoulder.

"Oh, child." Sean's mom pulled me back to her chest. "From what my ma told me about you and everything Sean has, I am so proud of you."

She and her hugs were unbelievable. My emotions had been a rollercoaster since I got here. Up and down with things I was holding in and new things coming out. With these hugs, everything was freed. I was going to be all right.

"Child," Ruby backed us toward the bed, "come sit down and tell me everything that you were going to tell my ma on this trip here."

"More like, tell us everything that happened that day," Sean grumbled. "Not once did you say your father hit my grandma."

"Hush, Sean," Ruby snapped.

Yes, Sean could hush. We didn't need to talk about the negative of that day anymore. What I needed to talk about was the positive going forward. Such as how I got justice for two people for my father's wicked mouth and ways in one situation.

Sean leaned against the wall with his arms crossed against his T-shirt with what looked like a band logo between his arms. Ignoring him, Ruby sat at the head of the bed and patted the pale green comforter on her left so I would sit next to her. At some point, Leon had moved to the rocking chair. Glancing at him, I gave him one of last night's between-the-flames grins, then glanced down at the bed beside me. I was excited to share with them my vindication on how the seventy thousand dollars came about. And...it would be nice to have him closer beside me.

It worked; Leon sat down beside me, then leaned over to kiss the side of my head. He placed his hand palm-up on his leg. With that look in his eyes, it was my turn to follow the other one's request. I slid my hand down between his arm and torso until I reached his hand. Instantly he took my hand and turned our hands so his was on top. Slowly I tilted toward Leon and peered up into his eyes. It was more than just studying his eye color; I was seeing the truth that eyes are the windows to the heart. At one point, the optometrist at the optical I formerly worked for explained to me that our pupils dilate when they are admiring the one they love. I assumed Leon's eyes were not the only ones making this hypothesis true.

"Dear lord," Sean snapped, "will you two knock it off already?"

Right. Turning back to Sean's mother, I asked, "May I start with that envelope first? I feel like I was finally able to get Miss Gemma Ann the justice she deserved."

She nodded her head. "Of course, child."

I went on to explain how I had just graduated from university last Sunday. I told them that two or three weeks ago, my father was packing for another fishing expedition. This one was going to be a whopper; he was leaving for six weeks to fish in South America. There was no way he was going to come back for my graduation—at that point, I didn't think he even remembered it was coming up. Knowing the answer already, I still asked him if he was going to be back in time. Of course, the answer was no. Fishing was his top priority. Regardless of that, he was going to buy my disappointment off me so I couldn't be upset at him for missing it. Now, I never asked for anything. Truthfully, I just wanted him to tell me that he was proud of me, but it was easier to throw money around. He left me a hundred thousand dollar check and the titles for my sports car and my everyday car on my bed while I was at work. There was also a note that stated the sports car must remain at their house and I could only drive it to have it serviced. When I got off from work, I noticed the check and the titles. The thing is, I was holding the title to his sports car, not mine. The color of mine was True and his was Imitation Blue—he never could get this straight. We had the same sports car, but his was handmade and limited edition; mine was worth a quarter of what his was.

I glanced around the room at them; they were going to think I was an evil person for the next part. "For some history of this sports car, when the original owner passed away, the family agreed to put it up for auction, so everyone had a fair chance at it. The auction was to take place at three p.m. on Friday. Everyone knew this attorney, Forrest Stevenson, was going to put everything down to get this car. Knowing Forrest was scheduled in court first thing that Friday morning, according to the whispers and my father's drunken celebration confession, he paid the family to have the auction moved to eight a.m. so he could sweep in and buy the car."

I held up my index finger and deepened my voice as I quoted my father, loosely, "'Because no'—I'm not saying that word he used—'has the right to drive a magnificent car as that one.'"

Ruby's head tilted as she looked at me. "Did he use that term?"

My lip curled with disgust and I nodded. "Yeah, I'm sorry." I held up my hands, shaking them. "Just hold on, I promise you there will be a happy ending for everyone but my father. Forrest Stevenson is a kind gentleman. He's my friend's uncle by marriage. I hide out at her house, so I see him often. It's to the point that he recognizes me as his niece as well. When I realized my father's mistake, the first thing I did was take the title to Forrest's office and offer the car to him. It should have been his car in the first place, and I wanted him to have it. I told him everything that was going on, how I acquired the title, and then about my sister's wedding. He had a couple other attorneys from other firms come into overview as I legally sold the car to him for seventy thousand, which is the book value, not the true value. Since I was kind to go to him first with the car and gave him a steal, he drafted a contract to help block my sister from having her dream wedding up here. I just got their contract yesterday; he is in the process of reviewing it for me to ensure they didn't put any loopholes in it."

Now this was awkward. I just sat there as they all stared at me. Maybe they were wondering why I didn't give them the hundred thousand dollars instead. "I traded my car when I crossed the border; I needed something more reliable and a little larger." I laughed. "It's going to be my home for a little while. I set fifty thousand aside for the property owner to sign my contract. My parents are going to come up throwing money around—I want to be fair and give the property owner some compensation as well. I'm hoping that they are sitting comfortably so they will take this money and invest it back into the property so it can stand for a hundred more years. For the remaining funds, I plan to give it out randomly to brighten people's day."

I think a normal person would have just taken all the money to start a new life elsewhere. However, I didn't want my parents' money anymore. There was a weird stigma tied to their money. I didn't want that feeling of them funding my new life. This needed to be me as much as possible. They could have offered me a million dollars, and I would still walk away from it or give it out to others. Gifts and money from my parents were guaranteed to be used against me later; nothing from them ever came without strings attached. For this reason, I had money that I had saved over the years from working and birthdays to help me fund my new life. This life was going to be all me, minus my new SUV.

"No." Sean's mother looked at me with wide eyes. "No."

No to what? I just rattled off a bunch of things she could be objecting to. It had to be the contract; I was just like my parents throwing money around to get what I wanted. In spite of that, this was different—I was trying to protect the property.

"As long as you are in town," she patted my leg, "you will be staying with us."

"Thank you for the offer, but I have my SUV all set up." I squealed a touch. "I'm going to be glamping." I had dropped a pretty penny on a plush down comforter to lay it down in the back. I had picked up a new pillow and blanket. I was set. If only I got a chance to try it out.

"What the hell is glamping?" Ruby glanced over to Sean. "Well?"

Sean's head lowered into his shoulders. "Don't ask me, it must be a crazy American thing."

"It's luxury camping... No, that's wrong, it's glamorous camping. I bought this amazing plush down comforter to lay down in the tailgate." I squeezed Ruby's hand. "I appreciate your offer, though I probably will only be in town for one more night."

With that last statement barely leaving my mouth, there was pressure against my left side, as if someone was leaning against me. Leon was hunched down as he peered at me with sad puppy eyes—more like crushing puppy eyes. Yep, he could ask for anything right now and I would probably tell him yes.

I leaned my head against his. From the corner of my eye, I could see that Sean's mother was watching us, but I didn't care. Leon knew that I had growing feelings for him, and it seemed like he felt the same. Those feelings would just push down the thoughts that I was leaving soon. My heart just wanted to stay in this daydream with him longer.

Ruby's eyes narrowed, then she glanced down at the floor for a second. Sitting back up, she ordered, "Stay."

Leon sat up to look over to her. "What?"

She chuckled. "Not you," she held out her palm at me, "her. Nora, you have no reason to leave. Stay, enjoy our beautiful town. Perhaps you will fall in love and want to make this your home."

I liked her optimism, yet I was going to crush it. "Yeah, until my father comes up here and murders me. He's seriously going to murder me for selling that car, then he'll desecrate my body when he finds out who I sold it to. And if he doesn't do it, my mother will be up here for destroying her baby's wedding. I will be accused of giving her another medical condition."

I could hear my mother's words echoing through my head: *"All I ever wanted is to walk your sister down the aisle. While I lay there dying giving birth, all I could think about was just that. And now you are destroying it; you are destroying this family. Just kill me now and get it over with. I know that's what you want and are trying to do; you are the reason for all my health problems."*

I wish it wasn't going to play out that way—I truly did love this place. It was a place like no other in the world. People were always so kind here, except Mr. Grumpy against the wall. The lake, the forest, and the castle all added to the town's enchantment. And then there was Leon, wrapping his arm around my torso, drawing me to him. And that's the thing; when it was just the two of us, I forgot about my grand mission. I was instantly distracted and enchanted by him; it was as if he had some magic about him that he knew exactly how to unlock new parts to me. Parts of me that I held reserved tight from other suitors. They never felt right, no matter how long I knew the guy. Last night and today, my heart had been thumping in my chest with excitement, like a child bouncing through the house on Christmas morning. It was telling my mind that forever isn't so far-fetched anymore.

The side of Leon's chilly thumb rubbed my cheekbone with the rest of his hand on my cheek. His bottom lip pressed his upper lip up as it tucked with his wistful grin. This instantly sent my bottom lip into a pout as I gazed up into his eyes. I think the reality of it was setting in for him as well as his thumb moved to my bottom lip and his lips pressed firmly against my forehead.

Sean's mother took my other hand, snapping me from Leon's embrace. "Nora." She spoke softly, as if she didn't want to ruin our moment but had something she needed to get out.

"Yes, ma'am," I turned toward her, although leaning further back so I could rest against Leon.

"Oh baby, it's Ruby. Please call me Ruby." She bit the inside of her cheek for a second, as if she wasn't ready to speak. "What did he do to you that day?"

"I got off easy," I gave her a grin, "except for the AC part. He made me change into my swimsuit, then he paid a taxi driver to drive me the long way home. Which was twelve hours instead of eight. He told the driver he needed to drive with the AC on high, he couldn't talk to me; the radio had to stay off; if I fell asleep, he had to wake me up; I wasn't allowed to eat or drink; and if I had to use the restroom, I would have to pee on the side of the road."

In all honesty, it was my favorite punishment to date, because it was the one that influenced me the most. What my father wasn't counting on was that with nothing but time I was going to dissect, study, and analyze everything Miss Gemma Ann had said to me that day. She was a beautiful lady inside and out who never once looked down her nose at anyone. I wanted to grow up to be like her—there was nothing wrong with being kind to even strangers. Mostly, there was nothing wrong with listening to your heart and believing in it.

"Oh, and he refused to look at me for a month. Which was fine because ninety-eight percent of the time when he looks at me, it's usually an angry glare."

Possibly letting them know my own father despised me was going to change their views of me. Perhaps it would help them understand why he disliked me. "My mother baby-trapped him. He truly hates children, especially girls. And to note, she didn't baby-trap him because she wanted a baby. She baby-trapped him because he comes from old oil money."

"What is wrong with your family?" Sean rubbed his eyebrows with his thumb and index finger, then stopped. "I thought you said your older sister is the favorite?"

"Without a doubt she is the favorite because she was born on my paternal grandmother's birthday. The odds have been against me since the day I was born," I chuckled.

Sean walked over to the rocking chair and sat down. "Now I am just confused."

"My father is my grandmother's favorite of the five children. I was told he is the spitting image of her father. And to my grandmother, her father was the greatest man to ever walk the earth. So, since my sister came from my father and was born on my grandmother's birthday, she is the favorite grandchild out of ten. It's no secret within the family. Favoritism runs high—just ask my eight cousins or my aunts and uncles."

"So she's favored by your grandmother, not your father?" Sean looked over to Leon. "Is she still drunk? I'm so lost."

I held up my index finger. "I'm hungover, not drunk. When my sister is around, there are times I can tell my father resents my sister for my mother trapping him with her. However, my father wouldn't do anything to upset my grandmother to lose his status with his mommy. He coddles my sister like no other to show my grandmother that he's an amazing father."

Sean's head swung, then he side-eyed me, loading more questions.

I held up the rest of my fingers to stop Sean. I already knew what was going to be asked. "I'm a black sheep because my mother and sister like to play victims. They need a villain so people can feel bad for them. I have never been what they say I am; it's all a smear campaign."

It's easy to become a villain when you try to reach out for

help for the things my mother and sister were doing and saying to me behind closed doors while telling lies to everyone. With no witnesses, it was my word against theirs. Two against one, and time after time I lost. As time went on, I just backed myself into a corner, distancing myself from my family, and remained silent. Here and there I would hear secondhand accounts of things I supposedly did or said to my mother or sister. None of it ever had any truth to it.

"Get your hands off her," Ruby sneered at Leon as she pulled me into her chest. "She's my baby now."

"Thanks," I chuckled, "but I don't need to be anyone's baby. I just need to get away from them so I can be free to be me."

"Are you sure about that?" Sean scowled as he gestured toward Leon. "Every chance you get, you are snuggled up to Leo."

Ruby's eyes lowered to Sean. "I have three boys," she grumbled before her tone softened, "so I never got a daughter. It sounds like you never had a mother. While you are here, let's just give each other what we missed out on."

I thought about her offer for a moment. It wasn't such a bad idea—her mother taught me so much in such a brief interaction. I bet, spending a few hours with Ruby, I could learn a lifetime of things. I could feel my cheeks raising as I looked up at her. There was one thing I endlessly wanted the experience of having.

"Do you think..." I paused; this was going to be such a weird thing to ask of someone, "...you have some time to teach me how to bake things like cakes, cookies, pies, from scratch?"

I knew how to cook—most nights I cooked dinner for my family. Baking, on the other hand, I had tried a few times but constantly failed. It was something I wanted to take up learning, although it felt like you truly could not get the full experience from a lesson off an internet video. From a video, I couldn't ask questions or taste if it tasted the same as theirs. I couldn't show a video tutorial the cake in the oven and ask if it needed ten more minutes. Ultimately, I had given up on this baking dream until I married. As goofy as it sounded, I was hoping someday to have that amazing mother-in-law who would take me in and teach me the family secrets.

Ruby's jaw clenched, her fists shook, and her eyes began to glisten. If it wasn't for the glistening eyes, for sure I would have thought I was in trouble. She wrapped her arms around me, standing up. "Yes, my baby," she squealed, "I will teach you whatever and everything you want to learn how to bake!"

"Really?" I squealed. The thought of spending the day with Ruby baking was too much; I let out another squeal.

"You're staying here tonight; we will start first thing in the morning."

CHAPTER 5

The more I thought about it and the more I stared at the white lettering against the smoke glass door, the more amused I was. The county office was open on Tuesdays from 2:22 p.m. to 4:44 p.m. That was two hours and twenty-two minutes, or 142 minutes. This county recorder was going to have an awesomely fun personality. Now I was even more excited to talk to them.

I looked back at Leon in his black T-shirt and dark blue jeans, sitting with his arm on the back of the bench. His lips were curled in with his eyebrow raised. He had to expect me to be upset since I had my plan, and now this was throwing it off-course. I chuckled at his silly expression as I walked over to the bench and sat down next to him.

"What?" I chuckled again. "I'm not even mad—this is more amusing than anything." I patted his leg. "Good for that person for sticking to what they like. I just hope on Tuesday at 2:22 p.m. I can hear about their twins that were born on Tuesday, February 22nd."

"Are you sure that you're okay?"

"Yeah, I find this funny." My shoulders dropped. "Do you want to hear someone that won't?"

"Not really." His arm lowered and he drew me to his chest. "Do you have to call her now?"

"I kind of have to at this point." I pulled out my phone from my back pocket and made that dreaded call.

"Marigold," she sneered from the speaker. "Did you get them to sign the contract yet?"

Oh yes, I was going to leave this call on speakerphone. Leon had heard about her—now he was going to get to hear her.

"No, sorry, the records office doesn't open again until next week, T..."

She cut me off. "Goddammit, Marigold, we sent you up there with a simple task. Why am I not surprised that you can't even handle this?"

"Marigold," Ivan's voice drowned out my mother's. "Hey, Flower, when are you coming back? Me and you have a date to go shopping together."

This couldn't be good; I knew how my mother was with Ivan when my sister wasn't around. Since he was asking me to go shopping with him, clearly Stephanie wasn't around. Just as much as I didn't like it when Ivan interacted with me, Stephanie didn't like it either. After a few of her brutal lectures, Ivan knew this as well. Unfortunately, he refused to listen to her or me.

"What are you two out shopping for?"

"Here, Mom, trade me. I want to talk to Flower, and you need to try this on."

"Oh, Ivan," she giggled, "you might need to come in here and help me try this on."

It had to be something inappropriate by the tone of her giggles. The first time I learned about their inappropriate shopping excursions was at my cousin's engagement party when my mother was going on about all the latex outfits Ivan had picked out for her to try on at the little sex shop they visited together. She didn't care who heard her. It seemed more as if she was bragging that a young buck was still interested in her. Ivan hitting on you was far from a compliment, though. He would hit on anything that had a pulse.

"In a second, Mom." A door closed—he must have left her

changing room. "I'm going to go talk to Flower about wedding stuff."

My head moved back and forth as I mouthed to Leon it wasn't going to be about wedding stuff.

"So, my Forbidden Flower," I hated when he called me that, "your sister wants a lingerie bachelorette party. Mom and I are picking outfits for your sister as gifts. She thought it would be a good idea to have my input. When you get back, we are going to go shopping as well." His voice turned seductive. "I've already found a few outfits I want to see you in."

Besides the fact that Ivan was disgusting, it was disgusting that my mother was trying on outfits that she was going to be purchasing for my sister to wear during intimate moments between her and Ivan. Boundaries were never a thing with my mother. If I spoke up against this, I was called names for being a prude.

Leon's brows lowered. His lips pinched together, not in a pucker to kiss either. This was the first time I could tell he was getting frustrated. This poor man didn't know what he was in store for. Fingers crossed this didn't ruin his mood for the rest of the day.

I needed to get this conversation moving before Ivan said something else. "I won't be back for a week or so. The recorder's office is closed. The nearest hotel up here is a few hours away. I'm going to go check out the cities until the recorder's office opens again." All right, that was a lie, but he didn't need to know I was staying up here. More than anything, I didn't want them coming up here.

"How about I come up there and keep you company? Your sister and I have a deal that nothing counts until after the wedding."

Leon crossed his arms against his chest and was biting the inside of his lip now. His aggression was pointed at me, but it wasn't meant for me. I couldn't fault him; this was Ivan we were dealing with. Ivan only knew how to be inappropriate.

"Shouldn't you be writing your vows? I thought Stephanie said you two were writing them."

"I've already written them." His voice changed back from excited to seductive. "Care to hear them?"

"Please." I could only imagine what he wrote, considering his grades were bought. "Enlighten me."

"Babe, going forward from this day, you are going to vow three things to me—"

With that, I hit the mute button as I stared wide-eyed at Leon. These were going to be awful.

Ivan continued, "A cold beer always in my left hand, a cig in my right hand, a full belly, a full bottom lip, and most important, empty balls."

"Nooo..." Leon whispered, "is he serious?"

I held up my index finger to Leon as I took the call off mute. "So, Ivan, you know it's supposed to be your vow to her, like to love her for all your days and such. It isn't what she vows to do for you."

"Whatever, Flower, how would you know? Have you ever been married?"

"No." I rolled my eyes—there was no getting through his thick head.

"Neither have I, so you and I should practice together for our wedding night. It will be so great that you and your sister will wrestle each other for me. Trust me, there will be enough of me for the two of you. Maybe...we all could make up together."

I stared at Leon's beautiful eyes, trying to distract myself from Ivan's words, which were only going to get worse from here if I didn't shut him down. I set my phone on my lap, then leaned forward and covered Leon's ears. "That horrible case of gonorrhea is back." I kept my head tilted down toward the phone. I needed to stop Ivan from going any further. "It's like the snow-covered Rocky Mountains in my underwear, and the smell is so potent it makes me gag."

"You know," by the noise in the background it sounded as if Ivan was walking back into the dressing room, "I don't get how you have so many issues down there when you are supposedly my untouched flower."

"Toilet seats," I quickly responded as I released Leon's ears and crinkled my face at him.

"Don't listen to her, Ivan," my mother chimed in,."She's a boring old prude that is going to end up marrying a poor loser someday." Her voice turned snarky. "Because she believes in love that is only found in the heart." Her cackling filled the air. "Apparently, I didn't change her diaper enough when she was a baby, because she is still full of shit. It's really unbelievable, it must have replaced all her brain cells. I am shocked that she even graduated college."

My lips pinched together and my jaw clenched as I inhaled through my nose. I completed my double major within four years while working and still graduated with a 4.0 GPA. The only thing she did after high school was intentionally get herself knocked up so she would never have to work a day in her life. Oh, and the kicker to all of that: my father was dating her best friend when they hooked up. There was no hiding this little fun fact; she loved bragging about it to all. Classy...

Poor Leon should have gotten up and walked away five minutes ago—I would have. I already had my own circus; I wouldn't want to be subjected to another one. It was time to change the topic. "I was thinking maybe we should just leave this poor property owner alone. This place isn't a wedding venue; there are wedding venues all over the world designed for weddings. Stephanie and Ivan could just pick another place that isn't this one."

"Nonsense, Precious gets what Precious wants. I am warning you, Marigold: screw this up and I will make you pay for it."

She meant literally, not figuratively. I had already been told to pay for the cake and the photographer and was also warned it wouldn't count as a wedding gift; I would still need to buy one for the bride, one for the groom, and one for the mother of the bride. My mother may throw money around in front of people, but behind closed doors, she was stingy. Case and point, for three years I paid for her cell phone until my father decided he wanted to get a cell phone. Her reasoning behind making me pay for the cell phone was that if I hadn't given her all her medical conditions, she wouldn't need a lifeline.

"Ohhh," Ivan cooed, "can I pick her punishment?"

"Well look at that, I have another call. I will call you in a week with an update, bye." Before they had a chance to say anything, I hung up my phone.

Leon pointed his finger at me as his brows veered inward. "If he comes up here, I'm going to have words alone with him. Don't be surprised if he is never seen again."

"Welcome to my world." Now it was time for damage control. "Which, on my end of things, is not diseased. And I don't care how much she calls me a prude; for myself and my body, I believe certain acts should be saved for the right one for that one special night that ties you together forever." I sighed and rubbed the nape of my neck. "I am sorry for what you had to listen to a moment ago—it is the only way I know how to shut him down. More so, I'm sorry for subjecting you to them. It was completely unfair for you."

His hand cupped over my fingers as his thumb ran across the top of my hand. Before he could say anything, my phone began to vibrate with a new call.

Quickly I glanced down to see Forrest in his blue-black suit with his back to his partner lighting up my screen. I squeezed Leon's hand once before dropping it. "I have to take this." I turned the phone on speaker.

"Good morning, Nora." Forrest's smooth voice filled the air. This man could have been a voice-over with that cool, calm voice. It was the type of voice that you wanted to close your eyes and listen to as he read you a book. Well...in my case,

I could listen to him read our contract to me.

"Forrest, I'm surprised to hear from you. I thought you would be out cruising around."

"Not yet, I have a few things to handle around here. Then I am planning on taking the missus up the West Coast next week. Let's get to business." When there was business on the table, he never dillydallied around. "I reviewed your parents' contract, and as we thought, they are trying to screw over the property owner. Buried in the back pages, there is a clause stating that if your parents invest more than the property value specified, they will have thirty days to claim ownership of the property."

"I don't understand—if we can't even find the owner, how do they know the property value to specify?"

"They don't." There was the sound of papers shuffling. "They are going from the nearest property sold. It looks like it was a deal between family members because the property was sold for twenty thousand dollars."

"What!" I yelped. "Her dumb moat is going to cost that much. They're going to steal this person's land right out from underneath them."

"And that's why we have that clause in your contract."

I rolled my head back and pinched the bridge of my nose. "With all things considered, I'm not so keen on telling someone what they can and can't do with their land." I brought my head forward. "What if they want to pass it to the next descendant?"

"I get it," Forrest's voice was becoming remorseful, "yet it's the only way to block your parents from going after this land or paying someone else to do it. Since you left, your mother has been running around town telling everyone that they bought a castle for Ivan and Stephanie as a wedding gift. From what I heard, they plan on turning it into a summer home."

I rolled my head toward Leon and slowly moved it side

to side as I closed my eyes. This was expected; I wasn't at all surprised. All it meant now was the game was on—they were going to be cutthroat to get that property. If this owner thought this was just a bad dream, once they told my parents no, it was going to become a nightmare for them.

"Nora." Forrest's voice deepened, opening my eyes. "I know how your parents' attorney operates; I wouldn't put it past him to go after the property owner for the property after one of his clients was injured there. When you find the property owner, tell them this and have them put up no trespassing signs at every entrance to the property."

"Do you want a new SUV?" I tittered as I tried to calculate in my head how much more I could afford to drop in stopping them.

"With you just starting out from scratch," Forrest chuckled—he knew what I was truly asking, "I will now stand beside you at a pro-bono rate. And since I am already involved in this web, give the property owner my business card. I will do everything in my power to help them take down your parents."

"Forrest, you are a saint! Thank you so much!"

"You're welcome, but you need to keep me posted on where and how you are doing, all right?"

"Of course."

That was just a roller coaster of calls, and by Leon's curved body and arms crossed against his chest, we weren't getting off that roller coaster just yet.

"What does the clause in your contract state?" Leon asked.

I picked up my laptop bag from under the bench. Then I drew out a red folder and a green folder. Opening the green folder, I handed it to Leon. "In nonlegal terms, it states that if the property owner signs this contract, they legally will not be able to sell or rent out the property unless it is for agricultural reasons for the next ten years. I fully intend on telling them about my clause."

He peered up at me before he flipped the folder open. "What if it turns out that the owner is a jerk and none of this is worth it?"

"If the owner is from here," I pointed to the section that I just quoted, highlighted in fluorescent yellow, "I have a hard time believing that they are a jerk. And if they are, Miss Gemma Ann wasn't, Ruby isn't, Trevor isn't," I chuckled, "Hank is far from it, and then there's you: not a jerk. Even if the owner is a jerk, all of this is still worth it because that property most likely contains a little bit of history from all of you. Maybe Miss Gemma Ann's great-great-great-great-great-great grandfather was a knight. Or...maybe Miss Gemma Ann's great-grandmother times six or something was the kingdom healer. Perhaps Hank comes from the blacksmith, or I'm wrong and it's you that descends from a blacksmith." I gave him a soft grin. "If they are a jerk and if I fail, it will all still be worth it because I have met some of the most beautiful people because of it."

Leon grinned to himself as he sat back, crossing his leg over his knee. He reached over, picking the contract back up, and began reading it.

I set the other contract beside him. "You're welcome to read both contracts, but you must give them back to me before Tuesday at 2:22 p.m. They are the only printed copies that I have here." I leaned over and kissed his cheek. "I'll be right back."

That got his attention; he lowered the contract. "Where are you going?"

Standing up, I leaned over and kissed his other cheek. "To the hardware store to buy every no trespassing sign they have in stock." With my thumb and index finger, I gently turned his head up and stole another kiss. "This poor property owner doesn't know about the storm brewing. I want to try and help them as much as I can," I softly whispered against his lips. It wasn't a romantic line, though the way his eyes opened to my own, it was the delivery that made it worth it.

His chilly fingers danced down my arm until they reached my hand. "Hold up." He stood and moved closer until we were chest to chest. "You can't just run off, leaving me with only a peck."

His head lowered, blocking the sun. Even with the sun behind him, his eyes shone. He never returned home to put his contacts back in, so these were his own eyes for me to enjoy. And I was enjoying them, mostly when I caught him looking at my lips then moving to my eyes with anticipation. Yesterday, that moment was only visible by the lowering and raising of his eyelids, but today it was that heart-jumping-with-excitement arousal package.

"It's just down the block." I let my bottom lip graze his. "I can see it from here. Plus, that was three pecks." That was far from enough for me. Despite that, I didn't want to be coming on too strong, especially after he had gotten a glimpse of my crazy American life. For sure it would shy away the strongest of men.

His arms tightened around me. "I need more than three pecks if you are going to walk away from me."

I was not expecting that from him after my two crazy phone calls. I was expecting him to come up with a cunning excuse to remove himself from this situation and perhaps even my life at this point. He had to have seen me as walking drama—I felt like it. I mean, I wasn't the drama, but there was way more in my life than there should be.

That wasn't going to matter; just as I had earlier, he raised my chin with his thumb and index finger. Between his lips, there was the spark, and my mind filled with images once more. And once more, my lips moved against his as if nothing was happening in my mind.

But everything was happening in my mind; I was back in the stable with Leon and that unholy son of Satan. Leon fell to his knees as the iniquitous man wiped his mouth with his arm, then let his tongue wipe the blood off his own skin.

Leon pushed himself up as the iniquitous man began to tremble. His arms were coated in thick black hair, possibly three to four inches long. His nose stretched out into a snout as his pointed ears perked. He wasn't trembling—he was shape-shifting. Leon was now face to face with a black bear. The bear curled its lip up, exposing its fangs to Leon, then rushed out of the stable into the dark as the king had just before him.

Oh no... This had to be my creative mind still under the influence of yesterday's events, which had included drinking a hallucinogen and endless talk about how many bears were here now. Soaked in the hallucinogen, my mind had to be filling in the other details of these horrendous visions.

Leon dragged himself over to his dog, which was lying in a small pool of blood. He had to know she was dying by her current state and the tears streaming down his cheeks.

No, no, no, this needed to stop now. No one ever told me about King Leon's pet dog; my mind should not be able to fill in any more details. I had seen Thelma's story play out; there should be nothing left in my mind to come to life.

Swiftly he wiped his eyes and leaned down, resting his head next to hers. "Gunner Louise, thank you so much, you brave girl."

Leon drew back, petting her head. "Since day one, you have continuously been brave and loyal. I'll never forget you, Gun-Gun." His eyes blurred with tears. "I'm so sorry." Once again he lowered his head to hers. "I'm going to free you of your pain."

Oh god... I had seen *Old Yeller* one too many times to know that there was no way I was going to be able to keep it together if a similar storyline played out in my head.

Leon's hand rested on my neck as his other hand moved down my back until he cupped my butt cheek, raising me tight against him. His lips didn't move from my lips as I breathed him in. My heart couldn't care less what was playing out in my mind; it was basking in the warmth from Leon as if he was the sun shining down on my chest.

From the blood dripping from the sides of his chin and the dog's still body, I knew what he had just done. Worst of all, I knew what he had become. I gasped.

"Nora," Leon drew back a touch, "are you okay?"

The answer was FUCK NO! How was I going to explain this to him? "*Hey, when we kiss, my mind wanders to a horror movie, but don't worry, you are the star vampire in these visions.*" Hell no—I didn't want to lose him. I just needed a distraction for now until I could figure this out. There had to be some dumb reason my mind was doing this, I hoped.

From the corner of my eye, I saw a tabby cat rub against the corner of the building. "Cat" fell instantly from my mouth, giving me a much-needed distraction.

His left brow lowered. "Cat? What do you mean by cat?"

Swiftly I wiped my eye; this was going to be bad. I didn't want to lie to him, but despite that, I didn't know what else to do. "There's a cat in the area; I'm highly allergic, not deadly allergic." I pointed to my left eye. "It's the craziest thing, only this eye will run. That is a sign that I am highly allergic, and since I can still breathe it is not deadly allergic." Lies, lies, lies... I was a horrible person to be lying to him. This was too big of a lie to even be classified as a silly white lie. I was awful.

He studied me for a moment with his head slowly shaking—he wasn't buying it. My heart dropped; I was a horrible liar. I think he was learning that. Although perhaps it was the pirate whiskey causing the hallucinations and he had experienced them in the past. He was waiting to see if I was going to speak up first.

And that was going to be another hell no from me. I wasn't certain enough to risk speaking up and opening that can of crazy with him if I was wrong. Quickly I gave him one more kiss. "I'm off to buy some signs. I'll see you in a few."

There was no way I was going to stay around any longer.

Worse than the visions, there was a growing pain in my chest that I had just lied to him. My heart felt betrayed for Leon; this was all wrong.

CHAPTER 6

This was too much for me. I had successfully made a pie that was, hopefully, edible. Leon needed to hurry up and answer his door so we could see if it was. I knocked again on the black door to his apartment above the bar. After working all night, he had to be asleep. I would be—or would I? It was a quarter after eleven; perhaps he was in the shower. I knocked again—my clock was ticking. I only stopped over to have a pie break, then Ruby and I would be starting a cake this afternoon and possibly cookies as well.

"Come in," came from a muffled voice from the other side of the door. "I'm in back, getting dressed."

The apartment was not like other apartments; it was a modern, open-floor concept. When you walked in, the kitchen was to the left with the living room just past it. To the right was a dining area, then a hallway with three doors. That stuff was common for apartments, but the two walls of windows weren't. Standing at the kitchen island to the left and straight ahead, the walls were windows from floor to ceiling. This wasn't visible from the street-side view of the building, so the windows had to be on the back side of the building. They lit up the dark mahogany apartment. The ceiling was a dark, glossy mahogany with thin beams dividing the ceiling into different rectangles. The herringbone-pattern flooring was a touch lighter mahogany than the other woodwork in the apartment.

I walked over to the kitchen, setting the pie and glass bowl of whipped cream down on the island. Running my fingers against the marble countertop, I admired how striking and modern the place was—as if it had just been remodeled. Moving on, now it was the matter of where he kept his plates and utensils. Not counting the cabinet above the refrigerator, there were six mahogany cabinets above the countertops and stove.

Utensils were easier than I had thought; they were in the top far drawer. With this luck, I was going to try the cabinet in the island first. I knelt and swung the cabinet door open before me. Success! There were two different size plates. I drew out two nine-inch black and grey-blue dessert plates and placed them on the counter.

"What are you doing in my cabinets?" Leon growled as I closed the cabinet door, exposing him kneeling in front of me.

"Eep!" I emitted a piercing squeal of horror as I fell back onto my butt. My shrill instantly turned into giggling as I rested my elbows on my raised knees. That was beyond dramatic; I think I scared Leon just as much, and it was a good thing there were no other apartments in this building, or someone might have thought something bad was happening in here.

"Oh, Nora, I didn't realize it was you." Leon's bottom lip pouted out a touch as he leaned forward. "I didn't mean to scare you."

Playfully I pressed his shoulder back while dropping a knee, although it didn't do much as he continued to move in for maybe a hug or a kiss. I may be new to reading his body language, but the way his eyes shifted to my lips, it was for the latter one for sure.

"Are you sure about that?" I rested my crossed arms just under my breasts, hiking them up a touch. Even with his desired gaze, I wanted to have a little more leverage just in case, because he did sound upset a moment ago. I couldn't blame him; I was in the wrong for going through his cabinets without his permission.

Leon slanted forward, sliding his hands around my torso, wrapping his arms around me in a bear hug. The right side of his lips curled up as he peered into my eyes with a spark of mischief. Ohh... I liked this little spark; it was contagious. I gazed up into his eyes, returning that mischievous grin as he dead-lifted me when he stood up.

Leon set me on the counter, releasing me just enough so I was able to free my arms. There was no second thought; they moved up to rest on his shoulders so I could run my fingers through his freshly showered curls that glistened in the light from the windows like after the first snowfall in the moonlight.

Although now I was too far from him again. With that, Leon tightened against me once more, drawing my thoughts away from his hair. With his head resting against my own and being tightly secured in his arms, this was a far better greeting than being scared.

His lips gently pinched my ear lobe for a second before moving to my cheek. "I wasn't expecting you this morning," he whispered. "I thought you were baking all day with Ruby."

"Baking..." I softly breathed out as his lips moved closer to my lips. However, before they connected, I remembered why I was here and how I had a time limit. Swiftly I turned my head and pecked his lips before sitting upright so there was a little distance between us. "I have a surprise for you," I squealed. He could go ahead and find my squeal a little crazed, but I had a little 50s housewife in me. I wanted to be able to please him in other ways, such as cooking and baking. That little daydream was only going to come true if he enjoyed my baking. "For second breakfast I brought you blueberry pie and whipped cream."

Straightening up more, I gave Leon my best Pan Am smile while holding the bowl between my right arm and torso. "The whipped cream was whipped all by Nora power."

Who knew that whipped cream was just a little arm strength, mixing vanilla, sugar, and heavy cream together? This was never something I had thought about until Ruby taught me this morning. I had to chuckle to myself; I think I might have given her a grey hair when I put all the ingredients in the bowl, then set it in the freezer to set up.

"You are a strange one," Leon chuckled as he moved his cool hand to my cheek, "but I wouldn't trade you for anything else."

His lips moved against mine—gosh, more than anything I wanted this. Despite that, it couldn't go too far. I didn't want any visions right now. I just wanted to enjoy his lips for a moment, then we needed to get back to this pie. With the horror from the first two visions, I couldn't imagine the next level of horror the third vision was going to entail.

That spark must have traveled down to his lips as I was filled with warmth while he stole my breath away. His lips persuaded mine to let go and enjoy this. I ran my hand up his chest as the patches of hair tickled it until my fingers glided over something warm and wet. There was more wetness in this one spot than there had been on the rest of his chest. This was odd. I glided my fingers once more over the spot to feel that his skin was disturbed. Slowly I moved away from his lips and rested my head against his head, so I was able to peer down at what I had touched.

What I was not expecting to see was a bleeding three-inch gash on his left pec a few inches above his nipple. That halted any visions, any more commands from his lips, and my pie excitement. My anxiety was rising; how does one get a gash such as this one on their chest?

"Leon," I cupped my hand under the gash, "you're bleeding."

"It's nothing." His left hand covered the gash as he reached over with his right hand for his shirt, next to the pie. "Don't worry about it."

I couldn't tell if it was a deep gash from my angle, but either way, it needed to be tended to. "Try again." I lowered his hand as I peered into his eyes. "Let me take care of you."

"Nora," his hand moved back to the gash, covering it, "I'm excited to try this pie you made. How about you cut a couple slices while I finish getting dressed?"

"Umm, no." I crossed my arms against my chest and glared at him. "If you are a good patient, I will reward you with some pie."

He snorted, a brow lowering. "Seriously?"

It wasn't my intention to come across as treating him childishly by rewarding him with pie after allowing me to bandage him up, but he couldn't just leave a gash such as that exposed. I had no other leverage here.

"Yes." Sternly, I leaned back.

"Fine." Leon covered the gash once more. "The first aid box is in the hall closet."

This was a quick fix; I think we spent more time going around if he was going to let me bandage it. And since he was a good patient, he was going to get more than just pie. Gently I kissed the bandage, then right above it on his cold pec.

"How is this even possible?" Leon chuckled. "You have flour in your hair."

"Baking with Ruby is the best! She is so fun and free-spirited. There was flour everywhere."

I was all in on learning from Ruby. Sitting at the counter before we started, I busted out a notebook and different colored pens. I was going to sit and learn from the Master in an observing session. The Master, however, had her own ideas; flinging a tablespoon of flour at me, she told me to put my books away and get into the kitchen. From there, it was all free-spirited fun, with some more flour shenanigans.

Gently Leon pulled the yellow ribbon on the bow holding my hair in a bun. My pop-can curls bounced down, exposing in the middle of my center part my heart agate. Without a doubt he preferred my hair down as this wasn't the first or second time he had let my hair down for me.

"What's this?" He picked up the rock and flipped it over from finger to finger. "You don't need this anymore."

"Ruby knew how much it meant to Miss Gemma Ann that I have it, so she wanted me to keep it."

He tapped my chest right above my left breast. "Your heart is right there," his right brow dropped as his lips puckered for a second, "covered in flour."

I guess there was more flour in my hair than I thought. Glancing down, my plum-colored T-shirt was now flour-coated plum. "Sorry about that." I reached down to the hem of my shirt and drew it up until it was off. I peered at him with a hint of naughtiness as I held my shirt over the counter ledge with my thumb and forefinger. "Is this better?"

It was fairer—we were both shirtless now, except I was in a bra. An eggplant-colored bra layered with black lace flecked with silver that screamed it needed to be shared with others. It also screamed it needed to be touched; the contrast between the satin eggplant underlay and rough lace was seductive to touch. I didn't happen to put this bra and matching thong on today; it was more by chance if Leon and I got a moment together today. I thought he may enjoy it.

I was right; Leon took a step back with his top front teeth pinching his bottom lip as he admired this new view in his kitchen, allowing me to enjoy my own view of him in his black gym shorts with a neon yellow stripe down either leg with his proud, pale chest sprinkled with white hairs. He was proof that you didn't need to be sun-kissed or superficial to be enticing.

Leon's fingers slid through the belt loops on my jeans, drawing me closer to the edge of the counter. The back of his fingers glided up my side then toward the center of the bra. I was right earlier—this bra screamed to be touched. The pad of his index finger skated along the edge between the fabric and my skin. His head remained bowed as he watched his hand complete its path.

In a flash, his hand cupped my right breast as his lips moved to my lips—again, only for a moment, then he drew back. Not as if he was timid, but more as if he knew how to get my pulse up. And I liked this sweet and soft side that turned a little devious.

My breasts were pressed together within Leon's hands. "Are you sure pie is the only reason you stopped by?"

I tugged at the tie on his gym shorts, drawing him closer to me, then I wrapped my left leg around him, causing him to reposition his hands. "This was for later if I got to see you again today."

One hand moved to my neck while his other hand moved into my hair, tightening a fistful. The desire for later to be now was demanding my attention.

Lost in his lips and the sweetness of the tip of his tongue, my mind flicked back on; I was back in that stable again. I watched as Leon wiped his mouth with his hand, then wiped his hand on his brown pants. He stood up and walked to the front of the stable, putting on a belt from which hung a sword. Then, in a flash, he took off out of the stable into the night as the others had before him. However, I stayed with him, watching him run through the forest, dodging trees and jumping over fallen logs.

Soon enough, behind him was the boreal forest made up of western white pine, white spruce, white cedar, and balsam fir. Before him was a cliff edge that overlooked the lake. I knew where this cliff was; I had seen it from exploring with my sister years ago. It was on the east side of the lake.

Below him was a red wall of jagged sandstone caves. He watched his footing as he moved closer to the edge strategically, as if he was looking for a certain spot. Next, he knelt and lowered his feet over the edge to what appeared to be a little lip on the side of the cliff. Then he took a step lower and placed his hands on the original lip and began to scale the side of the cliff, following the curve of the cave until he disappeared into its mouth.

Inside, he moved to the left and lit a lantern sitting along the back wall. He had to have been in this cave before; lanterns don't just magically show up. He placed the lantern on a large boulder at hip height. Then he fell to his knees and bowed down to the red stone.

When he sat up, the whites of his eyes were red and his cheeks glistened in the light of the lantern. Calm and collected, he walked over and propped his sword up in a crevice in the wall. After a deep breath, he charged the tip of the sword. The tip didn't even penetrate the breast of his white shirt before it fell.

Again, he propped the handle of the sword in the crevice. This time he placed a rock on either side of the pommel. Four steps back, he was against the opposite wall, and again he charged the tip of the sword. This time the tip pierced his chest an inch or two above his left nipple. His white shirt began to turn red around the silver blade.

His neck thickened, his vein bulging out to take center stage as he screamed out in pain while taking another step forward. His torso shifted to the left, dislodging the sword from the wall. It was only a second, but it felt like forever as I watched the sword dangling from his chest, losing its silver shine to the red cloak, before sliding down his shirt onto the pommel, then falling against the wall. His actions were pixelated with elbows out and his hands in wide claws moving to his head as he screamed out again.

There was so much in his screams—I could feel his pain. It wasn't the pain you felt in the back of your throat; it was the suffering he knew. My heart raced not with the physical passion my body felt, but with the sheer horror of what I was witnessing. This was so wrong; I shouldn't be witnessing this man as Leon trying to end himself in this manner or in any manner. This shouldn't be happening while the rest of me was living in a state of ecstasy. And it was—I could feel Leon's hand cupping my breast as his fingertips gently pressed into the upper side. His other hand rested on my neck with his thumb on my jawline gingerly controlling the angle of my head, his dominance balanced with his softness. I could feel that warmth within me increasing, giving me confidence. My lips knew exactly how to dance with his lips as if they had been practicing for years. With my left hand resting on the back of his neck and the right one on his lower back, I had the power to draw him in closer. My body wasn't being awkward with him in any form.

My jean shorts were still on and zipped up. Even with his hand cupping my breast, my girls were still safely secured in their holders. Leon was in his shorts with everything below his waistline leaning against the island. For no reason, my mind was in one of the layers of hell again with this hallucination, vision, whatever it was. There was nothing that we were doing at this moment that would have remotely tarnished my chances of wearing that pure white wedding dress someday. There was no reason for my mind to be hysterical like this. My mind needed to be turned off so the rest of me could just enjoy my Leon.

There was a commotion at the entrance of the cave. Slowly, Leon turned his head toward the enormous figure now entering the cave. "Leave, it's not safe for you," Leon whined at a man that appeared to be Sean's twin. Sean was already a fit, muscular brick wall; this guy was twice the size of him.

The man knelt before Leon, placing his hand on his shoulder. "Are you hurt?" he asked, his deep voice echoing through the cave.

"Gavin," Leon refused to look at him, "it's not safe for you to be here. I order you to leave at once."

"I will not leave your side. Are you hurt?"

"Gavin," Leon's voice rose, "you must leave now!"

Ugh... There was no turning it off. I wanted to just scream out like not-my-Leon had for this to end. As before, everything within me was muted. There was no justification for this happening for the third time. I couldn't blame it on pirate whiskey anymore; I hadn't drunk it since Thursday night. In fact, I hadn't had any alcohol yesterday or today. By now there would have been no alcohol present in my blood. Perhaps it was laced with something, yet this felt too real to be dreaming up while making out with Leon. Thelma only told us the description of the king after he was bitten. Not once could I recall hearing the tale of how the king tried to off himself after he was bitten. I had nothing to go from to create little details, such as feeling the heaviness of the air in the cave as if it was going to rain soon, or smelling the flames of the lantern mixed with the subtle essence of blood droplets that were stimulating my other senses.

I could distinguish which one was reality and which one was hallucination. I could taste the cool mint of my Leon's mouthwash or toothpaste with his kisses, but I could smell that weird metal smell on not-my-Leon's breath as if he had been sucking on pennies while he panted. The Leon next to me smelled fresh with the essences of tea tree shampoo in his hair, while not-my-Leon smelled of horse dust, hay, and sweat releasing those sweet endorphins. It was almost as if he had been working in the stable all night.

Gavin moved his face in front of Leon's. "Oh, lord." Swiftly he drew back. "What happened to you?"

Leon's head fell to the side, exposing the four puncture marks. "I was bitten." He turned to Gavin with tears streaming down his cheeks. "I don't know what's going to happen, and I don't want to hurt you."

Good lord, those bite marks made me realize how messed up I was. I was breathing in a man that was trying to kill himself after witnessing one of the most horrendous things playing out.

Gavin's chest collapsed as he fell back on his butt. He placed his elbows on his knees and pinched his eyebrows together.

"Gavin, please leave me here."

"I will not leave you," Gavin boomed. "I swore to protect you, and I still will." His eyes began to swell with tears. "I am so sorry I wasn't there to protect you. As soon as I saw the bear leave the stable through the window, I rushed out of the castle to you. I was too late—by the time I got to the stable, you took off, and I followed you here. I'm not going to let you down again; I will stand with you now no matter what."

Leon placed his hand on Gavin's shoulder. "You are my knight, but mostly you are my brother. My time is up. I need you to help me end this before someone gets hurt."

"No." Gavin shook his head. "I will not hurt you in any manner. We can figure this out together."

Leon stood up, pulling off his shirt and tossing it to the side. Next, he took the chain that contained two rings off his neck and tossed the chain next to the shirt. "For the safety of the people in this kingdom, there is only one answer."

Leon walked over, picking up the sword and handing it to Gavin. I watched as he fell to his knees, as if the weight of everything drew him down. Leaning forward, he stretched out his neck as long as possible. "I will never hold this against you. End this now so you can save me from becoming..."

This was it—I was going to have my answer to whatever happened to King Leon. But now I didn't want to know; I had seen enough. More than anything I wanted to snap out of this vision. I was about to witness the death of the man that I held in my heart as the standard. He was my symbol of pure love. Just the emotional aspect of watching a man in Leon's image was going to destroy me. Even with my Leon alive and well before me, I was never going to get that image of Leon beheaded out of my mind. It would haunt me worse than the description of Thelma's creature.

There was a warm stream running down the outer edge of

my left eye as Leon's lips caressed my right jawline, making their way down my neck. His hand lowered to my lower back, then he pressed against the back of my jean shorts, closing that narrow gap between us. His hands moved up, drawing my chest into his chest. The world needed to stop, as did my mind.

Gavin cut off Leon. "Don't say it. You are not and you will never become one. I will stay by your side night and day to ensure that darkness doesn't seep into your blood."

"It's too late," Leon snapped. "End me before you can't. I order you now!"

Gavin dropped the sword. "No," he whined, falling to his knees before Leon.

The silkiness of his lips was now on the middle of the side of my neck. For a second there was the pressure from the cool wetness of his front teeth gliding against my skin. The haziness or distraction from the cave was gone just like that. I was now hundred percent focused on what Leon was going to do. Was he going to give me a little love bite or the dreaded hickey? I wasn't going to open my eyes; I wanted him to have that permission to be himself. I could handle dealing with the hickey later.

His lips remained still together for a second, then swiftly he removed them along with his hands against my back. This wasn't what I was expecting—he had to have known that I was distracted. Possibly I wasn't as smooth in my movements while we were intimate with each other. There was a chance he knew I was stressed, or he felt the stream of tears from my left eye.

Leon's hands moved to either side of me on the counter, his head lowering without looking at me. "I will be back in an hour," he said, then he walked out.

Not just out of the kitchen—Leon walked out the front door, leaving me sitting on the kitchen island alone. His tone was so cold; he must have caught on that I was distracted and took it as I wasn't as into him as he was with me. Or perhaps he saw the little stream running down my cheek and thought he was being forceful with me. Either way, he had just walked out, upset, and I couldn't breathe anymore from being on this roller coaster.

CHAPTER 7

I sat there staring at the dark pistachio-green trim on Ruby and Gordon's white Dutch colonial house from behind my steering wheel. Leon had to have noticed earlier that there was something wrong with me. How was I going to explain to the man I had fallen for in a couple days that when he kissed me, I saw a horror movie playing out in my mind? He was going to think I was off my rocker. It was over; I couldn't continue to have these visions every time I was with him. This was unfair to him, and I wasn't going to be able to take much more.

This was too much. I was suffocating in my SUV. I opened the door, only to take off down the gravel road. After a mile or two, my surroundings became familiar. I was on the red gravel road to that old campground. This realization only pushed me to run faster. I was praying that I was going to find my clarity there.

The campground main office stood with boarded-up windows, rust patches on the teal-green metal roof, and absent of its best feature: Miss Gemma Ann sitting in that old wooden rocking chair, staring out at the lake. I would give anything to have her here right now; I needed her advice. She wouldn't judge me harshly if I brought this to her. I didn't know who to bring it to or how to even handle it.

With Miss Gemma Ann not here anymore, I did the next best thing. I walked down to that bay and sat in the water as

I had once before. Running my hand back and forth under the water, I searched for a rock that resembled a brain. I just needed a sign that I wasn't going crazy. This had to be some weird regression from my childhood.

The sound of the water splashing wasn't enough to pull me from studying the rocks beside me with my head resting on my arms, which were crossed on my knees. It could have been a bear at this point; I didn't care anymore. I wasn't going to move. The water splashed up against me as if someone had sat down beside me. It still wasn't enough to draw me from the rocks.

"Baby girl," Ruby calmly said, "what are you doing out here?"

I kept my face resting on my knees; she didn't need to see that I was adding a little salt to the lake. "I needed some air. I needed some clarity." I sniffled. "There's something wrong with me, so wrong with me. The worst part about it is he's starting to figure it out too...I don't want to lose him."

"What do you think is wrong with you that you're going to lose him?"

"You're going to think I'm crazy." I peeked over my arms. "I don't want to lose you either."

"Oh, baby," she tittered as she wrapped her arms around me, drawing me into her chest. "Never am I ever letting you go."

Inhaling deeply, I let it out. "There's a guy in town that my heart is head over heels for. I have never felt this way before for a guy, and I just love it. He seemed to feel the same way about me until today. He...he stopped in the middle of kissing and walked out. I ruined it." I looked up to Ruby. "Not that we were going to go any further than that." I didn't need her to think I was a hoochy chasing after all the local boys.

"Do you think he doesn't like the way you kiss and that caused him to leave?"

For how much he liked to study my lips, there was no way he didn't like the way I kissed. My head moved side to side. "I think he realized what was happening when we kissed."

"What do you mean?"

First stop on the crazy train. "My left eye will stream tears out, and I feel like my face goes flush in fear." I shouldn't have used the word "fear." It wasn't always fear—the last time had been more out of sympathy.

By her eyes bulging out, I realized I really shouldn't have said it.

"Is he forceful with you?" She didn't give me a chance to respond as she started to stutter a little. "I don't care who he is, I'll put him in his place."

"No." Moving back to my original spot, I dipped my hand into the water. "He's the opposite. He's...incredibly kind and sweet to me. He constantly keeps me close to him. If he could, I think he would put me in his pocket, and I wouldn't object."

"Baby," Ruby's brow lowered, "I'm lost."

I inhaled deeply again. "The best way to describe it is reading a book while watching television. Part of my mind is focused on him, while the other half is watching a vision play out in my head. Oh, and I cannot turn off these visions. Either they have to play out or something in the outside world shuts them down."

"What are these visions?"

There would be no turning back if I told her the truth. I needed to be prepared for the consequence of airing this out. She was going to find me insane and possibly tell Leon to run to the hills away from me. On the other hand, I had no one I could turn to for advice when it came to this issue. I could only imagine what my mother or sister would tell me. And it wouldn't be so simple to call a friend back home, either. With starting a new life, I didn't want my life in the States mixing with my future new life. There was a lingering fear that some-how it would get back to my family—then I would have to vanish and start this process all over again.

I was going to give her a preview of my crazy train. "The

first time we kissed, I saw a man in a stable. He must have been closing it up for the night. Well, from what I can gather, I think the story of Leon the Great is playing out in my head. Except, since I don't know what he looks like, I use *my* Leon's image in his place. In spite of that, the weird thing is he started out physically different. His hair was short on the sides with about an inch of length on the top. It wasn't white, it was dark chestnut-brown. His eyes weren't orangish, they were deep brown, almost black. That's...umm..."

"We have time." She had to have known that I was holding back; I've been told I can be read like an open book. "Go ahead and tell me exactly what you saw."

Turning away from her, I watched the waves roll into us. "I saw a king threaten Leon about refusing his daughter. He accused him of being arrogant, but it seemed more like Leon wanted to find love. I'm sure that my mind added that in because that's what I believe. Anyways, the king left, but soon after, Thelma's creature took his place. This creature had..." My heart raced—it was hard enough to witness it; I didn't want my spoken words to bring life to it again.

"Baby," Ruby softly spoke as she rubbed my back, "sometimes talking about what scares us is the best way to overcome that fear." Her hand rested on my shoulder. "You are safe with me."

With the warmth of her words and the comfort of her hand, the toxic words smogged the beautiful view before us as if it was the smoke of a wildfire overtaking the innocence of the sun's warmth. The fear fueled my voice to tell her every detail of what I witnessed. In my mind, I just kept telling myself I was already here. Maybe after hearing what I saw, she would have an answer to all of this. Or perhaps she knew the urban legend and could tell me if there was any truth to what I was seeing. I just needed Ruby to pull something from this vision to tell me that I was sane.

Ruby's lips curled in with her eyes widened, her head

moving up and down as she continued to listen to me in a state of horror. By her reaction, I was starting to regret telling her this, but there was a slight ounce of hope trying to remain lit within me. That hope was after all of this, she was going to tell me about her own hallucinations from drinking that pirate whiskey. And how the ingredient that causes the hallucinations takes a while to leave your system. Ultimately, the answer to all of this was going to be that I was stuck on a bad trip and needed to listen to Leon's warnings next time.

That hope was swiftly extinguishing as Ruby said nothing and continued to stare wide-eyed at me. My chest dropped; this wasn't going to end how I hoped. "For the most part, I don't think he caught on to this one. I played it off as if it was a side effect of my hangover. I *was* hungover. I had too much of his pirate whiskey—I mean moonshine—the night before. Not all of that was a lie; I was hungover. But I do not like lying to him." I tapped my chest. "I don't want to lie to him. I don't want him to think I'm crazy. I'm not crazy; I just don't know what's going on. The second time," I whined, the reality of it all was setting in, "I lied to his face. I didn't know what to do, my eye was watering, and I felt flushed. We were outside, so I told him that I was allergic to cats. There must have been a cat nearby." I was no better than my mother or my sister; at this point, I was the same as them.

There was a chance that Ruby was going to tell Leon about this awkward conversation in the lake. If that was the case, I didn't know if Leon would talk to me again. He should just run for the hills and free himself from my toxicity.

I bowed my head. "If you tell Leon about all of this, will you tell him I'm sorry for lying? In that moment I didn't know what else to do. My sister, who still lives at home, just bred her Persian cats. As of when I left, my mother has three and my sister has four cats. I'm not allergic to cats. I didn't want to lie to him, I don't want to lie to him ever. He deserves better."

He did deserve better; he may have walked out, but now

it was my responsibility to walk away. I could leave Journey and head south a few hours to Nellville until Tuesday. I had a friend back home who knew I wasn't coming back. She told me that if I ever felt lost or alone, to visit her parents in Nellville. They would take me in with no questions asked and help me with whatever I needed.

Swiftly I lunged at Ruby, wrapping my arms around her. "Thank you so much for all that you have taught me and listening to my crazed story. I'm so sorry for everything." The water rushed down my legs as I stood up. I swiped under my eyes with the side of my hand before walking toward the shore.

"Baby girl, come back here," Ruby ordered as she stayed in place, "and tell me how many..." Her hands trembled as she tried to find the correct words.

"Visions?"

"Yes, visions that you have had." Her tone was stern and direct; it made me feel as if I owed it to her to finish this conversation before leaving.

I walked back over to her and sat before her as if she was Miss Gemma Ann. "Three."

"Please tell me all about the last two visions."

"The second one was about his dog. What I left out last time was there was a dog in the stable with them. She was a beautiful golden-reddish dog with a black muzzle and paws. He called her Gunner Louise, Gun-Gun. My gosh, was she ever a beautiful dog... And protecting, she charged Thelma's creature without a second thought. Unfortunately, he had the upper hand and threw her into the pitchforks hanging on the wall. The tines pierced her torso... My heart broke watching this play out because you could see that Leon loved her." My left eye began to run, adding salt into the lake as my voice cracked. "He thanked her up and down for being such a loyal dog. Leon apologized just as much to her before—" I made my index and middle fingers into fangs. "She was his first." My voice grew louder in Leon's defense. "It wasn't Leon's fault, it was clear that she was dying, and he was just... *Old Yeller*."

"Leonora" fell softly from Ruby's mouth.

This wasn't good. It was the first time that she called me by my real name. And her poor eyes were going to be the driest eyes for how open they were without blinking during most of my story. It wasn't as if I was trying to scare her—she asked what I saw. Part of me still saw Miss Gemma Ann in her, and Miss Gemma Ann wanted me to be honest with her. I just don't think Ruby thought my honesty would be this horrifying.

She blinked twice rapidly. "What happened in the third vision?"

"It's not going to get any better." Slowly I shook my head side to side. "They all have a level of darkness about them. I think that's enough for today."

"That's all right, maybe it will help you clear your mind by talking about them."

For her sake, maybe it was best I try to find the positives and focus on them. "Leon tried to kill himself by stabbing himself in the chest with a sword." Or not—I needed to tone it down for her. "He knew what he was and was trying to protect everyone else from himself. Gavin ended up finding Leon."

"Wait," Ruby interrupted, "did you just say Gavin?"

"Yeah, there was a man that looked just like Sean but twice the size of him. He had such a calming voice and mannerism; you knew that you could trust him with your life. And Leon did—Gavin was his knight. Yet I think there was more there than just knighthood. They loved each other, not the way I am in love with my Leon, but the way my Leon and Sean are brothers."

Ruby's bottom lip was beginning to bounce. I wasn't sure if I should take this as a good or a bad thing. I placed my hand on her hand to ask the one question that possibly could solve this mess for me. I needed to know. "Is Gavin real?"

She nodded. "Yeah, he was. He lived around six hundred years ago. He was Leon the Great's right hand and his knight."

"How? How am I dreaming this up?" Never had I heard the name Gavin until Leon in my vision uttered it. "Am I having flashback visions? At first, I thought I was having a reaction to the moonshine that they were passing around at the fire. Perhaps there were hallucinogens mixed into it. Right here and now, I am sober. Which makes this a hundred times worse because it has to be me."

"It is you." Ruby stood up, causing the water to rush off her yellow summer dress.

That was most likely the right answer, but far from the one I wanted to hear. I remained seated in the lake. It was time for one of those bears everyone was so fearful of to come take me out since I was losing my mind. I was going to be free from my family for the first time only to end up in psychiatric help. I fell forward—the bears could come get me as I drowned myself in the shallow water.

Ruby grasped my shoulders and rolled me over, foiling my plan. "What are you doing?"

"Marinating myself in fishy lake water for the bears because there is something horribly wrong with me. These visions are awful. I can't live the rest of my life having them every time I am intimate with Leon."

"Oh, my dear, you are in love for the first time." She tittered as she held out her hand to me. "Your hormones are all over the place, filling you with creativity. Let's get back to baking and channel this energy."

"If that's the case, why can't I have visions of chocolate chips attacking me while I bake instead of these visions?" I whined. That would have the extra bonus of deterring me from eating sweets like I do. I rolled onto my back as I pictured a tip of a slice of cheesecake slicing my hand off. On second thought, no to baking horror visions.

Ruby bit her bottom lip as she gazed out at the lake, then

looked back at me for a second. "Gordon was getting jealous of me hogging you all morning. He would like to have some time with you to get some daughter time in as well. I think you are in need of some papa time."

It was hard to keep that awkward chuckle in; I could count on my hand how many times a guy in my life wanted to spend time with me in the father-daughter capacity. And never in any of those times was it with my father.

"Okay" dropped from my lips in a mixture of snark and disbelief.

"Then, later this evening, you and I will make milkshakes and watch comedies with the guy-who-gets-the-girl endings all night."

Ruby was oddly comfortable with this, but her reasoning didn't seem fitting. There had to be more to it than my hormones, or people would be talking about this all the time. For now, I was going to give her the benefit of the doubt.

CHAPTER 8

I watched as Gordon popped the hood to my SUV, which was parked on the gravel part of their driveway where I had left it earlier. He had incredible genes; he didn't look a year older than forty, though he had to be in his sixties with his eldest in his mid-thirties. Gordon's smooth heart-shaped face was perfectly holding his thin mustache that turned into a goatee, crawling two inches up the sides of his cheeks. These were great leading lines to his ears. Now, normally I didn't notice people's ears, but Gordon's were on the smaller side for a male, making them cute. Most of his features were on the smaller side. His eyes were narrower, closer to the bridge of his nose with smaller canopies. And since I had this new thing for noses—Gordon's nose was more to a point and not so predominant. What wasn't on the smaller side was his incredible smile. His all-upper-teeth smile was a mile of cheerfulness.

Ruby wasn't joking—Gordon wanted papa-daughter time to teach me all the things that a dad, daddy, pa, papa, or pops teaches his daughter. That was our first order of business; establishing our titles for each other going forward. I was now his baby girl, and he was my papa, dad, daddy, pa, or pops.

"Baby girl," Gordon propped up the hood against the built-in stick he pulled from the front of the engine, "tell me how you check the fluids in your car."

"Well, Papa, I would call Holly to schedule an appointment to have Ben look at them." I wasn't calling him Papa to be condescending. I knew that would get a smile out of him, and at this point I wasn't sure what title felt more natural to call him yet.

His black peppered eyebrows lowered, narrowing his eyes even more. "How do you change a tire?"

"Oh, that's an easy one." I smiled up at him again. "Have it towed to Ben."

Ben was our family mechanic; the man was amazing with vehicles. He could have an answer in minutes and fix it within a couple hours. Holly was his receptionist. She was as friendly as they came and always had a good story to tell. The only time I got to drive my father's cars was to run them to Ben, as I was my father's personal runner. I ended up getting to know Ben and Holly well by chatting with them when I dropped off the cars. Thankfully we never chatted about cars.

"What about when your check engine light comes on?"

"Oh, for sure take it to Ben A.S.A.P," I sang to him with a little zazz.

Gordon crossed his arms against his soft grey T-shirt. "Do you know how to pump gas?"

I was going to mess with him a little. "Ben does," I said, then I busted out laughing. "For real, I can pump my own gas. And I have a little hammer in my glove box for when something isn't working; I can hit it to get it to work until Ben can look at it for me."

"That's it—you're going to learn how to do some of this stuff. There's only one Ben, and he's not in your passenger seat to help you if you get stuck somewhere up here."

Before I could reiterate, Gordon pointed his index finger at me. "No hammers."

After two of the longest hours of my life—well, three, because Gordon had to look up how to do things on my SUV since it was the latest model and, according to him, "filled with cheap plastic"—I now knew basic car care for my new SUV. Truthfully, I should have put some money aside to see if

Ben would have come up here with me instead. That wasn't a knock on Gordon, either. There was no bringing my interest in vehicles to life.

Gordon slammed the hood down on my SUV. "All right, baby girl, it's time to do something fun."

I prayed it had nothing to do with vehicles, but my mind drifted to golf. For whatever reason, I felt like Gordon was a golfer.

His head angled to the side a touch. "Do you want to learn how to sword fight?"

Wait... I could have sworn that he just asked me to sword fight. By the bouncing of his eyebrows, I think I heard him correctly. "Umm... Yeah!" Forget golf, this was going to be awesome!

With my new love, Leon was still sitting in the back of my mind. And our visit together popped back in my head. Gordon wasn't around this morning while Ruby and I were baking, so Gordon and Leon must have been sword fighting earlier, and that is how Leon got the gash on his chest. That gash was brutal; Gordon must be as hardcore when it comes to sword fighting as he was about teaching me about maintaining vehicles for the last three hours.

"Wait," I shook my hands out in front of me, "only if you take it easy on me. This morning I bandaged Leon's gash up. I don't want any of those. Plus, I don't want to bleed all over my bras. All the pretty ones are not cheap, and now I have to live on a budget."

Gordon snorted then tittered—I don't think he was ready to have me as a daughter. "I promise to take it easy on you."

Gordon walked over to a large shed, not quite a garage, on the back corner of the property before the trees. I watched as he drew the keys out of his jeans to unlock the padlock. I was curious if it was a man cave with cases of swords like they have cases for guns. Or perhaps the swords were displayed on the walls on plaques of sorts. Maybe I needed to offer my assistance if he was going to pull out all the fencing gear because of my weird little bra rant.

Before I had a chance, Gordon walked out with two swords. The blades had to be about three feet long. I was not expecting massive medieval swords, more wobbly, thin fencing swords.

Gordon handed me a sword, the weight dropping my hand a touch. I was not expecting it to be about seven pounds and almost dropped it as soon as it was in my hands. I pointed the sword down at the ground. "Are these real?"

The sword was a cross with black leather closer to the midsection where the bars met. Above the black leather was a silver handle that came to a semi-round end. The silver handle was engraved with some sort of knotting, comparable to Celtic knotting I had seen in the past. That semicircle was engraved with a crest of sorts. I couldn't make it out fully, but it felt familiar.

"Yes, so be careful. You have Gavin's sword, and I have Bartholomew's sword."

"Hold up." I looked up from examining the sword. "This is Gavin—as in Sir Knight Gavin's sword?"

"Yes baby, Mama descends from Gavin, so it has been passed down the years to her."

I returned to admiring the sword. "She didn't even say it, but I can see Gavin in her, and holy cow is Sean his mini-me. Physically, that is. I don't know if Sean still hasn't fully warmed up to me."

"Baby..." The stress in his tone pulled my attention back to him. "What are you talking about?"

I could feel my eyes widen as I realized my mistake. There was no way I was going to tell my new papa about my visions. First, I wanted to stay in this fantasy of having a television sitcom father. If I could have picked my father at birth, I would have chosen Gordon. He was everything that my biological father, Dan, wasn't and everything I wanted growing up. Second, if I was his baby, I wasn't sure how he was going to handle hearing that these visions only came about when I was making out with a boy.

"Who is Bartholomew?" I piped up, changing the topic. After the few hours going on about different things with my SUV, I didn't want that same intense lecture from him about sex.

Gordon went back to wiping his sword with a cloth, exposing its shine in the sunlight. "King Leon's other knight. He had two: Gavin and Bartholomew. I descend from Bartholomew."

Gavin was King Leon's right hand, and Bartholomew was his left. Just like I believed as a child when I told Miss Gemma Ann that one knight was King Leon's sunset and the other was his sunrise. I guess this could be chalked up to just a lucky guess. Kings in stories usually had more than one knight. He would need one for day protection and the other for night protection.

"Did you know that all the swords have names?"

"No way," I said. This was just getting more and more interesting. "What are their names?"

"They were all given female names." Gordon winked at me.

I was going to venture a guess. "Was it because women are to protect the heart of their man?" If a man was going to share the sincerest part of himself with you, it was your responsibility to protect it from harm, including your own.

"No," he chuckled. "The proper way to use the sword is to stab someone in the heart. They were given female names because females like to stab men in the heart."

"That's not very funny," I grumbled. "I wanted romance."

"Fine," he tittered as he put his arm around me, "Gavin's sword is Idalia, because it means 'behold the sun.' Bartholomew's sword is Alba, which means 'sunrise.'"

I had seen King Leon take off with a sword with which he had tried to end his life. If Gordon knew so much about these two, perhaps he knew about King Leon's sword as well. "What about King Leon's sword; who has her and what is her name?"

"Sigrid, peace of victory. After he disappeared, everyone

assumed that he took the sword with him." Gordon leaned closer to me. "If you believe Thelma's story, there is a fable that has been told over the years."

I despised this stuff, yet Gordon was compelling, and I wanted to hear it. "Go on…"

Gordon held up the sword before his face. "It is told that the only way to free the king from his curse is for Sigrid to enter the chest of the creature that first cursed him." He moved the tip of the blade to my left breast, pushing it in just enough to indent my T-shirt. "But first, the tip of the blade must be coated in the king's blood and that of his true love. She must love him just as much for it to work."

That didn't make sense—in Thelma's recounting, King Leon was turned into a vampire. In all my forced years of watching horror movies, not once did a vampire have blood. They were considered undead; dead but functioning as if they were alive. And wasn't it because they had no blood that they were pale creatures? With that, how was it going to be possible to coat Sigrid in the king's blood?

Gordon took a few steps back. "After it has pierced the cold heart of the creature, it must be drawn out. This will only paralyze the creature for a moment, allowing you to—" he swung the sword in the air, "slice the creature's head off." He stabbed the sword into the ground. "And that is how you will free the king from his illness."

I couldn't take this anymore; this didn't make sense. "How does the king still have blood? I thought vampires lost all their blood after they were bitten."

"I don't know; it's just what I have been told." Gordon shrugged his shoulders. "How does one fall in love with a soulless vampire?"

Apparently, he wasn't up to trend on all the new vampire romance movies. "Well, in Hollywood, it just happens nowadays. Just go find the palest boy that sparkles in the sunlight or the other one that refuses to go out in the sunlight. What happens after the vampire's head is cut off?"

Gordon walked back to his shed for a moment. He came back with a canister and a small toolbox. He moved right beside me and peered into my eyes. "Spray his body in this bear spray, coat him good." He set the spray in my hand, then opened the little grey box. "Take the magnesium fire starter out of here and light something on fire. Throw the burning object on his body and get the hell away from him."

This no longer felt like a story—it felt as if he was giving me instructions.

"Be careful, he's a shapeshifter. From what I know, he prefers to take the form of a bear."

CHAPTER 9

The sun was up bright and early, and so was I. Between Gordon's teachings yesterday and my latest vision, I was curious if Sigrid was still in that cave. It wasn't that I believed King Leon had been bitten and became a vampire; I was starting to think that maybe it was a metaphor for depression. Possibly the king was depressed, and that's why he was begging Gavin to kill him.

If I was entering the realm of the paranormal, perhaps the king had succeeded at some point and his body was still in the cave. Giving me the visions, he was guiding me to him so I could help him finally have a proper resting place. He may have only chosen me because I was here to protect his legacy.

Even if it was the old king's skeleton or just the sword, I needed something from those visions to prove to myself I wasn't going crazy. These visions felt so real, and the more I learned about King Leon's time, the more little details were aligning with those visions. If there was something in that cave, I didn't know how I was going to explain it to anyone else, but at least I would have some peace.

With my purple camo tennis shorts on, my black tank top, cell phone in the arm case, bear spray attached to my shorts, survival case in my pocket, and my running shoes on, I was ready for my quest. "Hey, Papa and Mama," I yelled back into the house, hanging halfway out, "I'm going to go for a run before Mass. I promise I will be back and cleaned up before we leave."

"Baby girl, do you have your bear spray?" Gordon hollered from the living room.

"Yes, Papa," I yelled back.

"Papa" and "Mama" felt more natural for Gordon and Ruby. For whatever reason it felt more loving than the standard "Dad" and "Mom." "Daddy" and "Mommy" felt too childish for me to call Gordon and Ruby. I don't think they cared too much; they were just loving this new relationship. Sean moved into his own place a few years ago, so I think they both had been dealing with empty nest syndrome. For me, it was nice to feel what it was like to have that warm family.

After a mile or two, I stared down at the waves slapping the red sandstone wall, turning it a deeper red color. This wasn't helping—I was to enter a cave in which a vampire had tried to off himself, and the wall below the cave looked as if it had been soaked in blood. Fear was starting to rise; what if there was some truth to this? What if that was the cave where he took his victims to eat and let his leftovers drain out? My heart started racing, but no matter what, I needed to do this.

I followed King Leon's steps from the vision down the side of the cliff. Trying to keep my fear at bay, I reminded myself that King Leon was a noble man. I remembered my childhood promise to myself: the man I fell for was going to fill in every detail of King Leon for me. I mean, Mr. Bartender's likeness was already filling in the image of King Leon in my mind; I could only hope this meant I wasn't going to enter a cave of horrors.

Hanging on to the edge of the cliff wall was no easy feat. If Sigrid was in the cave, I wanted to bring her back to Gordon to care for her. After sitting in the cave for years, I couldn't imagine she was going to be as shiny as Alba or Idalia. On the other hand, there was no way I was going to scale back up this wall with a three-foot sword. I couldn't just drop her in the lake, either—I would never find her in the depths. This only meant that I was going to have to tell Gordon about the cave and skirt around what made me want to explore. Then maybe Gordon had a sheath I could borrow so I could it attach to my belt next time I came out here.

There were caves on either side of the one I was scaling, though they were open to the elements. This one curved and the entrance was tucked in the corner of the other one. In no way would any four-legged animal access this cave. Reaching up, I grabbed a loose rock. Leaning toward the entrance, I tossed the rock at the ceiling of the cave, then swiftly drew back. I didn't need to be the first case of the latest bat-caused pandemic.

Nothing... No sounds and nothing exited the cave.

I tapped my cell phone, turning it on to flashlight mode, then angled it forward. It was time to see if I was crazy. Placing my hand on the inside of the cave, I set my foot on the floor and pulled myself in.

The cave was as reddish as the exterior. Along the whole cave, which must have been about twelve feet tall and eight feet wide, was a foot lip. It was almost as if someone had carved a bench along the wall. It would be a good smoking cave for teenagers if they didn't fall to their deaths. In the back, there was another ledge with a clear glass lantern still filled with fluid. I placed my bear spray and survival kit next to it; they were uncomfortable to carry.

Scanning the cave again, a reflection on the opposite wall from the lantern kept drawing my eyes toward the silver shine. My heart stopped with my snort—it was a sword. And not just any sword; she had the same black leather handle, the same engraved knotting, and the same crest as Alba and Idalia. It was Sigrid. I had found her.

I knelt before her, running my fingers along the flat of the blade, admiring the fact that she looked as if Gordon came out here daily to care for her. The metal wasn't eroded, the leather wasn't flaking—she was perfect for battle. Except her tip appeared to have fresh blood on it.

There was no way that it was blood, this cave had to have been undisturbed for years. I didn't pass anyone on my trek out here, either. In the elements, blood would have dried within an hour or so.

I let my curiosity get the best of me and, like a dummy, touched the substance. Rubbing my thumb and index finger together, and only then did I notice that when I touched the blade, my ring finger must have been sliced. It wasn't some magical substance on the blade; as I watched the red drip onto the blade, I realized it was my own blood.

"Just great." I shook my hand. "Now I'm bleeding in a cave with nothing to stop it." I covered my finger with my other hand as I looked around to see if there was anything in here that could help. To the side of the entrance, there was something white. Slowly I moved closer to the white object.

These dramatics needed to stop; it was a balled-up shirt. Wiping my hands on my shorts, I held the shirt up, angled toward the light. The shirt had one slice in the breast, but otherwise was still in perfect condition. The placement of the cave entrance must have saved everything in here from the elements. It almost felt like King Leon had just been in here the night before. Shifting my grip to avoid getting blood on the shirt, I held it up by the shoulders to get a better look at it, only for clinking of a chain against the cave floor to draw my attention away.

Before me was a gold chain with two gold rings on it. The rings must have been older gold, because on the sides of the curved knots it appeared to be darker. Or perhaps it was the lack of lighting in here. I placed the larger ring on my middle finger and the smaller one on my index finger; they had to be a wedding set by the matching knotting. The only difference was the larger ring had a thin gold border on the top and bottom of the curved knots. With the rings still on my fingers, I walked back over to Sigrid and compared the knotting between the three.

All three of them were identical—they must have come from the same blacksmith. With that, I remembered once I told Leon all of this would be worth it, because possibly he came from a blacksmith, and it was his history I was protecting. I plopped onto my butt, resting my arm on my raised knee as I studied the rings once more. The sword before me was Sigrid, King Leon's sword. There was a chance that these rings belonged to King Leon's parents once and were given to King Leon after their deaths. Gavin and Ruby were related, and Gordon and Bartholomew were as well. Perhaps I was wrong, and Leon didn't come from a blacksmith or leather smith, but rather was named after his ancestor.

Beep, beep, beep... Beep, beep, beep... Beep, beep, beep...

My phone's ringing echoed through the cave. It was my timer—I needed to get back or I was going to be late for church.

With the excitement of having found pieces of Leon's history in this cave, I put the chain around my neck and headed to the entrance of the cave. I moved to the side of the cave, staring down at the water below me. If I wanted to make it back in time to give myself enough time to get ready, I was going to need to take a shortcut. I tucked the rings into my sports bra, held my nose, and jumped. Within seconds I was submerged in the cool water. Surfacing, I gasped, then swiftly began swimming toward the shoreline.

CHAPTER 10

Being raised for show, I endlessly had to be dressed to the nines. Nonetheless, if I was going to be the newest Hughes, I was going to bring the best version of myself to represent my new family. The best version of myself included perfectly blown-out hair into beautiful curls, perfect soft and innocent eye makeup, and just because this was our first family outing, I went all out and contoured my face. I wore my ankle-length canary dress with thick straps paired with a white knitted cardigan so as not to show my bare shoulders in the house of the lord. And to complete the innocent look, I wore my white Mary Janes.

Poor Gordon and Ruby soon learned the hard way that having a little girl was not like having a little boy. Because I wanted to be perfect, we all were almost late for the service. Despite that, when we arrived, it didn't seem to matter; everyone already had their own unofficially designated pews.

The small chapel had two aisles, possibly fifteen rows of almond-colored pews with teal bench cushions. The floor was tan tile while the walls between the stained-glass windows were red brick. There was a different scene on each stained-glass window. Two by fours pressed together to form the arched ceiling with a few random beams or alternating simple chandeliers with six lights. For the front of the chapel, they had used two by fours again, although they made an intricate pattern of almost staggered ladders pressed together on either side of the altar. In the middle of the altar hung the cross. Moving toward the pew, just before the three steps that spanned the altar were two brick podiums on either side.

"You're late." Gordon leaned past Ruby, grumbling softly past me at Sean as he entered our pew from the outer aisle in his black slacks and navy button-down.

"Yeah, sorry, something set off the security system down at the cabins this morning. I lost track of time when I was trying to track down what it was. I couldn't find anything."

"It might have been me," I said. "I ran past that place this morning when I was out for a run."

Sean angled toward me with his left arm resting on the back of the pew. "Did you stay on the road?"

"I did until I was past that property." I studied his deep brown eyes for a second. Something within me told me not to say the real reason I was out there this morning. "I wanted to go check out the cliffs on the side of the lake."

"No, it wasn't you." Sean leaned past Ruby and me, lowering his voice to Gordon. "There's been some strange things going on around here lately. Leo thinks that rabid bear is back."

Ruby sat back and looked over to Gordon, who looked right at me. "Baby girl, did you bring your bear spray out with you this morning?"

I gasped; I had forgotten it in the cave. Do I tell them what I was up to or just be vague? "I did, but when I stopped to rest, I think I forgot it out there. I'll have to go back out there after the service and get it."

"No," Ruby snapped, "it's not safe out there with that crazed bear running around. Going forward, I would like you to take Sean with you if you want to go out running."

Before I could say anything, chilly fingers pried my hands apart, then moved my right hand on to his lap. It was comforting but unexpected after he got up and left yesterday morning. And I never did visit him at the bar last night. Ruby's plan was in full motion—we had milkshakes and watched rom-coms all night. Between movies, she expressed that she didn't want me to leave yet; she was loving our time together and there was so much more for her to teach me in the kitchen. I didn't disagree. I was loving every minute with Gordon and Ruby.

I let my head fall to the side as I looked up at Leon, only for my soft grin to disappear—he had those awful contacts in again. He was so perfect in every other way: sky-blue button-down shirt with khaki pants, perfect translucent hair, and a smile that demanded yours to mirror it.

His expression also changed as one eyebrow dropped. "Nora, you're wearing makeup today."

"And you're wearing those contacts again."

"You look beautiful."

"I hate your contacts." I should have given him a compliment or told him the same, but it just slipped out.

"Baby girl," Gordon mumbled under his breath, "is that how we talk?"

"Sorry." I looked back at Leon. "I loathe your contacts."

From the corner of my eye, I saw Ruby throw her head back, then turn toward me. "We don't talk like that."

Sean snickered from the other side of Leon. "Someone's in trouble already."

I could do better than this. "I am sorry for my words. I feel that you have these two beautiful, rare gems that should be shared with the world, yet you hide them behind those horrendous contacts."

"Oh, good lord, baby girl," Ruby mumbled.

"Now, dear," Gordon patted her leg, "just remember what she came from. It's going to take some time to undo them from her."

Was I really that awful of a person? I looked over to Leon as his head moved side to side, then to Sean, whose head moved up and down with a dopey grin. I bowed my head; I needed to refrain from talking about those contacts any more, but I just wanted Leon to be Leon.

Leon squeezed my hand to get my attention again. "What did you do yesterday afternoon?"

And that was all it took to get me out of my shell. "Only the greatest thing ever." My excitement lifted my eyelids wider. "I learned how to sword fight. And I'm not talking about fencing—this was bowling-ball-heavy, two-handed swords. Original, back-in-the day swords. They even had names," I squealed.

Leon leaned right past me to Gordon. "You taught her how to sword fight?" The aggression in his voice rose. "Why are you teaching her this?"

Gordon's shoulders raised and dropped as he gave Leon a close-lipped smirk.

I didn't get why this was upsetting to Leon; they had done it earlier with each other. Maybe Leon was afraid that I was going to get hurt. Slowly I hid my left ring finger under my leg. That was the last thing Leon needed to see right now.

"He took it easy on me, mostly showing me the basics, and we played out a scenario of..."

"Baby girl, shh," Gordon interrupted. The service was beginning, and it was time to listen, not chitchat.

After the service, everyone headed downstairs for coffee and donuts. Leon waved the Hughes on but kept his hand on my leg so I would stay put. Here it was—we were going to have that awkward conversation about yesterday in the middle of a chapel. I needed to find a way to distract him from this conversation. Lying was wrong, and I was going to go to Hell for lying to him in here.

Leon put his arm around my shoulders and pulled me into his chest. "Why did you leave yesterday?"

Without looking up, I fiddled with his right hand resting on his lap. "You left first."

His head rested against my head. "I had to go handle something, then I was coming right back. I'm sorry."

Here was my ticket out of explaining my reason for leaving. I turned my head and kissed his cheek. "I'm sorry too."

The hair on the back of my neck pinched under the chain. I had forgotten the necklace; quickly I sat forward, flipping my hair, and undid the necklace. "I found something out on my run this morning." I clasped the necklace and moved it closer to my chest. "I know Ruby is related to Gavin, and Gordon told me that he is related to Bartholomew, so when I found these, for some reason, I felt like they had belonged to one of your ancestors. I don't know, maybe it's because I was practicing with Gavin's sword and I saw a little piece of their history. I was just hoping that these were a little piece of your history as well." I dropped the rings into his hand and closed his fingers over them.

He didn't say a word, just stared down at the rings. I hoped I was right, and they belonged to his family. If not, hopefully he could help me find their owners. It would be fun to find a piece of history hidden away for years, just waiting to be found so the stories about it could come forward.

Outside of my grandmother's teacups, there was no history in my family. Everything had to be the latest and the greatest. According to my mother, holding onto items that were not trendy or new was for poor people, so they felt like they had something. Because of this, I held onto that castle. It was someone's history that they wanted to destroy for one night. I might not have history in my family, but it didn't mean I couldn't protect someone else's history.

"Nora," Leon said softly as he looked over to me, "where did you find these rings?"

"Out on my run this morning." I waved my hand in the air, hoping it would stop him from asking more questions. "Somewhere on the east side of the lake or west. I'm not sure of my directions up here." There was that same feeling that I couldn't tell him exactly because it was going to open that crazy can in my head.

His eyes narrowed before returning his gaze to the rings.

"I used to wear this necklace every day after the death of my mother. When my father passed away, I added his ring. I thought I had lost this necklace forever. I could never find it, no matter how much I looked for it."

That did not jive with my vision—King Leon lived six hundred years ago or so. Maybe my visions were general clues to things, like a riddle or something. Perhaps a robber hid Leon's family heirlooms in the cave after robbing his apartment. He *did* live above a bar—not the safest place in the world.

Leon undid the clasp and drew the rings from the necklace. He placed the larger ring on his leg next to the chain draped over his leg. Then he reached for my left hand, turning it as he drew it closer to himself. I was so baffled by his movements that I forgot about my ring finger until it was too late.

"What happened to your finger?" His eyes widened.

Swiftly I looked down at my hand; it wasn't bleeding anymore, so I never bandaged it up or really looked at it again. I had sliced it from the tip of my ring finger down to my palm.

"Sigrid," I whispered to myself. "Darn her."

"What did you just say?"

I tittered and held up my hand. "This is my proof that I am a klutz." I closed my hand and hid it again. "You know that Ruby and I were baking yesterday." That wasn't relevant, but it wasn't a lie either. I was just going to let his mind fill in the rest.

"I don't think that you are a klutz." He leaned back into the pew, studying me. "I think that there is more to you than you are sharing with me."

What do you do when someone is calling you out? You call them out until the conversation gets so confusing it's dropped.

"Would you care to go first?"

His brow dipped as he snorted. Judging by that reaction, I wasn't the only one hiding something—he was as well.

"Oh my goodness, you are hiding something from me."

I turned toward him. "Did you leave me yesterday to go see another girl?" I turned away. "Or—what if I'm the other girl? Between Ivan, my sister, and mother I have seen every level of cheating."

That's all I have ever been exposed to. This wasn't a playful distraction anymore; it was starting to weigh on me that there was a possibility I was the other girl or something else going on. The first night he sent me to Gordon and Ruby's home, it was Sean that took me there. Then his behavior yesterday when he walked out. Was it regret?

"I am the other girl," I mumbled, but it didn't feel right. That didn't stop me from feeling flushed; this wasn't who I ever wanted to be. I could see how our situation would be perfect for someone to cheat. With me leaving soon, I was just one quick fling, gone before she ever caught on.

I stood up. "Excuse me." I turned to head out the inner aisle.

"Whoa, Nora." Leon grasped my right hand, stopping me.

"Let me go." I shook my hand free. "We are in the middle of a church."

Leon stood up against me, drawing my chin up. "Do you believe that I would use you as a side piece or ever cheat on you?"

His tone was stern—if I just said yes, this would be over. Be that as it may, I stared up at him until his image blurred. I had no actual proof that he left me yesterday for another girl. It was a horrible thing to accuse someone of when that wasn't even the real reason fueling my over-the-top reaction. I just needed a normal excuse to push him away. I was frightened that he was figuring out there was something wrong with me whenever we kissed.

My head moved side to side until my lips had enough confidence to work. "No, I believe in your heart... I just don't know how to explain yesterday morning between us."

His thumbs wiped the tears off my cheeks, then he bowed

my head and kissed the top of it, leaving his lips there. "That was my mistake; I shouldn't have walked out the way I did yesterday. I was caught off guard that you stopped over, and I had something to handle. I'm sorry."

I rested my head against his chest. "I am sorry for my over-the-top reaction a moment ago. It wasn't fair to accuse you of that when I knew it wasn't true. I'm sorry for yesterday as well; I was confused and left."

I don't know how he did it with the little gap between the pews, but Leon cradled me so I was sitting on his lap when he sat down on the pew. I rested my left arm on his shoulder and pecked his cheek. Playfully he leaned his cheek closer to my lips as if asking for another kiss. Pecks were allowed in church; he got another one. With that, it was tempting to see if being in the house of the lord would halt any visions.

"So, my little treasure hunter, I think I owe you a finder's reward for finding my lost rings."

"That's not necessary." With one arm around his shoulders, I rested my head against his shoulder, then left my hand on his pec as I closed my eyes. "This is all I need."

Giving him those rings was never about collecting a reward; it felt like he should have them. And at this moment, I didn't want anything from him except for him not to move. I missed him more than anything last night after watching rom-com after rom-com. I just wanted to snuggle up to him to make up for what was lost yesterday.

Leon's head rested against mine as he took my right hand into his hands. "These rings have been a symbol of love in my family for ages. I wore them on a chain close to my heart every day in hopes that one day they would be my symbol of love that I could share with my forever." He lifted my hand to his lips for a second. "I have a confession: the love that these rings have been through has felt to me as if it was something unattainable, especially one forever. Although, under the stars around that old bonfire, there was a new warmth, and now it doesn't feel that way anymore." Warmth was replaced with coolness as his fingers moved what felt like a ring onto my right ring finger. "This ring no longer belongs on a chain—it is the symbol of everything that is in my heart because of you."

CHAPTER 11

Sundays were for church and family dinners in the Hughes household. I guess when I was out on my run, Gordon was in the smokehouse throwing on the meats for today's dinner. After Mass and donuts, the guys left, including Leon, to go tend to the meats again. In honesty, I couldn't imagine that there was much to do other than let the meat cook. It seemed more like a reason to hang out and have guy time.

Which didn't matter to me; I was enjoying some more mama and daughter time with Ruby in the kitchen. Today's agenda was the sides and desserts for tonight's dinner. This was exciting to me, since today would be the first chance I would truly get to cook for Leon. And not only him, but for the Hughes, which included Sean's older brother, Calvin, but not his wife as she was on a business trip.

"Hey, Mama," a deep, strong voice echoed through the house as the kitchen door opened, stopping me in my tracks.

A gentleman ducked as he walked into the kitchen. My head tilted back as he moved over to Ruby before me. His statue would be best described as a gentle giant, as he was built like a bodyguard and stood over six-foot-five. His warm smile to Ruby raised his cheeks so much that his eyes appeared to close. It was lighting up the room, as large as he was tall.

"Oh, sugar." Ruby wrapped her arms around his enormous torso. "I'm glad that you made it up."

I couldn't move; I couldn't speak. I just sat there at the

counter, staring at Gavin before me. How was this possible? Everything about him matched my vision. Ruby only said that she was related to Gavin, not that he was her son. And if he was her son, how was that possible? My vision seemed as if it was from a different era.

"Come, Calvin." Ruby grasped his hand. "I want you to meet your baby sister."

My head fell further back as I stared up at him. "Gavin?"

"Calvin."

All I could hear was "Gavin" as I continued to stare up at him. "Gavin." I was losing my mind—there was no way.

He knelt in front of me. "Nora, I have heard wonderful things about you."

"I-I—" I stuttered. "I have seen you before; your heart is pure, and you are an honorable man."

"Oh," Ruby cooed awkwardly to him, "Nora here is a history buff and is confusing you with Gavin."

"No." I shook my head, then glanced over to Ruby. "I'm losing my mind. That vision is becoming reality." I held my right hand up. "I saw the rings in the vision; I found the rings from that vision. When I gave Leon the rings, he told me that they were his parents. I saw someone in Leon's image take the necklace off his neck and set them down." I gestured before me. "Gavin here was in that cave with Leon after he took the necklace off." My heart started racing and my hands began to turn cold. "Do you not remember King Leon pleading with you to end him?"

"So, I heard," he took my hands into his, "that Mama has been teaching you how to bake. I drove six hours just to see how good of a teacher she is." He chuckled. "I can say this because she's not here, but Stella, my wife, cannot bake or cook. It's awful—she even burnt water once."

"What?" I tittered at him. He must not have heard my last statement or didn't want to talk about such a dark thing in Ruby's presence.

"She needs lessons, so if Mama can harvest out your baking skills, maybe there will be hope for Stella."

"I'm not so sure about that." I glanced over to Ruby. "I mean, Gordon..."

Ruby cleared her throat.

I was still working on using "Papa" and "Mama" when addressing Gordon and Ruby. If he was one of their three sons, I wasn't sure how he would feel about a stranger calling his parents that. "Sorry—Mama is a wonderful teacher and I have learned so much from her, but only Papa has tried my baking. He's so kind I don't think he would have the heart to tell me if it wasn't good."

From yesterday, I still didn't think that Leon had tried the pie I had left him. He hadn't said a word about it to me, and I wasn't going to bring it up in case it was a flop. Leon had grown up with Ruby's baking and cooking. Even having the master teach me, I had a feeling, since I hadn't heard anything, that it was awful. It would have been easy for me to mix up the salt and sugar, and she wouldn't have noticed until it was too late.

Calvin leaned forward as his brow lowered. "Whatever do you mean?"

"He's enjoying having a daughter, so I think he would take it to heart to see me disappointed if he didn't like what I made. You know—when you see someone crying and you start crying kind of thing."

"Not Pa, Leo. I was talking to him last night, and he was going on about this pie you had made." He looked up to the left, squinting his eyes. "Now, what was it he said? Oh yes, he's never tasted a pie such as that one in his life. It was the best thing that he had ever tasted. It would be worth it to come up and try it."

"Mama's are the best." I snorted with a sideways grin. "Nevertheless, that was kind of Leon to talk it up."

Calvin was kind for distracting me from my mini meltdown. However, it was odd that he didn't question anything I had said. If it was me, I would be throwing a thousand questions on how a vision was becoming true. Calming down, maybe I was right earlier; these visions were clues to things now. There was no way he could be Gavin. Ruby would have behaved differently that day when I was talking about him. Besides, if those rings sat in that cave after all those years, just the air and temperature would have changed them.

"I'm Nora." I held out my hand to Calvin. "I am sorry for my behavior earlier—you remind me of someone else."

He flashed his pearly white grin before encompassing me in his arms. He stood up, taking me with him. "I've always wanted a baby sister. This is going to be awesome." He bounced us around the kitchen.

He squeezed a little too hard—now I had to pee. "Umm... Calvin." I tapped his shoulder. "May I go use the bathroom, please?"

"Oh of course." He set me down.

Walking down the hall from the bathroom, baby pictures caught my eyes. I guess I never stopped to look at them before. Now with Calvin here, it was interesting to see the difference between him and Sean. With their baby pictures including the other brother, Pharrell, it was like they were all just clones of Gavin. Possibly the next generation would carry Gordon's features.

I was still studying the pictures, trying to find Gordon in those boys, when I heard Calvin speak up. "Does she know?"

"No, and it's going to stay that way," Ruby almost ordered. "Leo doesn't want her to find out. I think he is afraid he's going to lose her if she does. And I don't blame him for not telling her; they're so cute together. She's so in love with him, and you can see he feels the same way."

"But I thought..."

"We all thought his end wouldn't be coming," Ruby interrupted Calvin, "but he told me that he was starting to feel weak and it's getting worse."

"When did this start?"

"About three weeks ago Gordon told me that Leo mentioned to him that something wasn't right. So, with that said…"

Instantly I felt heaviness in my chest as my heart dropped. This was the second time I had heard someone talking about Leon's health. It was almost harder the second time, as if it had become real. We all had a ticking clock in us, but to hear his batteries were running out sooner rather than later was excruciating. I could see why he didn't want me to know; he didn't want me treating him as if he was broken. And that's what I shouldn't be doing. If I could move past his awful contacts, I could bury this repeated forbidden knowledge as well.

"What are you doing?" Sean growled from behind me.

"Eep!!" I screamed—and not just a little scream. I was focused so on the picture while listening to Calvin and Ruby that I let out an ear-piercing, glass-shattering squeal. It was so obscene that I started laughing as I turned around and playfully punched Sean in the shoulder. "You are awful."

Sean's hand moved to his upper right shoulder, rubbing the spot I had just punched. "Is that all you got in you?"

My eyes narrowed. "You caught me off guard. I was admiring how cute of a baby you were and trying to figure out what happened to you."

Snickers came from the kitchen—I guess I wasn't the only one eavesdropping today. Glancing down the hall, I saw Calvin leaning out from the doorframe, bouncing with his snickers.

Suddenly I was spun around by hands on my hips.

"Nora," the panic could be wrung out from Leon's voice, "are you okay? I heard you scream."

He moved my head side to side, kissing my forehead with every movement. Then he moved to inspect my neck, continuing with the pecks only for them to move to my cheek. There was sincere concern within him that something happened to me. He must have taken my klutz comment to heart—however, it was sweet he was trying to comfort me.

"I'm sorry, I didn't mean to worry you." I took a step forward and threw one arm around him, placing my hand in the middle of his back. With my other hand in his hair, I slowly lowered his head onto my shoulder, then placed my head softly against his. "I'm fine, I was so focused on something else I didn't realize Sean snuck up behind me. Which resulted in an overly dramatic scream."

"Well," he softly whispered in my ear in a mischievous tone, "you did say you were a klutz. I was concerned that you tried to slice your ring finger off since you were baking again."

Oh boy, he fell into that trap, assuming that I had cut my finger while baking. I was just going to have to go with it for now. If the truth came out, there was no way he was going to believe I was having visions when we kissed. Or worse, he wasn't going to want to kiss me anymore.

"I have another one," I chuckled.

His head moved up before me, his eyes lowering to my lips first, then moving up to my eyes. "I might need that left one someday."

Even with those awful contacts, it was still hypnotic whenever I caught him giving me this look. It was tempting to give him what he wanted; nothing could compare. But now we had an audience of my two older brothers and my mama. For sure Sean would say something to ruin the mood if he had to watch us kiss.

Leon took a step back, raising my hand, showing me the cut. "This needs to be wrapped in chain mail then bubble-wrapped."

I crinkled my nose at him. "It would stink to high heaven if you did that. That weird metal smell on skin mixing with sweat." I made a subtle heaving sound. "At that point my left toe would be the better option."

"My gosh, baby girl." Ruby grasped my hand, cutting in between Leon and I. "What happened to your hand?"

"Wait." Leon's brows lowered, and not in his fun baffled

way. "This didn't happen when you two were baking?"

My goodness, why was he so concerned about a small cut on my finger? It couldn't be that he was afraid of the sight of blood, as it wasn't bleeding all over the place. It didn't even sting when I washed my hands. It was the weirdest cut to date; I only noticed it when he kept bringing it up.

Leon snorted, then growled, "Gordon."

"Oh no, no, no." I squeezed Leon's cheeks together until his lips puckered. "It happened when I was out on my run. Fun fact, I didn't even feel it or realize what happened until I looked down and saw blood. But hey, it's not bleeding and is still attached."

This is what happens when I lie; it snowballs until it smashes into the truth. Well, hopefully that was enough of the truth to get Leon off this topic.

"No more teaching her how to sword fight," he sneered, taking my hands as his head turned toward Gordon, "got it?"

"It didn't happen when he was teaching me how to defend myself with the sword. Leave Papa out of this—he teaches me the coolest things."

"Leo, you know that it's sworn in our blood to protect and that includes the princess," Gordon growled back at him. "In today's world she needs to know how to protect herself."

For the most part, I hate being called "princess" or "queen" by men—it is just corny to me. But hearing it from Gordon's lips, my heart bubbled with joy. It wasn't just some corny line; he was fully accepting me as his daughter. There were no objections from me—he had to be the coolest dad ever, full of love and vast knowledge of the most random things.

"Why does she need to know how to sword fight? That's just asking for her to get hurt again."

"She never was even close to getting hurt," Gordon snapped back.

Leon held up my hand. "This cut is clean, and for how long it is, it's from a sword."

"Now, I never said it was from learning sword fighting with Papa." I waved my index finger at Leon playfully. "From your assessment, you must have had your fair share of cuts, but that doesn't mean I have or will. We were not being reckless."

"Seriously, Nora," Leon grumbled.

"Serious. I got it this morning when I went out for a run." I reached over and tried to move Sean before me. He stayed put like an ornery older brother. With that I moved in front of him and pointed back at him. "If I promise to take Sean running with me, will you all just drop it, please?"

Calvin started cackling. "Good luck with that. I don't think Sean knows how to run."

"Really?" Sean sneered playfully at Calvin. "Want to race down the road and back?"

"Calvin," I pinched the bridge of my nose and squeezed my eyes closed, "that's not helping."

This wasn't fair for Leon to be upset with Gordon, I just didn't know how to skirt around the topic enough to get Leon off Gordon. Telling him the truth wasn't an option; there was still something within me holding it back. The only thing I could pull from was Gordon's words that I needed to know how to protect myself.

"Leon please let it go." I locked my left hand into his right hand and held them up before us. "I'm not broken, but I may not be the strongest either. Papa is trying to protect me the best way he can: by showing me how to protect myself. Just like Ben won't be in my passenger seat if my SUV breaks down, Papa isn't going to be there if a guy like Ivan overpowers me. And that's the thing, I have been able to deflect Ivan for the last ten years, but these last couple years it's getting harder and harder to get him to leave me alone. Having Papa teach me self-defense, even if it is sword fighting, gives me some comfort I will be better prepared for when that day comes."

Leon's shoulders dropped as his head fell to the side. "I

will never allow him near you again."

"Life doesn't work that way. It's only a matter of time if I fail."

Everyone in my life back home said that Ivan was harmless—even I joked about how gullible he was. Regardless of that, there were more moments than there should be when I felt helpless for the last ten years. Without the support of others, I tried different ways to block Ivan. When I was younger, I installed a lock on my bedroom door to keep him out of my room. Susan, my mother, removed the door because I must have been hiding something if I put a lock on my door. I tried to explain to her it was because of Ivan, but she wouldn't hear of it. I was hiding something from her. Dan, my father, just told me I was jealous of Stephanie and was trying to cause drama in the family. I even tried talking to Ivan, but after ten years, he thought it was a cat and mouse game.

"I am here to protect you. Swords are dangerous—that's why no one uses them nowadays."

There was no stopping my bottom lip from becoming dominant as I gazed up at Leon. "Please don't put restrictions on the relationship that Papa and I have. Let him give out what he feels is best for me."

"I'm going to teach you how to use these guns." Sean put his arm around me.

Leon's head moved side to side as he glared at Sean.

"Just hold on, Leo." Sean removed his arms and flexed. "For our first lesson together, I'm going to teach Nora how to punch." He snickered the same way Calvin had from the doorframe. "The only thing hers did to me was stun me for a second for how weak it was."

"Whatever, weakling," Calvin boomed at Sean, "you need lessons more than she does."

It was fun to watch these two go back and forth with each other. It wasn't damaging daggers; it was all lighthearted bantering.

"I'm sorry." Leon's chest dropped as he held out his hand to Gordon. "I just don't want something happening to her."

Gordon took his hand. "That's what I'm trying to prevent." His head turned to me as he held Leon's hand still in a firm handshake. "No one is going to touch you ever. Here or in the States, I swear."

Dinner went off without a beat—far different from family dinners I was used to back home. First, everyone helped; it didn't fall onto one person to do everything. Second, Gordon wasn't glued to the television while eating dinner. He was engaging and present but mostly cheerful. As a matter of fact, the conversations in general were cheerful; there was no drama, no complaining, just laughter and positivity.

After dinner was cleaned up, we sat around playing card games for a while before ending up around their firepit. The firepit was one of the best ones I had ever seen. It was sunken into the ground in the formation of a door lock. In the middle was a large, roundish white plant pot, around which was a bench with removable peanut-shell-colored cushions and one armchair at the head of the pit. Ruby ended up in the armchair while Sean sat to my left. Gordon and Calvin sat talking to each other on the other side of Leon, who was on my right.

As the night progressed, Leon was slowly inching closer and closer toward me with his head and torso against my chest. It was more than cuddling; judging by the squinting of his eyes and random squeezing of my hand, he was in pain and it was getting worse. This was a difficult situation—I knew there was something going on with Leon, but he didn't want me to know what it was. I kissed the top of his head, then moved my hand over his eyes. Perhaps the light from the fire was too much for him.

I glanced over to Ruby. She knew what was going on and possibly she could help. With her arms dangling off the sides of the chair and her mouth cocked open, she was out cold. Sean was going to be no help; I still didn't think he was fully accepting of me just yet. I glanced up at Calvin, who was towering over us, blocking my view of Gordon. In my heart I prayed that he was loyal to Leon as Gavin was to King Leon.

Calvin's eyes met mine as he hid his bright smile with his lip folding in. He bowed his head, then closed his eyes.

I rested my lips on the top of Leon's head, telling myself Calvin wasn't experienced in helping Leon. From what I was told, Calvin was a professor of medieval times, history, literature, or something like that.

Leon huffed out; he had to be getting worse. Perhaps dinner wasn't sitting well with him. Gently, I moved his head before my own to study if he was looking greenish. I still didn't understand how he was not albino.

Leon let his forehead rest on my forehead. "I'm sorry," he said, then he moved his head to my shoulders while tightening his arms around me.

I ran my hand through the hair on the back of his head. "How about I go get you some water? If it was dinner, it might help." Whenever I was sick, I always craved comfort, even if it was just being tightly wrapped up in my comforter. Resting my head against his, I softly whispered, "I'll make sure to get a blanket as well. It's a perfect night to snuggle under a blanket by the fire. Ruby is asleep, Sean's been on his phone all night, and Calvin and Gordon are wrapped up in their own conversation; it will be like it's just us under the stars."

Leon moved his forehead to my cheek. "Okay."

I squeezed his hand one more time before standing up. "Is there anything anyone would like me to bring them? I'm going to run into the house real quick."

Sean swirled the last bit of his beer around in his bottle, then tilted it toward me without saying a word. He was going to enjoy having a little sister now for this reason, no longer the runner by seniority anymore.

With that, I headed back to the house only for a massive cat to rub against my leg before I made it to the patio door.

He must have stood about two feet tall and about three feet long with his onyx feathered tail. He was perfectly groomed; no way was this a stray.

I squatted down to itch the underside of his black neck. "Hello there." I didn't know the Hughes had a Maine Coon. "If there was a king of domestic cats, you, sir, would be him."

The cat put his paws on my lap as if he was going to jump up. I had a moment to give him some love, so I sat down. Instantly he crawled into my lap and up my chest, so his face was near my face. His left paw lifted off my breast, curled, then returned to my chest again, only for his right paw to repeat the same steps.

"Well, your Royal Highness, I think that you are more of a Viking breed, but an Egyptian name would be more suitable. The Egyptians would just eat you up." I itched the top of his head; I knew cats loved this as much as Leon did. "With that being said and since Bastet was a female, you will be Ra."

Bastet was portrayed with a feline head and a female human body. The tying factor between Bastet and Ra was that she was his daughter. She was the goddess of protection and good health. Leon needed both of these right now, but this mammoth before me was male. There were other Egyptian gods of health and healing, but Ra was more fitting for this fellow.

The cat rubbed the side of his face against my face. I could feel his fangs glide against my chin. He was marking me as his friend. Way friendlier than any of my mother and sister's Persians, though in the cats' defense, Susan and Stephanie only interacted with them when they were kittens for the first few weeks. When the cats reached those weird teen years, they just got another kitten to replace them, and the current one would be given away after a couple years, supposedly for Susan's health issues. With this I learned never to get attached to their cats; it hurt too much after the first couple were given away.

I itched the sides of his face. "Ra, it's nice to meet you. I hope someday to have a beautiful, friendly cat such as yourself."

"Is Nora talking to someone?" I heard Gordon questioning from the firepit. His voice almost sounded as if there was a hint of trepidation in it.

That was my cue—I needed to get a move on it. I braced Ra against my chest with my head tilted against his. "If you are a good kitty, I'll go find you a kitty treat in the house."

I was going to bring him down to the firepit for the others to enjoy him while I got my blanket, water, and a beer for Sean. I pushed myself up, holding Ra against my chest, which was no easy feat—it was like holding a toddler.

When I got closer to the firepit, Leon was hunched over with his elbows on his knees and his hands in his hair. Gordon had moved to the other side of Leon and was speaking to him.

Ruby was still out and Sean appeared as if he had drifted off as well.

"I found your kitty by the patio door." I took a step closer to the firepit. "Since I didn't know if I could let him in, I brought him down here. He's a beautiful cat. I didn't know you guys had a Maine Coon."

Sean sitting up instantly stopped me from taking another step. I noticed Calvin and Gordon's eyes widening as if Ra was the Egyptian god before them. Perhaps Ra wasn't supposed to be outside.

"Baby girl," Ruby rolled her head and sat up, "we don't have a cat."

That would explain why I hadn't seen him yet. In that case, he must have belonged to the neighbor. I itched under Ra's ear as I admired his coat. The deep black and cool grey was an astonishing color match for his fur. For sure he could be a show cat if he fit in with the other standards.

Ra's head turned as he gazed up at me. My mind was taken back to where I had seen another animal recently that was this black and cool grey. My heart started to beat faster: King Leon's horse in the stable was the same coloring.

"Nora." Leon looked up, startling me out of my thoughts.

Instantly Ra hissed at the fire, then jumped from my arms onto the grass and took off into the trees.

"Ra!" I watched him disappear into the darkness, still lost as to why he was the same color as King Leon's horse. "Kitty, come back," I whispered. I didn't mean for him to get frightened and run off. There was something about that vision and Ra that I couldn't tie together. Perhaps a little more time with Ra and I would have been able to piece it together.

"Nora," Leon moaned as he fell onto Sean's lap.

That cleared everything in my mind. "Leon!" It felt as if I flew over to him; I didn't feel my body until I knelt before him.

He didn't push himself up, his head still resting against Sean's lap. His eyes squinted as if the pain was becoming unbearable. His torso curved in with his knees rising to his chest. This wasn't right; he needed professional help at this point. It could be any number of ticking time bombs. I ran my hand against his cheek as I held his hand tight.

"It's time to go to the hospital." Leaning in, I kissed his forehead. "I promise I will stay there with you."

Back home I had a friend that studied in Nepal and was dating a guy from Balvin, two hours north of Nepal. They were getting serious with each other, and with a surprise break in classes she decided to go stay with him for two weeks. She ended up finding him curled up in a ball, lying on the bathroom floor in severe pain. Ultimately, I remember her telling me that they barely made it to surgery before his appendix could rupture. With the curving of Leon's torso and the pain he was in, this had to be appendicitis as well. And if it wasn't, I didn't care—I didn't want to risk it.

"Nora," Leon clenched his jaw in pain, "I need you to go inside and stay in there."

"No," I snapped. That was ridiculous. "Let me take you to the hospital."

His head dipped to his chest so I couldn't see his face. "Go inside for me, please, Nora."

"I don't need to go inside; I need to take you to a hospital."

Calvin moved his arm behind Leon's torso then drew him up to his chest. It was as if Leon was a rag doll, his head and arms hanging limp. Except he still had a hold of my hand.

Sean slid down off the bench before me while Gordon moved in front of Calvin and Leon.

"Nora." Sean held out his hand. "Come with me."

My brows lowered as I glared at Sean before shaking my head. Leon needed to go to the hospital, not lay out here and die. I wished that someone would just tell me what was going on or at least let me stay with him.

Leon kissed my hand one last time before dropping it. "Please," he gasped, "go with Sean."

At this point I was paralyzed with confusion and fear. I just stared at the backside of Gordon. There was no hiding Leon's health issue from me now—we were in the middle of something that deserved an explanation. I didn't get it. Nothing they told me about his health was going to change how I felt about him. I just wanted to be able to get him the help he needed. Or if it was Leon's time, he needed to be around loved ones.

The popping sound of knees beside me drew my attention away from Gordon's back. "Come on, baby girl." Ruby placed her hand on my shoulder to stabilize herself. "Calvin is going to take him to the hospital. He's going to be all right. Let's go in for the night."

I wanted to stay with him, even to the end. I get that the Hughes were his family, but I loved him too. I was suffocating in my swelling storm of tears. "I want to go with him."

"We need to go," Calvin boomed over some commotion. "Take her inside and do not let that cat in the house!"

Sean lifted my arm up, reaching around my torso, then hoisted me up over his shoulder. Softly he rubbed my back and calmly spoke. "He's going to be all right; Pa and Calvin are going to be there for him. Please, Nora, trust us."

Sean sat on the floor next to my bed, telling me stories about when he and Leon were younger and other stories about him and his brothers until he fell asleep. After some convincing, I was able to talk him into going back to his own room to go to bed.

There was no way I was going to sleep until I got to speak to either Calvin, Gordon, or Leon. I sat on the far side of the bed with my knees up to my chest and my arms resting on my knees. This was the worst—I just wanted to know what was going on with Leon. He had no reason to hide it from me; it wasn't going to change anything. I was going to stay with him until the end. No matter when that was going to happen, he deserved to have everyone beside him.

I could have sworn I heard my name whispered. Yet at this hour, my mind could have been playing tricks on me. I was exhausted.

The bed shifted and sunk in as a chilly hand crept down my side to my back. His forehead rested against mine. "I never meant to scare you earlier. I am so sorry."

I already knew that he didn't want me to know about his health issue. This was going to be difficult to get around. I didn't want to ever repeat tonight. "You don't have to tell me what happened." I dropped my legs and straightened out. "But I want you to promise me no matter what you will let me stay by your side."

His lips found my forehead as his hand slid under me and the other tightened on my back. Gently, he rolled onto his back, moving me onto his chest. I locked my arms under his neck as I straddled him. I hid my face in his neck, just wanting to breathe him in forever.

"I didn't know what was happening. I didn't know what

was going to happen. All I knew is I needed to keep you safe... I didn't want that to become your last image of me."

Comfort didn't last. I sat up on my knees.

"Please," Leon patted his pec, "come back."

"I don't want to hurt you—what if laying on you is going to cause whatever to happen or make it worse?"

The room was dark; a cloud must have moved in front of the moon.

"Nothing you'll ever do will hurt me." His hand ran through my hair along the side of my head. "I'm better now that I'm next to you again."

I ran my hands up his chest, my left hand moving behind his neck. My right fingertips barely touched under his chin. I couldn't see him, but I could feel him. "Promise me," I ordered.

I don't know why; I didn't even wait for his answer. There was no second guessing. I had almost lost him. My heart was going to show him how important he was to me.

He breathed out and I breathed in. His hands moved to either side of my cheeks, stabilizing me as he lowered back to the bed.

Softly he kissed my lips, "I need you," then kissed me again. "I need you beside me for my forever."

CHAPTER 12

Beep... Beep... Beep... Beep... Beep... Beep...

Leon was laying on the couch, and I was laying on his chest, taking an early afternoon nap. With everyone back to work, Leon and I had gotten to spend yesterday and today together. Yesterday afternoon, he showed me how awesome it was to take a little catnap on the couch with the sun providing a warm blanket. Well, I was Leon's blanket—until the alarm on my phone ruined it.

I rolled my head so my forehead was flush against his chest. "I have to go," I mumbled into his chest, "but I'll be right back."

In the back of my head, I was hoping that when I walked to the county recorder's office, there would be an "out sick" sign on the door. That would give me another week to enjoy this new life up here and another excuse so my family wouldn't have a reason to come up here yet.

Leon's hand rubbed up and down my back. For how cold his hands were, the softness of his hands made up for it. "The office will be open next Tuesday, please just stay."

He was right and I wanted to stay, but I had no excuse to give to Susan about why I hadn't gotten her contract signed. As much as I didn't care for my biological family, I was not a good liar. "I need to do this." I tightened my arms around his torso. "Then I will be right back for this, so don't move."

His lips moved to the top of my head. "Please just wait until next week."

"They're going to come up here." Pushing myself up, I sat on his hips. "I can't let them get to the owner first."

Just as the door said, the locks clicked open at exactly 2:22 p.m. All I could do was chuckle to myself; this was going to be a ride.

A little fella was sitting behind an old reception desk surrounded by stacks of papers.

"Hank," I shrieked, thrilled to see him again. That would explain the weird hours—this must have been his second job.

Hank looked up as I walked in, pushing his large glasses up his nose. Then he tittered. "Frank, to be correct," he responded cheerfully.

He had to be Hank's twin. Now it was a matter of whether they shared the same personality. "Oh my, I am so sorry. I'm new to town, and I met a gentleman that looks just like you the first day I got here."

Frank moved a sheet off the top of the stack, stamped it, then moved it to another stack. "Oh yeah, Hank said he picked up a pretty thing off the street and left her for the bartender. It's about time that the old bartender settled down with someone. Hank thought you would be a good fit."

Wow, he was an honest one. I thought Hank was just messing around with Leon. I think I owed Hank a beer. "You don't say—well, your brother has a good eye for that kind of stuff."

That drew Frank's attention toward me, resting his arms on the stack of papers before him. "Do tell."

I wasn't one for kissing and telling, but there was nothing wrong with telling him how I felt. "Yeah, that bartender is something extra special. I'm going to have to buy Hank a beer to thank him."

He leaned forward. "You and the bartender?"

"Well, I did just leave his place to come here. And speaking of, do you think you can help me find an owner of a property up here?"

"Sure thing, what is the address?"

Do castles have addresses? There couldn't have been more than one up here, so he had to know what I was talking about. "Umm...the castle just north of here."

His head turned slightly as his eyes lowered. It felt as if he thought I was up to no good or something. "Sterling's castle?"

That wasn't helpful. The only last name I knew up here was Hughes, and only because Gordon had talked to me about taking their last name when I changed my last name. "Excuse me?"

"Your bartender owns the castle, and the bar, in fact."

"Did I say castle?" I tittered. "Silly me. I meant the campgrounds by it." I leaned against the counter for more of a dramatic effect. "You will have to excuse me, my mind has been in the clouds since I got here. It must be a different elevation than what I am used to."

It wasn't; I just didn't want him to know the truth. Leon was the first person I told my plans to. He had heard my conversation with Forrest and read both contracts. Why didn't he just tell me the truth from the start? I could have told my parents no, then move forward with cutting them out of my life instead of reading Stephanie's hourly dumb texts, dealing with Ivan hitting on me, or listening to Susan's snarky calls every few hours. This was more than frustration; it was a new pain of disappointment that Leon had hid this from me.

His new deceitfulness was stabbing me in the chest, ruining that perfect man I had seen. The lump grew in my throat as the more I thought about it, the more I bordered on volcanic. Right here was not the time to erupt. If it was going around town about Leon and me, I didn't need to air anything out here. Mad or not mad, this wasn't how I was.

I stayed a moment longer chatting with Frank, trying to play it off as I was only here for the campgrounds before I marched back to the apartment as a little ball of fire and gas. Leon wasn't going to get as much kindness as I had just given Frank.

Unsurprisingly, the door was unlocked. What I wasn't expecting when I returned, however, was to see Leon and Sean sitting on the couch, facing each other. Correction: they were not just facing each other. Leon had his hand on Sean's cheek while they were embraced in a kiss—not a peck, but a scene to which 70s porn music would provide the perfect score.

"Oh my god—was that a trick question in the church to see if you could get away with it? What are you two doing?" I turned back toward the door, not wanting to know that answer. "Forget it. I'm sorry for interrupting you two." I slammed the door before either of them could say anything.

"Nora," came a mumble from behind the door, "hold on."

There was no holding on—I didn't want to hear what he had to say. I knew what I walked into; it didn't need to be explained. I rushed out the door, down the stairs, and into my SUV before I could even tell if they had followed me out. I just wanted to be alone so I could try to wrap my head around everything that had happened in the last thirty minutes. I knew just the place where I wouldn't be found and could pull myself together enough to tell Gordon and Ruby goodbye.

CHAPTER 13

Not wanting Sigrid to fall onto me, I lowered her beside me, then drew my knees up to my chest, resting my arms on my legs and hiding my face. I left the cave dark; I didn't want to see the light right now. My heart was mourning and wanted to hide in the darkness. It wasn't the fact that Leon kissed him—it was the feeling of betrayal. His words from the church shattered through me, then out with my tears.

"My Queen," echoed from the entrance of the cave, "there is no reason for tears. Wipe your eyes. Together we will show him true revenge."

The voice was familiar, though I couldn't place it. That didn't matter; I wanted to be left alone and wasn't in the mood. "Sir, please leave. I came here to be alone."

"I can't." His voice moved closer. "I have seen how black your heart is," he snickered, "for you to fall for a monster."

Who was he to tell me I had a black heart, especially as it was bleeding red right now? "He is no monster, and that is none of your business. Although you are right about one thing, my heart is black; it's traditional and powerful." I sneered. "It's not for a man like you who can't respect my wishes and just leave me be."

"I will never leave you; we will be together for eternity."

"Lame." My nose curled with disgust. Even feeling that worthlessness from catching Leon with Sean, being hit on was the last thing I wanted right now. "Clearly that line has never worked for you in the past if you are using it on me now. Rewrite and go try it on someone else, I'm not interested."

"Do you know who you are talking to?" His voice rose as he growled at me.

An alert on my phone lit up the cave, and inches in front of my face was a bear snout. The air was filled with the smell of blood as his cold snort penetrated my face. His lip curled up, exposing his fangs. My heart dropped as my phone went dark again. I had seen that snout before—I knew who was before me.

My left hand felt around beside me until I found Sigrid's smooth blade. I followed the blade to the handle, then slid her alongside me. Before turning on the flashlight on my cell phone, I lowered my left leg over Sigrid, concealing her from the creature before me.

I peered into his beady, blood-red eyes, my heart thumping like it was ready to leave me in fear. All I could do was try to tell myself he was just another guy chasing after something he was never going to get. I needed to amp myself up; he had me cornered. Again, I tried to tell myself I had been in this spot before. If I could keep Ivan at bay all these years, I could take him on as well. Ivan may be a pig, but I had never been face to face with a bear that I knew at any moment could give me King Leon's fate.

The longer I stared into those horrifying eyes, my internal words flipped from a joke of a pep talk to Saturday afternoon with Gordon. His final warning echoed, then my mind flashed to when Gordon placed the tip of the sword into my chest. Goosebumps raised on my arms and there was a chill. He had been preparing me for this very situation. And I wasn't going to let his training go in vain—I was going to prove to him his new baby girl was his little knight as well.

There was no fleeing the bear; if I was to stand up, he would overpower me. I needed another plan of action. My mind raced back to Thelma. She had told me that whatever this thing was before me thrived on taunting his victims. I was going to play off that to buy myself some time to come up with a plan.

My head dropped to the right, the worst position in front of a vampire, but I needed to make it believable. "How did you get in here?" I didn't wait for a response as I pointed at his paw. "I mean, I barely made it in here and I have fingers. With those claws there's no way you scaled that cliff."

The bear moved back a couple inches as it sat down like a dog on its butt with its front paws before him stiff. His head cocked to the side a touch, making him slightly less horrifying and sort of cute. Or it would have been cute if he wasn't here to damn me for eternity.

I still had no strategic plan to save myself, so I was going to continue to confuse him. Raising my elbow up, I pointed behind me. "Is there, like..." I paused, playing dumb; people tend to open up a little more if they think you can't comprehend them. "...a trap door or something behind me?" I crossed my arms against my chest. "That would have been totally helpful to learn earlier."

I felt as if I was losing my damn mind talking to a bear in a cave.

Chin up, shoulders out, and breasts perked, I was going to feed into his game so he would come to me so I could introduce him to Sigrid. Since I had already been cold with him, I needed to ease into it. "Okay, Sugar Bear, what is your name?"

The flashlight timed out on my phone and the cave went dark.

"Shit." I fumbled with my phone, trying to turn it back on. "Shit...shit... shit." My fingers trembled; the fear was getting ready to discharge from my eyes.

"It's all right." A chilly, smooth hand rested on my ankle. "Please calm down. There's nothing to be afraid of here."

What?! There's a talking bear that exposed his fangs at me in a cave that now smells of blood. Because he is a vampire.

I'm so freaked out that there's no light in the cave and now I can feel a human hand on my ankle.

The flashlight flickered on, and kneeling in front of my feet was Thelma's words in human form. My head sunk back as I peered up at him. Peeking through black hair were long, narrow ears. There was no hair protruding from his ears that I could see, nor in his nose, for that matter. In fact, that whole account of his missing nose was incorrect; he had a nothing-special nose. It seemed as if he had been given those dilation drops before an eye exam, which was odd because my phone flashlight was lighting up the cave. And though I didn't want him to think I was giving him *that* look, I saw his lips were normal. There were no gaps or fangs peeking out.

On second thought, maybe seduction was my answer to all this; he called me his queen, and I was going to direct this situation. My bottom lip folded in, and I took it between my front teeth as I gazed at his lips for a second longer, then my gaze slowly moved up to his eyes. "What is your name?"

The corner of his lips curled up with pleasure. "Kek..."

That was not what I was expecting his name to be. I couldn't hold it in, and rudely I interrupted him. "As in the gamer slang for laughing?"

"No," he growled. "I am Kek, God of the Darkness of Chaos."

That was worse...

My piano teacher's son, an archaeologist in Egypt, would send her ancient artifacts. Her walls were adorned with engraved slabs, shelves filled with marble and gold statues. In the piano room next to the hexagon aquarium filled with guppies and mollies was a little chestnut end table with a frog statue on a plaque engraved with hieroglyphics. According to her son, it was a representation of Kek, God of the Darkness of Chaos.

The man before me was a shapeshifter of a bear, not a frog. I could see that frog statue in my mind—something here wasn't right. "Are you like the second or tenth generation of

Kek? Because the Egyptian Kek I know of was a frog. I mean, does Egypt even have bears?"

"Oh," he cooed. It must have excited him that I knew my Egyptian history and mythology, because his hand moved up to my shin and back to my ankle, sending goosebumps up my legs and down my arms—and not with pleasure; it was horrifying to have him touching me in any manner. I saw how he paralyzed King Leon that day.

"My Queen, I can take many forms. Up here in the north, I prefer to be a bear. Back then, I was learning my forms and could only become a frog."

Oh, the questions just kept popping up in my head, and my filter was lost in the darkness of my fear. "Why did you come to Canada? I mean, did something bring you here?" It fascinated me, wondering why someone would want to leave a warmer climate to move to the freezing tundra. Or for him, to leave a country that was still rich in Kek's history.

His head bobbled a little as if he was thinking about it, then it stopped moving. "I enjoy the cooler summers up here."

I struggled to stifle my snickers. Besides fear fueling everything right now, the God of the Darkness of Chaos preferred the cooler summers as if he was a snowbird. I pinched my lips as his image blurred a touch from my giggling tears. This was possibly the worst thing to be doing; he could kill me instantly if I offended him.

That didn't stop my mouth, though. "You're a snowbird, eh?"

He gave me a sly grin. "No, but if you want to be a bird, I will teach you how to change forms."

That was sobering. According to Gordon and Thelma, vampires could shapeshift. Was he insinuating he was going to make me a vampire? Everything within me froze.

"Hey." He itched his dagger fingernails into my leg as if to relax me. "I would prefer you to stay in your natural form. Your beauty is unparalleled."

Holy shit, an Egyptian god just openly and directly hit on

me. My mind was racing—this was insane. I had to be going insane. There's no way he wanted me; this had to be a case of something he wanted but couldn't have. Or perhaps my black hair and emerald eyes reminded him of another pharaoh that he missed in Aaru.

"Umm...thank you," I peeped.

I needed to get my head back into the game. I couldn't let him have me. It was getting weird by his gawking at me and my lack of self-control.

I leaned my head to the side, still peering into his eyes. "Why would you want me as your queen? There's not one thing about me that you know. Do you really want to spend eternity with me if all I do is annoy the crap out of you?"

"I've been watching you all week." His cold hand ran up my ankle to my shin and back, his serrated nails gently scraping me. "You are my queen and after I change you, I am going to parade you all through town until that old king dies from a broken heart for all of his kingdom to see."

I wasn't sure I understood his explanation, but I was too focused on how to get him closer to me. "If I am going to be paraded around, I want to get my hair done, and you, sir, are getting a manicure. Those nails are awful."

After insulting his physical appearance, the flashlight on my phone timed out, leaving the cave in darkness once more. "Shit," I grumbled again. Normally, I wasn't one to swear unless I was severely heated, but now curses were slipping out with my fear.

Taking a second to calm down, I realized the darkness may be in my favor as an idea registered in my mind. "Kek," I whispered seductively, "can you see in the dark?" I needed to know this; I didn't want him to see Sigrid coming.

"No." I felt his hand glide up my leg again. "All I need is to be able to feel you."

What!? The God of the Darkness of Chaos couldn't see in the dark—how was that even possible? I mean, it was great for me, but baffling nonetheless.

"No more lights." His tone was stern but mixed with his own seduction. "I don't want to frighten you. The moon should be the first one to see you in your true form, then he will illuminate you for my own eyes if he is pleased."

It had to be a little after 3:00 p.m. It seemed like it only took seconds with King Leon and it did. It may have taken a second, but I wasn't a halfwit. My mortality wasn't the only thing he was after.

Kek paused. "I can feel your blood rushing through you. There's no need to be frightened; it will take a second then it will all be gratifying afterwards." He snickered to himself, and I tried to choke the disgust back down my throat. "You won't want to leave this cave for a week."

Goddammit, ewww... Even Egyptian gods were lame. That last line was out of Ivan's handbook. But I needed to know his plan. The more I knew, the better chances I had to create a plan to get myself out of here, mortal and pure. I thought back to that first vision, when King Leon instantly moved to Gunner Louise after Kek left. "Won't I need to feed?"

"For tonight, I have everything you need," he purred. "You will feed from me."

And back to being horrifying and disgusting. My leg moved further out in the darkness, then I felt his leg against my other leg. He had to be kneeling at my knee now. If I could get him to lean in, I could introduce Sigrid to his heart.

I leaned forward until I could feel his cold breath on my nose. He smelled of blood. My chest caved with disgust as my stomach turned with the thought that I was going to have to go full seduction mode if I wanted him near me. Even with the fear and disgust, I had no other option right now—he wanted me.

"What am I to wear to said parade as your queen?" Slowly I drew back with each word, hoping he would follow my words to my lips. "Are we going modern, medieval, Egyptian, or Greek?"

His cool breath remained on my lips as I sat back into position. His presence was uncomfortably close; it was now or never. With a flick of my wrist, I slid Sigrid out from under my leg, then thrust her forward while keeping her at a slight angle.

A piercing scream echoed throughout the cave—I had made contact with him. With this excitement, I thrust forward a few inches more. Holding the sword in one hand, swiftly I turned back and tapped my phone, turning on the flashlight again.

There he was: the God of Darkness of Chaos knelt before me with Sigrid a few inches in his chest near his left pec. His head was tucked in, so there was no access to his neck. His hands dangled on either side of him.

"Fuck yeah!" I yelped as I was overcome with excitement at my success. Truthfully, I didn't think I was going to succeed. That just made my next words even sweeter leaving my mouth. "You better fucking bow before me, God of the Darkness of Chaos!"

"Nora." Sean's voice echoed from the entrance of the cave, stopping my showboating and returning me to reality.

"Ummm... Sean?"

"Are you—" He paused for a second. "Are you all right in there?"

Sean was here, and instantly I felt like that green piece of Jell-O from that old dinosaur movie.

"Seriously, Sean?" My fear returned as my eyes followed up Sigrid's silver blade, which was now turning red. "No. Oh god, I just stabbed Sigrid into Kek. The Egyptian God of the Darkness of Chaos is before me with Sigrid penetrating his chest." My hands trembled. "This is Thelma's creature—he wasn't just an urban legend. Oh my god, he told me I was going to feed off him." All my disgust was coming out as word vomit. "We were going to spend a pleasurable week in this cave together. He was going to take my mortality and virginity."

My chest raised and dropped. I had just stabbed the man that claimed he was Kek, an Egyptian god. I was going crazy. I just stabbed someone. He had to be some mentally unstable man just pretending. In no way was it possible he was Kek. I don't even think Kek was a real person, but more of a myth.

"Oh lord." Panic rose in Sean's voice. "Nora, you need to finish this before he comes to. He's only going to be paralyzed for a few seconds, then he will regain consciousness."

"You expect me to do what?—I'm done." I couldn't take my eyes off the black hair before me. "Get in here and do it yourself."

"I can't. If I come in there, he can overpower me, then he will kill you for this. Just do it," Sean shrieked, then his tone mellowed out. "I believe in you. Please listen to my words and finish him."

The black hair moved up, exposing blood running down his cheeks from his eyes. It was almost as if the color was draining from his irises as they turned a whitish-grey color. His fangs appeared as he spoke. "He's right and wrong." His arms still dangled at his sides. "I am going to kill him and your old king, then I am still going to take you as my queen." He sneered. "You belong to me. For this you will bow before me until I forgive you."

With his last statement, rage blazed within me. "The fuck I am," I growled as I drew the sword from his chest. "I am an American." I leaned forward and jeered. "I bow for no king, and the fuck I belong to you!"

His head dropped to the side as his brows lowered. It was almost as if he wasn't expecting me to have that much fire within me or had never been rejected before. My words must have shattered his old-ass ego. Either way, his perplexed expression wasn't helping gain access to his neck. It was slightly amusing as it reminded me of when he did it while in the bear form.

"Seriously!" Sean yelled.

Sean yelling drew Kek's attention to the entrance of the cave. He extended his long neck, giving me the perfect target. Swiftly I swung Sigrid, slicing his neck through as if it was a hot knife through butter. His head dropped and began to roll with his jaw extending open then closing. Quickly, I moved back on the ledge, watching the head as it passed by me. I pointed Sigrid down and tried to spear the top of the head.

"Nora" echoed through the cave.

"What, Sean?" I snapped as I tried to stab the head again.

"What's going on?"

"I'm a—" I tried to spear it again but missed by an inch. As gruesome as it was, I felt like I was playing whack-a-mole. "—little busy."

I moved a little to the left, slamming Sigrid down, making contact with the head. She sliced through the front part of Kek's head. This was beyond horrifying. It was time to get off this emotional roller coaster. I just needed to get out of this cave of horrors.

I glanced over to the lantern, bear spray, and survival kit sitting on the ledge as Gordon's recipe for a little pyro fun echoed through my head. I popped the cap of the bear spray, coating the head and then the torso that finally collapsed, spewing a foul odor of death into the cave. I took Sigrid in my hands, shaking her free from the decapitated head. It wasn't like hot butter anymore; she must have been caught on a bone or something as I shook her again. Finally, when she was freed, I swung her at the top of the lantern, shattering the upper half and only leaving the bowl of fuel exposed.

I stared down at my phone. It was only inches away from Kek's severed head—not where I wanted to reach down. Ugh... I rubbed my forehead; I needed my phone. Once that battery came in contact with the fuel and flames, it was going to wipe this cave of horror from history. I lowered my leg until the tip of my shoe touched the screen. Just as slowly, I swiped my leg over to the left and toward the bench so I could reach down and grab it.

"Sean," I yelled as I held the phone by my thumb and forefinger, rushing back to the broken lantern, "can you swim?"

"Of course I can..." There was an unsure tremble in his pause. "Why?"

I dropped my phone in the bowl, then drew out the magnesium fire starter. "I need you to jump into the lake and swim as fast as you can toward the shore." Cheerfully, I sang to myself with my head bobbing side to side and a shake of my hips. *"Because I'm going to blow this motherfucking cave up."* It had to be relief, or I was losing my damn mind for what I just had done, but oddly I was starting to get giddy.

I admired the red droplets mixing with the golden liquid in the bowl. "Yeah, Sean...try to make sure you stay under the water until you are to the shore."

"No," he whined, "I can't leave unless you are with me." His voice was starting to crack. He must have been fearful that I was going to sacrifice myself.

I walked over to the entrance of the cave and wrapped my arm around the stone wall. "I'm going to be right behind you, but I need to hear you jump into that lake."

I felt the warmth of his hand on mine and heard the angst in his voice. "Promise me?"

"I don't need to promise you," I tittered. "If you saw or smelled what is in here, you wouldn't need to ask that." I released his hand. "Now go so I can get out of here."

The cave echoed with the sounds of a splash below as I studied the horror before me. The flashlight from my cell phone was still on, even with the ports being submerged in liquid. Kek's body was highlighted lying there. He was dressed in matte black slacks with a glossy, fitted long-sleeved shirt. He wasn't overly built like the Hughes men; his shoulders were the widest point on his body, but otherwise constituted a natural six-foot build.

The horrors before me were swiftly changing in my mind to who the person below me could have possibly been.

Studying his body was putting a human element to the god/ vampire. Perhaps he was damned at one point the same way that King Leon had been. Kek was known as the God of the Darkness of Chaos, but I truly didn't know what that meant. Even with his title, he could have had a few good traits about him. A few times he tried to provide me with comfort—in fact, not once did he harm me or even try to. This was sobering. All I could hope for was that I had freed him.

"Be at peace and I am sorry," I whispered to his still body.

The air was becoming suffocating with the heaviness of the smell of blood; it was time to leave. I drew up the hem of my shirt until it was off, then I knelt, bunching up the shirt as I struck the magnesium fire starter into the fabric. It took a couple tries and a few breaths, but when there was an adequate flame, I threw my shirt onto Kek's torso, watching as the fire spread up his body. More than anything I wanted to turn my head away, but I needed to see if the flames would follow the bear spray path to the lantern. I never wanted another terrible thing to be able to play out in this cave again, even if I had to blow the cliff face off.

I walked backwards, watching the orange flame dance its way up to the lantern that contained my cell phone. It was now or never. Turning around, I raised my hands above my head and dove out of the cave. The lukewarm water engulfed me, welcoming me. Rocks began to sprinkle above me like fireworks falling from the sky. It was such a surreal feeling; this was my celebration for my victory of taking down the one that damned King Leon. And this was going to be the only celebration—I had no intentions of ever repeating what happened in that cave. Well, except for Gordon, as I had followed his directions. There was no hiding it; I was still that little girl desiring to hear her papa tell her that he was proud of me.

I stayed underwater until I made it around the bend in the lake. It was a beautiful summer day—without a doubt there would be people out on the lake fishing or just enjoying themselves. There was no way I was going to surface right below the cliff; I didn't want to be pegged at the crime scene. I couldn't imagine the trouble I would be in if the proper authorities found out I ruined a landmark.

Spinning in the water like a mermaid, I stopped when my backside was parallel to the lakebed so the water could push up on my back, surfacing me. The lukewarm water was replaced with the warmth of the sun. With the water sloshing in my ears, my mind drifted back to yesterday: laying on Leon's chest as he showed me one of the best parts of his oversized windows. My heart ached to be back in that fantasy again.

I didn't want a heartache right now; I didn't want to feel anything. This afternoon had been an emotional roller coaster like no other. I just wanted to be still, allowing the water to gently rock me while it whispered comfort into my ears and softly kissed my lips. I closed my eyes and remained still.

Occasionally the sounds of boats grew louder, but nothing grew loud enough to indicate closeness to me. Until the sound of sirens began to grow louder as they neared. I had been fortunate enough that none of the other boats came near me—I wasn't going to move. The aches in my arms and legs were telling me I was going to stay put a little while longer; their boat could go around me.

The water became more disturbed, then there was a massive splash. This wasn't the ocean; nothing in the lake could take me out like a shark. Raising my left arm, I popped up a thumb up, hoping the boat driver would leave me once he realized I wasn't just a dead floating body.

Thick stone arms wrapped around my torso from below me, and instantly I was submerged for a second before I surfaced in a coughing fit.

"I wasn't—" I gasped for more air to finish my statement, "drowning. I was just relaxing out here."

He thrust me up as his forehead rested in the middle of my back. "I should have been there to protect you. I'm so sorry for failing you today," Sean whimpered into my back.

"Sean." Gently I ran my hands up and down his forearms. "I'm safe now. There is nothing to worry about."

I wish that was true.

Sean spun us around and before me was a maroon boat with big golden letters that spelled out "Game and Fish." My eyes blurred the image of Gordon in his fluorescent orange life jacket with his hand out to me.

"Sean, hand her up to me," Gordon ordered with that Game and Fish authority voice.

In more than one way, I felt like a little eight-year-old as Gordon took me in his arms and hauled me into the boat. Gently he set me down on one of the boat chairs before kneeling before me.

My head bowed, keeping my shorts wet with my tears. "I'm so sorry," I mumbled. "I... I..." I stuttered, about to confess to the Game Warden that I blasted the caves off the cliff.

The boat rocked with Sean kneeling before me as well. "She killed him."

"What!?" Gordon and I both snapped at Sean simultaneously.

"I know Kek's voice, and I heard him talking to her. Before I jumped into the lake, I peeked into the cave to see his body on the ground and his head a meter away from it," Sean blurted out instantly.

Folding my lips in, I sat back. That for sure shut off my tears as I could see Gordon's wide gazed fixed on me. He didn't say a word, just sat back, sinking into his shoulders.

"I can explain." I raced to get the words out. "I went in the cave to get away from everyone after I caught Leon and Sean making out. I didn't see anyone in the cave when I got there. Then a man started hitting on me. He turned into a bear and back into a man. I'm so sorry, but he wanted to damn me so I could be his forever." I whined, "I didn't mean to kill him, but I did. I'm so..."

Gordon flung forward, wrapping his arms around me,

muting my word vomit. He pressed my face into his chest with his hand on the back of my head. I didn't know what this was; yes, it was a hug, but was I in trouble?

Gordon released me but kept his hands on my shoulders. "Did he touch you?"

My torso sank while my shoulders stayed put in his hands. "Yeah, my ankle up to my shin."

With that they both backed away from me to raise my leg to inspect it. After they pulled off my shoes and socks and fully inspected my legs, they stared at each other as if they had more to ask but were unsure if they should.

Gordon cleared his throat after a moment. "What did you stab him in the heart with?"

"Sigrid. She was left in the cave when King Leon tried to kill himself after he was bitten."

"Okay," Gordon nodded, "what about his head?"

"I sliced it off and speared it."

Gordon's head bobbed again, then stopped. With a slight turn, his eyes narrowed. There was a new protective papa scowl. "Why is your shirt off?"

It wasn't scary, more endearing. After everything, I was going to have a little fun with him. I leaned forward a touch and whispered, "I needed it to get Kek's body hot and disturbed."

Gordon's jaw clenched as his eyes widened. I folded my lips in to pinch my mischievous smile from growing. I had witnessed the Hughes bantering with each other, and I kind of wanted to be part of that family dynamic as well.

"Leanora Ann Hughes, you better not have been taking your clothes off for a man. And I don't care that he is a god; your," his hand moved in a circular motion around my body, "is not for display until after you are married. And even then..."

"Pa," Sean backhanded Gordon, then pointed to me, "she's messing with you."

I was an open book; I couldn't hide my snickers as they made me tremble. "It's missing because I used it as tinder to start his body on fire." I don't know what was with me today, but I sang that same song from earlier. *"It got hot in there, because I blew that motherfucking cave up with his body in it."*

"Oh, baby girl." Gordon engulfed me once more in his arms, taking me with him as he stood up. "I knew! I knew you had it in you! I'm so proud of you!"

Sean wasn't joining in our celebration; I noticed that he picked up a lit-up cell phone behind the steering wheel on the dashboard then swiftly turned to us. "We need to get back— Leo's at the house."

"No." I shook my head back and forth. I had been through so much today, I didn't think I could take anything else. "I don't want to be anywhere near Leon right now," I growled. I didn't want to be around him or see him. I wasn't so keen with Sean right now either.

"Baby girl." Creases appeared between Gordon's brows. "Why?" Slowly he lowered me again. "But I thought...?"

"Yeah..." I grumbled as I crossed my arms against my chest and glared at Sean. "I was under the same impression until someone over there had his tongue down Leon's throat." Welcome back to that emotional roller coaster where rationality was lost.

Sean snapped his index finger at me. "No."

"Oh, I'm sorry, did Leon have his tongue down your throat instead? I mean, what the hell, Sean, it was obvious that there was something going on between Leon and I. Were you jealous or did you two have something secretive on the side going on?" That could explain why he had been continuously cold to me from the start; I was a threat to his love life.

"Sean," Gordon growled, "what the hell is she talking about?"

"Ugh, Nora." Sean pinched the bridge of his brow. "Leo knows about what's going on with you. We have been working together to figure it out since he found out, because Leo is concerned about you." His hand dropped. "He doesn't want to do anything to make you uncomfortable."

"Really." I wasn't buying it—it sounded more like a lame excuse. "Because walking in on you two making out sure as hell made me uncomfortable." I had never felt such a lost feeling in my life until I witnessed them earlier. There wasn't a part of me that thought Leon would ever do this—he was my Adonis. Despite that, I saw them together with my own eyes and there was no denying what they were doing.

Sean lowered to my level with his face closer to my own. "We all have insecurities and his greatest one right now is losing you. He knows about what happens when you two are intimate together. We were running out of theories to test."

"Leonora Ann," Gordon grumbled, "you better not be getting..."

"Pa, stop." Sean held out his hand before Gordon. "It sounds pretty PG-13; kissing is the furthest they've gone."

Wow, I may not be one to kiss and tell, but Mr. Bartender sure sounded like the opposite. Not cool. I was not impressed.

Sean took my hands after he studied my scowling face. "He loves you and is trying to do everything he can just to have a normal life with you."

I should have been listening closer to Sean, but Gordon had taken a call. Not a pleasant call, judging by the way his hand covered his mouth as he stared at Sean. His eyes closed as his head nodded. Sean grasped his mouth in the same manner that Gordon had and bowed his head. This wasn't going to be good. My mind started racing. What if I had killed an innocent member of this community? Or there was a warrant out for the person that destroyed the cliff? It could be any number of things—none of which were going to be good, their reactions told me.

Sean's head rose, showcasing the redness in his eyes. "We need to get her to Leo before it's too late."

CHAPTER 14

It was too late by the time we made it back to Gordon and Ruby's house; Leon had been placed in the spare bedroom on the main floor. Before they would allow me to see him, Gordon and Ruby sat me down on the couch between them, each taking one of my hands.

"Before you go in there," Gordon leaned his shoulder against mine as he took a breath of courage, "you must understand that it's his time and you will be saying goodbye to him."

His time? His time was eighty years from now—he was twenty-six, it couldn't be his time. What was wrong with them for believing that it was his time? Sure, they all knew about his illness, but that didn't mean one should just give up and accept it. Leon didn't seem as if he was one to back down; he was going to make it through this just as he had the other night.

Ruby leaned closer to me, her large marble eyes drowning in tears. "He's lived a long, beautiful life."

"No." I shook my head slowly. I had no control over my actions. Releasing my hands from theirs, I snapped, "He's twenty-six years old. What is wrong with you two to believe that he has lived a long life? His life isn't over and—" I tapped right above my left breast, "I am not giving up on him." This was so wrong. I didn't care what I was walking into; I was going to do everything I could to make sure he got to live that long, beautiful life.

My confidence quickly faded as I saw Leon's lifeless body lying in the middle of the bed. His chest hardly moved up and down. My eyes dropped to see Sean kneeling before the bed with his head down as if praying for him.

"Sean." His name flowed from my lips at the sight of him as if begging him to tell me the plan. Surely, being Leon's closest friend, Sean knew how to help him.

Sean's head rose, and swiftly he wiped his cheeks with the side of his hand before he walked over to me. He held out his arms and engulfed me as I moved closer to him. "I'm so sorry." His hands moved to my shoulders. "I'm going to leave so you can say goodbye to him."

My head moved side to side. He was Leon's best friend; he shouldn't have been giving up on him so easily. I glared into his eyes, my blood boiling, infuriated that everyone was just giving up on him. "You will go call the local doctor to come here now," I sneered. "You and I are not going to give up on him."

"Nora..."

"No." I wasn't going to give him a chance to fight me on this. "I don't care what anyone else says; you will listen to me."

"He loved you so much." His arms tightened around me. "Thank you for giving him the love back."

"You know what love is." I pushed myself out of his arms. "Believing what your heart tells you. My heart is telling me to fight for the ones I love. I fought Kek, a fucking Egyptian god, from making me his queen," I tapped my sternum, "because no matter how mad I was at him the last time I saw him, my heart still belongs to this man! I may not have Sigrid, but I will put up a greater fight to save Leon! Go call the doctor at once!"

When the door latched after Sean left, I moved Leon's arm up and laid against his chest. With my arm on his chest, I held his other hand and laid still. I didn't know what to do next. All I knew was that I wasn't going to say goodbye to him.

The door opened once in a while, and I could hear people entering and leaving. Prayers were whispered around me. I remained still, praying for Leon; praying for their prayers to be transformed to a speedy recovery. It wasn't fair for people to be praying for him to rest in peace—they should have been praying for his health and longevity.

Since Kek was real, I even prayed to Osiris, God of Death and Rebirth. I prayed to the benevolent god to refuse Leon if he came to him and resurrect him. I prayed to Hathor, Goddess of Love, to protect our love and bring him back so it was able to grow. I prayed to every Egyptian god I could think of that possibly could save Leon. Moving from Egyptian gods, I prayed to Aphrodite to see the love that Leon and I had so she could save him, allowing our love to continue to grow. I even joked that if she found him appealing, she could have him as long as she saved him. Then, as a Christian, I prayed to the one true God that I grew up believing in to awaken Leon and for forgiveness for praying to other gods. I repeated this cycle over and over, praying that just one of them would answer my prayers. After going face to face with Kek, I didn't care who it was.

"Baby girl." Ruby gently shook my shoulder. "Come on, baby, you need to eat, it's been almost two days."

I remained still, trying to figure out how it could have been two days already. It felt as if it had been an hour. Either way, it didn't matter I wasn't going to leave Leon's side.

"Please, baby girl," Ruby pleaded again, her voice filled with tears.

If they weren't going to get the care for Leon that he needed, I wasn't going to move. I remained still.

"Gordon," Ruby yelled out the door.

Within seconds, the room was filled with rushing footsteps. He must have thought something had happened. "Ruby—"

Panic echoed throughout his voice. "What's wrong?"

"She can't stay like this; it's been two days, and she hasn't moved. She needs to eat."

"Baby girl, come out and have dinner with us, please?"

A little too fast, I sat up and, lightheaded, collapsed back on to the bed. There was no way I could hold up my body right now. From everything in the cave and laying here with him, I couldn't support myself anymore. Instantly I curled back up to Leon. "If he doesn't eat," I mumbled, "I do not eat."

"Baby." Gordon rubbed my shoulder. "He's unconscious, he can't."

"Yes, he can," I growled. "Why hasn't a doctor checked him out? He could be hooked up to an IV. This isn't fair to let him die. This isn't fair for him to listen to everyone praying for his death. It isn't fair for people to be giving up on him the way that they are. If he dies, I die, because I am not giving up on him. I pray to Hathor and Osiris to spare him and bring him back. I pray to the God above to see that he is loved here and to spare him. I even prayed to Aphrodite to see his beauty and save him."

"Gordon, who are Hathor and Osiris?"

"Egyptian gods that I prayed to." Inhaling, I pushed myself upright, then glared at Gordon and Ruby. "I defeated the Egyptian God of the Darkness of Chaos in that cave, which means they are real as well." My elbow wobbled under my weight. "If Leon dies, I die. Hathor will ensure that we are together, and Osiris will welcome us to the afterlife."

"What is she talking about?" Ruby's voice was filled with trepidation. "We need to get help now."

My elbow gave out, causing me to fall onto the bed. As my eyelids slowly closed, I rested my head on Leon's stomach. "Please don't give up. I promise I'll never give up on you."

My jaw chattered as coldness creeped through my arm. A sharp pain in my hand drew my attention to it. Translucent tape held a needle in the vein on top of my right hand. No, this was wrong—Leon was to have the IV, not me. I released Leon and began to peel the tape off my hand.

"No." Sean rushed over to me, grabbing my right hand. "Leave it be."

"No, let me go." My jaw chattered again. "This isn't fair—he needs it, not me."

The bed sank as Sean sat on its edge, holding my hand above my head. "Breathe, Nora."

I couldn't. I stared at Sean until he was blurred. How could they give me an IV, but not Leon? "This isn't fair to him," I sobbed. I just wanted another chance with him; I wasn't ready for our story to end like this. A six-day story wasn't fair. I wanted a lifetime with him. It couldn't end like this; he had been my King Leon from the start, and no one was ever going to replace him. Every part of me was telling me not to give up on him, but now I didn't think I was going to have any control over it. Ruby had said that it had been two days, which meant that Leon could have gone too long without substance within his body. The body can only go so many days without food or water, and that enormous brunch spread I made for him Tuesday morning wouldn't sustain him that long.

My heart must have been trying to give me comfort as my mind was filled with images of Monday and Tuesday. Monday morning, Leon squeezed me tight into his torso as he asked me if I wanted to go back to his place for breakfast. Me being me, I stated we could only if I got to cook for him but he could pick what it was. Of course, his response was the items had to be my favorite to make or eat. With that, we spent a good part of both days in the kitchen. And, well...there was more than just cooking and eating going on.

Sean didn't say anything. With his other hand, he moved my head toward the other side of the bed. Leon lay there still, but there was a clear tube that ran from a silver pole to his left hand.

I turned back to Sean. My eyes were swollen with tears; I could no longer see anything. "Really?"

"Yeah, stubborn little baby girl got her way. And I have a feeling this isn't the last time you will, either. Anyways, yesterday when you blacked out, the doctor was called, and both of you two have been hooked up to IVs since."

Now Leon had a fighting chance to overcome whatever was going on in his body. That's all I wanted for him from the start—for people not to give up on him I wrapped my free arm around Sean. "Thank you so much!" Swiftly I kissed the side of his cheek. "You are the best for this!"

He grinned slyly. "Am I your favorite brother?"

I cocked my head—never did I ever think I was ever going to hear those words slip from Sean's lips. Sean had been starting to warm up to me more, yet I passed it off because I was now the youngest, whom he could bark orders at. However, those Hughes boys had a competitive streak with each other. "Always."

He wrapped his arms around me. Just as parental hugs were new to me, this sibling hug was also. I felt secure against his hard arms and chest, and perhaps it was because he had shown up at the cave, but I also felt safe in a new kind of way.

That was, until I couldn't contain my shivering anymore. I was freezing, and this was the worst kind of freeze—I felt it from the inside out. This was awful; I couldn't stop shivering, my jaw started chattering, and my hands felt numb. I shivered my way out of Sean's arms. "Are they punishing me for earlier or something?"

I glanced over to Leon. His body had already gone through so much with his autoimmune disease and probably was going through so much now that he was unconscious; chill didn't need to be added to his list. Hopefully he wasn't going through the same thing I was right now.

"I guess they keep the IV bags in the refrigerator until they are needed."

My hands were so cold that I couldn't feel Leon's normal chill in his hand. I lifted my shirt to just below my breast, my torso curving in as I studied my little rolls. I had once heard that to help treat hypothermia, skin to skin contact was the best way to bring someone's body temperature up. I at least knew it provided comfort to newborns—just maybe I could give Leon comfort as well. I took Sean's hand without asking and placed it against my stomach.

He drew his hand back, his brow dropping. "What are you doing?"

"I can't tell if my body is physically cold—I need to know if my stomach is warm." My lips moved into a reassuring grin. "Please?"

"Nora..." Sean's eyes widened. "Are you?"

He had to be kidding himself; I had been here for six days, and I didn't come up here knocked-up either. "Seriously?" I snapped. "If my body is warm, then maybe I could give him some comfort."

With a sigh, Sean's massive hand moved back to my stomach as his head turned away. "Your stomach is warm."

I just wanted to lean into his hand, his warmth taking me right back to laying in the sun with Leon. Sean should be the one laying against Leon, but I already knew he wasn't going to humor me if I pleaded my case to him. On the way back to the house, he was a broken record, continually telling me how much he didn't enjoy the kiss they had shared.

Leaning down next to Leon's right ear, I softly whispered, "I am going to remove the right side of your shirt, then I am going to lay up to you in my underwear. I don't know if it's going to help, but I hope it helps you warm up."

I moved his shirt up, then pulled his right arm through. I stood up and took my shorts off. Then I pulled my shirt off until it hung from the bend in my right elbow. This was the furthest it was going to go, with me being tethered to my own IV. Raising Leon's right arm, I moved it around my shoulders after I laid against him.

Sean didn't say a word as he lifted Leon's left arm above his head, then my right arm above my head. From the closet he pulled out a blue fleece blanket. He tucked the blanket into our sides before lowering our arms. Then he draped the light throw blanket on the edge of the bed over our exposed arms. He was delicate with all his movements to ensure that he wasn't going to hinder the IV lines. With a gentle kiss to my temple, Sean walked out of the room, but not before pressing in the lock on the bedroom door handle.

CHAPTER 15

On Saturday, Ruby and I took a road trip to Sadiespain, a town two hours away, to buy supplies to assist with Leon's care. I hadn't brought up my idea, but with the two-hour drive, I decided it was time to share my care plan with Ruby. The plan that sounded perfect in my mind was to move Leon back to his apartment so I was able to take over as his caregiver. This would allow everyone else to resume their normal lives, and since I still needed to talk to the castle owner, I was stuck in Journey.

It went about as well as I expected—after a few lectures and going back and forth, Gordon was dragged into the conversation. I could feel my hands starting to tremble as we waited for him to pick up the call. My saving grace was that Sean was with him. I still held on to hope that I was Sean's favorite sibling and he would go up to bat for me.

Gordon didn't tell me to knock it off and just listened to Ruby. It wasn't a scream fest that would back me into a corner of anxiety; rather, it turned into a levelheaded family discussion with them out fishing and us driving to go shopping. Each person took a turn to debate their case. Gordon's main concern was the physical aspect of being a caregiver, while Ruby was more concerned about the fact that I was fresh out of university, and she wanted me to be dedicating time to my new life. But it was Sean that swayed them to allow me to become Leon's main caregiver. He spoke about the moments he had watched Leon and I together all the way up to this morning. After everything, there was no one else Leon would have wanted to care for him more than me, according to Sean.

Sean not only stepped up for me, but he also stayed beside me to help me get in the swing of things. He helped move Leon back to his own apartment and took the day off to assist me in every way. After getting Leon settled in bed, I sent Sean home so I could have a private conversation with Leon. It wasn't that I didn't trust Sean, but in a relationship, not all conversations were meant for the world.

"It's just you and I in your apartment now." I weaved my arm between Leon's torso and arm until I was able to take his hand into my hand as I stared at the ceiling. "So you and I need to have a discussion. I don't know if you overheard any of the conversations at the Hughes' house, but going forward I am going to be your caregiver. Whatever we had prior to Tuesday afternoon is now on hold."

It had to be put on hold; I didn't think that Leon would ever cheat on me with a female or even a male, but I did want an explanation as to why he couldn't have been honest with me and told me the truth about the castle. It wasn't as if it was going to add more value to his appeal—I was already beyond smitten with him. Finding out he was the owner of the castle only added frustration. I was now in a state of vexation that he didn't trust me enough to just tell the truth. I had been one-hundred-percent honest with him from the start. He knew my passion behind protecting the castle, and he read each contract word for word. I just wanted his honesty.

For now, it was pointless to lay here and become bitter about it. I was going to move forward as if Frank never told me the truth.

"That doesn't mean that I don't care for you or am going to stop caring for you. I am doing this because I want to be as respectful to you and your body as I can. There is no way around this until you open your eyes and can care for yourself.

I am going to be up in your business. To help with this I am always going to tell you what I am doing before I do it. You are going to be put on a schedule so you know what to expect throughout the day. With that said, you are not going to be rotting in bed. I have a wheelchair, neck brace, and sunglasses; you are going to get out of this apartment and get fresh air."

Tuesday morning, my alarm went off an hour before the sun was to rise. This was intentional; every morning we were going to get up before the sun so we could watch it rise together. This had to be his reasoning for having an east wall of windows. Leon was in his wheelchair with his neck brace on, while I sat beside him holding his hand describing the ever-changing sky.

After the sun was up, it was time for some physical therapy. I had purchased a deck of cards with each card demonstrating a different stretch or yoga pose. Unsure if it was helpful, I convinced myself that it was helping keep his muscles limber and preventing bed sores. For whatever reason, I was fearful that a bed sore was going to be the one thing that took him down. From the sore he would get an infection, and it would spread, shutting down his organs. Within weeks he would perish from that one little bed sore.

Not on my watch, though—with the fear of sores came a strict hygiene routine. I would brush his teeth with a water pick and dentist suction tool once in the morning and again before bed. I would spritz his mouth to help avoid cottonmouth. And to prevent chapped lips, I would apply lip balm on his lips in the evening. For every part of him, I had a procedure to care for him. There were times throughout the day I hoped that he wasn't conscious.

As expected, the first week was the hardest to get into the groove of things mentally and physically. By the end of the second week, I had it down, and it seemed other people were becoming more accepting of everything as well. No longer were they giving me disgusted looks when I went to get groceries with Leon, instead being polite and friendly, even acknowledging Leon.

Our evening went from praying for Leon to rest in peace to hanging out telling stories to me while Leon rested in the recliner. It was constantly someone new each night. It was as if there was a sign up at the church; every evening a different family would show up. Of course, they would call first to see if it was all right to visit and when to come. Most of the time they would offer to bring dinner with them, although with time on my hands in the afternoons while I let Leon rest, I would make dinner for our guests.

By that second week of the bar being closed, Sean and Trevor decided it was time for it to reopen. I had to agree with them; I wasn't sure of Leon's financial situation, but regardless, I didn't want him to lose the bar. Since I still had funds from graduation, I was going to manage the bar pro-bono and my tips would be donated to Leon. Sean and I would run the bar Thursday to Saturday. I would open the bar at 5:00 p.m. and he would come help when he got off work an hour later. The bar would stay open until midnight on those days. For Leon's evening care, the community stepped in and created a sign-up sheet in the bar for whoever wanted to stay with him while I was managing the bar. It was amazing how much this community rallied around Leon.

CHAPTER 16

Just after opening the bar, I was in the back room organizing the latest delivery Hank had left me. He was truly a godsend when it came to the supply order for the bar. I could pour a beer, but I had no idea what needed to be ordered or how many items to keep in stock. This industry was a whole new world, and he was teaching me new things every day.

The door chimed. I popped my head out past the swinging door. "Just a minute." I had stacked a few boxes too high while I was looking for the new inventory.

Since Leon couldn't object, I was going to introduce two new cocktails tomorrow for our first round of Friday Fight Night. Just to change things up a bit, each Friday I was going to make two new cocktails and at the end of the night everyone could decide on which one to keep for the next round. At the end of this, with the masses deciding on it, I was hoping to add the winning cocktails to Mr. Sterling's mostly beer menu. Again, with the help of Hank, tonight's contenders were the Classic/Dirty Martini vs. the Vesper Martini. I wanted to get the ingredients separated from the normal inventory, so I was prepared for tomorrow's battle. Thankfully not much needed to be purchased for these new recipes; both called for gin, while one also had vermouth and the other had vodka and Lillet. I learned this from watching videos on the internet while Leon rested.

My lack of knowledge in this industry was irrelevant to

the community. Throughout the night, everyone of age would pop in to have a beer and say hi. It was starting to feel as if they were doing it to support me as much as they were doing it to support Leon. Case and point, Miss Wanda, a nondrinker, would come take her seat every night to have a cup of tea with me right when I opened the bar. She would tell me stories from her years, her perfect curls bouncing as she giggled at herself.

"Good evening, Wanda," I greeted her as I walked out from the back room, only to notice from the corner of my eye another customer sitting around one of the wooden tables near the back wall. I poured the hot water into the cup with a gold trim for Wanda and patted the counter. "I will be right back. I need to go help that other customer."

She didn't even need to face me—by her big, puffed-out 80s hair I knew exactly who it was. Although it was odd that she was alone. Stephanie or Ivan had to be lurking around. Susan never went anywhere alone just in case someone tried to attack her. She was unbelievably narcissistic; in her mind, every man wanted her for her beauty. I grew up listening to the countless tales of men that tried to follow her to her car or hit on her. For protection from these men, she made sure someone was always with her out in public. To be truthful, it felt more like she used this to try and get the attention of Dan.

I took one more look at her fried hair and turned around. I was in my rights to refuse to serve her; I wasn't taking a salary, or even tips—everything went back in the cash register to help Leon get back on his feet. As awful as it sounded, it wasn't like Leon was going to fire me for refusing service to a customer. Most likely a nonpaying customer, at that. When Susan found out I was volunteering here, she was going to expect free drinks.

A hand tightened around my neck, forcing me backwards until I hit the wall. Then Dan raised me up so I was just barely on my tippy toes as he peered into my eyes. This was his signature move when he was raging. In the bar's low lighting, I could see the anger discoloring his features.

"Where is my car?" he sneered as his spit splattered against my face.

I glared into his eyes without saying a word. I owed him no answers; everything I had done was legal. If it wasn't, no matter how much Forrest wanted that car, he would never have gone along with the sale of it.

Dan's hand tightened more around my neck. His face moved closer to mine. His repulsive breath stung my eyes more than his hand tightening around my neck. I wasn't going to give him the gratification of showing fear. He was just going to feed from it and things were going to get worse. I was going to stand my ground. I wasn't the little girl he could just intimidate anymore. I had no fear of him, no respect for him. His hand around my neck was validation that I had done the right thing.

His hand tightening more around my neck was proof that he knew this as well. His elbow moved up as he slammed his body into mine, releasing my neck for a second to reposition his hand. "Tell me where my car is or else!"

"My car is with its rightful owner," I calmly replied.

"Bullshit," he growled. "That was my car, you stole it from me."

My eyes bounced from Dan to Susan, who sat cocked in the chair with her arms across her chest, smugly grinning. She looked as if she was enjoying this. What kind of mother could enjoy watching her husband physically attack their daughter? It wasn't that I needed her protection; it was the realization of who these people really were. I had known they weren't the best, but this was justification for leaving.

"I do not fear you." I glared back into Dan's greyish-blue eyes. "I have faced evil. Your eyes hold more evil than Satan's first knight, but you do not frighten me."

Wrong answer—his other hand swung up and back, slapping me across the mouth. His ring must have caught my lip;

I felt warmth trickling down my chin.

"Where is my car?"

"I do not fear you. I have no respect for you." I made sure to emphasize the "p" so my lip splattered blood on his face.

"I am your father," he growled. "Show some respect."

I chortled. "You are no dad, father, or papa. I wasted my life chasing after your approval, only to realize it was unattainable. With the realization that you are so wrapped up in yourself and will never see past yourself, I no longer have respect for you. You have no clue what it means to be a father or ever have earned the right to be called one."

His hand tightened more against my neck. "I am the greatest father. You should be lucky to have me. Instead, you are nothing but an ungrateful brat! Always stressing your poor mother out, making her sick. I shouldn't be surprised that you stole my car."

Susan liked to blame me for all her illnesses. She would intentionally make herself sick to make it believable, either taking pills, faking a migraine, or shoving her middle finger down her throat. More than once, she had said her doctor told her that I caused her asthma, stomach issues, and her aortic aneurysm. With Dan never around to witness the truth, he would listen to her and blamed me for everything as well. I was far from the cause of her illnesses; I was petrified of getting in trouble growing up. I was never out of line, never late, earned good grades, started working on my own, and volunteered.

Stephanie, on the other hand, told her teachers that Dan was physically abusing her. Unlike me, I never witnessed them ever laying a hand on her. She later confessed to me that she was going to run off with a friend and Dan had found out about it. After that, she became untouchable, and she knew it. So anytime Stephanie messed up, the blame was passed to me. In Susan's own words: "You will always be here to take it, and Stephanie will fight back." She was right; I had nothing to fight back against them with. I was the black sheep in the family. I was in the shadows of Susan and Stephanie until they were bored and needed a villain.

"I legally sold my graduation gift," I calmly said, knowing this was going to enrage him even more. He wanted an altercation, but I wasn't going to give him one. "The gift that you left me before your trip."

"Lies," he shrieked and drew back his other fist. "Tell me right now where my car is or else."

"You will never see that car again." I gasped. "I had five attorneys from four different firms present at the sale. They all watched surveillance footage from that day. I told them everything from our talk about you not attending my graduation to after I found the check and titles. Nothing I did was illegal; the car was legally sold to its rightful owner. Go watch yourself on the surveillance videos if you don't believe me."

Dan was paranoid that someone was going to steal from him. His office had cameras pointing at his safe, above his desk, and a few in the hallways throughout the house. I knew about all the cameras, but I hadn't watched any of the footage until that day, when I had a feeling it would be useful and turned over the footage to Forrest.

"NO ONE," Gordon boomed as I was released from Dan's grasp and fell to my knees, "touches MY BABY GIRL!"

When I lifted my head after catching my breath, Dan was curled up in a ball. Gordon must have kicked out his legs to get the upper hand against him, since Dan was pinned against me.

Gordon grabbed Dan by the chest. "You think it's fair to assault someone smaller than you? Let me show you what it feels like." He punched Dan square in the face, then allowed him to drop to the floor.

"Pa," Sean yelped as he rushed over to Gordon.

Gordon didn't even take his eyes off Dan. "Take your sister upstairs and have Mama call Dr. Dangle." He kicked Dan in the torso as Dan tried to pick himself off the floor. "This ass-hole had her by the neck." He kicked Dan again. "I want her checked out."

Susan grasped her chest. "I feel lightheaded from fright." She gestured toward Gordon. "This behemoth assaulted my husband."

I pushed off my knee and stood up. "How dare you call Papa a behemoth," I sneered as I moved before her. Dan may have height against me, but Susan was a few inches shorter than I was. My shoulders rounded and my back hunched as I glared down at her. I pointed my finger down at her like a gun. "Behemoth? Have you ever looked at yourself? You may look like the next day after a one-night stand from the 80s on the outside," I cackled, "but inside you are far more monstrous than any evil creature that was ever portrayed in your horror movies that you love so much."

Sean slid his hand around my stomach, drawing me back to him. "I got this, Nora." Gently he spun us away from Susan, then whispered in my ear, "Go in back."

"He is not your father," she snapped at me.

Peering around Sean, I growled, "He has been more of a father to me in just the short time that I have known him." I pointed to Ruby, who had come in with Gordon, without tak-ing my eyes from Susan. "She is more of a mother than you will ever be." I shook my hand again at Ruby. "Just five min-utes with her and you could see it for yourself if your head wasn't so far up your own narcissistic ass!"

Susan scanned the bar with her palms up, pretending to be in disbelief. "Do you see how she talks to me? I am her mother." There was a sniffle—she was loading her crocodile tears. "I had a traumatic pregnancy and almost died. Hear that, Marigold? I almost died so you could live. Then I did die, because I gave up so much of my life to give you the best possible life." Her hands rose to her face, her head dropping as she whimpered.

No one moved, and after a minute Susan realized this. She glared up without a single tear or messed-up makeup. Her eyes scanned the bar again, and I could see her frustration growing with the fact that she wasn't getting her way in here. She was one of those people that demanded attention as soon as she entered a room. She needed to be the center of attention.

"Don't let Marigold fool you." Susan's voice rose. "She's as ugly inside as she is outside."

From the corner of my eye, I saw Peggy roll her eyes, then return to talking to Sharon. Frank glared at Susan under his eyebrows, then took a chug of his beer. Chauncy didn't even look up as she let out a sarcastic "Yeah, sure" before dropping another coin in the jukebox. Everyone in the bar went back to what they were doing before the showdown, ignoring Susan and her little rant.

Susan's hips shifted as she placed her hands on them and snickered. "Not that I would expect you to see this, since you are all just a bunch of backwood-bred hicks."

Never did I want anyone in here to be subjected to her toxicity. Bar nights were supposed to be fun nights, not like this. My blood boiled as I lunged around Sean. I was going to give Susan the attention she wanted.

Swiftly Sean grasped me and swung me away again as Susan held out her hand, gesturing toward Dan. "See what her lies did to my poor husband, her father. She stole his car, then she got her father assaulted for her own wicked ways."

"She's not the thief." Ruby walked with her arms open so Sean would release me to her. She brushed the hair away from my face and inspected my lip with her hands gently on my cheeks. With a stern tone and matching glare, Ruby looked over to Susan. "The only thieves in here tonight are you and your husband for stealing away her childhood. And it doesn't take a backwood-bred hick to know that you are a psychopath. Just in case that word is too big for you to comprehend, it means that you are a dishonest, exploitative, manipulative, and narcissistic person."

Susan looked Ruby up and down. "And who do you think you are?" she sneered.

"I am Leonora's mama, and you will not tell lies about my daughter." Ruby looked back to me. "Her pure heart saved us all."

Susan noticed Trevor walking in and instantly rushed over to him in tears. "Please, sir, help me, those awful people have assaulted my husband, and I am fearful for my life."

Trevor stopped and scanned the bar, his gaze fixing on my face. "Nora." He rushed over. "Sean, what happened to her?" His eyes widened. "Is he back?"

Without a doubt, "he" was Kek. Leon, Trevor, and Sean were close; I wouldn't be surprised if Sean told Trevor what happened that day. I think it was slowly trickling out around town.

"No," Gordon held Dan's hands behind his back, "that was the handy work of another evil man right here."

Trevor stayed with Gordon while Ruby and Sean took me in back to clean me up. I wasn't sure if it was because of what had happened in that cave or because Leon couldn't be next to me, but Sean always remained fixed at my side.

Sean hoisted me onto the stainless-steel table next to the sink as Ruby went over to grab the first aid box. It wasn't as bad as everyone was making it out to be; I just had a cut on my lip and a sore throat. However, it was enough mentally to keep my head lowered in shame that these beautiful people had been made part of my unnecessary family drama.

Sean gently lifted my head, his eyes on my busted lip before moving to my blurring eyes. "So that was the infamous campfire-story Dan and Susan." The pad of his thumb swiped the tears from my cheekbone. "They will never get near the castle. Please don't cry. It's protected."

My shoulders rose with my inhale, then dropped. The castle hadn't even crossed my mind—there was another matter we needed to talk about first. Dan and Susan were not going to stand for this type of humiliation, even if they didn't know a soul in the bar. By not cowering to my knees below them, I had started a power war. There was no way they were going to allow their disobedient daughter to do this; if word drifted out, they knew it could damage their reputation. Well, I had already made Dan look like a fool by selling his prize possession to Forrest. After tonight, Dan would be out for my head on a stake, because no one dared to cross the almighty King Dan. Just like that day he threw me in the cab and sent me home, he was going to do something to crush me to show me he was the one with the power.

"I know how Dan operates," I babbled through my tears. "He's going to retaliate against me." This life wasn't just about me anymore; Leon was my top priority. "I need you to swear to me that you will be here for Leon and continue his care."

After tonight's altercations, I could see Dan marching down to the police station and filing an assault charge against me. I may not have laid a hand on him or Susan, but they were notorious for misconstruing information. It was going to be my word against their word, since the bar patrons were not going to be present when I was hauled in.

Sean blurred before me. "Promise me you will take over Leon's care if I have to leave," I whined as I grasped Sean's upper arm. "Please promise me. It's in your blood, I have seen Gavin's loyalty. I see Gavin in you. I know you are loyal. Stand by Leon the same way Bartholomew and Gavin stood by King Leon. Please... Sean."

I felt his warm breath on my face. "You're safe, nothing bad is going to happen to you. I am here to protect you."

"It's not a matter of safety or protection for myself." I wiped my cheeks. "It's the matter that he is going to retaliate against me. It wouldn't have mattered two months ago, but it does now. Please be there for Leon, give him the same care that I have."

"Hey, nothing is going to happen to you. I am your brother, no one is going to hurt you ever again."

"Please, Sean, this isn't about me, it's about Leon. I've been typing Leon's daily schedules and care instructions." I leaned forward, drawing my phone out of my back pocket. "May I have your email address to give you access to them?"

"Baby girl," Ruby squeezed my hand, "we all will be here for Leo if something happens. I promise you that we will care for Leo just as much as you have. Please don't worry, I promise you this."

"Thank you." I leaned forward, wrapping my arms around Ruby.

CHAPTER 17

Once upstairs, Sean and I found Wanda sitting next to Leon in the chair with her head down as she held their hands to her chest. It was a sobering image as the realization set in that Wanda was the one who alerted Gordon earlier—it had been his night with Leon.

Sean walked past me to head straight for the kitchen. He was on a mission to raid the refrigerator. His appetite was as large as his muscles were; he was endlessly hungry. I couldn't imagine Gordon and Ruby's grocery bill each month feeding three Seans.

"My gosh," Wanda gasped as I raised my index finger to my lips, trying to mute her. It didn't need to be talked about in front of Leon. It was still unknown if Leon was aware of his surroundings or just in a deep sleep. I was holding on to the hope that he was still there, listening to everything going on around him.

I shook my head as I took Leon's hand. After kissing it once, I rested it on his chest before I kissed his forehead. "Thank you, Wanda, for sitting with Leon while Gordon helped in the bar tonight."

Sean growled unnecessarily from the refrigerator door with a forkful of chicken parmesan in his mouth. On the way up to the apartment, I had told him that I didn't want to discuss any of the events that unfolded at the bar in the apartment. Of course, his response was that Leon had the right to know what was going on in his bar. Which was fair, but his second reasoning stung a little. Sean told me that I wasn't being my true self for Leon. Even in his condition, Leon would have wanted me to be me, good or bad.

After downing all the leftovers and two slices of cake, Sean left to walk Wanda home. I knew Sean wasn't going to let what happened go until Leon got the full awful story about all the drama I brought to his establishment. He didn't need this stress, and I didn't want him to think that I was messing things up for him. I just wanted Leon to wake up and walk right back into his life as if nothing happened.

Once the apartment was free of extra people, I curled up to Leon on the recliner, closing my eyes and resting my head against his. I had told him that everything was going to be put on hold, but even being unconscious, he was comforting. I just needed him right now.

Resting my cheek against his, gently I rubbed my fingers in his hair. "I know I told you that everything between us would be suspended, but more than anything I need your comfort. I miss you so much." The tears carried my soft words down our cheeks to his ear. "In the next few days, things might be changing. There is a strong chance that I may not be here for a while. This isn't my choice at all. If I had my way, I would stay beside you until your eyes open again." Gently I kissed his cheek. "He's going to retaliate against me, and I might not even get this for a while."

The tears were starting to dance between his stubble and my cheek, so I moved my face away from his. After wiping off the tears, softly I kissed his cheek and resumed our original position. "Please don't give up—even miles away, I will never give up on you."

His breathing was soft and steely; I imagined it as waves rolling in. It took me back to the lake with Miss Gemma Ann.

"I believe," I tenderly whispered, "she saved me for you."

As he said he would, Sean returned. It was time to put this

day to bed. I moved Leon from the recliner to his wheelchair and wheeled him to the kitchen. Grabbing his IV bag, I placed it on his lap, then wheeled him into his bedroom.

Sean watched from the doorframe with another slice of cake as I backed Leon's wheelchair beside the bed. "Why don't you take tonight off? I'll drive you out to the folks' house, then come back to handle things here for the night."

It was sweet of him to offer, but he didn't know our nightly routine. Generally, he went home after we closed the bar for the night. Leon's bedtime routine was just between us, but with the uncertainty in the air, I was going to have to share it with Sean. I already knew what his answer was going to be if I asked him to continue it, so I would have to sway him into it.

I locked the wheels on the chair and blurted out, "Are you going to take a super-hot shower, then lay against Leon in your underwear?" So much for swaying him into it.

"Seriously?" Sean walked over, setting his empty plate on the nightstand. "Why would I even consider doing that with him?"

I moved the IV bag to the nightstand. "Because his IV bag must be refrigerated, it's like an internal polar challenge circulating through your body. I turn myself into a lobster, spoon up to his backside, and cover us up with a blanket just like that first day. I hope that it can counter the coldness from his IV bag."

Sean reached for the sides of Leon's torso, then stopped for a second. "Leo, I'm going to move you to the bed for Nora. Then help her get you ready for bed. Once you are settled in, I'm going to take her home to Pa and Ma's, then I'm going to come back here." Gently he moved him onto the bed. "Don't worry, man, I'm not going to snuggle you ever."

"Come on, Sean, you're missing out. Cuddling with Leon is the best." It was, and earlier was the perfect example. Even with the stress of the evening, I had fallen asleep in the chair with Leon.

"I'll take your word for it." He gently lowered Leon onto the bed. "Let's get a move on this so you can clock out."

Leon lay there in his black sweatpants and white T-shirt.

"That's not what this is." Sitting down on the edge of the bed, I rubbed Leon's hand. "This isn't a job."

Sean removed Leon's collar. "Are you going to tell him what happened?" Then he moved and pointed at Leon's chest.

I nodded to let Sean know that it was all right to take Leon's shirt off, then I glared at him when my head remained still. "Nothing happened that needs to be discussed," I stated, trying to keep my voice positive.

"Your neck and..."

"Shh," I cut him off as he untied Leon's drawstrings, then I mouthed, "No!"

"Nora, you tell him everything." Sean's hands slid under Leon's waistband and tugged down his sweats. "Every moment, every blade of grass, I've even seen you explain in detail what everyone walking down the block was wearing and about their strides."

Slowly I shook my head as I pressed my lips together.

"Fine." Sean gazed into my eyes as he continued to lower Leon's pants. "Have you told him about what happened that afternoon?"

Gingerly I rubbed the back of Leon's neck, easing the pressure the closer I got to the front of his neck. "Are you talking about the afternoon I caught you two making out? After which Leon fell into a deep sleep?" I glanced up at Sean and gave him a wink. "Now you are going to have to finish that kiss to awaken him."

"We talked about this already," Sean grumbled, sitting up with his head cocked as he stared down at Leon's black boxer briefs, which had an arrow on the left leg pointing up, the words "THE MAN" below it, and an arrow on the right leg pointing to the middle with "THE LEGEND" beside it. It was hard not to miss, as the arrows and text were bright gold.

Sean's eyes widened. "What the hell!?"

I started giggling uncontrollably. "Are you sure there isn't something that could change your mind?" I was exhausted from everything today; I wasn't surprised that my mind no longer had control over my mouth.

"Fuck no!"

I fell onto the bed giggling as I inched my way up to Leon's ear. "I'm sorry, I put that bonus pair on you this morning, and Sean just saw them." I kissed his cheek. "You are a legend in every way."

Sean dropped Leon's sweats across his hips, trying to move on from what he had just seen. "First of all, that's not possible, and I know that you don't believe that."

The fun was gone with Sean's deep tone. I watched Leon, frozen in time, as I glided my thumb across his cheek. Who knew what I believed anymore—no one knew why Leon slept and wouldn't wake up. I had no one to turn to for answers about why Kek wanted me. Me, of all people; he could have had anyone else. Why, after all these years, did he desire me as his queen?

I gave Sean a wistful grin, then returned to Leon. "I never believed that Egyptian gods were immortal, until one was propositioning me with lame pickup lines."

Sean's eyes widened. Nothing about my experience in that cave was fun or funny. I didn't know how to handle what had happened; I was just trying to make it lighthearted. He wanted his answers, and I had refused to go into detail about what happened, though he was present for part of it. He didn't need his mind filling with nightmares.

"Nora, it's all right to talk about what happened in there with me."

"There's nothing to talk about. I gave you and Papa the rundown of what happens when guys use lame pickup lines on me."

He pointed his index finger at me. "Comments like this concern me that he did more to you than you are letting on. I am here to help and protect you in all ways."

CHAPTER 18

Ever since the cave, I felt as if there was someone constantly watching me from the shadows. On the evenings when I was off from the bar, I would go out for a run after dinner. The whispers in the trees would always send me back to Kek telling me how he had been watching me. With his eyes sliced and incinerated, it was impossible for this to be happening now. But the rustling of the leaves and the breath of the breeze had my mind in hyperdrive about what else was lurking out there.

At the bar, I never felt this way. I had met the entire town, and no one was a stranger to me anymore—well, until my latest shift, when a lady and gentleman dressed sharply in navy-blue uniforms and neon yellow patches on their breast with fluorescent white letters that spelled out "Border Security Officer" walked in. It was odd that they were this far north, or I guess it could also be this far south. Either way, Journey was too far from either border for them to be here on business.

Walking behind the bar, I set my dish towel down. "Are we on duty, or may I buy you each a beer?" I was nosy about what brought them to the little town and was going to sweeten them up. Or perhaps they had a good story to tell.

"Working," the dark-haired lady sneered. "I'll have a Coke." She was broad as she was stern. Her aged face, possibly mid-forties, had seen the sun one too many times. There was no cheerfulness to her pencil-lined lips. Perhaps there wasn't a good story to get out of her judging by her sour face.

The younger gentleman with bronze glasses and a warm smile glanced around the bar behind me. "I've wanted to own a pub. How long have you owned this place?"

"Oh, I don't own it." I filled a clear glass with Coke, then placed it before the lady, whose badge read "Klein." Glancing over to the gentleman, I gave him a wistful grin. "My friend had a medical emergency; our friends and I are running the bar for him until he recovers."

The gentleman leaned forward so I was able to read his last name—Walhaug, according to his badge. "How's the pay?" His breath was sweet and minty. "Is it enough to cover the bills and then some?"

That made me chuckle. "I'm not being paid, and all tips go toward the owner's medical expenses." I pointed to the door. "There's a sign." I turned back to Officer Walhaug. "So what will it be? It's on the house."

Before Officer Walhaug could answer me, Officer Klein crossed her arms against her chest. "Let me get this straight, you are working here for free?"

"Yep." I nodded. "That's what you do for loved ones when they are down." By the looks that they were giving each other and their questions, it felt as if they were working on a case.

"So," Officer Klein set her glass down, "where are you from?"

It was odd that she would assume I wasn't from here. "The States." My heart was starting to race as I realized I was their current case. Dan had to have turned me in for working undocumented at the bar. He wasn't going to win, though—I was going to fight. "And you know that I am in my legal right to be here. I've been up here since the first of June; it hasn't been one hundred eighty days."

The immigration law was if you were staying more than one hundred eighty days, you would need to apply for a visa. On my phone I had a countdown on the number of days I had left before I would need to leave. If Leon was still in his current state, I was going to go back to the States on Wednesday,

November 22nd to stay with a friend for the long holiday weekend, then return on Wednesday the 29th.

"Regardless, you are working unsponsored," Officer Klein snapped back at me.

She felt like the type of person that used the badge as a power booster. This wasn't going to end well for one of us. I was going to stand my ground with her. No matter what, I was going to be here to care for Leon.

"I don't need to be sponsored to volunteer. Maybe you should go read your own law book again, like I have. I know that I am in my right to be here if it is within one hundred eighty days and I am not taking any form of payment for services provided."

"I would bet anything that is just some story that you are feeding us and that you are being paid under the table, which is working illegally."

"Ms. Carter." Unlike Officer Klein, Officer Walhaug spoke softly. "We will need to talk to the owner of the bar. We have been unable to reach him; do you know where he is?"

I glanced up to the ceiling and closed my eyes. "He has a medical condition and is not taking visitors right now."

"Produce the owner, or you will go with us right now," Officer Klein growled.

CHAPTER 19

As they demanded, I brought the officers to Leon. This was wrong on so many levels; I was not breaking any Canadian laws, and Leon was not a roadside attraction for people to gawk at. He was a person with a medical condition, and my words should have been enough for them.

Gordon swiftly stood up from the couch as we entered the apartment. I was thankful it was his night with Leon and not someone else. I didn't know if he had any pull as Warden of the Game and Fish department, but still I was holding on hope that he knew someone who could help in this situation.

"Baby girl, who are they?"

"Border Security Officers." I inhaled deeply, the pain in my throat letting me know that tears were on deck. "I've been turned in for working undocumented." Swiftly, I turned toward Officer Klein and sneered, "Which is false."

I walked past Gordon, leading them into Leon's bedroom. Once we were all in the room, I gestured toward Leon and growled, "Are you satisfied now?"

"Yes." Officer Klein walked over to me. "Come on, we are going now."

"Going where?" Gordon questioned as he moved in front of me. I didn't need Sigrid; I had a protective papa in front of me now.

"Pa!" Sean rushed into the room; someone downstairs must have told him about the officers, judging by the level of anxiety in his voice. "What's going on?"

Officer Walhaug calmly explained the situation to Gordon and Sean as I sat on the side of the bed, taking Leon's hand into mine. With the way Officer Klein was behaving and the mellowness in Officer Walhaug's voice, I had a feeling I wasn't going to be allowed back into Canada for a while.

"Until this is straightened out, Ms. Carter must return to the States." Officer Walhaug continued, "I understand the circumstance, and on a personal level I apologize, but cases like this can take up to two or more years to resolve. During that time, she is not allowed to enter Canada."

My head dropped as I raised Leon's hand to my lips. This couldn't be happening; I couldn't leave him in this condition. "No, I can't leave him that long." I looked up to them as the tears streamed down my face. "I am his main caregiver."

"It doesn't matter." Officer Klein locked her arm around my arm, lifting me from the bed. "Let's go."

She was no better than Ivan or Kek trying to force me into something that was wrong. Male or female, I wasn't going to stand to be ordered around like this.

I turned to face Officer Klein, only inches from her face. I glared into her eyes. "If you take me right now without getting the proper care lined up for Leon, you will have blood on your hands. I will go back to the States and get on every social media platform to tell the world about how I was falsely accused of a crime that I did not commit. Then I will tell them the story of how I was here to care for my love and you frightfully ripped me away from him." I leaned in closer. "What you may not know is that in the States right now the media likes a good law enforcement brutality story. This—" I gestured between us, "a female officer from the Great White North that is being unlawfully unfair to an American here to save her love—this battle between us is going to spread faster than your wildfire smoke that pollutes our air every summer. And that's just the start of it. Our battle will catch the eyes of some bigwigs that I go to church with. They will have already calculated how this story of injustice will help their political careers if they become the hero of it when they take it to Washington. They will approach me after Mass to hear my brokenhearted story. While that's going on, the masses of social media warriors will come out to protest this unfair treatment. They will picket outside your house. Your children will be asking your partner why there are people outside the door holding signs saying Mommy is a murderer."

I took a step back, tilted my head, and crossed my arms against my chest. "Get ready to explain to your children and the world why you let an innocent Canadian citizen die."

Officer Klein's lips puckered until she finally spoke. "She has two hours to make arrangements, then Officer Walhaug and I will be escorting her out of the country." The apartment door slammed after she walked out.

"Hot damn, Nora," Sean chuckled, "that was savage!"

I walked back to the bed, sitting on the edge. I bowed my head until it rested against Leon's shoulder. I had two hours left with him, and I just wanted to lay here alone with him. Although that wasn't going to be possible.

"Ms. Carter." Steps neared me. "Please be aware that I can't leave your side until we cross that border."

"I understand, Officer." He wasn't as abrasive as Officer Klein, so I was going to give him the respect that he deserved. "Officer Walhaug, please make yourself at home. I can handle all my business from this apartment."

"Thank you and you are welcome to call me Devin."

"Baby," Gordon rubbed his hand on my back, "I'm going to have Ma come over so you can teach her how to care for Leo while I get this straightened out." His voice deepened. "Sean, you remain at her side until further notice."

"Papa, I also need Sharon from the bank to come here." Sitting up, I noticed Leon's chest was rising and dropping swiftly. He had to have heard everything to have that reaction.

"Devin and Sean, I need you two to step out of the room."

"Ms. Carter, I can't…"

"His breathing is stressed," I interrupted. "I need to calm him down. Please just step outside the door."

They walked out as I laid down beside Leon, then rolled him over so he was laying halfway on my torso with his head resting on my chest. "Please don't worry. I'm going to get Forrest involved, and he is the best. I'll be back before you realize it."

I kissed the top of his head. "We need to get excited; the Master of Care is stepping in for me. Mama is going to take over the care for you during the day. And at night it's going to be like the good old days when you would have a slumber party with Sean."

I worked out everything with Mama and Sharon, leaving me an hour with Leon. I didn't care if he was going to crush me; I was about to enter another world without air. My life had revolved around him long enough that I felt even more lost than the day before I graduated from university. I remained in a tight embrace with Leon until that final knock echoed through his bedroom—it was time.

CHAPTER 20

Officer Klein followed us in her cruiser while Officer Walhaug drove my SUV to the States. I may have been in my own vehicle with Gordon beside me in the back seat, but I felt like I was that twelve-year-old girl again in the back of the cab being punished for Dan's unjustified temper. I didn't speak the entire trip back. All I could do was stare out the window at the blurring familiar sights.

At the border in Portal, Gordon moved to the driver's seat as Officer Walhaug returned to Officer Klein's cruiser. Gordon spoke to me as we descended further into the States, yet I could only pick out his tone, not his words. After an hour in, I think he gave up talking to me. It wasn't that I was ignoring him; I felt dead with disappointment. I had failed Leon and messed up the Hughes' lives.

The landscape became even more familiar; we were back in Puth. Gordon glanced up in the rearview mirror. "Baby, I have made arrangements for you to stay in an old friend's apartment. All I want from you is for you to take care of yourself until we can get this straightened out with the Canadian officials."

The words were still not with me, and all I could do was bow my head with the heaviness of my tears. When I raised my head again, we were stopped at an elite apartment complex in town. There was no way I was going to be able to afford to live here with only a thousand dollars to my name.

"No," I mumbled from the back seat. "Take me to the north side of town, I can't afford to live here."

Gordon pulled into the parking garage. Once he got out, he opened my door. "Don't worry about rent; it has all been covered." His thumb brushed my cheek. "Please don't cry, I will fix this. For now, let's get you inside. It's been a long night."

Footsteps neared as I exited my vehicle, and soon enough there was a gentleman walking toward us. I knew that rounded body and white hair. I knew the sharpness of his hooked nose, his gap-toothed smile, and those dimples. My heart began to race.

"No, Papa, please don't turn me over to him," I whined as I grasped Gordon's arm. "Please, no, he's going to turn me over to Dan."

He was Joe Salary, a kind soul that repeatedly took an active interest in my life whenever we were around each other—and the only time we were around each other was on fishing trips where families were permitted to attend.

Before Gordon could say anything, Joe hoisted me into the air. Moving to the center of the aisle, he bounced me. "That's my girl!" he squealed with excitement. "I always knew that you had it in you!"

"All right, Joe." Gordon walked over and patted his shoulder. "She's had a rough night; we need to get her upstairs."

"Oh, yes." Joe lowered me, then tapped my chest. "I believed in you. I knew that you were going to do great things someday. I just never realized how good this vengeance would taste."

"Joe" softly fell from my lips. "What?"

He tapped my heart, and instantly it hit me—he knew about Kek. The story of Joe's wife started to replay in my head. From the whispers and gossip of my biological parents' inner circle, Stephanie and I learned that, before I was born, Joe was more like my father back in the day: fishing came first, family was for show, and money was thrown around for status. That all changed when Joe came back from a fishing trip. His wife was supposed to pick him up from the airport, but she never showed up. Another member of the fishing party ended up giving Joe a ride home. Ultimately, Joe found his heavily pregnant wife sitting in the gazebo at four in the morning, pale white, without a pulse. The coroner ruled that she had bled out from a complication from her pregnancy, but the whispers said that there was no blood around her body or even within her or the child she was carrying.

After our first trip to Journey, Stephanie liked to scare me by telling me I was going to have the same fate as Joe's wife, and a vampire was going to come for me because I was the same age the child that was never born would be. I passed it off as jealousy because Joe was always kind to me.

Warm tears rolled down my left cheek. "She was right," I whispered, staring, paralyzed, at Joe. "Stephanie was right, he took your family from you."

"All right." Gordon wiped my cheek. "It's late, or it's early; either way, this isn't the time for this conversation."

Joe's lips pinched as he nodded twice. "I would have never allowed you to go to Journey unless I fully believed in you." He took a step forward, pulling me into his chest. "I'm so sorry, but you needed to be the one to do this. Even at a young age, I could see that it was already written in your fate. Miss Gemma Ann saw it as well—we both knew you were destined to save Journey from that monster and save the king. He was a monster that taunted that poor kingdom long enough, not everyone had the protection of Sigrid. He killed my wife and unborn child to show what happens when someone ruled by the curse leaves the kingdom." His voice rose. "He was a bored, sick monster that enjoyed putting fear into others. I was far from perfect, but she was. Never in a million years did she or our unborn child deserve that fate."

"Okay," Gordon moved his arm between us, "that's enough for tonight."

CHAPTER 21

Lori was gracious enough to give me back my position at the optical. She had met my family and understood what had happened the first time I was forced to resign. Going forward, I was going to work Monday through Friday, 8:00 a.m. to 6:00 p.m., and on Saturdays from 9:00 a.m. to 4:00 p.m. It was cheaper for the organization to pay me overtime than to hire another person part-time.

I couldn't live in self-pity forever, so I did the next best thing: I made my schedule chaotic, an idea planted by a former dance partner's older brother. Russell had happened to stop by the optical for his appointment and left with a new pair of contacts and a new bartender. I wasn't surprised that Russell had opened a bar; our paths had crossed a few times over the last few years at parties. The man loved to party; beer pong, dancing, and even just sitting on the couch chatting—he thrived in this atmosphere. Being underage, there was nothing else to do in our little boring town at night, so house parties it was. Sitting on sketchy couches chatting with Russell was how we had grown to truly know each other.

Thursday was going to be my first day at the bar. I thought I was bartending at a little dive bar, as Russell had told me, but it turned out it was the trending bar. Scheduling ahead, you could pay a fee for the bar to be transformed into whatever theme you picked off the list. During my orientation, Russell had shown me the schedule. It was mostly bachelorette parties that wanted Egyptian themes. Thankfully, this option was only open for Saturday nights. After almost becoming an Egyptian goddess, it wasn't appealing to me to dress up as one anymore. At least the schedule was a little more appealing; I would be working Thursdays and Fridays from 7:00 p.m. to 1:00 a.m. and on Saturdays from 5:00 p.m. to 1:00 a.m.

And since that wasn't enough, I picked up a grocery store bakery shift. This position paid differential pay and offered a ten percent discount on my groceries. Another perk was that they had a gas station attached to the store, which meant I could get a ten percent discount on my gas as well. This made the 3:00 a.m. to 6:30 a.m. shifts on Monday, Tuesday, and Wednesday a little more bearable.

Three positions seemed like a lot, but I needed to be earning as much as I could. Earnings from the bar were going to be funds that I lived from. I was living rent-free in Joe's apartment building; I honestly didn't have too many expenses. All earnings from the optical were going into a savings account in Journey to cover lost wages for Ruby, because she promised me that she would take over as Leon's prime caregiver. Earnings from the bakery also went to an account in Journey, but this one was a checking account with to help cover Leon's medical expenses.

My need to keep moving went beyond the money. I had people relying on me at all hours. There was no way I would let any of them down. That wasn't who I was—I would rather bleed myself dry than fail them. Thankfully that determination was saving me from the chance to stop and comprehend all that had played out over the summer. I couldn't allow this to happen; the darkness needed to stay where it was. I guess a little had a chance to slip through as I was now frightened by what I couldn't see in the shadows.

Today was a fresh day with a new mission. I was heading to one of the universities in Balvin, a town two hours southeast of Puth. Balvin had two universities: one was the engineering school, and the other was the medical school. My goal for the day was to sit in on one of Dr. Wally Walizer's classes so I could speak with him afterward. It would have been simpler if the school had just published his office hours so I could schedule a meeting with him, but since they didn't, this was my Plan B.

It wasn't going to be too difficult to blend in with the other students. The school offered undergraduate and graduate programs. I would slide right in since I had just graduated with my undergrad degrees. All I could hope for was his class was in a lecture hall so I would be able to sneak into the back unnoticed until the lecture was over. On second thought, the new semester had only begun last month, and I could get by stating I was a late entry. To make this line believable, I had my old backpack. Thankfully, I hadn't cleaned it out yet and still had two of my finance textbooks.

I smoothed my skirt as I took the desk in the back row in the far-left corner, praying I was going to remain hidden in the dark so the dean wouldn't call on me. I drew out my textbook and my notebook. I was counteracting this, by what I was wearing. I had on my white lace skirt with a navy shirt. My hair was tied up in a high ponytail with a white silk scarf. I should have been in a hoodie and jeans, but I wanted to be presentable for Dr. Walizer.

Odd as it was, I was kind of giddy to be sitting in another lecture. I loved school and learning new things. I graduated with a bachelor's in science in accounting and another in finance. I could have added another business degree or two, but the university kept revamping the curriculum and it was getting old when the classes I needed were dropped. Never in my four years of studies had I taken a medical course. Today was going to be a new experience. All I could hope for was that I didn't sit there like a deer in headlights, because I had no clue what he was lecturing about.

Students who appeared to be my age began to funnel into the classroom, taking desks all around me. A gentleman walked in, then leaned against the front desk with his legs kicked out and arms crossed against his massive chest. His narrow ocean-blue eyes, which reminded me of Trevor's eyes, shone under the fluorescent lights. They would have been more appealing if he removed the scowl off his face and the air of arrogance he projected as people told him good morning and he didn't even flinch.

Yes, he was leaning against the front desk, but there was no way he was Dr. Walizer. To me, Dr. Walizer—or, according to his online profile on the university's website, Wally—was an older fella with thirty to forty years of teaching under his belt. This arrogant lad before me couldn't possibly be thirty. His hair was a molasses color in the sunlight. His brows were the same color and provided a visor for his gorgeous blue eyes. His nose had a couple waves about it, but it was the tip that matched the slit in his chin. His face structure was that of a classic black-and-white superhero; strong and defined.

His eyes moved to mine. Swiftly I lowered my head and opened my corporate finance textbook, paging through it as if looking for a specific page. This wasn't the attention I wanted to draw to myself. All I wanted was his attention at the end of the class, not now and for sure not during class.

I peeked up through my eyebrows to see his gaze had moved to the window. Leaning forward, I tapped the girl in front of me in the bright red hoodie. Her ponytail swung as she turned around.

"I'm new in this class," I whispered, trying not to draw his attention back to me. "Is that Dr. Walizer?"

"No, thank god." She tittered as she leaned closer to me and whispered, "Wally is one of the best professors you will ever have. This fool before us is Nick Yaman, one of Wally's higher-class students. I heard he is brilliant, but he has the worst bedside manners. Wally is making him teach his classes to teach him some humility while Wally is caring for his wife." She leaned a little closer. "She just had surgery for cancer. If it went well, Wally should be back late next week."

"Thanks." I fell back into my chair. That wasn't what I wanted to hear. Not that Leon was going anywhere, I just wanted an answer or a magical formula to make him improve. Crossing my arms against my chest, I glared at Nick with disdain for the whole situation.

I had two options: sit this class out or get up and walk out. These choices teeter-tottered in my mind. If I stayed, there was a chance I might learn something. If I left and came back next week, there was a chance that Nick might still be teaching this class. When Dr. Wally returned, Nick might fill him in about the student that kept walking out of the class each week. I didn't want to ruin my reputation with Dr. Walizer because Nick spouted off.

"That is not the class textbook," came a strong, stern voice beside me.

I guess I didn't need to decide—it was about to be decided for me. Or was it?

I flipped the book closed. "Have you ever had one of those days when nothing is going right?" I gazed up, giving Nick a sideways grin. "I was in such a rush this morning that I grabbed my roommate's corporate finance textbook. I mean, come on, Universe, give me a break. It's my first day here." I waved my left hand. "Don't even ask me my name; I'm probably going to get it wrong," I moved my index and middle fingers like they were running. "Just go pick a name off your roster and make sure it's a pretty one; my real one isn't."

Nick's right eyebrow rose, then he walked to the front of the class again. My little dramatics had worked; he wasn't ready for someone like me today.

Class was fascinating. I had no clue what they were talking about, but despite that, I pretended to take notes and stayed attentive toward Nick. Soon enough, the air was filled with textbooks closing and students rising. To be courteous to the other students, since I didn't have another class, I remained seated until they left.

Nick's arm stopped me from passing the desk. "I wasn't informed that there was a new student added to this class."

I gave him an awkward grin. "I'm new; it's my first day."

His arm rolled, exposing his palm. "I would like to see your student ID."

"Seriously?" I chuckled. "In my four years I have never been asked for my ID before. I mean, honestly, who carries it around?"

He leaned to the side and drew out his wallet from his back pocket. Then he flipped it open, holding it up to me. On the left was his driver's license, and on the right was his student ID.

With a snort I moved my purse in front of me and dug out my old student ID from the University of Puth and handed it to him.

"What is this? That ID isn't even for this university or valid anymore."

I was screwed, or was I? Perhaps if I filled him with lies and truths, it would confuse him enough and he would just let me go. I leaned closer to him to study the ID. "My goodness, this isn't the University of Puth?" I stood up and placed my hand on my forehead. "I must have taken the wrong highway down when I was kicked out of Canada." Swiftly I reached over and plucked my ID out of his hand. "I am so sorry about all of this, I must be going," I said, then headed for the door.

"Miss Carter," Nick boomed with force, "halt."

Standing in the doorframe, I did as I was told.

"Get back in here and tell me why you are really here."

My head dropped. I didn't want to get into this with him. "I am here to see Dr. Walizer about a personal matter, and since you are not him, I am leaving. Thank you for the lecture, it was fascinating, but I do not regret my decision to go into accounting and finance at all."

"I have the next two hours off. Since you are not a student

here, you can accompany me to lunch."

I glanced back, watching him pack the textbook into his black leather messenger bag. "Leonora," he glanced up, giving me a close-lipped grin, "I would like to hear about you getting kicked out of Canada, so what do you say?"

"It's Nora, and I was kicked out and banned for ten years." I leaned my back against the doorframe. "A loved one slipped into a coma unexpectedly. I was his prime caregiver, but to give him a break from me, I was running his bar three nights a week. Turns out even if you are not being paid or accepting tips, a POS BSO will still get in your face for working without sponsorship. I couldn't get sponsorship; the owner was lying in the apartment above the bar unconscious. I may have let it slip in the heat of the moment that the BSO, which stands for Border Security Officer, was going to have blood on her hands and how I was going to destroy her for it."

Nick moved the strap over his head. "So you came here for professional advice from Dr. Wally in regard to your loved one?"

"Yeah. I'm drowning here not being up there to help him." I shrugged my shoulders. "I thought maybe I could get answers, advice, pointers, or anything I could to help Leon recover sooner. So, there you go. Thanks, Nick, but I'm guessing you are a busy man." I held out my hand to him. "It was nice to meet you."

CHAPTER 22

Nick came across as a man who got what he wanted without any effort. I had to be the first girl ever to say no to him—multiple times. He did not take it well, because after the fourth "no" it was interesting to watch this cold, stern guy pout for not getting his way. When that didn't cause me to surrender, he shifted to stating I owed it to him for being a distraction in his class. To be fair, I could have handled the situation better, so I agreed to take him to lunch.

We ended up at a nice restaurant a few miles from the campus—Nick's choice since I was new to Balvin. It was far from a restaurant the average university student would go to for a simple lunch break or even could afford. Thank goodness I had passed on the hoodie and jeans today; I wasn't entirely sure they would have let us in. There was a classiness about this restaurant. The floor was tiled black and white, and the walls were a grey-blue with gold pinstriping. From the ceiling hung standard light bulbs encased in a translucent green glass globe. The round tables seated four and had deep blue and green velvet armchairs with gold feet. It felt like the set of a 50s movie and was incredibly impressive.

"All right, Nora." Nick moved his white cloth napkin to his lap. "For the next two hours, I will be your Dr. Wally Walizer. Let's start from the beginning: what is Leon's medical history?"

I was starting to have a good feeling about this lunch.

Nick had been paying attention to me earlier because I had only said Leon's name once. "I don't have access to his medical history." I set down my wine glass filled with water. "I was unconscious when the doctor was called in, and we are not married."

Nick's head cocked to the side as his brows dropped. I probably shouldn't have said I was unconscious. I needed to get this conversation on track before Nick started asking about that.

I raised my left hand off the table to stop him from saying anything. "I do know he has some sort of a condition—I guess you could say I saw one of his episodes. In spite of that, my family wouldn't tell me what was going on. At first, I thought he was having appendicitis for how much pain he seemed to be in, but my family was acting weird. When I saw him again, he seemed perfectly fine."

Nick sat back in his chair and crossed his arms against his chest. His biceps were thicker than my thighs. "You have no clue if he has a condition, disease, illness, or anything else?"

"Leon doesn't want me to know about his health issues. I overheard my mama tell my older brother that Leon is concerned about my reaction." AIDS, cancer, an autoimmune disease—none of that mattered to me. I meant what I said; I was going to stay beside him to the end. I shook my head. "When I first met him, by his physical appearance I thought he was albino, but he told me he wasn't. From there I just assumed that he had some autoimmune disease. He's pale, his hair is white, his skin is like a sheet of copy paper, and his eyes are a pinkish-orange color."

His brow lowered. "How does your family know what's going on, but you do not?"

I inhaled deeply and held my breath; this was about to get confusing for him quickly. "They aren't my biological family. Once I get a little more money saved up, I'm changing my last name. When I went back to Canada this summer, I returned to pay off my biological father's evil ways. Long story short, the Hughes took me in and asked me if I would take their name. I met Leon and the Hughes all at the same time."

Nick's hand moved up to his eyebrow for a second. "This is going to take longer than two hours." His hand dropped. Resting his arm on the table, he leaned in as the corner of his lips curled up, giving me a readable grin. "What are your plans for this evening?"

"I have dinner with a good friend that happens to be my landlord. I'm sorry, I can't cancel on him. I know that he is keeping an eye on me for my papa."

"Bio dad or adopted dad?"

"I wish to never see my biological father again after what he did to me or speak of him again. Going forward, when I say 'Dad,' 'Daddy,' or 'Papa,' it will be in reference to my adopted papa."

The conversation shifted before the crazy train could pull up, and we just chatted about the most random things. I learned that Nick was originally from Balvin, an only child, and loathed teaching college students. He said he would much rather teach preschoolers that didn't act like they already knew it all. From the sound of it, it was a good thing he went into the program that he did. What made him more personable to me was that he loved concerts. He also had an interest in Egyptian history and mythology.

Even with what happened with Kek, I still held a friendly conversation about my piano tutor's son and what my brothers did for a living.

Nick turned his plate so the sliced chicken breast on top of his salad was parallel to him. "Let's get back at it—why were you unconscious?"

"Leon has been unconscious since Tuesday, June 6th of this year." That was all he needed to know; he didn't need to know why I was unconscious or about the events leading up to that point. It didn't matter how much he enjoyed Egyptian mythology.

"Okay, since you don't know his medical history, what were you planning on talking to Dr. Wally about?"

I rolled my glass on its edge. "Mostly if there was a way to help him overcome this sooner. Or if we should be providing him with better care."

"All right, let's start with your care practice first."

I stabbed my fork into a cherry tomato. "I tried to provide Leon with as much comfort as possible while still being practical. Everyone said it was his time and he was moving on, but part of me felt that wasn't true. I may be wrong; however, I feel as if Leon's body is in that final battle with whatever he has. And it's not that it's going to kill him, but he is growing out of whatever it is."

Nick wiped the corner of his mouth. "Having his medical file would be handy right about now."

"No joke," I tittered. "From caring for Leon, I don't think he is fully unconscious; it seems more like his body isn't functioning, but Leon is aware of his surroundings."

"This is getting interesting. Please tell me how you have come to that conclusion."

I bit my lip. It wasn't that I was violating Leon in any manner, but part of me felt like Dr. Nick wasn't going to take hearing about our bedtime routine well. With a deep breath, I let out my nervous word-vomit explanation. "When Leon was moved back to his apartment after a few days, I became his prime caregiver. He has never needed breathing assistance; this is important to note. The first night I gave him his IV bag, which sits in the refrigerator all day, I noticed his breathing changed. It stopped, like he was shocked by the cold, then eventually mellowed out. I know that IVs are not fun when the solution is cold, so the next day I got Leon laying on his left side. Before getting into the shower, I got his bag set up on the pole, then I went to turn myself into a lobster, spooned up to Leon, then plugged him in. His breathing remained consistent."

Nick shifted in the chair; his head cocked to the side. "I don't know what you mean by a lobster."

"Hot shower," I explained. "I would take an incredibly long, hot shower to physically heat up my skin."

"That can't be good for you."

"Physically, probably not. Mentally, it's heaven to stand under the hot water, burning everything away."

"You should be taking cold showers. It prevents muscle soreness, improves circulation, can increase metabolism and immunity." Nick sneered as if reading from a medical book.

Even a doctor's advice wasn't going to take away my tranquil showers.

"Anyways—I need to point out this disclosure before going forward. Well...maybe I should have added it before the whole lobster chat, but oh well. Now, I did not do anything that might make Leon feel uncomfortable. I constantly told him what I was going to do with his body beforehand. I felt this was important, considering our relationship."

"Define your physical relationship with him, prior to him becoming comatose." Nick spoke to me as if he was building Leon's file in his head as a doctor—however, I had caught him a couple of times giving me the look that I missed so much from Leon.

My lips puckered. "Pure and harmless."

"Wow," Nick grumbled as if disappointed that he wasn't getting any juicy details, "you do not like to give simple, basic answers."

"Fine," I snapped with annoyance. It should have been my silence, my right. "Within the six days of being around Leon when he was conscious, not much happened. I'm pure, like the first snowfall of the year, and he's respectful."

"Six days," Nick yelped. "After six days you became the prime caregiver to a stranger." He rubbed his forehead. "Go back to the hot showers and finish that statement for me."

I had already finished; either Nick wasn't paying attention or just needed to hear it again. "I would plug his IV into his port, then snuggle up to his backside in just my underwear so he could have some warmth to combat the coldness from the IV."

Nick's head rose. "What?"

I shrugged. "I thought it would feel like a giant heating pad. You know, like those pink colored ones that are filled with water."

"I'm going to remain quiet." He inhaled. "During this time, I would like you to explain your care for Leon and the reasoning behind it."

Good—he needed to remain quiet. He was becoming unnecessarily stressed for some reason.

"I noticed Leon's breathing would change as if to respond to other things. To me it felt like he was still in there mentally, but his body wasn't working. With that I gave him care as if he was paralyzed from the neck down."

"Excuse me." Nick set his fork down on the side of his plate. "As if he was tetraplegia?"

"I'm not sure what that means, so it's more like he was quadriplegic. I had him on a schedule." Since Nick wanted details, I went into every little detail about Leon's daily schedule and all the activities it contained until the waiter stopped over for our plates.

This was my chance to make up for disrupting Nick's lecture and having him sit through this crazed lunch. I slid my debit card against the bottom of the plate as the waiter picked it up. The waiter nodded down at me, and I winked back at him.

Playing it off as if nothing happened, I continued. "Our afternoons were normal: running errands, going to the store, making dinner, and so on."

Nick held up a hand. "You would take Leon outside of his apartment?"

"Yeah," I said. "The first couple times, people would give me funny looks. It's a small town, so after a while it became the norm and people would say hello to both of us when they saw us. It wasn't like I was hauling around a dead, limp body; Leon was dressed, wore sunglasses, and had his neck brace. Besides, in the evenings, a different family would come over for dinner and to pay their respects to Leon. He must have been a great person to be loved by the whole town the way he was."

The waiter returned with my receipt—now I was going to be busted. I kept my head down as I filled it out. I wasn't sure if Nick was one of those guys that like to flash money around and pay for everything or be thankful.

"What is this?" he sneered. "No, I asked you to lunch—you are not paying."

I handed the receipt back to the waiter and hushed him along. "It's a fair trade: lunch for your professional opinion." Which I so far had not received and wasn't sure I wanted at this point.

Nick huffed. "My professional opinion is six days is not long enough for you to be imprinted into his memory. Let's say that Leon is aware of his surroundings, which I do not believe—he does not know who you are. At that point you are just a stranger who could be adding stress to him since he can't figure you out."

Whoa... That stung. "His body responds to different things," I snapped. "I am no stranger to him." There was no way I was a stranger to Leon. In my heart I hoped even that first interaction at the bonfire was enough for his heart to hold on to me.

"Okay, Nora," Nick held up his hand to mute me, "have you ever seen a coma patient leave a hospital bed?"

"I have only seen actors pretend to be coma patients on television, and you can't believe everything you see on television."

"Trust me, they don't, and that is why they are portrayed that way on television. Nora, his body needs to be left alone to rest and recover, not hauled off clothes-shopping and paraded around town."

This was far from what I was expecting to hear, and for whatever reason I felt defensive. "It was to the local grocery store and to the park. I thought letting him lay in the grass under the sun would be good for him, considering we get vitamin D from the sun." Fresh air, warm sun, and vitamin D; I didn't get how that wouldn't have benefited Leon's body or soul.

"Most likely, you have put more stress on his body. After so many days in a coma, a person's chance of waking up decreases."

"No," I gasped, trying to squeeze back the tears that instantly sprang into action.

Nick rested his arm across the table, palm up as he leaned toward me. "I'm sorry to say, you have unintentionally given Leon a death sentence."

"What?" I grabbed the napkin off the table to dab the corner of my eyes. Even if Nick was right...no, he had to be wrong. There was no way. I gave Leon love with everything I did. He was never meant to lay in a bed until the end of his days and rot. His muscles needed to be moved. He needed fresh air, warmth, and comfort.

"If there is a chance for him to recover, I highly recommend that you cut off all contact with the patient going forward."

"No," fell from my lips again. I needed something to give me a reason to still have contact with Leon. Sucking in air as if it was confidence, I said, "Yeah... No, that's not going to work. See, Leon and I are in the middle of reading a suspense novel. I think it's more harmful to his mental health if he doesn't get to hear the ending."

"What?" Nick's arm slowly drew back from the table to cross against his chest.

"It's going to be a no," I sternly stated, holding my ground with Nick.

"Think about it, Nora."

"It's a no," I growled.

"How is Leon going to know what is real if he can't open his eyes? If he is even awake, he may be confused. Then you come along reading a suspense story to him, and Leon may be thinking that is his reality now. We don't know what kind of activity is going on in Leon's brain without the proper scans. So how would Leon know reality from fiction?"

I tried to open my mouth to debate, but Nick held up his hand. "You may have the best intentions, but you have no experience to be messing around with Leon in any manner. If you want him to have a chance at living a normal life again, you need to cut yourself from his life."

As Nick's image blurred, part of me knew that he was right, since he was the expert. "Can I tell him goodbye?"

"No, Nora, nothing."

I wanted to scream out in pain, as King Leon did when he stabbed Sigrid into his chest. It was time to leave. I stood up without looking at Nick. Swiftly I thanked him for his time, then turned around and left without saying another word.

I was so distraught by Nick's words; I wasn't even sure how I made it back to Puth. I don't remember moving from my vehicle when I got back to the apartment complex. I sat there in a trance-like state, staring straight out the wind-shield. It wasn't until Joe texted me to let me know he was at the restaurant that I robotically moved my gaze to my cell phone sitting on the passenger seat.

Doing as I was told by a professional in the field, I didn't call Leon. It didn't stop there; I was so ashamed of myself that I cut communication to everyone. I pushed everything that happened in the last couple months down and went about my life, going from a shift at one job to the next. My change in mood was easy to pass off as I was exhausted from my posi-tions.

It only took until Wednesday morning after not responding to Sean's text messages to get a threat from him. He texted me that if I didn't respond to him soon, he was going to come down and check in on me. With that, I told him I would call him later in the evening after dinner and my run. In truth, there was one person I needed to call first to apologize and say goodbye to.

Of course, silence answered the phone. I took a deep breath—there was no way I was going to make it through this call without crying. I exhaled, the pain in my throat building up. "I'm sorry for not calling sooner, and I am sorry for calling. I spoke to a professional about you, and I was informed that everything I was doing, including this call, is wrong. I am so incredibly sorry. I thought that—no, in my heart I *felt* that you were still in there listening to your surroundings. I thought that keeping you mentally and physically active was going to help you recover sooner. I didn't realize that I was killing you instead." I wiped my nose with the side of my hand. I knew what was going to happen with this call. I could have been better prepared with a box of tissues.

"Please believe me that was never what I wanted, I just wanted to help you recover. I fell in love with you so incredibly fast and hard; never in a million years would I ever want to do anything to even hurt you. Let alone kill you. And now that sounds backwards. Just speaking to you now is hurting you, because after six days, I couldn't have imprinted on your mind. But you did my heart. Leon, I am so sorry. Please be well and I love you. I'm so sorry."

The only way to end the call was for me to hang up. Pushing that little red button for the last time felt like Sigrid stabbing into my chest.

CHAPTER 23

I had just handled my first Friday night at the bar after working all day at the optical. I sat there at the measuring desk, dazing off. I had forgotten how tiring the night shift could be. I just needed to find my groove with all these positions.

"Nora," Lori chuckled, "how about you go on a coffee run? At this pace there is no way you are going to make it through another late shift."

"Don't—" I covered my mouth as I could feel another yawn coming on. "Excuse me, sorry. Don't worry, I got this. I just need to readjust myself to late night bar shifts again."

"Mmmm...kay. Is it worth it?"

I pulled my left arm across my chest to stretch it. "I made over eight hundred dollars in tips last night. Yes, it's worth it. Plus, tonight is an Egyptian theme night; I can rock that look." That didn't mean I wanted to be rocking that look.

"If you keep yawning, you are going to mess up your eye makeup."

To save time, I had done half of my eye makeup this morning. Thank goodness I did; it took a thousand tries to master the black, gold, and green-lined look. Mostly because my hand would start to tremble anytime I moved the eyeliner pen next to my eyes. After quite a few pep talks and cotton balls of makeup remover, when I closed my eyes, they perfectly resembled a hieroglyph from Kek's original times.

While I tried to focus on fixing my makeup in the standing

mirror resting on the measuring desk, the door chimed, drawing my eyes from the mirror to the gentleman that walked in. I didn't even need to get up; I knew his massive build from a mile away. Regardless, I had no idea why he was in Puth—we hadn't spoken since our lunch. I never gave him any of my contact information outside of my name.

Nick didn't enter the optical as if he was looking for me. After one glance to the side, he moved straight to the men's section. Perhaps this was an odd coincidence and he was just here looking for a set of frames. I watched as his head slowly moved up the frame board. His mischievous grin grew as he watched me from the vertical mirror. When our eyes met, he slowly moved back and pretended to look at frames again.

"Hello, sir, Nora will be right with you," Lori cheerfully chimed as she conveniently picked up the phone and acted as if there was someone else on the line.

Now I was trapped. Inhaling, I stood up and walked over to Nick. Acting as if I didn't know him, I gave him space and stood a few feet away from him. "Hi there, I'm Nora. May I help you?"

"Perhaps you can." Nick turned toward me and leaned against the counter beside him. "My vision has been messed up since Monday. Everything is now dull; I can't seem to see light anymore."

This wasn't the first time a guy tried lines on me here. I had a feeling I knew how this was going to play out.

Swiftly I reached past Nick to a pair of thick, black, square plastic frames from the top shelf. These frames were nicknamed "BC" because they were birth control for men. Most customers enjoyed trying them on just for fun.

His head cocked to the side after he put on the glasses, admiring himself in the mirror. "Well look at that," he turned back to me with a Superman smile and dilated eyes matching the black frames. "It worked!"

I pinched my lips, trying to remain composed.

Nick tilted toward me. "Do you have them in green as well?"

That was it—his tone was so stern I couldn't hold back. My shoulders bounced with my snorts, my eyes watering a touch. Glancing back at his eyes, his brows danced, turning my soft giggles into crackles.

"There's my light; I thought I lost her." He engulfed me in his arms, drawing me into his stone chest as he petted the back of my head.

As awkward as it was, I just needed the comfort of a hug more than anything. It almost made my heart ache. I imagined I was in Sean's arms as he surprised me by coming down here to let me know Leon was awake and healthy. I just wanted to live in this illusion until it came true.

With this we were even, but that didn't mean I wasn't going to play around with him a little. I wiggled out of his arms. "Come with me." I locked his arm into mine. "We need to get you to Doc right away. If your vision is better with a nonprescription clear demo lens, there may be an issue."

He stopped and looked down at me. "There is something seriously wrong—on Monday, you were not supposed to buy lunch. I was the one to ask you out. Go out to dinner with me tonight so I can make it up to you."

I should have known that was coming, but it didn't stop me from feeling awful. He had driven all this way to ask me to dinner only to be rejected. Even if Nick was right about Leon not remembering me, my heart wasn't going to give up. I wanted to hear it leave Leon's lips before I truly let him go. I didn't know how I was going to explain this to the expert without him throwing more statistics at me.

My head dropped as I felt my tears shifting from silliness to sorrow. "Nick," I whimpered.

Gently he raised my chin so he could look into my eyes. "I know... Let's go to dinner as friends tonight." The corner of his lips curled up. "I owe you a meal."

"I'm going to need a raincheck; I have to work tonight at the bar."

"Ask her," Lori coughed, "out to dinner," she coughed again, "after her shift." Lori bent over, coughing and grasping her chest.

I rolled my eyes. "Maybe someone should quit smoking," I sneered at her.

Nick's eyes bounced from Lori to me, then to Lori again, before returning to me.

"Oh, leave her be, she's fine. What is really troubling her is I work at a bar full of drunks that have been ogling me all night." I patted Nick's chest. "It makes for great tips."

"Actually," Lori was magically healed as she stood up, "he should stop by before your shift ends to walk you home."

I led Nick to the measuring desk to sit down, giving Lori a wide-eyed stare over my shoulder so she would realize this was the guy that had earlier in the week told me my backward care was killing Leon.

"What are you really in town for?" I didn't want to be his only reason for driving so far.

"I had an interview for a residency at the hospital up here first thing this morning."

"No way—you got kicked out of the one in Balvin? Was it for your poor bedside manners? One of your real students told me that's why you got stuck teaching Dr. Walizer's classes while he was out."

"No." His brows veered in as he grumbled, "Wally is my uncle. My grandfather is the director of the neurology department in Balvin. The two of them plus my mother, who is the director of the cardiology department at the same hospital, felt that it would be beneficial if I split my neurology residency between the hospital in Balvin and another hospital where I am not related to most of the department directors."

"Did they hire you?"

"They did. So what I was really hoping was this local Puth

gal that I met on Monday could show me the best area of town to get an apartment in. Then to thank her, I was going to take her out to dinner."

I liked this softer, playful side of him. Even if I didn't care for him much on Monday, or for his advice, he was still willing to help me. I could at least return the favor. "My buddy Joe owns the building I live in; I could ask him if he has any vacant apartments. When do you start?"

"Next week—but here's the thing, this is only temporary. I can't get tied down in a year lease. Plus, I am only going to need a place Wednesday night until Sunday morning."

Sitting back in my chair, I crossed my arms, then raised my fist to rest my chin on it. Well, that changed things. I don't know how Joe would handle the rent amount for an apartment that was only going to be used part-time. It's not like Joe could rent the place out those other days and I don't think Nick would want to pay rent on two places.

I did have a fully furnished spare bedroom with its own bathroom. It would be like getting an assigned suitemate at the university if I had stayed on campus instead of living at home. Then there was the fact that everyone had helped me out, and with Joe's approval I could pass it on to him. "I have to ask Joe first, but if he approves of it would you like to stay in my spare room?"

"Nora—" There was a bang from the front desk. "Nooo..." Lori's muffled whine drifted out from behind it. I could only guess that bang was from slamming her head against the desk in disappointment. She wanted me to date him, not invite him into my apartment. And, in her mind, my bed.

I ignored her, wanting to hear what Nick had to say. "Aren't residency shifts ten to twenty-eight hours long?"

Nick nodded with a weird, pleased smile. He wasn't going to refuse my offer if Joe approved it. Now, he needed to understand that if this happened, it wasn't going to be what he thought it was.

"You will be working the same days that I pull my doubles at the optical and bar. We are never going to be around each other. Except depending on when you get to town on Wednesday and when you leave on Sunday. Which isn't a guarantee either because I go to church every Sunday."

I wasn't exactly afraid of having this mountain of a resident doctor staying with me. He wasn't frightening, and he was showing me sides of himself that clearly none of his students had seen. Between Ivan and Kek, I was confident that I could handle him on my own. Plus, my bedroom door had a lock, which I used every night anyways. In the back of my mind, I hoped he was going to see we were only going to be friends. From there, maybe he would be more open to helping me with Leon.

CHAPTER 24

Theme nights brought in people left and right; I was tripping over myself trying to keep up with drink orders. For fun, DJ Justin would ask the crowd some random Egyptian god trivia, and the first person to get it right would win a shot. If no one could solve it, I got a chance too. Even with everything with Kek, it was still fun to get to apply my Egyptian knowledge. Since I couldn't drink while working, a couple guys thought it would be nice when, every time I got a right answer, one of them would give me a hundred-dollar tip.

I didn't know if people tipped like this at other bars in town, but I'm guessing not. Our crowd mostly consisted of the owners' buddies from their high school all the way up to university years. For that they kept the prices of drinks cheap. Not as low as Leon's prices; from what I could tell from working there, he had to be barely making even. I don't think he knew that he needed to raise the prices with the increasing inflation rates.

"Our Queen!" Justin's voice echoed through the speakers of the bar. I still hated being called that, especially dressed as I was tonight. It was too close to reality. "The crowd can't figure out which dude was the dog head."

"Anubis," I yelled as I finished pouring the latest cocktail order for Lana, our waitress. "He's a jackal, not a dog-headed man. He was known as one of the gods of the dead. He guided souls to Osiris, who was the god of the deceased."

The lights flickered, the sound of a horn blaring sounded through the speakers, and the crowd hollered as confetti rained upon them. I think they were having more fun letting me answer the questions because Justin would make it as if we were all winners. I think it was also helping Lana pull in larger tips.

A man in a jackal face mask with long black hair approached the bar. He was dressed to the T in a depiction of Anubis. His exposed tan chest shone with a golden glow. From the corner of my eyes, I could see the girls' eyes following the mystery man as he walked over to the end of the bar, taking the last stool. I glanced over to Lana, who was fanning herself with her drink tray as she shot me a wink.

His mask stayed facing me as he crossed his arms against his chest, leaning back a touch. By his arrogant body language, she could have him. Even if Leon wasn't in the picture, I had no interest in being with someone that was going to spend every waking moment of his life in the gym.

He may not be impressive to me, but I was curious who he was. "Anubis, how did you not know that answer to the last question?"

"Because I didn't know that you had to dress up to enter the bar tonight." He pulled the mask off and set it beside him on the counter.

No way—Mr. Bad Bedside Manners was before me, dressed as Anubis. My goodness, if his students could see him now.

"This is the first outfit I could find," Nick grumbled.

"Nick," I chuckled with disbelief, "let me know you are outside, and I can get you in without a costume."

"Thank god." His shoulders dropped a touch as they relaxed. "I'm not here to play dress-up and silly games."

The man needed a beer; his fun attitude from earlier was gone. "Well, since you did, I'll buy all your drinks tonight."

I should have thought about that statement a little more as a young thing with her hair tucked perfectly into her headpiece, dressed as Nefertiti, strutted up to Nick. Forgoing the stool, she sat on his exposed leg, rested her arm against Nick's shoulders, and ran her fingers through his hair.

"What will it be, my lord?" she purred drunkenly.

Forget getting him drinks, now I was worried about who he was going to bring back to our apartment each night. Lori was going to enjoy hearing these tales of the flavor of the night—however, I could already see her disappointment that it wasn't *us* together, cuddling in each other's arms.

"All right, you two." I still had a job to perform. "What will it be tonight?"

Nick rolled his eyes as he shook his head. Little Nefertiti was already three sheets to the wind to not notice Nick's discomfort. With that they were getting shots.

I began to pour tequila into the first glass when Justin called out, "Continuing with heads, who had a frog head?"

My right hand began to tremble until I could no longer hold the tequila bottle and it fell, bouncing on the anti-slip mat below. My left hand grasped the shot glass so tightly, I could feel the glass breaking in my palm. The tequila burning my palm brought me right back to reality.

"Nora," Nick snapped, then growled at his little Nefertiti trying to be sweet on him. "Get off me. I am working, and I need to go help the bartender."

"Queen Nora," Justin sang, "do you think you could help them out?"

I don't know what just happened, but I didn't want to be the one to answer this one. I didn't want to provide firsthand knowledge about Kek to anyone. From our time together in that cave, I learned a few new things about him, but he wasn't a simple myth anymore. He should never be spoken about or idolized in any manner for the lives that he destroyed over the years.

"Nora," Nick leaned over the bar, holding his right hand out to me, "are you all right?"

Glancing at Nick, then to the crowd, I realized I was being

ridiculous. Kek was defeated and blown up and Journey was freed. "Well, Justin, this is a trick question." I ignored Nick and continued to the beer taps with my left hand behind my back. "Heqet was the frog-headed goddess of fertility. But Kek was also depicted as a frog."

"Heqet is correct!" Justin bellowed. "Before we celebrate her victory, I would like to point out that this is Nora's first week working for us. And in no way was she given the questions or answers ahead of time." Justin held his hand out toward me from the DJ booth. "She must be a true Egyptian goddess to know all the answers."

"You would be surprised how close I was to becoming one," I muttered.

"Mr. Anubis," I walked away from Nick to the sink, "you are not allowed back here."

"Give me your hand," Nick ordered, "and tell me what happened a moment ago, or I will take you home right now and tell everyone it's a medical emergency."

I slapped my hand palm-up into his. "I'm tired and something caught me off guard that turns out was nothing. Are you satisfied now?"

"No." Nick angled my palm into the light as if looking for glass. "I would like for you to go put more clothes on." His tone was still stern, and completely uncalled for.

"Coming from the man in only a shendyt." I leaned into his face. "These men are harmless. I have dealt with far worse than drunks. Take a look at what you are wearing first before you judge me."

My outfit wasn't as revealing as his. I was in a pleated black minidress with a gold collar that covered the straps. Across my hips I wore a wide fabric belt and golden cuffs on my upper arms. My legs were on display, but I stood behind a bar, so it didn't matter.

"Queen Nora." A man in the middle of the bar broke my glare away from Nick before he could say anything.

"Yes, my pharaoh," I cheerfully stated as I strutted toward him. Nick needed to relax while I got back to work. "What can I get you?"

The night carried on. I ended up pouring Nick a beer, but otherwise I was too busy to interact with him for the rest of the night. Which was okay because he seemed to keep himself busy dodging all the little goddesses throwing themselves at him. I was almost surprised to see him sitting there after the last customer left and we began to flip the chairs up.

"All right, big guy." I sat on the barstool beside him and nudged his shoulder. "It's time for you to leave." I was a little excited that he hadn't gone home with someone; I didn't want to walk home by myself after my minor freakout earlier.

The dark crescents just below each of his lower eyelids indicated how exhausted he was, but his wistful grin indicated he wasn't ready to end the night quite yet. Nick pressed his shoulder into my shoulder and peered up at me. There was that softness reappearing. If I was single, I may have asked him to come home and cuddle with me.

Nick stood up and held his hand out to me. "I would like to walk you to your car."

I had a feeling that I was about to disrupt his softness again. "May I walk you to your car instead? I live two blocks away, so I walk to work."

His hand dropped and his eyes closed as his head rolled forward. "You walk home every night, alone, carrying your tips with you?"

"Yep, I only live a couple blocks away. It's a waste of gas to drive it here when I can just walk."

Leaning closer to me, I could smell that the mint tucked in the side of his cheek was not enough to overpower the IPA from earlier. "Are you struggling with money?"

"Oh, gosh, no. I have three jobs. It's more like I just don't have a lot of it since I gave everything away this summer."

Perhaps it wasn't me that Nick was sizing up, but my

apartment. He may be second-guessing if it was a good idea to move in with me if my apartment was two blocks from a bar. In his eyes this could be a sketchy district. Oh, was Nick ever in for a shock, a bigger one even than when I realized he was in a shendyt in public.

Tonight, I needed to ease his mind about everything—the idea of a roommate was starting to grow on me. Especially when I wouldn't be coming home to a dark apartment on Egyptian-themed nights since I was handling this so well. And this life wouldn't be as lonely anymore. Since I came back, I hadn't jumped back into my Leonora Marigold Carter life. I loved my friends here, but part of me felt like I failed since I was right back at square one.

"Do you have a place to stay tonight?"

"After I drop you off," Nick checked the time on his phone, "I was just going to head back to Balvin."

As much as I wanted to shower first thing when we returned to the apartment, it didn't happen. I had a new guest that had driven up to hang out with me after his interview. It only felt right to hang out with him on the oversized white leather L-shaped couch after he had stayed the last half of my shift at the bar.

Nick looked around the apartment from the couch a cushion away from me. "This apartment is amazing, but not worth three jobs amazing."

Snuggling myself into my throw blanket with my knees against my chest, I peered out the oversize windows at the skyline. "I live here rent-free."

"How?" His jaw dropped. "Do your parents own the building or something?"

The surprise in his tone drew my attention back to him as I slowly moved my head back and forth. "No, a friend does. The bio set likes to buy cars with their money, not property. My adopted set are hardworking, modest people. In fact, my mama took a leave of absence from her position to take care of Leon. All my earnings from the optical go toward offsetting her lost wages." I fiddled with the white tassel on my blanket. "She knows about the account, but she's not taking from it yet."

"And the other two positions?"

"The bakery, I benefit from the discount and my earnings go into a checking account to help purchase medical equipment and or supplies needed—"

"Let me guess," he interrupted. "For Leon."

"Yeah, so I live off my earnings and tips from the bar. Just tonight I made almost three grand in tips."

"That's because you literally looked like an Egyptian goddess and even had the guys falling to their knees before you. I'll come back next week having to address you as 'My Queen.'"

Just hearing him call me that name made me quiver. "No," I sneered.

"What?" Nick tittered.

"I got myself into a situation this summer, and now I despise being called Queen. I can handle a few drunk guys throwing it out here and there, but please don't."

I wiped my left cheek as I felt it becoming warm with moisture. Part of me wished that when I crossed the border into the States, all the nonsense in my head was going to be gone. This was the first familiar sign it wasn't over yet.

"Oh, Nora, I'm sorry. Are you comfortable telling me what happened?"

The words began to flow from my mouth before I realized I was talking. "I had gone for a run, and this man cornered me. He started telling me how he was going to make me his queen and parade me around town. Me being me, I asked him a bunch of questions. Truthfully, I was trying to annoy him so he would realize I wasn't what he wanted. It didn't work—at one point he told me that he had been watching me all week and wanted me for himself. I had to change gears and let him think I was warming up to him. It was the only way I was going to get him in the correct position to overpower him." I shrugged. "It worked; I was able to free myself."

"Did he…" His tone deepened. "…touch you?"

"Only my lower leg and ankle. You must understand that I do not fear the mere man." I looked back at Nick. "After that day, I fear what is hiding in the darkness. So, just to forewarn you, I sleep with my bedroom door locked. It's not that I don't trust you—it has nothing to do with you. I've done it since I returned to the States."

"Why only since you have returned to the States?"

"I always had Leon next to me at night. Now, I stay alone in this oversized apartment."

"Is he in jail now?"

"Sigrid took care of him; he is no more."

"Who is she?"

"Just an old silver gal that stood for peace of victory." None of that was a lie, it was just the outer crust of the pie. He didn't need to know the inner workings of that mess.

Nick stared out the window into the darkness of the night. "Even if I get my own place, every night that I'm in town, I will make sure that I am off a quarter to the bar closing. I will be either walking or driving you home going forward."

"Nick, really that's not necessary. I'm not allowed to drink while working. I'll be able to drive myself home."

"He's not going to be the last creep that is going to be drawn to your friendly demeanor, your kindness, or even your beauty. Someone else is going to try something with you. As far as I know, Sigrid isn't here to protect you now."

"I couldn't save her." I bowed my head. "We lost her that day."

Nick ran his hands through his hair. "I'm almost glad you're banned from Canada—I feel like there is more that happened, yet you are either protecting yourself from having to speak the words that could bring it back to life, or you are protecting me from hearing the truth. Either way, I saw enough tonight, and it will never happen again when I am around."

CHAPTER 25

Russell had approached me on Monday just before the optical closed. It was his younger brother's twenty-first birthday on Wednesday. For his birthday, the bar was his for the evening. Lana and I were each offered a huge bonus for working at this party. With that kind of money, I assumed there was a catch, and there was. It was a party of the gods: poor Lana had to wear a sheer tulle white toga that draped over only her nipples and crotch. She was to be a Greek goddess. And—no surprise—I was their Egyptian goddess. I was to wear a loincloth, the backside of which was a gold G-string. If that wasn't enough, the only other part of my new uniform was gold nipple pasties with dangling gold chains.

I didn't want to do this—it wasn't right. It was too much of my body exposed. Nevertheless, it was Russell's father pulling the strings. The man ruled with his big, bullheaded walrus temper and money. He got what he wanted and made sure his sons did too.

Unfortunately, twenty thousand dollars after taxes was too good to pass up, and we were still entitled to any tips, though that wasn't that appealing considering it was an open bar for the night. The thing that made it more bearable was guests were allowed to look but not touch. Russell also promised that he would allow Nick to come in at closing time to walk me home. Fat chance of that happening—I could only imagine the lecture I would get if Nick saw me dressed like this in public.

All around, it was a difficult situation, but Russell had always been good to me. I didn't want to cause trouble between him and his father by refusing or leaving them hanging. With Lana already agreeing, I agreed as well. Now I just needed to get my mind in the game.

By my lunch break on Wednesday, I still couldn't shake the feeling I was betraying Leon. I wanted to clear my conscience.

"Hi Leon, this is Nora. If you remember, I took care of you for a while. Anyways I know that I'm not supposed to call you anymore, so I am sorry for this call. Umm..." This was dumb; he could be sleeping or away from his phone. I just needed to get it out before I made it worse.

"For my bartending position I have been offered a lot of money. I mean, a *lot* of money. Russell's father bought the bar for the night to celebrate his younger son's birthday. Normally I don't work Wednesday nights, but I have to work tonight. Russell promised that he would let Nick, my roommate, walk me home afterwards."

I took a deep breath—time to get it out. "Of course, there is a catch: my uniform for the night is pasties and basically a G-string with a loincloth in the front. I'm sorry, you're probably wondering why I'm telling you this, but I'm not comfortable doing this. I don't feel it's fair to you. I guess I just wanted to be honest with you. I'm not doing this because I want to. I'm only doing this because I need to."

Later that evening, I leaned in the doorframe to the office of the bar. Russell sat there behind the particle-board desk with his feet resting on its top, focused on his phone. He was not traditionally handsome, but he wasn't ugly either. He was just Russell: average height, standard build, not husky or fat. He did have squeezable cheeks. His dirty blond hair was already starting to recede, so he tried to keep length on top to cover it.

Unsurprisingly, Russell had chosen not to go with a theme

and wore a black button-up with khaki slacks.

"What is this?" I chuckled, pulling his attention away from his phone. "I thought we all had to dress up."

"Yeah, I forgot my toga back at university a few years ago."

I had heard stories about his university years from Jordan, the other bar owner and Russell's best friend. They were wild and still are—however, Russell was way milder with me. Jordan, on the other hand, was Jordan; an HR nightmare in the sweetest way possible.

Jordan came from old farm money. His family owned most of the northern part of the state and farmed all of it. He and Russell were friends from high school, and that friendship carried on over the years into business partners in this bar. With Russell mostly running the bar, Jordan would make his appearance here and there, brightening everyone's day. It was hard to have a bad day with Jordan around; he knew how to get a smile out of you.

"Well, it's your lucky day—I still have the second pair of pasties you gave me."

He snorted. "I appreciate that you are going along with this tonight. I don't care what my father says. If anyone gets grabby with you, I will kick them out."

"Thanks." I was more focused on how I was going to be moving about basically naked; I had forgotten about the male factor. If I just stayed behind the bar and faced forward, I had nothing to worry about.

"Well, hello...my goddess." Jordan leaned against the opposite doorframe as he tilted toward me. "I swear you should have been born in another time, there would have been statues in your honor everywhere still today."

Dressed as a Greek god was sure fitting for him. Jordan could have been the model that Michelangelo used to carve David. He had the height Russell was missing. His muscles were built from years of farming. His neck was long and strong, only touched by his dirty blond hair curled out at the right length. His upper lip had the fullness under his predominant nose and brow line.

My head rested on the doorframe as I subtly breathed in his hypnotizing cologne. I just wanted to close my eyes and drift away into it. "Perhaps it's only Egyptian gods that want me."

"And this Greek one as well." His big, cheeky smile gave him away. I knew that he was scheming as his eyes slowly moved up my chest. "I was thinking, after our shift tonight, how about a threesome?"

"Dude." I straightened up then waved my hand in front of my chest. "I am going to spend all night with my chest hiked up in the kitchen sink trying to soak off these pasties." My eyes widened as Russell snickered. "They are, like, superglued to my nipples."

The party ended up being a blast with about sixty people present. Justin kept the trivia rolling as I poured drink after drink for Lana to usher out. Most of the night everyone spent dancing out on the floor. I had gotten into my own groove, even forgetting my outfit in the darkness of the bar. This wasn't what I was expecting at all. The only time Russell had to step in and save me was when his own father would sneak behind the bar for a dance.

In no time, it was closing, and the guests began to funnel out as we started to flip chairs—except for one that I had never seen enter the bar. He sat at a table in the back corner with his arms crossed against his chest. His brow was lowered, and his lips were pinched. My heart dropped as I placed my arm across my chest. I was in trouble.

For a man that was vocal about everything, Sean didn't say a word until we entered the apartment. It was like walking the walk of shame as we navigated home in silence. I almost wished it was Calvin here instead. Calvin had always been softer to me.

"What were you doing tonight?" Sean sneered as we walked into the dark apartment.

"Working—now keep it down." I walked over to the sink to get a glass of water. "Nick works early in the morning. I don't want to wake him up."

"I don't care." He raised his voice almost to yell so Nick would hear him. "This is wrong; you shouldn't be living with a male before you're married. Pa and Ma wouldn't even let you stay the night at Leo's, but now you are living with some strange man."

That wasn't fully true, but Sean didn't know this because he stayed at his own place. "He's not a strange man, and we are not living together as a couple. He's my roommate with his own room. We are hardly ever around each other. Plus, they know he's staying here, and they are cool with it."

"Only because he babysits you during your bar shift." Sean leaned against the white marble island. "Where was he tonight? Of all the nights you needed him there for you, he wasn't even there."

Nick's head popped up from behind the couch. "You told me that you were going out with friends tonight," he growled, "not working. Why were you working on a Wednesday night at the bar?"

"Nick," I tittered, "what are you doing up?"

Oh man, I was in serious trouble tonight. They might not have known each other, but I had a feeling they were going to feed off each other. That was, if Sean didn't let all his aggression out on Nick first. They were both powerful men, but if I had to put money on either of them, it would be Sean. Nick was more of a Superman; Sean was a Hulk.

Nick moved his arms to the back of the couch. "I stayed up to make sure you made it home safe." His hand rolled as his index finger pointed at Sean. "Who is he?"

"This is the youngest of my older brothers, Sean."

"Wait." Sean's head spun around. "You lied to your roommate about where you were tonight?"

Lowering my head, I pinched my lips and gazed up at Sean.

"This is not the Hughes way." Sean walked over and fell into the armchair. "What is going on with you?"

"It's not like I made this suggestion or wanted to do this either." I slid down the couch next to Nick. "I had to do this. It's done and over. Please drop it so we all can go to bed." More like they could go to bed while I tried to figure out how to unglue my nipples.

Nick glared at me with his arms crossed against his chest. There was no way he was going to drop this. I had lied to him while he sat up waiting for me to make sure I was safe. This was going to be an awful night.

I rested the side of my head on the back of the couch. "I'm sorry for lying about where I was tonight," I whispered to Nick, praying my softness would warm him up a little. "It was a private party for Russell's little brother. At all times I was safe. Jordan and Russell had my back all night. In fact, Russell even chased his own father out."

"Sure they did," Sean sneered. "They are the same guys you said made you wear pasties and a loincloth tonight." He sat on the edge of the armchair. "I saw how every single guy there checked out your itty-bitty tiny gold things on your nipples and the string up your butt."

"Twenty grand after taxes just for looks." I sat back carefully, adjusting my arms under my breasts. "Totally worth it."

"Twenty grand!" Nick shrieked. "What did they make you do for twenty grand?"

"Bartend, that's all. I was safe. It was harmless, easy money."

Nick's eyes moved over to Sean as Sean's head slowly moved back and forth.

"You are selling your body," Sean grumbled. "It's not acceptable. How do you think Leo would feel about it if he knew this was going on?"

Sean didn't need to go there. He was Leon's best friend; he would know if Leon would have been accepting or not. That was worse than anything tonight. My heart ached as a pain grew in my throat, letting me know there were going to be tears soon. "Leon knows," I gasped, trying to push that lump down. "I told him. And once I'm paid, I'm moving the money into his checking account. I can only imagine the debt he has with owning a bar that is not that profitable."

"Six days, Nora," Nick sneered. "He is not your responsibility. Let his family handle his debt, not you." He sat back with his disappointed scowl fixed on me.

"He's right, Nora, Leo's financial situation is not your problem. You do not need to be working three jobs to support him."

"I'm supporting Mama as well. Can I just go shower, please?" I puffed out my chest. "They're starting to hurt," I whined to Sean with my chest deflating. "I don't think it was the brightest idea to use surgical glue."

Nick's brows lowered as his eyes bounced from my black T-shirt to my white tennis skirt. "Even over-the-counter surgical glue isn't something that you should be messing with." He pointed at my chest. "Why did you use surgical glue? Better yet—what did they make you do for twenty grand?"

"Sean, cover your eyes," I stated as I stood up before Nick. "I am going to show you my assigned outfit, then we all are going to drop this. You two are going to go to bed so I can get these things off."

He was going to freak; I didn't dare look up as I stepped out of my skirt. Then gently I raised the hem of my shirt up, making sure not to snag it against the chains.

Nick didn't say a word. His hands moved under my legs as he cradled me against his chest.

"Oh no you don't," Sean growled, instantly beside us.

"Chill out," Nick snapped as he walked us toward his room. "I'm going to help remove the glue."

"There." Sean pointed to the island. "You are not allowed to take her in your room ever or set foot into her room."

Nick did as he was directed and set me down on the island,

then went to his room to gather supplies. Sean rolled his eyes at me then shook his head in disappointment. This disappointment was the worst feeling I had felt in a long time. I bowed my head; there was no holding back the tears.

Sean blurred as I glanced up. "I'm so sorry. I didn't want to do this, but I didn't want to let down Jordan and Russell." I wiped my cheeks with the side of my hand. "Then there was the money. I just want him to be able to wake up to resume his life as if nothing happened that day."

"No tears." Sean wrapped his arms around me, drawing me into his chest. "Please quit all these jobs."

"I can't..."

"Why do you feel that Leo is your responsibility?"

That was easy. "Because I love him."

"Well," Sean rubbed the back of my head, "he's one of my best friends, and I love him as well. But that doesn't mean I need to be working three jobs for him. Why do you think you need to?"

Leaning back, I held up my ring fingers. "If this ring was on the left hand, no one would be questioning me why I was working three jobs. Just because it is on my right hand doesn't mean that I don't honor it the same as if he had put it on my left hand."

When Nick returned, Sean raised his hand to cover Nick's eyes, then covered his own eyes as well. "The two of us should not be looking at her breasts. Let alone her nipples."

"Knock it off." Nick slapped his arm away. "You are just dragging this out longer."

I wasn't expecting it, but Nick had a soft touch with me. He constantly checked to see if I was all right and would forewarn me if he needed to peel some of the glue off or tug a little on the chain. He gave me the utmost care.

If only Nick and Sean could get to a friendly level with each other. Occasionally I would catch them glaring at each other. Mostly because Sean was right on the other side of me, leaning in, watching to make sure Nick didn't try anything.

With the tension in the room between Nick and Sean, I thought maybe a little humor would help. "I take it this isn't the first time that you had to remove pasties from a lady's chest."

His exhausted eyes moved up to mine. "This is a first and hopefully the last. What made you think it was a good idea to use a whole tube per nipple?"

"The chance of exposing myself to strangers is a little unnerving."

Brring...Brring...Brring...Brring...

Sean's phone began to ring. "Augh," he grumbled, "I need to go take this in the other room." He looked over at Nick. "Touch her in any inappropriate way and you will lose your own nipples."

When my bedroom door closed, Nick's hands slid me closer to the end of the counter, so he was now between my legs. His hand moved up my side until it cupped my left breast. His head leaned in as if to rest against my head while he inspected my now-exposed nipple.

"A lady of your caliber should not be selling her body in this manner." His words warmed my chest as he moved back to my right breast. "It's not necessary—I will provide you with a life of luxury."

"I don't need a life of luxury; I'm trying to help my family and Leon."

"They are not your responsibility." His voice hardened. "You are punishing yourself for nothing."

Suddenly there was a sharp pain. "Ouch!" I yelped.

Sean rushed from the bedroom. "Nora, are you all right?"

I pressed on my breast, turning my nipple up. There was a bleeding quarter-inch gash.

Swiftly, Nick reached for a paper towel. "I'm sorry. I thought it was going to be released differently."

Nick went back to being extra gentle. And from that moment,

Sean didn't care what Nick's explanation was; he didn't leave my side and stayed in my room with me on the other side of my oversized king bed. Of course, he filled the darkness with his thoughts about Nick. For my safety, I needed to kick Nick out before something could happen.

CHAPTER 26

Our lunch breaks at the optical were flexible as long as Doc wasn't booked back-to-back with appointments. Thursdays, like today, his mornings were booked solid. To balance that, Doc liked to take the afternoon off. This meant Lori and I would need to stagger our lunches so the optical could remain open. Lori had a few errands to run, so she wanted to take her lunch after me.

After this was established, I texted Nick to see if his lunch break was going to be about the same time as mine. Most days I would just go home for lunch, but today it felt like it might be a good chance to meet up with him. If I could brighten his day by surprising him with lunch, perhaps it would brighten my day as well.

The air was fresh, and the sun was out. I had the bar shift tonight, which meant stepping it up for better tips. Since it wasn't a theme night, I had on my tight, forest-green jumper with a V-neck and sheer sleeves that had a sequined floral pattern on the cuffs, elbows, and shoulders. The chest was lined with slightly darker forest-green sequins. I was radiating in the sunlight, even down to my gold peep-toe pumps.

"This is already the best lunch break." Nick leaned over and kissed my cheek, snapping me out of my thoughts. "It's good to see your smile so bright again. What brought it out?"

Leaning over, I picked up his lunch. "To be honest, I was thinking what it would be like to be a bird."

He wore a black fitted T-shirt with navy scrub pants, his ID clipped to his pocket. This life would be so much easier if I could choose love with my mind instead of my heart. He was designed to attract all the females. His eyes were intriguing, his chest was thick and proud, and every part of him was etched in stone. Nick was beyond intelligent and caring. But my heart said no; it belonged to someone else. All I could do was pray that he found the one that would give all of herself to him. He truly did deserve all the happiness and love that he gave to me.

"Marigold," a voice shrieked, stopping my heart.

Oh no, it couldn't be her. Not today—this lunch was supposed to pep me up to get through the rest of my shift and the next one right after.

"Marigold," she snapped again, her tone getting harsher, growing angry that I wasn't acknowledging her. She huffed as she moved right before us. "You will answer me when I call you," she sneered as her fake eyelashes narrowed around her diarrhea-brown eyes. Her lips pinched in her frozen Botox face. "Why have you not been answering my calls?"

"My phone was in a fire, and I haven't had a chance to get a new one yet." Not fully a lie. I wasn't about to give her my new phone number so she could call and harass me every hour.

"But you had time to get him." She flung her hand palm-up at Nick.

Nick held his hand out to her. "I'm..."

No, there was no way she needed to know his name or his position. Quickly, I interrupted him. "This is Brice Harvest." I gestured to Susan. "This is Susan," my tone dropped, "my mother."

Her hip shifted out as she placed one hand on it. Her eyes moved up and down Nick with the cock of her head. I knew she was brewing up questions for him, and they were not going to be appropriate questions, judging by the way her lower lip was tucked in as she eyed him.

"So, Brice," her voice was a mixture of sweet and sultry, "what do you do here at the hospital?"

I spoke up before he could answer. "He works in laundry. In fact, his lunch is almost over, so excuse us."

Her eyes moved up and down his body again as her upper lip curled with disgust. "Damnit, Marigold. Do you want to be poor the rest of your life?"

This was going to get ugly fast. I adjusted Nick so his arm was around me and I could still hold his hand. I didn't care about his reaction; I was going to show him her true colors. "His position in the hospital doesn't define the value of his love toward me."

"You are a thick little girl. Do you want to end up living out of a car? There is no way he will ever be able to provide for you on that salary. I taught you better than this; he has no value. He's nothing more than what you keep on the side when your husband is out of town. My daughter will not associate with a man of this pedigree." She held out her hand to me. "You are coming with me."

I shook my head. "How dare you talk like that?" I growled. "You know nothing about him. His heart is just as beautiful as his body. You have no right to judge him in that capacity. To this day, you still know nothing about love. The value of one's love is not found in their wallet, but their heart."

Susan crossed her arms against her chest and shifted her weight to her leg behind her. "Of course, he's staring in your purse and not at you. Leonora Marigold Carter, open your eyes and take a look at yourself. He's only using you to get ahead in his life. By the way you dress, he knows you come from money and wants a part of it." Her eyes narrowed as she glared at Nick. "Even I can see that he doesn't love you."

That was a lie. I didn't know if he fully loved me, but there was something there. I wasn't going to correct her, though. She wouldn't listen, although Nick would. I didn't want that to cause that storm between us later.

"Like Ivan isn't doing that? Between you and his parents, where do you think he gets his money from?"

"He comes from money; Stephanie will have the same life I have soon. For you, this," she gestured at Nick, "is going to drag you down. Once you have nothing left, he will leave you for the next girl that he's probably been cheating on you with." She tilted forward and sneered. "It's going to feel so good to tell you once again I was right."

That was enough—I was going to put her in her place. I leaned forward into her face. "He loves me for me, and I love him for him. And that's all of him; mind, personality, and mostly heart. Just because you cheat and everyone else in your inner circle cheats does not mean I do. Does not mean Brice does either or that he will. Why can't you understand that money and sex do not equal love? Love is being beside someone when there is no one else to be there. Love is being there for someone when they are having a bad day, good day, and everything between. Being able to share all your dorkiness with someone and they just love you even more for it. There is no monetary value placed on love, and it is not through a man's penis. It is possible to not have a physical relationship with someone and still love them."

Her chest puffed out, then she snorted. "Your father will not stand for you making a mockery of us. He will cut you off; there will not be a big princess wedding or him walking you down the aisle."

I sold his prized possession; already there was never going to be any of that. I was dead to him. "Unlike you, I don't need his money," I growled. "I have my own. I don't need a huge wedding with a moat or bats glued to lights. If you want to talk about mockery, there is your mockery. Her wedding is going to be a roadside attraction. It's going to be an abomination, and everyone present is going to laugh about it."

"Why should I take advice from you?" she scoffed as she

eyed Nick up and down again. "You have no taste."

"Don't. Walk away. There is no reason for you to be standing here. I have made my choice; I will no longer be a Carter."

"After all the things I have done for you." She sniffled. "I have always gone up to bat for you, but you stand here and degrade me like you wouldn't care if I died."

Her crocodile tears weren't generating as fast as she wanted them to. She sniffled again. "I'm going to go home and lock myself in my bedroom. When you come over to make dinner, you're going to find out what your words did to me. This is going to haunt you for the rest of your life, knowing you drove your loving mother to her death."

My head cocked and my eyes rolled. "Are you done?"

"I want dinner on the table at six along with my apology gift." She turned and walked away.

Sitting back down on the bench, Nick and I watched as Susan began to limp the closer she got to the emergency room. By the time she made it to the door, she was dragging her leg behind her. When someone came to her assistance, she hunched over, grabbing her chest.

"I'm sorry for all of that," I told Nick. "But you needed to see the real side of her. I have a feeling that she is going to start popping up in my world now that she knows I am back." Gently I placed my hand on his upper arm. "I'm sorry I lied about you, but if she knew that you were a resident here, it would have been a whole fake act."

Nick leaned forward and picked up his pop. "I don't get how the girl that will fight her own mother on love is so afraid of letting love in." He sat back again as his head fell in my direction with that same look from when he found out I was paid twenty grand to wear pasties.

"I am far from afraid to let love in. I have a whole new family that I love as if we were blood."

"No, Nora, that's not what I meant."

I knew this, but I didn't want to get into it with him today.

"I'm not afraid of your love. I am in love with someone else."

"Six days, Nora," Nick growled. "Six days. He's been unconscious for how many days?"

I twirled my ring as I looked down. "Three months, three weeks, and one day."

"Nora," Nick took my hands into his hands, "please understand the chances he wakes up are slim. There's even a chance that when he wakes up, he's not going to remember you at all. He may even be a different person, who knows. Regardless, I know that six days wasn't long enough for the love that you are fighting so damn hard for."

"Untrue—it took me less than six days to know I loved him."

He peered into my eyes. "Did he ever say 'I love you' in those six days?"

My head dropped; I didn't want to say it. Nothing I said was going to appease the expert.

His index finger and thumb lifted my chin.

"No, all right? He never said it in those six days, but it didn't mean he didn't feel the same way." I drew back and wiped my cheek with the side of my hand before any of my tears had a chance to fall.

Nick sat up and wrapped his arm around my torso, drawing me into his chest. "At some point you need to move forward. All you are doing is wasting your life on nothing more than lust. This isn't worth it unless you truly knew how he felt."

"How would you know?" I growled through my tears. "Have you ever been in love?"

"I do know, but I can't get her to stop throwing her life away for someone that is most likely never going to wake up. Quit all your jobs, and I will take you away from all of this. Your family will never find you."

"No." I shook my head. "I have people depending on me; I can't quit."

CHAPTER 27

I walked into the optical, collapsed at the first station, and slammed my head against the black-speckled teal measuring desk that was right out of the early 90s.

"I take it that your lunch break didn't go well," Lori chuckled from behind the adjusting counter in the back.

"Susan ran into us on her weekly trip to the emergency room to restock her pills. We were sitting on the bench in the green area before the emergency room entrance. It was awful, she got in Nick's head, and then he started questioning me about love."

"Why don't you just give that boy a chance? He only took that residency up here to be with you."

Nope, it wasn't going to happen—in fact, I would rather have given Kek a chance. Life would have been so much easier if I had surrendered myself to Kek. There had been no progress with Leon, and I was tired of living this life. Working three jobs and getting nowhere in life was starting to wear me down.

I stared down at my pumps; there was a black scuff on the right shoe. "On paper, I should be falling head over heels in love with Nick. He's on a very successful path, his body is sculpted perfectly, and he has a classic handsomeness about him. He doesn't always behave like it, but he is kind and caring. I'm well aware why he picked those days for his residency up here. We've talked about it; he's concerned that because I dress on the more seductive side when I bartend, he thinks the wrong guy is going to follow me home. He wants to be here to protect me from others."

"See," Lori cooed, "he's the gentleman that you need: handsome, caring, protective, smart."

"Please stop," I growled. "I don't need his protection. I took down Kek the Egyptian God of the Darkness of Chaos myself; I can handle a mere drunken mortal."

The sound of frames falling on the floor drew my attention to the man in the men's section. I turned and noticed how sharp he was dressed in a suit with a white collared shirt peeking up from his jacket collar, the jacket fitted against his shoulders. He wasn't overly built, his body tapering as my eyes moved lower down his body.

"Oh you," Lori chuckled again. "Is that what we are calling Ivan now?"

There was no way I could be honest with her about Kek. It was just best to move on. "I don't love Nick; I don't want to be with him. I only let him live with me to help him out. It would be dumb for him to rent a place for only a few nights a week. And yes, I will admit it, at first I was using him for professional advice on coma patients. Now I don't dare say anything to him about Leon; he is so covetous. It upsets him to no end that I will not just give up on Leon and move onto him."

"Nora, at some point you need to allow a conscious person in."

"Now you just sound like Nick," I mumbled.

"He's right! You are finished with your studies, so it's time you move onto that next phase of your life. Why can't you just give Nick one chance?" Her bottom lip with mauve cracked lipstick pouted as she held up her cigarette-stained index finger. "One chance."

"How about," I chuckled, "I'll trade you Bob for Nick. At least Bob enjoys my baking."

"Don't tempt me; I might just take you up on that."

I sat back, crossed my arms, and threw my head back. I just told her I didn't love him. Maybe if I started listing off the traits I didn't like about him, she would move on. "Not that I have ever slept in a bed with him, but I don't like his morning breath. It's horrendous and reminds me of another foul smell that I never want to smell again."

It's like the smell when I cut off Kek's head. It gets trapped in my nose, and I can't get rid of it or get past it.

"He's handsome until his real smile appears—there is something about his upper left canine that makes me feel like I can't fully trust him."

In my mind I saw Kek in bear form snarling at me when Nick gave that wide Pan Am smile. It's not his fault, but I still can't get past it.

"He refuses to go running with me. This is the only time he will say something sexual to me, but he believes there are better forms of cardio. With that said, he appreciates that I am saving myself for the right one. Now on the other hand of the exercising thing, he wants me to start going to the gym with him to start lifting. Umm...no, he's massive, I don't want to be a muscular female. I have enough muscle strength for what I need."

"It might do you some good to start lifting; this is the thinnest I have ever seen you. Are you eating?"

"Yes, I am eating," I growled.

"Okay... But those are physical things that Nick might not have control over."

"Fine. I once fell asleep on him while watching a movie. Literally slid to the side and landed on him in my sleep. I wasn't trying to snuggle or anything. I honor what my ring means. Anyways, he woke me up, freaked out that I had drooled on him. It was a tiny spot, not even a quarter size. I love to cuddle, not that we do, but now I'm afraid to sit next to him in case I fall asleep again. I'm a drooler; I can't control it. He's not going to be able to handle me."

"For a man that is endlessly staring at your lips when he stops in on Wednesdays, that's a little dramatic."

Well, at least she saw it too. "I know, right?" I chuckled. "Good luck to the first girl that makes out with him. He's going to make her pat down her mouth every couple minutes."

Lori shook her head, her brown and grey hair unmoving. "Why can I even picture that?" She gave me a mischievous grin. "It's you that I can picture as the girl."

I wasn't going to acknowledge her last statement. "Nick is incredibly vocal about his dislike for me taking my long, hot showers. It doesn't affect him in the slightest. He has his own bathroom and doesn't pay for utilities. Which is clear by the fact that he leaves every single light on in the apartment before he leaves for work."

When caring for Leon, I constantly tried to remain positive even if I didn't feel that way. Part of my long, hot showers when I got off work was breaking down in disappointment that he still hadn't woken up. I was praying that I would close the bar and find him sitting up in bed one night. There was no holding back that disappointment in finding him lying there day after day. In the States, it's the disappointment of not receiving that one phone call that makes my showers longer.

"You two need to learn to accept each other's quirks. No one is perfect."

I held up two fingers. "Strike two: unlike Bob, he doesn't like my baking. He'll start lecturing me on how baked goods are horrible for your body and I shouldn't be wasting money on making that crap. Says the man that drinks a pop every morning at breakfast and another at lunch and another with dinner."

I liked the thought of homemade baked goods; they're comforting and make people happy. Plus, there were more harmful chemicals in the pop he drinks than in my blueberry pie.

"He's crazy—I like your baking, and it has come a long way since you got back."

That was warming to hear. "Thanks, Lori."

"So, what's strike three?"

With a deep breath, I said, "He's growing impatient that I just can't magically flip a switch and forget about Leon. In his words, Leon has with me. Nick, being the expert, likes to remind me that you can't imprint on someone's heart after only being together for six days. He doesn't even sugarcoat it; he just throws it out there that after being in a coma for over thirty days, the chances he wakes up drops every day. I know why he is saying it, but it still hurts as much as the first time he said it."

"Ohh," Lori's voice echoed with compassion, "Nora..."

I blinked the first row of tears out. "He apologizes for being so crude when I start crying. Then he will tell me that he doesn't want me wasting my life on something that isn't going to happen. That I would be so much happier if I just let Leon go. A couple times he has told me that I would be free from working because he will provide me with a life of luxury. I don't want to be a show wife. Mostly I don't want to be his wife."

Lori walked over to the other side of the measuring desk. "That boy needs to check himself. He was up here within four days of meeting you."

"I know, right?" I snorted, wiping my cheek with my hand.

She turned and took my hand into hers. "He is somewhat right. You are killing yourself here to support Leon up there. Your earnings from this job go to his caretaker, the grocery store goes to another account for his medical expenses, and you are living off a bartender wage. You need to cut back; I can see you are breaking down. Physically it's starting to show. I love you, but you are turning into skin and bones, and I'm worried. At this rate, even if Leon comes back into your life, there will be nothing left of you for him."

I wasn't going to touch on the topic of my body right now. "See, I know what love is; it's supporting the one that you love the most when everyone else is just counting on him to die. It's not all physical or poetry or even about money; it's being the one that is there the most when the other one needs it. I am doing this so his life is easier when he wakes up. It's already going to be hard enough when he realizes that he had slept almost four months of his life away. I don't want him stressing about money. And yes, money isn't everything, but since I was banned from there, this is all I can do to be there for him."

"Nick is jealous of this and most likely only says that crap to you because he is. Nick sees how much love you have in you and wants a part of it. As a doctor, he also sees you being self-destructive when you don't need to be pushing yourself this hard. If Leon is the man you say he is, he would be upset with you as well."

"Please don't say that—life is hard enough already. I don't need to be sitting here thinking that he is in that line with the rest of them." He was going to be when he found out that my reckless care was killing him.

"Quit your second and third job. If I can survive on our wages, you can too."

"It's not all just going to Leon; I am compensating Ruby for her lost wages. He's not her responsibility, but she is still kind enough to care for him."

"Why is he *your* responsibility?"

I was so tired of defending myself to everyone. It was my choice to dispense my time and money however I saw fit. "I was the one that fought everyone to keep him alive. When they all were saying their goodbyes to him, I went on a hunger strike until he was put on an IV."

"Are you still on that hunger strike?" Lori didn't wait for me to answer. "Did you eat on your break?"

I threw away my lunch as I walked away from Nick after

our argument. There was no way I was going to eat after going around with him and Susan. Nothing sounded appealing anymore, especially the sandwich I had ordered.

I bowed my head. "No."

"That's it," Lori huffed. "If you are not going to quit those other jobs, I am forcing you into paid leave for the next two weeks. Effective when I get back from lunch."

"Wait, what?" She couldn't do this; the optical didn't have enough staff to cover my shifts for the next week. "I can't take time off; we don't have the coverage."

"Oh yes we do," Lori tittered. "Doc and I have been discussing this. I guess he brought it home to Grace as well. She wants to help again and will be covering your shift for the next two weeks." Her tone turned stern. "I highly recommend you consider quitting your other jobs before you come back or move into your field of study."

That was a threat. I wasn't fully studied up on if there was a law that an employer could make you terminate your side jobs. However, I did know that we were in an At-Will Employment State. Which meant you could quit a job without notice or your employer could terminate your position without notice or reason. Grace was Doc's wife; she had replaced me when I was forced to quit the first time. I also knew that the last of Doc's four children had just gone off to further their education. He had made a few comments here and there that Grace was thinking about doing something to keep herself busy during the day.

All I could do was stare at her as the tears streamed down my face. I didn't know what to do anymore. Everything around me was collapsing, and all I was doing was trying to help others.

"Nora," Lori urged, "you need to do this. Something in your life needs to change before there is nothing left. We are not doing this to be mean—we are concerned about you." She sat back in the chair across from me. "Plus, you need to lay low for a few days since Susan knows you are back in town. We all know that she will be up here barking orders at you first thing in the morning."

She knew Susan too well and she was right. When I didn't show up later to cook my welcome-home meal for them, she was going to be waiting at the door full of fuel to gaslight the crap out of me. Not to mention, if Dan found out, he would have me by the neck again for upsetting Susan.

I tittered as I rubbed the back of my neck. "Maybe I should call Sean and see if he will come down for a few days. I may be able to handle Kek, but Dan is just looking for a reason to get rid of his embarrassing offspring."

That was a thought; if I was being forced into this break, maybe I could talk Sean into coming down so we could go on a trip together to get away from everything for a few days. Right now, Sean was the only one that I truly felt comfortable with.

Lori looked past me to the male section. "He looks like he has decided between the two frames. Go help this gentleman, and I will be back in an hour. Tootles."

The door chimed as Lori walked out. I turned the standing mirror toward me and tried to compose myself. "I'll be with you in just one second, sir."

Closing my eyes, I took a few breaths, trying to calm myself down. I thought more about it; I could take a couple weeks off from here since they were going to be paid. During that time, I could work out a new plan moving forward. Or even a couple plans for moving forward. Possibly get my résumé out there since I was banned from Canada anyways.

I could feel vibrations of my chair gliding across the carpet, turning me parallel to the desk, as if someone had their foot on one of the front legs. I kept my head down—he must have known I was crying. A hand gently lowered on my lap, palm up.

"I would like to exchange this."

One by one, his fingers uncurled to expose the heart I had left for Leon when I was deported.

It was more than what he was holding—it was the voice that paralyzed me for a second. The realization that he was before me now caused me to slide forward until I fell to my knees, bowing my head into my hands. I had dreamt of this day a thousand times; it had played out in my mind with every daydream. Although the only thing racing through me was the thought that I had almost killed him. "I'm so sorry," I whimpered.

"Why?"

"It was never my intention to harm you. I thought every-thing out. The goal was for you to come back to a normal life. I thought physical therapy would help your muscles prepare for when you got up. Then I was concerned the physical ther-apy might have been too much, so I tried to relax your mus-cles with a massage. I'm so sorry, I know what it feels like to have a cold IV, so I thought it would be comforting to have some warmth against your body to combat that. I was contin-ually respectful of your body."

"Nora, will you please look up at me?"

I wasn't done yet. "And it was more than just your body, it was your mind as well. Your body responded differently to things; I thought you were still in there. I guess it could have been in my mind, but I didn't want you laying there bored or feeling as if we forgot about you... I—I—" I gasped for air as I forgot what I was saying. "I'm so sorry, I didn't know the care I was giving you was harmful until a professional told me it was. I'm so sorry, that was never my intention to hurt you."

"Nora..."

Just the way he said my name was indescribable. However, the guilt of being the one reason he wasn't recovering as he should have been was suffocating me. "If I hadn't been deported, who knows if my awful care would have killed you. I am so incredibly sorry. Please believe me, I never intended to hurt you. I was hoping it was going to help you recover sooner, but I was told all it did was the opposite. I never wanted that for you."

"Okay, that's enough." His hands pressed into my torso and thrust me forward until I felt his chest against my chest.

Without a second thought, I wrapped my arms around his neck and hid my face in the nape of his neck. His powerful cologne and his own essence seeped into my nose, down into my heart. I held on even tighter. I never wanted to believe it, but parts of me were starting to think I would never have this again after being deported.

"Please don't apologize for anything; everything you did was right. Every night when you would spoon up to me after your shower, I just wanted to tell you how much it meant to me that you were there. Later in the night, when you would move me back on my back so you could snuggle up to me, I just wanted to kiss the top of your head as it rested on my chest. Every morning when you would hold my hand and describe the sunrise, I just wanted to tell you not even that sunrise could compare to your beautiful heart."

"You were awake," I mumbled, feeling everything within me freeze. Perhaps that meant Nick was wrong about all of it.

His head rested against my head and his fingers moved into my hair. "I was because of you. Even after I betrayed you with Sean, you still never gave up on me. This is unfair for you to be punishing yourself—it's me that you should be upset with."

That wasn't true. New relationships were delicate, like flowers, and that situation was a fist of rage. It could have been misconstrued at any point. I understood why he pulled Sean into it the way he did. I could see why Leon didn't just come out and ask me about it; I refused to tell him the truth as well.

"No." I pressed further into his chest, tightening my arms around him. "That was all my fault because I hid it. I lied to you that morning, to your face, about the cat, and that Sunday too many times. I was so frightened that there was something wrong with me, because my mind was playing out these hells only when..." I couldn't even say it; there was that delicate flower in my palm. My voice lowered. "I'm afraid of losing you."

Leon's chest rose as he inhaled, holding his breath for a second. His chest dropped as the words flew out of him with his air: "I withheld things from you as well out of fear of losing you. But I love you too much for it to be like this between us anymore, I need to tell you the truth."

He didn't need to define his health issues to me. All I needed to know was how to care for him. I reached up without moving from Leon and felt around for the tissue box. "It's okay if you are not comfortable sharing your health issues with me." I lifted my head and wiped Leon's suit jacket with a tissue before wiping my nose. "All I want is to be able to stay at your side. Well...and proper care instructions from a professional."

"Oh, Nora." His tone was more stressed as he lowered my head back to his shoulder.

"I'm sorry." I sat back on his legs as I dabbed my eyes again. "I'm not being very respectful towards you. I'm sorry for making a mess on your jacket."

I could picture Nick up in arms that I left bodily fluid on his nice suit jacket. There was no way he would have handled it; he would have gotten up and walked out. A week later I could see myself receiving a dry-cleaning bill from him. That man was in for a rude awakening when he moved in with a girlfriend—he was soon going to find out we weren't dry, plastic dolls.

"You are apologizing too much for no reason." Leon's index finger and thumb trembled as they raised my chin. "I love you."

My eyes widened. Up until this moment, I thought Leon

was before me. But now I saw a guy with incredibly dark hair, full eyebrows, and black eyes. His skin was golden. This wasn't my rare, pale-haired, copy-paper-white, blush-eyed man. This was the first man from the visions when we kissed; this was King Leon.

No, that wasn't possible. I didn't know King Leon or what he truly looked like—plus, he died centuries ago. This had to be Mr. Bartender Leon Sterling before me. My hands started to tremble more with my racing heart as I tried to work this out. Perhaps something changed within Leon while he was unconscious, and he wanted to be a new person after he woke up.

I needed this to be Leon before me; I needed proof that it was. I leaned forward and wiped his cheek with a clean part of the tissue, then sat back and examined it. Maybe he had gotten a spray tan and that was why the color wasn't wiping off. Again, leaning forward, I parted his hair; there was no new growth or dye stains. Putting my expert skills to work, I studied his eyes for little contact rings, but I couldn't find anything.

Leon tilted forward, his brows curved in, giving his forehead an interesting pattern of wrinkles, almost like the pattern of a thumbprint. The corner of his lips tucked in as he peered at me for a moment.

Before me was King Leon, not my Leon. People could tan and dye their hair, but it all felt natural on him, not processed. I just needed one thing to show me this was Leon before me. Anything to prove that this was my Leon and not Kek shapeshifting into King Leon.

My heart was not slowing down as I sat there, frozen, trying to figure out how I was going to prove this was my Leon and not Kek. I had an idea—there was one place I knew a beautician would never dye. Leaning forward, I tilted Leon's chin up as he had done with mine, then pushed his nose back.

"Nooo," I whined, "you trimmed your nose hairs."

Leon rubbed his nose. "Nora," he tittered, "what?"

I didn't look up as I unbuttoned the first two buttons on his shirt. My mind flashed back to that day in the cave when Kek had told me he could take many shapes. I remembered Gordon telling me something about blood, but I couldn't fully recall what it was.

"I might have failed," I whispered to myself as I moved his shirt, exposing his collarbone. There were his two little moles stacked with the third one just to the side over his collarbone. Could Kek have known about these moles?

"Nora, what are you doing?"

"I... I..." I leaned away from Leon; I needed to be cautious with him just in case. "I mean, Kek told me—" I drew my hair forward, covering either side of my neck. Sinking down, I hid my trembling hands in my crossed arms, "that he could take many forms. That day, he was warming me up to be his queen. Ruby and Sean told me there was no change in your condition since I left." A lump grew in my throat. "I'm a touch leery," I squeaked.

"Wait, what?" Leon didn't give me a chance to respond, panic and rage rising in his voice along with the heat in his face. "Kek was what with you?"

This was all getting confusing. Nervously I ran my hands through my hair, tugging it out straight, then letting it fall onto my shoulders. This Leon before me was not the Leon I left in Canada. There was something off about this situation; perhaps I had messed something up with Kek. "I feel like I missed a step in Gordon's directions on how to kill Thelma's creature, Kek."

"I need for you to be honest with me right now." Leon brushed my hair off my shoulders, exposing my neck. "Did he touch you?"

"Yes, but it wasn't anything to get this excited about. He had his hand on the lower part of my leg."

Leon's hands rested on my neck with his thumbs stabilizing my head so he could peer into my eyes. "I don't care if it was just your leg. He has no right to touch or even be near you. Now that I am mortal, he's going to die for that."

My gaze fell onto his nose as I became fixated on the word "mortal." It wasn't directly spoken to me, but they all knew of Kek from how he taunted the kingdom of Journey over the years. I could see how Leon would want to kill Kek, but despite that, I couldn't get past why he would say he was mortal. Kek was a god, not a mortal.

I didn't release his hands, holding on tighter as I tried to stop my trembling. "Mortal?"

Swiftly he wrapped his arms around my torso, drawing me to his chest. He squeezed tighter as his forehead moved against mine. "I love you," he said, the words skittish and broken as if something awful was going to happen.

There was so much going on in my mind. I remained silent as I tried to figure out why he was starting to break down. His words were so broken—had I said something wrong, or were my trembling hands making him uneasy?

"Please," he whimpered against my lips. "You would say it to me every night and again every morning. This may be my last time to hear it again."

Oh god, he had to be dying. That was the only possible reason I wouldn't be able to say it to him again. Or, worse, Leon was coming down here to tell me goodbye because I was banned from Canada and there was no way he was going to give up his life for me. Whatever the reason, I didn't want it to be the last time.

My eyes swelled with tears as I drew back. "I'm not going to say it if it's going to be the last time. Nothing happened between Kek and I, and for sure nothing has happened between Nick and me. There has never been another man that has stopped me from loving or being loyal to you. There is nothing I can do at this point about being banned from Canada, please don't punish me more for it."

He shook his head slowly. "No, Nora."

"You're dying." I didn't give him a chance to respond. I pulled his head back to my head. "I will never stop telling you that I love you until the day I die," I whispered before my lips decided they were going to keep his heart pumping.

There was that spark of his tongue between the silkiness of his lips, but this time all it did was cause Leon to fall backward. Thankfully I had my hand on the back of his head, so he didn't slam onto the floor. Leon rolled over so he was above me. He gazed upon me the same way he had once through the flames.

"One more time." His lips brushed my lower lip.

"I love you."

His eyes closed as if he was breathing in my words, then there was a deep inhale. "I am not Kek. I am the same person you met in the bar this past summer and," Leon sat up, bringing me with him, then rested his index finger on my lips, "I am the same man from your visions. As you saw when Kek damned me, I lost all my coloring six hundred years ago."

I just squeaked with his finger pressed to my lips, my eyes doubling in size.

Leon moved my head upright and kept his hands on my cheeks. "I'm six hundred thirty-two years old. Kek bit me when I was twenty-six. I was damned for the last six hundred six years."

I couldn't move; I just stared at him, trying to replay in my head what he had said. There was no way.

His shoulders dropped. "I love you."

Even with the stories and visions, Kek was unbelievable until he was in that littoral cave with me. In this moment, after everything, I couldn't see Leon lying to me or telling me this tall tale. Telling a girl that you were six hundred thirty-two years old was certainly not the way to win her heart back. Or he was the world's worst at pickup lines.

If Leon was six hundred thirty-two years old, that would mean he would have been twenty-six in the late 1300s to early 1400s. Leon the Great was the last of his dynasty to rule during that period. This would mean that the Leon before me was the same Leon from my visions.

I closed my eyes and held up my index finger, needing a moment longer to work it out. This new knowledge felt useful in figuring out what I had missed that day in the cave. Perhaps it had to do with *"freeing the king from his illness."* My Leon's illness was never an autoimmune disease; he had been bitten. I broke the curse when I killed Kek in that cave. That's why he slipped into a coma at the same time those events unfolded—his body was becoming human again or ridding itself of evil.

Or did I hurt Leon by not killing Kek properly? I dazed off, staring at Leon as I replayed that moment with Gordon, Gordon holding up the sword before his face, saying *"It is told that the only way to free the king from his curse is for Sigrid to enter the chest of the creature that first cursed him, but first the tip of the blade must be coated in the king's blood and that of his true love. She has to love him just as much for it to work."*

That vision snapped me out of my daze. Swiftly I turned over my left hand, exposing the red kiss that Sigrid gave to me. I had bled on her blade.

With giddiness rising in me, I unbuttoned two more buttons on Leon's shirt. I moved his jacket and shirt over and pushed my finger in his chest just left of the scar. I held my left ring finger up to him, exposing my scar. "Do you love me?"

His head fell to the side a touch as his chest deflated. "Every day since that first one I have loved you. I didn't know it was possible, but I love you more than I will ever be able to show you in the years I have left."

I hadn't failed. I had successfully killed Kek and freed Leon. Everything was bubbling within me; this was too much.

"Guess what, my fellow mortal?" I placed my hands on Leon's cheeks and drew them together until his lips puckered. *"You can't kill Kek for touching me,"* I sang, *"I already killed him."*

I bounced my eyebrows. "Want to hear how?" I didn't wait for him to find his words. "Sigrid bit me the first day I found her in that cave with the rings." I tapped his scar with my right elbow. "She still had blood on her from when someone tried to end himself. Gordon taught me that piercing Kek's heart would only paralyze him. Doing as I was told, I sliced his head off, then, because it wouldn't stop moving, I speared it." I smiled up at Leon, whose color was close to copy-paper-white again. "I lit him afire, then I blew up the cave... Well, actually, I blew up the whole face of the cliff. There are no more caves on that side of the lake. They are never going to allow me back in your country when the proper officials find out."

Leon looked like a deer in headlights. "Nora," he mumbled, "Sigrid..."

"Unfortunately, I didn't take Sigrid with me when I jumped into the lake, so she's gone too. Please forgive me, my mind was in kill-and-survive mode."

I backtracked to tell Leon everything that happened, from that day after I left his apartment to when they first hooked us up to the IV. I spared no details; this was the first time I had told anyone about everything that went down that day, and I was proud of myself for being able to talk about it.

After stealing a peck, I released Leon; he was going to need some time. "Sean has been getting on me since it happened to tell you this. I don't know why he didn't just tell you; he was there for part of it. Gordon could have told you as well since he is the only other person that I have told about what happened in that cave. I didn't—well, first you were unconscious, but mostly I didn't want you to think I was crazy. I mean, a girl that you barely know tells you that an Egyptian god who first appeared as a bear, then transformed into a human, approached her in a cave to proposition her to be his queen. There was no telling this man no either, because I guess he had been watching me all week and liked what he saw. Anyways, it's a terrible story. I'm not a fan of talking about morbid and gruesome things. You didn't need to hear it while you were unconscious."

Leon rubbed his chin. "He's dead?"

"Yes, sir." I was on an adrenaline high, thrilled it was officially over. "In Susan's fucking face that I don't know what real love is. In Nick's fucking face for saying that I'm afraid of love. I don't know about this king stuff yet—" I stole a not-appropriate-for-work kiss, "but I fucking love you, Mr. Bartender."

I pushed myself up, then glanced down at Leon. He was going pale as he sat there, paralyzed. I don't think he realized Kek was dead until this point. He must have thought his curse was lifted in another way.

I walked over to the closet in the examination room, pulling my makeup-removing wipes out of my purse, reminding myself this was exactly why I hated wearing makeup. My face was a mess of mascara. I ran the wipe back and forth, walking to the mirror and exposing the reason why I *had* started wearing makeup. Purple crescents underlined my semi-sunken eyes. Lori wasn't wrong—I looked as if I could have walked the runway in the 90s. My body had shrunk, my bones protruding. I was never hungry and sometimes lost track of time. Outside of working, I lived more in my daydreams than in reality.

My self-examination was halted as I was swiftly spun away from the sink. Leon's hands moved to the back of my thighs, then hoisted me up, the wall creaking as I was slammed against it in all the right ways.

His lips moved down my jaw to my neck. "No more Egyptian gods, vampires, and for sure no Nicks," he growled, sealing his words with warmth on my neck.

I ran my nails through his hair, drawing him back to my lips. I liked this new powerful tone within him. His words were thick and dominating, that trepidation from earlier nowhere to be found. There was nothing we were hiding from each other anymore.

"Your Majesty." My lips moved to his only long enough for him to desire more. "Are you envious?" I purred. It was indifferent using that term with him, though I wanted more of this newly confident man. The man that I had thought I was losing more and more with each passing day.

His gaze moved from my lips to my eyes as the right side of his lips moved up slyly. "You are mine."

I clenched my fists as my arms rested on Leon's shoulders, trying to hide the new trembling within them. Leon's words took me right back to that cave for a split second.

That split second lasted too long; Leon glanced behind him, then tightened his grip around me. He walked backwards until he fell onto the examining chair. His thumb glided beneath my eye, his palm warming my cheek. "What happened, Princess?"

My teeth pierced my bottom lip. "Umm... I thought I heard the door chime."

"No." Leon bowed my head, resting his lips on my forehead. "Please tell me the truth."

Drawing back, I scanned his eyes. My heart fluttered with how enchanting he was in every way, my *King Leon*. "It wasn't your tone or your words, it..." *Breathe*, I told myself, *it's going to be okay*. "It sent my mind back for a second to..." I didn't want to say it; I wanted to be a strong knight.

"I think," he glanced up to me with that sly grin again, "I know how to fix this." His hand warmed mine, his thumb rubbing my palm for a moment, then he drew his hand away, taking my ring with it.

I was a mess that he wanted no part of anymore. Who could blame him? He came back to a trembling shell. In hindsight, I should have listened to everyone else when it came to pushing myself so hard.

My spiraling thoughts halted when Leon took my other hand. "I'm yours, Nora." Gently he placed my right hand on my lap, then picked up my left hand, sliding the ring onto my ring finger. "Forever yours." He raised my hand and kissed the ring.

For the hundredth time this afternoon, my eyes blurred Leon's image. "I love you."

"I love you too. But losing you that day was one of the hardest days of my life. Then when that nitwit doctor told you to cut ties, I think I died for a third time. I don't want this anymore unless you are beside me. I need you, Nora. I need you beside me every day. I don't want to wake up another day without you beside me." His thumb rubbed across the ring. "Once that lady comes back, let's go home."

Those words just shattered my heart and pushed out more tears. I wanted to go back to Journey more than anything, and even more than that, I wanted to be with him. "I can't—I was deported for not being sponsored while working up there and then I was banned for ten years for putting a BSO in her place."

The front door chimed. I hoped that it was just Lori returning from lunch. Though, by the sound of heels clicking then the measuring desk chair being drawn out and a purse dropping on the desk, it wasn't Lori.

"Marigold!" The screech carried across the showroom floor to the back room. "Get out here now!"

Of course it was Susan—she could smell the happiness, and she was here to destroy it.

"Fuuuckk," I growled, dropping my head onto Leon's chest.

"I heard that," she snapped. "Get your ass out here now!"

I took Leon's cheeks into my hands. "Whatever you do, do not leave this room until I come get you." I kissed his forehead. "Promise me."

"Nora." Leon grasped my hands, lowering his brow. "What's going on?"

"Satan's foot soldier is here. I don't want her to know about you—not because I'm ashamed of you. It's more that I love you too much to want to expose you to her toxicity."

Susan was sitting at the second measuring desk, trying to smooth out her crow's feet when I closed the door. Her eyes bounced around my body, landing on my face. "Jeezus, you look like ass." She gestured toward me. "Go put your face back on before you scare all the customers—or, worse, a potential husband—away."

I didn't move past the front desk, leaning against it with my arms crossed, counting down in my head how long I was going to give her before I kicked her out. Any second with her was a second too long. Standing up straight, I moved my shoulders back. "You have no business here." I pointed at the door. "Exit the same way you entered."

"Marigold," she sneered, "is that any way to talk to your mother? Especially after I talked you up in front of that low-life loser earlier today. You should be thanking me; he's going to be pulling out all the stops for you tonight."

"Talked me up? More like you degraded him. It was awful. You should be ashamed of yourself."

"No, his body is the only thing he has going for him. Tonight he's going to prove his value to you with all that he has." She sat back in her chair, studying her pointed, blood-red acrylic nails. "You need to break them so they learn to worship you. I expect a thank-you gift tomorrow—you are about to have the best sex of your life."

"For fuck's sake, there is more to life than sex." I sat down on the other side of the desk. "What do you want?"

Her index finger curled as if she was scooping the air. "Your new boy toy for a few hours tomorrow, then let's just say we are even."

Oh lord, this was going to be another Ivan situation. "No," I growled.

"You don't say no to me." She leaned close to my face, "I will destroy you."

"Go for it." I started cackling. "I have nothing."

"You have no idea who you are dealing with. I want your

little boy toy to get Mommy her happy pills. Tell him he will be satisfied with his reward for obeying the monarchy of this family."

"You are disgusting to think—"

She cut me off before I could finish. "If you want him welcomed into this family, he will earn his place with me first."

"So you're telling me," I sat back and crossed my arms, "the only way you will allow me to bring a man into the family is if he steals pills from the hospital for you?"

"And—" She sat back in the chair, examining her nails again. "I get him for an afternoon to teach him the ways of the family."

Why couldn't the ways of the family be teaching him how to cook family recipes? Every time Susan made these comments, my stomach acid stung the back of my throat. More than anything, I wished I could say that she was joking, but she wasn't.

"There is no way your father is going to stand for you dating someone of his pedigree. You need me to gain your father's approval, but first I need to see if this new guy is worth it."

This was expected, but still awful. Nick was a person; this conversation should never have taken place. I held out my arm toward the door. "It's time for you to leave. I'm working."

"Tsk, tsk. Marigold, don't talk to me like that. I will have you fired from this little ridiculous job. Better yet," her eyes bounced around the optical, "I will have your father buy it and just close it for the hell of it."

"Good luck, not everything is for sale and not everything is yours." I cocked my head to the side. I was going to get under her skin a little. "Oh, by the way, you are not this god that you think you are. Brice has standards; there is no way in hell that he would ever bow down to you in any fashion."

"Right," Susan snickered, "just like he's with you for your beauty and love."

On second thought, I didn't need to lower myself to her level anymore. Especially when I had my future in the other room waiting to take me home so we could start our life together.

"It's time for you to leave, and not just out of this optical, but out of my life. I don't think you see it, but I have been distancing myself from the Carters since the beginning of the summer. It is at the point now that we need to move away in different directions and peacefully cut each other out of our lives. Goodbye, Susan."

"You ungrateful shit." She leaned into my chest with her purse clenched against her. "After everything I have done for you! I was the one that stopped your father from killing you that day in the bar. I was the one that got you this job! I am the only one in the family that stands up for you when they all are talking awful about you. And you want to cut me out of your life!? You should be begging me to allow you into my life."

Forget bear spray—I could have used her toxicity to blow up that cave. Everything she was saying was a lie. I had seen her pleased smirk as she watched Dan pin me by the throat. The family talks because she is the one that loves to stir the pot so she can feed off the drama. I got this position for volunteering as a favor to one of my former high school teachers.

The door chimed; this time Lori walked in, carrying a few shopping bags. She loved to run errands on her lunch breaks, so in the evenings she would have more time to spend with Bob. His health was starting to decline; it was no secret his day was coming sooner than later.

"Susan." Lori took one step back. "Get out of my store now!"

Susan's eyes narrowed. "It isn't over until I say it is over," she sneered, then stormed out the door.

I rushed to the door after it closed. I wouldn't put it past Susan to come back in and start round two. With my back to the door, I held the lock bolt in my trembling hand. I felt so incredibly guilty and relieved for telling Susan goodbye. Even if it only lasted until tomorrow, I still stood up to her.

I felt a knuckle run down my arm, then Leon took my hand into his as if he was trying not to startle me. "Nora." Gently he tugged me toward him. "Come here, Princess."

I stepped into Leon's arms, and his left arm moved around to my back with his hand resting in the middle, his right hand slowly lowering my head to his shoulder, then gently he rested his head against mine. I closed my eyes as he softly spoke.

"We are going to take the next couple days to tie up any loose ends that you might have down here. Saturday I have to get Pharrell from the airport, then we are taking you back to your real home. After today, I hope that we never return here again."

The examination room door closed, and Lori stood behind the front counter, watching us with a comforting smile. She looked at peace, and I hoped it was because she could see what I saw when I looked into Leon's eyes and what he saw when he looked into my eyes. I wanted her to see the truth and hoped any notion of Nick and I was washed away from her mind.

When she realized I was watching her, she pointed and mouthed, "Who is he?"

I shifted my arms and tapped the ring on my left hand with my right index finger.

Lori started squealing as she walked into the examination room and slammed the door.

Leon dropped his embrace. "Is there a piglet in here?"

My giggles were soon drowned out by Lori's "Woo-hoo" from the not-soundproof examination room.

Her head popped out, face beet-red. "Sorry," she said, disappearing again behind the door.

Leon pulled me back to him with his brows hooded. His lips pressed against my head. "I think it's time to go back to the apartment."

Before I could say anything, Lori emerged and spoke first. "That's a great idea. Stop at the restaurant across the street before heading home. Nora's favorite is a Number Three, no cheese, but with raw onions. Get it with a side of sweet potato fries and get her a chocolate, marshmallow, banana malt."

That sounded so good—Lori knew me too well—but I had foregone a morning run to get a big batch of chili in the slow cooker. It was supposed to be rainy for the next couple of days, so I thought it would be a good time to bust out my chili recipe.

"I have chili in the slow cooker at home, it should be ready in a couple hours." The chili may have been for Nick and me, but now I had a reason to make some cornbread without his complaining. Leon seemed to love everything that I made for him in Journey, and now I could cook for him again.

I caught Lori watching Leon as he held his hand out to me. She looked over her glasses, leaning back with her head cocked. "Well, doesn't he seem like a good reason to take some time off?"

"Not just some time." Leon wrapped his arm around my torso with his hand resting on my hip. "I would like to resign her from her position so I may take her home. Excuse me, let me introduce myself." He held out his right hand. "I am Leon Sterling."

Lori was an animated person, and before Leon she was no different. She looked as if she was going to explode, her lips pinched as she trembled, trying to remain composed and not squeal again. She had two extremely masculine sons; just as with Ruby, I had become Lori's work daughter over the years.

Lori took a step forward, grasped Leon's hand with all her force, and thrust him into her chest. "I'm just so excited to meet you," she squealed with pure delight. "I'm Lori Smithstone and I approve Nora's resignation."

In the parking lot, there was a moment of calmness as I sat staring out my windshield. It may have started as calmness, but it was growing into panic, fueled by the realization that everything was stacked against me.

"I can't quit. I'm not allowed into Canada for the next nine years, ten months, one week, and three days!" There was more than that—he was King Leon. He was a *king*. Marriages didn't work the same way for the average person as it did royals. I was a mutt through and through. I couldn't tell you my heritage because my family didn't care; life was about them, not their ancestors. "I don't come from a royal bloodline." I lowered my head against the steering wheel. "None of this is going to be possible. I just need to go back in there and tell Lori it was a mistake. I can't lose this job." My heart was racing, my hands were going numb from all the trembling.

"Nora," Leon's hand felt cold in my sweaty hand, "are you all right?"

"I... I..." I couldn't breathe. "Do you like cornbread?"

CHAPTER 28

The lingering remnants of my dream replayed in my mind: Leon pinning me against the examination room wall. My eyes stayed closed a little longer as I tried to keep that dream alive in my mind. I could feel the warmth on Leon's breath and the silkiness of his lips. Then I could feel the fear rising within myself when Leon shapeshifted into Kek and spoke those dreaded words.

That was enough to get me going for the day. It was a little after six in the morning; I worked at nine and I wanted to go for a run to clear my mind.

After brushing my teeth and washing my face, I slipped into my favorite running shorts, white with teal pineapples, paired with the matching teal tank top with the built-in bra. Nick should have left for work at six, so fortunately I wasn't in for a lecture about modesty. He would have classified it as too seductive to be worn in public because the tank was more of a bralette and the shorts were a little on the cheeky side. But this was my favorite running outfit; I wanted to wear something uplifting if I couldn't remain in last night's fantasy without a horror ending.

"Seriously, Nora," Nick grumbled as I walked out of my bedroom, "is that really what you wear to go running every morning?"

I walked into the kitchen. "Can you not today? I already don't feel the best this morning; this run is going to be hard enough." I felt like I had a horrible hangover and had gotten hit by a train. I had taken some aspirin, though I figured the fresh morning air was going to help clear my mind.

"No, Nora," Nick pointed his finger at me, "you are not going out for a run this morning."

"I want pancakes," I whined. I knew this was going to get under his skin. "So if I want to wear my favorite running outfit, I need to go for a run. Maybe you just need to go with me to make sure that I am safe."

"Or," he griped, "maybe you should go put some real clothes on and stop running around in your underwear."

It was after six—he should have been at work. My hand trembled as I raised it up to pull a glass from the top shelf. "Go to work," I grumbled.

The trembling continued as I filled the glass up from the tap, with Mr. Doctor watching my every movement. There was an ache in the pit of my stomach.

Setting my glass of water down—there was no way I was going to be able to hold it up to my lips with Nick watching—I went over to the refrigerator. If Nick was still here, I could just make us breakfast. At this point, it didn't seem like he was going to let me out the door.

In the refrigerator was the whole slow cooker, base and all. I wanted to chuckle, but I could tell Nick was on the edge this morning. I studied the slow cooker; there was a first for everything. "Umm... Thanks for putting the chili away last night. Why are you still home?"

Nick was standing behind the refrigerator door when I closed it. "Because I told the hospital I needed the rest of the weekend off when Russell called me to find out why you hadn't shown up for your shift. I was going to go back to Balvin today now that you are safe to have my mother check out my heart. But since you have decided to run around in your underwear in public again, I'm staying put."

"Blah, blah, blah." I wasn't really listening to him—I was

hungry. "Hey, if I make you eggs, sausage, and breakfast potatoes, will you at least try the pancakes if I make them?"

"No." Nick crossed his arms against his chest, leaning against the refrigerator.

My head dropped to the side. "Please," I whined. "I want pancakes, but I don't just want to make them for myself." This man was unbearable at times. He wanted a relationship yet despised my cooking. How was the relationship going to work? I didn't want to eat out all the time. It was these little things that would turn into big things and proved we weren't meant for each other.

I glared into his eyes. Though he was physically huge, I wasn't intimidated. "Maybe eating some pancakes will give you enough comfort to relax a little. I am wearing the proper clothing to go out running. And if you want to start on something that is bad for you, my pancakes are not going to rot your teeth out like those gross pops you drink all day. Do you think your mother is going to be happy to hear about all the caffeine you drink? I don't have a medical degree, but I still know that they are not good for your heart."

"Are you done?" Nick sneered.

"Nope." I gave him a sly grin. "My pancakes are good hangover cures."

"I'm not hungover," he grumbled, "are you?"

I pouted, pushing out my bottom lip. "Please? I will even make it into a fun shape for you."

"No," his head nodded toward the living room, "but he might."

"He might?" I glared at Nick. I was already tired of his attitude this morning. "Do you have a guest?"

"Ugh." Nick pinched the bridge of his nose. "How many times did I tell you that you were pushing yourself too much for no reason? Life is not a fairy tale; he's not going to remember you. Just like you didn't remember him or me when you decided to bring a guy home yesterday."

"No." I shook my head. "There's no way I brought a guy home."

But Nick wouldn't joke about something like that. Oh god, I was feeling sick—what if it was Ivan? Susan could have told him where I was. I wouldn't put it past him to drug me after all these years of rejections. At this point, there was no telling what happened. I already didn't feel right and couldn't recall most of yesterday.

"No, no, no." Nick swiftly wrapped his arms around me, preventing me from falling. "That's enough of this; you are not going to work today." He examined me, leaning closer. "You don't remember bringing a guy home last night?"

I just wanted to drop to the floor and curl up in a ball. I couldn't remember going to work at the bar or even eating yesterday. There was a knot of fear and confusion growing in my throat—I could remember our lunch together, then it got sketchy from there.

Nick's broad hands pressed my head into his stone chest. The warmth of his breath warmed my ear. "I'm not mad at you—truthfully, I'm more worried about you than anything. I will handle this guy situation for you, but first you have to promise me that you will come back to Balvin with me and agree to every test that I request."

He didn't give me another moment to think about it, his hands moving to my face so I would look into his eyes. "Nora, I'm serious about this; you need to come back with me. This isn't normal for you to not remember last night's events or for me to find you passed out."

Inhaling, I pressed my hand to Nick's chest. I had two shifts today, then I would take it easy tomorrow. "I'm fine." I stood up and reached for my water glass, glaring at my trembling hand. It was only going to make things worse in Nick's medical-driven mind. "I have tomorrow off, so I promise you I will take it easy."

"It's Friday, not Saturday." Nick pressed his hand against my forehead.

"Nora." Another masculine voice reminded me it wasn't just the two of us.

The way he said my name wasn't the way Jordan, Justin, Russell, Sean, or even Gordon did. It was soft and sweet, filling me with warmth, then with sorrow that it was just a hallucination.

"Nora," Nick said, "do you think you are okay to make it back to your room by yourself?"

I inhaled again. I was being ridiculous, drowning myself in sorrow. I had messed up last night and the guilt was overwhelming. I just needed to pull it together and handle the mess that I created. I swiped under my eyes swiftly. "So, pancakes are off the table. How about French toast? I know that you eat sandwiches, so it's sort of the same thing, but you can't pick off the ingredients from the bread."

"No, Princess, I will make you pancakes and anything else you want. As long as you promise me to eat."

The way he said "Princess" took me right back to that first vision when King Leon had said it to the other king. This wasn't a simulation to fill me with horror, but a trigger to yesterday's events. He had called me Princess in the optical yesterday. This was Leon, coming into the kitchen, offering to cook me breakfast—not a strange man or Ivan.

"Wow." I giggled; I didn't know what else to do. Yesterday was such a blur. "What happened yesterday?" I was tired and slightly out of it, but Leon still felt like a dream.

I watched as Nick glared at Leon; however, Leon's attention was directed toward me. Not checking me out, but with the same worry that filled Nick's eyes. This likely wasn't the grand reunion that he had envisioned, and certainly wasn't the one I had. I needed him to stop worrying about my health. I was fine.

"Did Susan drug me or something after she left the optical?" I asked awkwardly. "I mean, I wouldn't put it past her to do it. She likes to hand out pills like candy so she can flex her medical knowledge."

"Did you drug her?" Nick sneered at Leon.

"Get real, man," Leon growled. "I did not drug YOUR GIRLFRIEND."

Wow, this was getting ugly fast. My shoulders dropped and my head fell to the side—it stung to hear Leon call me Nick's girlfriend. My bottom lip trembled, tears loading onto their exit deck. "Why did you call me that?"

Leon gestured toward Nick. "That's how he introduced himself to me. He even made me sleep on my own couch."

"Did you call Sean? He would tell you the truth." I didn't wait for Leon's answer, I was in full panic mode. "Don't believe Nick," I grumbled. "He's territorial over me. Not because I am his girlfriend but because we are friends that look out for each other. Like yesterday, he *pretended* to be my boyfriend so I could show him Susan's true colors. And I guess last night."

"I was just protecting you," Nick interrupted. "I came home to find a random guy here with you. And what needs to be highlighted was the fact that you were passed out. I've been watching you drain your batteries, and I was concerned that he was taking advantage of the situation."

"That's fair," I gestured at Leon without removing my focus from Nick, "but why did you make him sleep on his own couch when we have another bedroom?" After the words left my lips, I realized I had repeated Leon's words, and they were not correct.

"Leon...*your* couch?"

Leon splayed his hands wide, palms up. "My apartment."

I could see him having an apartment in Joe's building, but I didn't understand. "Joe's apartment?"

He shook his head. "My apartment complex—all four buildings."

I tried to think back to that first day back in Puth, but it was all a blur from the horror of being ripped from the only place that felt like home. This was too much to add to everything else today.

Nick's lip curled and his eyebrows lowered. I knew this look; this was his disappointed look. It had to be registering who Leon was.

I gave him a wistful grin before glancing back to Leon. "Did you introduce yourself to him last night?"

"No." Leon sat back and crossed his arms against his chest. "The man was on a roid-rage. I just told him I was Sean's older brother."

That wasn't helpful—Nick and Sean hadn't hit it off with each other. Sean was way too vocal about Nick staying in his lane. Here and now, I could see Nick's new frustration, but these boys turned into two-year-olds while I was sleeping. "Both of you just introduce yourselves to each other and work this out."

"I am Nick Yaman." Nick leaned across the counter with his hand out. "Nora and I are only roommates. Well—I appointed myself as her personal bodyguard."

I couldn't help but grin. Despite how much he criticized me on various things, I still appreciated him. "That is true and no matter how much you drove me crazy, I always appreciated you. You are one of the good ones. Don't let anyone tell you different."

"I am Leon Sterling," Leon said proudly, breaking our moment. "For watching over my Leonora Ann, you are welcome to stay in this apartment until the end of your residency."

He was the second person to call me Leonora Ann and I liked it. There was a sense that when I set out in June, I had succeeded in becoming me and losing Leonora Marigold. My life may not look like I wanted it to, but to them I was Leonora Ann.

That thought only stayed with me for a second as my thoughts drifted right back to Joe. He was the one who took me in; he was the one who agreed to allow Nick to stay with me.

"But Leon—" I gestured around the apartment. "I thought

this was Joe Salary's place."

"No, he manages the properties for me so I don't have to come down here to do it. In fact, with everything now, I am considering selling all my properties in the States." Leon tapped his chest.

I recalled that night around the fire when all Leon did was try to keep me close to him. After that, he never stopped trying to keep me close. Leon endlessly made me feel wanted.

My mind flipped again as I walked over to Leon, returning to that parking garage the first night in Puth. My teeth sank into my bottom lip as I stopped at the stool before him and leaned against the island. "Speaking of Joe, were you aware of his little scheme ten years ago?"

Leon stretched his arm out to me. "No." He shook his head slowly, then stood up when I wouldn't take his hand. "I would have never allowed it to happen." His arms tightened around me as he drew me into his chest. His head rested against mine as his soft words warmed my ear. "Even with these results, if I could go back in time, I would have stopped you from ever entering that cave. This is never what I wanted for you."

He moved back to examine me, and all I could do was stare at him until he blurred. I did believe him, but my tired mind was playing out the different scenarios that could have happened if I failed. Ultimately, my mind froze.

Leon's thumb wiped across my cheekbone. "Gordon and Joe only told me the truth the other day since they said that they had told you the truth. To me, you were my promotional prize for ordering so many boxes of fountain syrups." He gave me a soft sideways grin. "It was the best thing that I had ever won. I have never felt so rich in my life."

"I take it that you are not going to return me." I wiped my other cheek off and chuckled. "Though, if you wanted to, I think I have warmed Peggy up enough that she would take me in."

"Nope, you are mine now." His lips rested on my hair. "Do you feel all right?"

"I'm just tired; I haven't been sleeping well." I didn't want him to know why I was exhausted. I didn't want him to feel like it was his fault for my current state.

I straightened up in his embrace and watched as his eyes moved up to my bun. His beautiful, bold new features felt so surreal. I was just waiting for Kek to transform into his real self before me.

"Is something wrong?" Leon whispered so as not to let Nick hear. "You look confused."

My mind drifted back to that hallway as I listened to Calvin and Ruby talk about Leon and me. His greatest fear was that I was going to find out the truth and not see him as him anymore. Never until this point had I ever looked at him differently.

"I'm sorry—when I close my eyes, I'm with you. With my eyes open, I still go back to what I said in the optical. I'm not used to the new—er, the old you—yet. And this has nothing to do with age or your past condition or even you, really. He's dead, but in the back of my head I am waiting for him to transform before me." No matter how quiet I was trying to be, Nick was just on the other side of the island. I wouldn't put it past him to be listening, considering his feelings about Leon.

"Nora." Leon's hand moved to my bun. "It was never fair for you to end up in that cave with him. Again, it was never what I wanted for you. I can't imagine all of this is easy for you." My hair fell on my shoulders as he released my hair tie.

This was his signature move; I assumed part of the motivation behind it was because Kek wouldn't have known about it. It was the most comforting thing he could do. What wasn't comfortable was the fact that it never once crossed my mind this morning when I put up my hair where my heart came from. I just plopped it on my head as I fixed up my bun.

"What is this?" Leon chuckled as he lifted my heart from the top of my head and held it out into the sunlight.

"Dude, that was lame," Nick snickered, pulling my attention away from Leon.

I watched as Nick scooped a cup of flour from the jar and plopped it into the flour sifter. Next, he added four teaspoons of baking powder, a quarter-teaspoon of baking soda, and then half a teaspoon of salt.

"I don't care who you are." He sifted the dry mixture in the clear glass mixing bowl. "Magic tricks to pick up a girl are just as corny as pickup lines."

"It wasn't a magic trick." Leon tossed the rock over to Nick. "Maybe you should ask your roommate how many years she has had a rock hiding in her hair."

I held up both hands and mouthed "Ten years" to Nick.

Nick frowned. "What?"

"Ten years, Nick. I left it with Leon when I was deported, but yesterday he gave it back to me."

"You can just keep it." Leon tapped his chest. "I have her heart right here."

"Right... After six days," Nick grumbled as he stirred in the buttermilk.

Leon rested his arms on my shoulders and peered down at me. "Well, if you can't see that there is something special about her after only spending an hour with her, there must be something wrong with you."

Brring...Brring...Brring...Brring...Brring...Brring...

Lucky for Nick, a cell phone in the living room was ringing, breaking the moment.

"I need to get that." Leon leaned in and gave me a swift peck. "I love you."

He took his call in the office as I sat up at the counter before Nick. The man that hated all baked goods, pastries, and anything else in that category was making pancakes. This was just too much; never did I think I would see this day.

All I could do was grin at Nick in bemusement. "Why are you making pancakes when you don't even like them?"

He flipped the pancake onto a plate then poured more batter into the skillet. "I may not like them, but that doesn't mean I won't make them for you." Nick glanced up. "You never got the chance to see me. We never got the chance to live together because you were constantly drowning yourself in work."

I peered into his eyes until I couldn't take it anymore. With a huff, I turned my sights toward the counter. "I was never going to look at you the way you wanted me to. From the start you knew about Leon, so I don't know what you expected to happen between us."

"What about now?" He moved another pancake over to the plate. "Were your six days still worth it?"

"Yes." If I was realistic, it might have been a "*maybe*." I had spent less than two hours with Leon since he returned. But my heart was telling me I was right.

"Do you trust him? I'll take the next week off and stay here with you if you do not trust him." He didn't even give me a chance to reply. "Maybe that's a good idea. I'm going to stay in town this week."

"Whoa, calm down. If you are taking a week off, it will be for a vacation to relax. Hanging out here seems like it will be far from relaxing for you."

"I know, right?" Nick's lip curled up, exposing his dreadful tooth in his mischievous smile. "You two are sickening to be around already."

"Not yet," I tittered, "but when I get some energy up, it's going to get worse."

"Oh, god," Nick whined.

Since he was using the skillet on the island, I pulled out two pans: one for eggs and the other for sausages. They felt like fifty-pound weights—I needed to pull it together.

With the sausages cooking, I leaned back and nudged Nick. "Will you eat scrambled eggs?"

"Only if you put cheese in them."

For whatever reason, this excited me. "Hey, there you go." I bounced his shoulder again. "I like this positivity."

"Oh, whatever." He rolled his eyes, then returned to the pancakes. "I've never once complained about your cooking."

It was as if I wasn't present at breakfast; Leon and Nick carried the entire conversation about the apartment, the complex, and I couldn't even tell you what else as I zoned out a few times. In spite of that, it wasn't enough to not notice how Leon was true to himself. He was a charmer and a man of his people. It was as if Nick forgot his vexation with Leon and they were just two guys hanging out.

"All right, you two." Nick stood, picking up his plate. "I'm going to pack up to head back to Balvin." Moving the plate into his left hand, he held his right hand out to Leon. "Great to finally meet you. I will be in contact with you about this place."

Nick then set his plate down, holding his arms out to me. "I'll always be here for you when you need answers or protection."

"Or as a friend to randomly text me to remind me how awful hot showers are for you. I don't need you worrying about me; I'm not going to dress like I did when I worked at the bar anymore. But I am so incredibly thankful for everything you have done for me." I stood up on my tippy toes and gently kissed his cheek.

CHAPTER 29

Leon cleaned the kitchen while I sat at the island and kept him company. I offered to do the dishes, but I wasn't allowed to do anything but relax thanks to my current state at breakfast. Leon kept a close eye on me, making sure I was eating and tapping me a couple times when I zoned out. Leon, being Leon, would feed me a chunk of his pancake so I could try his syrup-to-pancake ratio or for some other silly reason. He would squeeze my trembling hand under the table and give me the softest grin, a silent promise to take care of me. This was never what I wanted him to wake up to.

After washing dishes, we hung out in the living room watching a movie.

The front door clicking woke me up as Leon slid off the couch. "No," I mumbled as I let myself fall into the balled-up blanket now in Leon's spot. I was on the upward swing, feeling a little better after breakfast and my little catnap on Leon, but that didn't mean I was ready to give it up yet.

Leon's arms slid under me. He curled them up, causing me to roll into his chest in the cradle position.

"What are you doing?" I chuckled. "I thought we were going to snuggle on the couch a little longer."

"I heard what's been going on down here, and you worked yourself up yesterday because of everything." He stood up and started toward the bedroom. "Then you just collapsed in your car. And today—"

I cut him off. "I'm sorry." I didn't want to talk about it. "There was an altercation with Susan, then Nick and I got into it. I wasn't expecting to see you, then Susan showed up again. All at once everything was falling apart and, worse, everything I was working toward was collapsing. I was just released from the one job that I enjoyed. I don't enjoy working in bars, and for the bakery it's educational but tiresome at four in the morning. The worst of all of it is I am banned from entering Canada for the next ten years. Even if you wanted me to, I can't go home with you. And I would never make you leave your kingdom for me. I can't describe what I felt or what happened next. It just didn't feel good." So much for not talking about it.

Leon curled me tighter against him for a second longer, then lowered me onto the bed. I had no objection; I just wanted to take a nap, preferably for the next nine years. Perhaps, since we were dealing with paranormal things, he was going to put me under a spell and let me rest for the next nine years. Then he would return to the States and wake me with a kiss, just in time for me to be able to enter Canada again.

I tightened my arms around his neck. "Stay with me," I whispered.

"Forever." Gently he straddled my waist, tightened himself around me, then rolled me onto his stomach. "I am going to be here to take care of you."

After fearing the darkness for the last couple months, I felt safe again. Leon's darkness wasn't wicked; it was full of strength and authority. Everything was going to be all right—I just needed to surrender myself to these new paths.

My lips moved to his forehead. "I want you next to me in any form, as long as it's still you."

His hair, his skin, and even his eyes had changed, but his lips had not. They were still inviting me to make his heart my home. My hair shadowed us into our own little world. His lips lit everything within me, guiding me down his jaw to his neck as his warmth moved up to my fingertips. His chest collapsed for a second as my bottom lip glided against his neck.

I didn't need a vision to realize what I had just done. I had kissed him in the same spot that had marked him damned for the last six hundred years. "I'm so sorry." I moved from him onto the bed.

I had seen Kek give him that damned kiss. I deserved to spend eternity alone.

"That's it." Leon got up and went into the bathroom.

I drew up my legs to my chest and hid my face in my arms. Nick was right—I was toxic to Leon.

I heard the tub faucet running, though I had never used the tub; I preferred showers over baths. Though, this was weird. Did he storm out to take a bath? I peered over my arms to see Leon returning to the bedroom in just his black boxer briefs.

Moving my gaze up, I admired how Leon's former salt-white hair was now like pepper speckled against his chest. He was no longer copy-paper white; his chest was a new, desirable gold.

My head dropped into my arms as I felt a rush of guilt flood over me.

No sooner did I drop my head than I was thrust over Leon's shoulder.

"Umm," I tittered, "what are you doing?"

"Someone lost her luster." His hand ran up and down my back. "I'm going to see if I can find it again."

"I didn't lose my luster." I closed my eyes, my stomach starting to turn. "I've been told I have been nothing but toxic to you. For your safety, it's best if you just go back to Canada."

Leon lowered me, dropping my legs into warm water, then my torso. "The only—"

"Wait," I interrupted him, "do you still have your underwear on?" I was still fully dressed in the tub.

"Yes," Leon chuckled as he lowered me all the way into the tub. "Now, I was saying..."

Sitting back, I squinted, a mischievousness smile curving my lips. "You do know that they invented these machines that wash your clothes. Nowadays you don't have to bathe and wash your clothes at the same time."

A perplexed look dawned on his face, the corner of his lip quirking and a thumbprint design appearing on his forehead. I started giggling like a fool at my own corny joke and his expression.

"There she is." He stole a peck then climbed into the tub opposite me. "Like I was trying to say, the people around here are toxic. You are not like any of them or remotely toxic."

It wasn't like I wanted to throw Nick under the bus, but Leon needed to know a professional had given me that advice. "I'm not so sure about that—Nick was the one that told me. He's a professional when it comes to that stuff."

"Yeah, I know." Leon pinched his eyebrows together. "I'm trying to give him the benefit of the doubt, considering he was never taught how to deal with a vampire transitioning back to human. Plus, he watched over you like a hawk. It drove Sean crazy, but I respect him for doing something I couldn't do."

"That one night Sean came down, you should have seen them together. I thought Sean was cold with me the first time we met; he was ridiculous to Nick. All Nick was..." I needed to stop—that night was not something I wanted to talk to Leon about, ever. "Anyways, I agree with Nick that I am toxic to you... I just kissed your neck, even after I saw what happened to you. I should have known better. That wasn't acceptable. I need to do better, and I am sorry."

"Not toxic," Leon crossed his arms against his chest, "just awesome, and going forward it should happen more often." He winked. "Daily—actually, since all you have is time on your hands now, hourly."

"Hourly?" I looked down and grabbed the hem of my tank top, pulling it off. I felt like I was being constricted by a snake; wet clothes were the worst. Especially now with my body on the fritz. "Someone is a little needy." After trying to wring out some of the water, I set the tank top on the edge of the tub.

"Nora," Leon rubbed his hand up my lower leg to get my attention, "are you all right?"

His hand on my leg sent me right back into that cave with Kek. Swiftly I drew my legs to my chest, brushing my leg off as if there was something on it. I wrapped my arms around my knees, trying to calm myself down.

"Hey," Leon moved closer, "did I do something wrong?" The worry was heavy in his eyes.

"Of course not." I leaned in and gently placed a sweet kiss on his lips. "You know, sometimes I startle easily." Leon had heard me scream many times after he or Sean had startled me, so I figured this was believable.

"Your giggles after your screams were always the best. Not saying I was trying to scare you, but still the best."

"I know that you would never." I gave him a soft grin, but there was one burning question that I wanted the answer to. "What happened?"

His hips shifted and his hands sunk below the water. "May I wash my underwear while I tell you?" His lips puckered as he tried to hold his laughter in.

I was going to call his bluff; I drew up one leg and pulled my shorts off under the water. Then I let the shorts hang off my index finger. "Would you mind doing mine as well?"

He snorted. "Are we even now?"

"If it's making you uncomfortable, you'll have to look away while I stand up. There is no way I am going to be able to get those back on in the water without sloshing everywhere."

"No, no." He fussed under the water for a second, almost breaking the water tension with the side of his face. "So how far back do you want to go?"

"From the start, minus the things I have already seen." There was no sense in making him relive that horrible day, though I wanted to hear the reason behind it. I was also curious where I fell into this; was I going to be his fifth, sixth, or possibly seventh wife? True love had to break the curse; was it possible to have more than one true love over the years?

"My mother, in today's world, would have been classified as a Scandinavian princess. Even without today's technology for communication, my parents grew up knowing each other. They were best friends from day one, so when it was time for my father to take a wife, there was only one choice for him. Above all, they were best friends until the end of their days. My mother passed away from an illness and a week after her burial, my father passed away from a broken heart. A week later, at twenty-three, I ascended to the throne."

With his legs to the sides of me, I sat forward with my knees against my chest again. The tub was comfortably long, but I wanted to be a little closer to him.

He tapped one of the switches on the wall. "Their love was pure." The lights turned off, then there was another click, and I assumed he had tapped one of the other switches as the ceiling lit up like the night sky filled with stars above. The twinkling lights weren't enough to see Leon, who was still across from me. The sound of another click filled the air, and a soft blue glow from below drew my attention from the ceiling to the water.

"This is incredible." I glanced back up to the ceiling.

"I take it that you never tried the switches?"

"I never used the bath; I like my hot showers."

"I like your hot showers too," he chuckled. "That was the best part of my day, combatting that torture line you hooked me up to."

"Torture line," I tittered, "more like your lifeline. I would have thought your other line was more of a torture line."

"Yeah," his blue eyes widened, "that was too. When the coldness began to creep up my arm, it was okay, because I knew that you were going to be right next to me." He tapped his pec with his finger, though only his middle finger made contact with his chest. He wasn't talking with his hands; he was signaling me to him. Perhaps the water was cooling off and he wanted something warm against him. Truthfully, he didn't need a reason; I wanted to be next to him.

I scooted around until my back was against his chest, his arms around me. His fingers intertwined with mine.

"It was soothing to listen to you softly talk about plans for your future that included me and our future family. That was my lifeline. I only wish you got to be more you throughout the day."

"I didn't want to do anything that would make you uncomfortable. Before that afternoon, I just wanted to be in your space. Afterwards, I had to put all that aside—it wasn't fair to you since you were unconscious. I needed to be respectful, not that I wasn't before, I just needed to be cautious then and now."

"No," he tightened his arms and his head moved between my shoulder and neck, "you don't." He kissed my neck, playfully growling at me. "I'm human now." His teeth tickled my neck.

I had so many questions; more and more kept popping up. "Have you—?"

I stopped, feeling like it wasn't a good idea to go on. I understood he did what he needed to survive, but it had been hard enough to see Gunner Louise's fate.

"No." He sat back. "Strictly animals. Mostly foxes, rabbits, coyotes, or anything that was becoming a nuisance. Since I could survive on that, I never touched humans, and I couldn't change anyone—I only had upper fangs; I would have needed lower ones to do that."

I couldn't imagine this was very comfortable for him to talk about. I started to move forward, back to my spot, but I didn't get very far. He squeezed me against him.

"Please stay," his cheek rested against mine, "unless you are uncomfortable."

"I think it's more like I'm going to make you uncomfortable with all my questions."

The water sloshed around the tub and over its edge. I don't know how he managed it, but he turned me around so we were face to face. Then he dimmed the tub light so there was a soft glow just as above us.

"Never have you made me feel uncomfortable or even like I was a monster, but now it feels like you see me as broken. And yes, the last few months have not helped that, but I am not. Physically, I am a twenty-six-year-old male, just like Sean or Trevor." His hand moved to my cheek. "I'm sorry that everything happened the way it did. Despite that, in so many ways you healed me. Let's just go back to the Monday before that afternoon."

That's all I wanted; that peace of sleeping on his chest on the couch with my mind and body still. Yet I couldn't get past what I heard that Tuesday afternoon from Frank. And Leon was the only one that was going to be able to clarify it for me.

I leaned forward. "You knew my plan—why did you make me wait to hear it from Frank instead of just telling me the truth?"

"Because I wasn't ready for you to move on. I didn't want to hurt you, but with all things considered, I needed you to move on. I was cursed and there was no way around it. How was I supposed to tell you that because of love, I could never love someone?"

"You never loved me?"

"Oh, Nora," his eyes were glistening pools, "I loved you and I love you. That is not what I meant. My curse prevented me from ever moving forward with someone."

It felt like he was moving forward with me that week and I didn't notice anything holding him back. "I'm lost."

"That day you saw Gavin with me in the cave, what you didn't see was that Bartholomew was the one that chased down Kek. Bartholomew had him cornered, and Kek told him that the only way he could die was if my true love killed him. He explained to him everything that Gordon taught you and told him I couldn't just bite her so we could live happily ever after. Only I was damned and I couldn't pass it on. Kek told him to watch his neck—the first time I tasted human blood, I was going to be complete. Going forward, I would only be able to live off human blood. Starving me was the only way for him to kill me."

That didn't answer anything, only opened the door for more questions. Kek couldn't have been created just to destroy Leon. They were from two different time periods. There had to be more to Kek. "I don't get how only your true love could kill Kek... What if he bit a thousand other men?"

"He could have bitten other people, but not that many. Every time he transformed someone; he would age. It would take a decade off his life to the point that if he bit too many people, it could kill him. And when he died, we were all to die as well, or so we thought. Oh, and I didn't know this until afterwards, but having him around that week was weakening me. Just being in his presence for long enough could have killed me. At the time, I thought my curse was coming to an end and I was going to perish."

Crossing my arms against my chest, I let myself fall into the side of the tub. That really didn't answer my original question, but the next question was already on deck. "Why didn't a past lover step up and free you? Over six hundred years, at least one of them should have loved you enough to do it."

I was fishing; I wanted to hear how many lovers a six-hundred-thirty-two-year-old man had. On second thought, it made me cringe—what if he was like Ivan back in the day? Maybe this wasn't a good idea to be in the bath with him, let alone sitting on his lap.

It was too late now, but that didn't stop me from slowly sliding against the wall back to my end of the tub.

"Nora," he rested his arms on the outer edge of the tub, "what are you thinking right now?"

"How many girls Ivan has been with times six hundred."

"No, not even close. That week before my father passed away, he told me that I was expected to take a wife to be our queen. He added that kings all around the world were going to throw their daughters at me. He told me once my heart had found her, I would be the richest man alive. For over six hundred nine years, I have held onto his words. Even before that, I held onto finding the love that I saw between my parents. I was never going to ask anyone to take on Kek for me. I wasn't human; we would never have a family. I never aged, but she would until she would be gone. I would have gone from the richest man to spending eternity the poorest to lose her."

It must have been a lonely six hundred six years watching everyone around him progressing in life while he stayed put. Then losing them and watching the next generation repeat the same cycle. I wouldn't fault him for remaining a bachelor either.

So why was he being sweet to me when he had no intention of finding love? What was I to him? He had told me that he loved me right away, but now he said he wasn't going to love anyone because of his curse. He told me I was his professional caregiver, but he wanted me instead. This was getting more confusing. I just needed to stop asking questions.

I drew my knees up to my chest again. I was going to sit here and just listen to what he had to say. Even in the warmth of the water, I still had a chill and a weird sense of unreality.

Leon cut off my spiraling thoughts. "But there has only been one and she was an accident, a total accident. I wasn't supposed to fall for her—she told me her plans a thousand times. She was going to handle a few things, then leave to start a fresh life somewhere else. That was the thing: she was going to leave, so there was no time for anything to start up between us. I could enjoy her, then not worry because she would be gone before anything got serious. Love is supposed to take time to grow and bloom."

Was I just his toy for the week? The anger within me was

enough to cause my hands to shake and my fingers to tingle. I was no one's toy; I believed in Miss Gemma Ann's words and was saving everything for that one, not to be someone's loaner toy for a week.

"Strike kissing to awaken your one true love off your list as well," I grumbled. Maybe everything we had ever been told about love was wrong. Perhaps we were to find our own stories and not just believe fairy tales. "That's another fable I learned wasn't true." I huffed as I rested my cheek on my arm and lowered my voice. "It's possible that I belonged to Kek, since I was just your toy." Keeping my mouth quiet wasn't working well.

"Are you all right?"

His words bounced through me, my heart racing, my fingertips numb. I had a sinking feeling that things were going to go sideways soon. "Truthfully, no." At this point, I had nothing to lose. "I am so confused, and the more questions I ask, the worse it gets. I'm listening to you, but one moment it feels like you have the same feelings for me that I do for you, then the next it feels like that's not the case at all. But I get it. I didn't slay Kek in the name of true love. I didn't even know that you were cursed, six-hundred-thirty-two-years old, or even a king. I killed Kek because this crazed bear turned into a god that was talking about making me his queen and killing another king. I thought it was some old guy in Europe. I didn't care. I even told Kek I am an American, I bow for no king. They serve no purpose in this modern world anymore; they are just a tourist attraction."

"Nora..."

"What?"

"Nora, please," Leon moved closer to me, "you need to take a couple breaths for me."

Not happening—I was volcanic. I was mad at myself for falling for him and the nerve of him to just use me for a week of fun when I thought it was more than that. "No," I sneered as I pointed my trembling index finger at him. "What I did out of love was fight to keep you alive when everyone kept telling me it was your time to go. Fuck that. I didn't know that you were transforming back to being a human; I didn't know that you were the king. The only thing I knew was in my heart I loved you and was going to do everything I could to save you. Because it didn't even take me six days to know that I loved you. From the sounds of it, all you were doing was being sweet on me because I was leaving anyway. To drive it home, you must have staged that make out session with Sean."

"No," his head moved side to side, "not even true."

"You got what you wanted; I left Canada. In fact, you're free—I'm banned there for the next ten years."

"Okay," he wrapped his arms around me, then leaned back so I was against his chest again, "no more questions for today. This was too much, and I can tell you're still not even feeling well."

I tried to push myself up, but his arms just tightened around me. Faintness was creeping through me; I had nothing left to fight him but my words. "You are a jerk like the rest of them to think you were going to just use me for a week and an asshole for making me believe it was more."

CHAPTER 30

Slowly I lifted my eyes to see the blurry white numbers on the mirrored alarm clock—5:30. That meant Nick was leaving soon for work. I needed to catch him before he left to ask him a favor.

Gradually I got up, wrapping myself in my blanket, and waddled past the kitchen into the living room, only far enough to fall onto the couch. "Nick," I whined, "I don't feel well. At 7:45 will you call Lori and tell her I have a doctor's note to stay home today?" I felt like a sleepless ball of anxiety. Mr. Know-it-All was right; I was burnt out and breaking down. I rolled to face the back of the couch. "If I tell you that you were right about the jobs and agree to go lift with you every Sunday, will you please write me that note?"

Someone crawled onto the couch behind me. It wasn't Nick—it was Leon. "No," I whined as I rested my head against the cushion. I didn't want it to be him.

"Nora," he whispered, "do you want me to move?"

"I don't even want you here because that means last night was real. And if last night was real, I'm supposed to be mad at you for using me as a toy or something."

His head lowered against my back. "No, I wasn't using you. I was so torn up about everything. More than anything, I wanted you to stay because I wanted you. The man that was cursed because of love was in love with you. I was all mixed up with emotions. First, I was frightened you were going to get hurt somehow. That fear was starting to come true when Ruby told me about your visions. And that's the second thing; I couldn't confront you about them because I was afraid you were going to find out the truth about me. Sean was my only option to see if I was causing them. I was also hoping that Sean and I could work out how to stop them."

"Sean already told me about that day," I grumbled. "He doesn't like the way you kiss."

Leon rolled me over and peered down at me, looking slightly disgruntled with pinched lips and raised eyebrows. "In my defense, he was kissing a monster." Something must have snapped within him, his playfulness leaving as he lowered his head so I could no longer see his face. "For the first time in six hundred six years, I felt like my old self again. In your eyes I wasn't a monster; in no way did you treat me differently or were overly cautious with me; you only saw me as Leon. I was playing with fire, and I knew all that was going to burn up if you didn't leave soon. I needed you to leave before the truth came out. Once you found out I was a monster, I would never be your Leon again. The sparkle in your eyes when I gazed into them would be replaced with fear."

Curse or no curse, he deserved to feel love. He had been trying to protect me from his curse. But I did not believe he was a monster. Hank would have never left me with Leon that first day if he thought he was a monster.

"No one—" I itched a path to his ear, "including yourself— had the right to call you a monster. In no way do I believe that you were a monster in all of your six hundred thirty-two years. In the last six hundred six years, all you had was a unique dietary requirement."

His soft, warm, wet cheek pressed against my cheek, his arms tightening even more around me. I could still take shallow breaths; I was going to let him have this moment without saying anything. His lips moved to my forehead, then he met my eyes. "Can I marry you? I mean, I plan on asking you properly, but I don't want to spend another minute of my life without you in it."

I wanted it all with him, but it wasn't possible. "No, I'm sorry."

Leon sat up as my words stabbed him. "What? Why?"

"I'm nothing—it would destroy your life to marry me. After six hundred six years, that would be unfair to you. I can't do it." This was the last thing I wanted, but it was the right thing to do.

"Princess," he lowered himself onto me, "please believe me, I wasn't using you. More than anything I didn't want you to leave. Losing you would destroy me. I love you so much."

"It's not that." Tenderly I ran my hand through his hair. "I am legally banned from your world. It's so unfair to you."

"No. After today, Leonora Marigold Carter never existed. Leonora Ann Hughes is a birthright citizen of Canada."

"Excuse me?" How was I going to disappear after twenty-three years? There are so many records; a person can't just be erased.

His lips curled up. "You don't stay twenty-six for six hundred six years unless you have friends in the records office. I hope you don't mind—we erased Nora Carter. Your parents thought that you should have your grandmother's middle name."

"What?" I stared into his eyes. The six-hundred-thirty-two-year-old man before me wasn't kidding around. He was being serious.

Sitting up, he raised my left hand as if he was going to kiss my ring, but it wasn't there. His brows hooded as he gazed down at my empty finger. After breakfast, I tried to wash the dishes and pulled my ring off while I was filling the sink. When Leon kicked me away, I swiped my ring, and it must have been out of habit that I put it back on my right hand.

"Sorry." I held up my right hand, then hunched down as I began to pull the ring off.

Swiftly Leon intercepted and removed the ring, then raised my left hand. "I'm doing this backwards again. This is your wedding band; I have your engagement ring back home." He moved the ring to the tip of my finger. "My father was right; after six hundred fifteen years, it was worth the wait. I wasn't looking, I wasn't expecting, but that first night I became the richest man. When I thought our chance had passed, you stayed beside me no matter what. I have never met someone that viewed love the same way I did. I would wait another six hundred thirty-two years just to have you in my life for six days." He slid the ring down my finger. "I want to take you home—*our* home that you were fighting so hard to protect. I will give you my heart, and it will always be me. The words you spoke to me every night I want to make true. I want your words to come to life. I want our family. I want to be able to show you that love I felt the first night forever. I will always be your warmth, like after a hot shower or an oversize mug of tea. I will always stand beside you even when everyone is going in the opposite direction. I will always follow my heart when it comes to you. Leonora Ann Hughes..." His head subtly raised along with his eyebrows. Straight creases appeared in his forehead—this wasn't the fun, baffled look; this was his sincere look. "Forever?"

I placed my thumbs behind his ears with my fingers in his hair. He moved against me as I lowered onto the couch. His legs shifted and I wrapped my legs around his. Every part of me was going to answer his question. I needed his forever; it needed to start now. I needed him near. I wanted to feel every part of him against me, almost as if we were one.

The way we were moving together, we were going to need a short engagement. There was no way I was going to be able to sustain my promise to myself. He felt so natural and right, he could have whatever he wanted right now as long as I got him.

His lips grazed my neck. "I feel like this is a positive distraction to soften your answer." His lips moved to mine. "Still amazing, but that cliff is going to be fatal for me if we are playing on the edge."

"No," I whispered to his lips.

"No?" he whined as I sank further into the couch under his weight. "Do you need some more time?"

I wasn't saying no to his original question; I was saying no to his anxious thought. "I mean yes."

"I understand." He pushed himself off me. "It's understandable. Everything is moving so fast now." His eyes were glistening. Gingerly he ran the side of his index finger against my cheek. "I don't want to lose you again." He reached for his T-shirt, draped over the back of the couch, then started to put it back on.

"Leon, stop." I pushed up on my elbows and he froze, with only the top of his head peeking out of the shirt. "You're not on a cliff," I chuckled. "The only thing I need is you, forever."

With that, the shirt was off again, and we were right back where we were a minute ago. He had to have some form of enchantment left in him—he was the best medicine, and my headache was gone.

A clear thought popped into my head. "Let's go to Sans City. It's an hour flight, and it takes fifteen minutes to get a marriage license. We could be married before five today."

He kissed my cheek. "I've already looked into that, but—" his forehead moved to rest between my breasts, "I've been sworn to not marry you until we return home."

"Really?"

"Yep, your parents want to be present." He continued without lifting his head up, "Gordon wants to be the one walking you down the aisle, and Ruby is holding on to having a little bride." Leon's head lifted. "And it's 7:00 p.m., by the way," he said, then his head plopped back to its original position.

It was a good spot, perfect for head itches and to hide my puzzled expression as I tried to figure out the date. Had I slept the night or only for a couple hours? "Umm...is today Friday or Saturday?"

"And with that," his head rose again, "I need to get some food in you. One more fainting episode and I have been instructed to take you to Balvin."

It was odd that he would have to take me to Balvin. I didn't know anyone in... My eyes rolled back when I realized why. "Why did you call Nick?" I whined. "He didn't need to be involved; he would just say it's from eating baked goods."

Leon moved to the other end on the couch, putting his T-shirt back on, then puffing his chest out. "More like I know that I'm striking and women faint in my presence—despite that, twice is too many times." He winked at me. "It's my stunningly charming smile."

"Well, the first time it was your smile, the second time it was your eyes. Maybe you should keep all your clothes on going forward. I really don't want to meet old man Dr. Walizer."

He turned toward me, seriousness in his eyes. "Nick thinks you need to have your head checked out. I told him he's just jealous of my masculinity."

"Serious," I chortled.

"Well, I'm a hunk again, so that part was true. And I did call him; he lived with you for at least the last month. I want to make sure there wasn't anything else going on besides the exhaustion."

I'm sure that Sean had filled him in on Nick's real intentions for me. Even so, he was trying to still look out for me. For that, he got a kiss on the cheek.

His hand moved to my forehead as if checking my temperature. "I will make you whatever you want to eat." He stood up, drawing his phone from his back pocket. "I know how to follow directions and find tutorials online."

Later, I laid in bed with my back against my pillows and my knees up waiting for Leon to finish up in the bathroom. We were to pick up Pharrell from his flight to Puth in the wee hours of the morning, and with my little blackouts, it was time to call it a night.

My mind drifted back to that first day and feeling like I was on a gameshow when Leon lifted that box off the stack I had carried into his bar's back room. Although now, I could imagine the gameshow host in his black tux asking me, "For a chance to win a lifetime with Leon, what caused Leon's pale condition?" I would hold my hands up to my chest with my fingers interlocked as I bounced about. "Albinism!" I would shout out with uncertainty. The gameshow host, with his pencil-thin microphone and note cards in one hand, would rub my shoulder to tell me I was wrong but had one more chance. Again with uncertainty, I would peep out "Autoimmune disease." The gameshow host would lean forward, bouncing on one leg while he declared I was wrong. The crowd would gasp, and my heart would drop as the host straightened up to explain that I would have to go to the final round: defeating an Egyptian god to cure the king of his vampire disease if I ever wanted my fairy tale ending with Leon.

Leon sank into bed beside me, his arm sliding under my raised knees as I sat against the headboard, halting my gameshow woolgathering. Swiftly, he pulled me further down the bed, so my head rested on the pillows.

"Thank you," he said, smiling softly.

I studied the purpling in the inner corners of his eyes and the sunken skin below. He didn't have to say any more than that—I knew what he was thanking me for. Running my fingers through his hair, I lowered his head to my chest. I didn't need a grand thank you or even an apology; he wasn't indebted to me.

CHAPTER 31

The airport parking lots were being renovated, which meant Leon could only be dropped off at the doors and I would need to move the vehicle to another lot. I would be required to stay with my vehicle or it would be classified as parking and we would be charged sixty dollars. Parking for fifteen minutes for sixty dollars was a nope in my book. Leon was going to run in and get Pharrell while I stayed in the vehicle.

Leon leaned across the center console, his eyes studying my lips in the glow of the orange streetlight shining down through my windshield. "I'll be right back," he said. "I love you."

It wasn't that I was complaining, but it seemed Leon was releasing every "I love you" that he had bottled up over the last few months.

"I love you too." I leaned in and gave him a peck. Pharrell's plane had landed as we pulled up to the airport, and I didn't want to keep him waiting.

I was incredibly excited to meet him. I was going to spend the entire eight-hour drive asking him questions. I could only hope Pharrell was more welcoming—like Calvin—than cold, like Sean had been at first. If he was like Sean, there was no way I was going to be able to crack him within the timeframe we had driving home.

I sat there bouncing between one local radio station and the next. The stations were only playing grunge 90s music and the AM station wouldn't come in clearly. Growing up, I never got into the grunge genre, and at this hour there was no chance I was going to now, either. Turning off the radio, I stared out at the landing field before me. The lights flashing on the ground lit up the night sky, taking away its natural beauty. Between being worn out and the boredom of staring out at the lit-up nothingness, I was going to fall asleep sitting here.

I hopped out and headed to the tailgate of my SUV. Pharrell was going to have a couple suitcases with him. He wasn't just coming home for a week; from what I was told, he was taking a three-month sabbatical. Pharrell intended on taking over a couple of Calvin's classes to lecture and was scheduled to present at a couple of museums up in Canada. I hoped he liked the idea of having a little sister, because I wanted to tag along when he went to see Calvin and to hear his lectures at the museums.

Kicking my leg under the bumper, where the sensor to open the trunk was—nothing happened. I swung my leg again. Nothing. This was baffling. Not wanting to walk around and deal with the manual, I crab-crawled under the bumper to feel around for the sensor. Gordon had taught me that these sensors were in the worst location and could easily become covered in dirt. There was a good possibility that was the case now. I hadn't washed the SUV since I bought it, so the sensor could have been covered in dried mud or gravel dust.

A cold metal disc dropped onto my chest, then I heard the gears release as the trunk swung open. With the disc in my hand, I inched out, stood up, and brushed my backside off. Leaning into the tailgate under the cabin light, I examined the disc. It was the size of a quarter, mostly black with a thin silver band. The back side seemed to be a magnet. Testing my theory, I placed it against the button on my jeans. It held in place. I reached back to grab my cell phone to look up the logo. I had an eerie feeling, remembering how Kek had been watching me. Had our paths crossed before I ever traveled to Journey?

Suddenly, cold metal tightened around my wrist behind me, cuffing me. It made no sense; I wasn't illegally parked and I had stayed with my vehicle. There were no blue and red flashing lights or sirens. A split second later, someone moved against me, pinning me against the side of my tailgate as I tried to free my trembling hand. Fear rose within me as I felt his body up against my backside. I wasn't being arrested; this was something more sinister.

"Let me go," I screamed as I squirmed and thrashed, trying to knock him over so I could get away. Running toward the crowd exiting the airport was my only option at this point. I didn't have the confidence that I had with Sigrid to physically fight him off.

His arms tightened around my torso, pinning my arms into my back. His head moved beside my head for a second, and I slammed my head to the left, trying to stop him. Instantly there was a sharp pain in the muscle between my neck and shoulder.

I screamed in pain. "Who bites someone on the shoulder?" I growled as I tried to slide out of his grasp.

The pain was excruciating, throbbing as blood rushed through my body in fear. With the wetness of their mouth on my shirt, I was unable to tell if I was bleeding. I didn't dare look; I didn't want my face next to his face in any manner. I had more leverage using the side and back of my head than I would with my face.

One hand moved around my neck and another moved over my mouth. Before I could bite down on his hand, there was warmth breathing into my left ear. "Flower, quiet, we don't need an audience."

With his words, I instantly thrust my hips and legs. After years of rejection, he was going to make sure I couldn't reject him now. I was in the middle of a dark parking lot in the wee hours of the morning. I should have just circled the entrance as the other cars did, instead of sitting in this dark parking lot by myself. Now all I could hope for was Leon and Pharrell to hurry out before Ivan had a chance to get anywhere with me.

That was it—I needed to distract him. He wasn't the brightest, so I would be able to buy enough time for the guys to help me. "Don't you have a flight to catch?" I growled at him.

"Nope, but since you are going to take off in the middle of the night, I thought I should give you a going-away present." He chuckled, then his tongue ran up my left ear. "And fulfill two of my fantasies at once."

Leaning my head further away from him, fear was now leveling with disgust. There was no way he could have known I was here unless he had been following me. "How long have you been watching me?"

"Tracking," he corrected me. "Mom followed you from work to your apartment. See, she had a feeling that you were up to something, and it wasn't getting her an apology gift. I got myself involved when I called her to see if she wanted to hang out. She said no because she was on a stake-out, and I was sold." He kissed up the side of my neck to my jawline. "Man, am I ever glad that I called her today."

I was going to throw up if he kissed me like that again. I knocked my head back, trying to bash his head. "She's stalking me? Why? All I ever do is go to work—nothing worth being stalked over."

He forced himself closer, his mouth next to my ear again. "She told me about your laundry boy," he growled. "How dare you cheat on me?"

"I am not yours," I snapped as I tried to kick him off balance. Even cuffed, I could still run for help. "Ivan Miller, you are engaged to be married to my sister. Get this sick fantasy out of your mind. It's never going to happen."

Both hands moved up to my neck with force. "You will be mine and only mine."

"You will never get away with this, Ivan Miller!" I screamed again, hoping someone would hear.

"I already have," he cackled. "Mom said I should live out my dreams. See, your sister fell asleep, so I carried her to bed. Mom and I are sitting on the couch watching the latest remake of a 70s horror movie. With your father on another overnight fishing trip, no one will know the difference. Mom said she would be my alibi. It will be your word against hers and Stephanie's. No one will believe you. No one has ever believed any of the lies that you have ever told. We all know the truth: you are an agitator. This is going to be vindication for all the years of stress and agony you have caused Mom."

He was right—after all these years of her making accusations that I was a horrible person, no one was going to believe me. Somehow, she was going to spin this around so she could be the victim in all of this.

Ivan purred into my ear, "this is going to be two of my fantasies—no, three of my fantasies: your flower, public place, and dominating." He bent me over the tailgate, pinning me down as he forced my mouth open and shoved something in, then pressed his hand over my mouth so I couldn't spit out the chalky pill. "Mom even gave me something to help you relax. She told me to tell you that once you let it happen, you will see that she was right about everything."

My adrenaline rose as the pill dissolved on my tongue and trickled down my throat. There was nothing to spit out at this point. I needed to act fast before it had a chance to get into my system. I kicked my leg out to the side but failed to make a connection with his legs. I did it again with my other leg with the same results. Ivan must have been standing wide-legged behind me.

"Four," I growled as I tried to push myself back. "Murder. The only way you are going to get me is over my dead body."

Instantly we fell backward, Ivan slamming onto the pavement. Without a beat, his legs intertwined with mine. He rolled over, pinning me against the pavement while smashing my face into it.

"Your wish," he growled as his hands tightened around my neck, "is going to be granted."

"Your alibi isn't going to be enough to save you from this," I gasped, thrashing.

"Silly girl, my parents' money will get me out of everything. This will just be classified as some random homeless attacker. I'll finally get what I want, Mom will finally be rid of her headache, and Stephanie will no longer have to share the spotlight with anyone."

With every breath getting harder, I knew I needed to scream. Someone surely would hear me; I could hear voices in the distance now. With everything left in me, I sucked in all the air my lungs could possibly hold, then released the longest ear-piercing scream of my life.

Ivan pulled me back by the neck, his hands quickly shifting to my hair, slamming the side of my face into the pavement. Warmth pooled beneath my temple, trickling down my cheek to my mouth, and my eyes drifted closed.

CHAPTER 32

This had to be the third time I had woken up in bed feeling like a train had hit me. As before, I prayed the last thoughts that filled my head were nightmares. I just wanted to wake up in Leon's arms like that Monday before everything. There was nothing better than being in his arms with the warmth of the sun on us.

But there was no warmth here; the air was sterile with the smell of bleach. There were no birds singing sweet songs, just beeping and footsteps. I didn't know where I was, nor what day it was.

Rat-tat-tat…Rat-tat-tat…

I heard the tapping of knuckles on wood. "Knock, knock." Forrest's calm voice soothed the silence.

If Forrest was here, my nightmare might have been real.

"And who are you?" Calvin growled as footsteps neared me. Or maybe it was Pharrell—perhaps they sounded alike. Calvin should have been back home since classes had been in session for the last two months. He had no reason to be in Puth at this time.

"Calvin," my hand was released as Leon spoke, "I called him. This is Forrest, Nora's attorney. She trusts him, so I trust that he will help us find a way to destroy Ivan."

This was worse than a nightmare, it was a new type of hell. I was in the Hell of Ivan, directed by my very own mother. My mind raced, trying to remember what had happened in that airport parking lot so I could figure out what level of Hell this was. There was Leon's "I love you," crappy radio music, my tailgate, being slammed into my tailgate, Ivan's malicious intentions, and the warmth on my cheek combating the coolness of the pavement... I couldn't get past that point; did I get away? Did someone hear my scream? Did he...? There was no part of my body that didn't ache.

"Is she conscious?" Forrest's voice grew louder—he must have been walking closer to me.

"At this point," from my left Nick spoke up, "she should just be asleep."

I had to be at the hospital; Nick was here, Forrest was here, Calvin was here, and so was Leon. It was just a party in my room—a slightly awkward party with me just laying here. This wasn't what I wanted. If Ivan... I didn't want to be around anyone. I just wanted to curl up in the bottom of my shower until everything could be washed away.

"I don't want to put any more stress on her, let's make this quick before she wakes up," Forrest ordered, then continued, "Here's the bad news: the airport parking lots are under renovations, their security systems were not up Saturday morning. Although Nora's SUV has four backup cameras that are activated by movement. She first activated the cameras when she found the tracker attached under her car. It is not the time to go into detail, but it recorded the entire conversation between her and Ivan. Susan, her mother, was stalking her, and they planted a tracker on her car. Ivan made a comment that Susan gave him something to help..."

"He drugged my baby!?" Gordon shrieked from across the room, interrupting Forrest. His tone was raspy, as if he had been crying prior to his outburst.

I almost wished he wasn't here. I couldn't imagine how he took getting that phone call. At this point I didn't know how he was ever going to see me as his brave baby girl anymore.

Footsteps neared the bed. "You never told me that he

drugged her," Gordon continued to yell.

"No one in this room except for Nora has a right to her medical chart," Nick growled back. "Even if you were legally her father, in the States she is protected."

"What I was going to say," Forrest cut in, "was Ivan drugged Nora with something Susan supplied him. I guess it was to help Nora relax and for Ivan to have all night. Susan was going to be his alibi if anyone asked where he was. This attack was premeditated. I'm going to destroy Ivan and Susan for..."

"Why didn't you just kill him when you had the chance, Pharrell?" Sean boomed from across the room, heat and passion in his every word. Sean wasn't joking around; he was furious and broken at the same time. "Do you not understand what she had already gone through for us and our kingdom? I don't care if I got life in prison. I would have killed him."

"Hey," Gordon snapped. "Sean, go sit down and leave Pharrell alone."

"Death is too easy," someone scoffed. "He is going to pay for this." It had to be Pharrell—his voice reminded me of Calvin's but was hoarse. "I slammed his face into a car and punched him twice. No one touches our princess," he snarled.

It wasn't hard to see that Pharrell descended from a knight and grew up with brothers. With how Gordon taught me to defend myself against Kek, I could only imagine their training was more severe. Ivan wouldn't have known what he was walking into.

"It should have never happened." Leon took my hand again, but this time he sandwiched it between his hands. "I should have never left her in the car. I had even heard her mother threaten about the dumbest thing of all, getting her prescription drugs. But never in a million years did I think a mother could be this awful to orchestrate an attack on her daughter for not getting her the drugs."

"Excuse me," Forrest said, "what?"

"On Thursday at the optical, I heard her tell Nora that she had to get her new boy toy to steal her happy pills to earn his place in the family."

"I was far from her boy toy," Nick sneered.

"Hey, man, I am just repeating what I heard."

"Moving on," Nick huffed. "Last Thursday, I met her mother. From the first moment we met, I knew what she was after, so I had her medical file red-flagged for prescription drug abuse." He snickered. "No one was going to talk to Nora that way and get away with it. Get me on the witness list—I will testify against Susan Carter."

A for effort on Nick's part, but Susan was cunning when it came to getting her drugs. Forget medical networks; she bounced from clinic to clinic, doctor to doctor, until she got what she wanted. State borders meant nothing. She enjoyed going on shopping trips out of state, then magically devolving with some kind of fit, and we would end up in the emergency room for six hours as they tried to figure out what was wrong with her as she screamed in pain. Half the time I think they just caved so she would be quiet. It was unsettling to hear and most likely stressed other patients in the emergency room as well.

"I might take you up on that," Forrest continued. "They are going to put up a fight, throwing their money around. I am going to try to have the trial moved out of Puth at the last minute. For right now, Leon and Pharrell, Ivan is pressing charges against you two for assault."

"What?" Pharrell shrieked. "He was the one on top of her undoing his pants when we pulled him off her. Besides, it was only a face to a car hood and two punches to the face—hardly an assault. Oh, and the hood was plastic, not metal." Pharrell huffed. "If he's going to press charges against me, let me show him what assault really looks like."

What a great first impression, laying on the cold pavement bleeding from the head with another man on top of me, possibly naked. Please, not naked... My heart started racing. After all these years, Ivan had never gotten this far with me. He had never been this aggressive, either. Yes, I knew this day was coming, but never did I think he was going to try to kill me. He didn't smell of booze or narcotics any more than he normally did. This had to be fury stemming from jealousy. Or Susan got in his head by gaslighting him.

"Thank the lord you two stopped him when you did. With that being said, in Puth we have a Good Samaritan Law. With the camera surveillance and audio of his confession about what he was going to do to her, he will not be able to touch you two."

Hopefully, no one was watching me; my chest deflated with relief. Once again, Ivan had failed. He still didn't get what he wanted.

"This conversation needs to be taken to another room." Leon's voice was no longer calm and cool; it was filled with authority and power. "Nick, is there a conference room we may use for a meeting?"

"Yeah."

"Until we are home, Nora is not to be left alone again. Sean, you stay at the door of her room, and Calvin, you stay in here with her. Nick, I want you to be present at this meeting. Gordon, you are welcome to join us. And Pharrell, you're involved, so you'll be joining us as well."

Leon couldn't have predicted that this was going to happen. Not even I thought my mother was this messed up.

"I'm going to call my grandfather to come sit with Nora until we return. Once he gets here, I'll take us to the conference room."

Footsteps drew away from the bed. Leon kissed my forehead and told me he loved me. Chatter remained at what must have been the door to the room for a minute or two. Then I felt the right side of the bed lower as someone sat on the edge beside me.

"Nora," Nick whispered, "you are at Sacred Heart Hospital in Balvin. It is Monday, October 2nd. In the early hours on Saturday, Ivan Miller attacked you in the airport parking lot in Puth. Leon and your brother stopped him before he had a chance to..." There was a pause as if he was trying to find the courage to finish his statement. "Let's just say you were still fully clothed when they found you. However, you were unconscious and bleeding from the side of your head. Pharrell called emergency services while Leon called me. I had you flown here to be under the care of my family. As of right now you are on my grandpa's floor being treated for slight swelling in your brain and undernourishment. My grandpa is coming to sit with you. If you need anything, ask him, not the nurses." Nick squeezed my right hand, then his footsteps disappeared.

I needed to hear those words; it was more of a relief than Nick would ever know. I didn't have to see sorrow in anyone's face or hide my own emotions.

"Nick was telling me that you are a professor at U of C—what do you teach?" The voice wasn't familiar, but it had a calmness that had grown with age. It must have been Dr. Walizer. I must have fallen asleep after Nick left, because I didn't remember hearing footsteps enter the room.

"Ancient religion and mythology," Calvin replied. "Mostly I focus on Egyptian mythology."

"No way, that is fascinating. Whatever made you decide to take up teaching that?"

Calvin had to have known the vampire that bit Leon was an Egyptian god. Perhaps he took up studying it to try to find a cure for Leon. Calvin taught Egyptian mythology, and Pharrell was down in the frontlines digging it up. They were the modern-day versions of Gavin and Bartholomew, protecting their king.

"Let's just say I knew someone from Egypt that got me interested in it."

That wasn't what I was expecting; Leon was from Canada, not Egypt.

Footsteps stomped into the room. "Why does Nick only have one patient?" demanded an annoyed female voice, pulling me from my thoughts. "I have other residents in my office complaining to me about favoritism."

"Nick shouldn't be working at all." Dr. Walizer's voice remained calm as he spoke. "Nonetheless, I am using this as a lesson about bedside manner."

"Giving him one patient to focus on is not teaching him anything," she sneered.

"He only has one patient right now because he is learning the hardest lesson."

"Why? Do they not have family or something?"

"Heather," Dr. Walizer's voice rose, "I expect better from you than this. It doesn't matter; we care for all our patients with compassion."

"We don't have time to dedicate ourselves to one patient," she snapped.

"Nick is seeing what it is like to sit on the side of the bed when someone you care about is laying there." He must have been gesturing toward me in the moment of silence. "She is his friend from Puth. The same friend that gave him a place to stay while he did his residency up there. She was attacked at the airport when she went to pick up her brother."

"Oh, shit." She must have sat down in a vinyl chair; I heard a squeak and a hiss. "How's Nick handling this?"

"He's beating himself up. This was the first weekend he was away from her."

That wasn't something I wanted to hear. This wasn't Nick's fault at all, and he couldn't have prevented it. Susan was out for blood the moment she handed those pills over to Ivan. She was the only one that could have prevented this from happening the way it did.

"How far did her attacker get...?"

"From the sounds of it, just enough to subdue her. Her

brother and fiancé pulled him off her before he had a chance at anything."

Hopefully, they weren't watching me—even just hearing this again caused my chest to drop with relief. If only every person that walked through that door could start their conversation with "Ivan failed."

"Where is Nick now?"

"Sitting in on the meeting with her attorney. She's just asleep, but he wanted me at her side since he couldn't be. As awful as this is—and my heart goes out to this poor girl—Nick needed this. I feel in my heart this is going to bring back that human element to his practice."

"Hopefully not too much, we still have a job to do."

"Well, now you have your answers." There was a clapping sound, then Dr. Walizer said, "Heather, let's go teach other residents about not jumping to conclusions, fairness, and compassion."

I wanted to get up. Laying here while everyone was studying me was awkward. Not to mention, I didn't want to worry anyone, and I needed a distraction from my own head.

Opening my eyes, I saw a normal hospital room; on the wall before the bed was a white dry-erase board riddled with black marker. To the left was Calvin, head down in a book. His index finger glided down as he prepared to turn the page. To the right was a door—the bathroom, I assumed. A drawn curtain concealed the main door.

Looking down, I saw my right hand was poked with IVs. Next to my left hand was a plush, rose-pink cushion with black puppy dog eyes angled in and slightly darker pink, cheerful cheeks. It looked like an emoji, but stitched to its hand was a sword. It was cute and, even despite everything, my lips curved. My guess was it was from Gordon.

"I—" I gasped as I picked up the pink cushion, forgetting until this moment that I had been screaming as my throat was crushed by Ivan. "I should have saved Sigrid," I whispered as I studied the cute little plush. "I knew that it wasn't Kek. Even if I had failed, I still feel like Kek never wanted to hurt me more than he had to while converting me. Ivan drugged me and still slammed my face into the parking lot. Ivan was more of a monster that day than Kek ever was."

"Kek was at peace with death prior to meeting you." Calvin delicately spoke up from his book. "He hated this modern world. His plan was to undo all the chaos he had caused, then he was going to kill himself. He had no reason to rough you up."

"Are you sure?" My head fell to the side and my eyes lowered to the bed. "He told me that he was going to make me his queen for eternity. In no way did he come across as it was in death. He even said he was going to kill Sean and my king."

"To kill the king, he needed to be in his presence long enough—otherwise, it would only weaken him. Kek was hanging around in the shadows a couple weeks before you arrived. No one knew, and it wasn't until the night before I met you that I received a letter from Kek stating his intentions. He didn't believe in technology and his letter got lost in the mail."

I glanced at Calvin. "Were you two friends?"

"I wouldn't say we were friends—he liked to sit in on my lectures and give me grief if something I presented was incorrect."

I snorted as I pictured Kek up in arms as he stomped down the stairs of the lecture hall, snatching the dry-erase marker from Calvin's hands, then teaching Calvin and his students the proper way to draw his hieroglyphics. Calvin would cross his thick arms against his chest, leaning on his back leg while the rest of the class would stare motionless at the deranged man sitting in their professor's chair.

That was a nice little mental break from my current affairs. "Was he at least kind to you when he would interrupt your class?"

Calvin nodded. "Oddly enough, he was."

"Were you ever fearful of him?"

"I was not. At one point in their childhood, Bartholomew, Gavin, and Leo made a pact that they would be brothers for life. From that pact Kek was unable to touch Bartholomew, Gavin, or their descendants. In fact, Kek was unable to touch anyone in Journey as long as Leo remained there. In a way, Journey was Leo's hunting territory and no other vampires could hunt there."

"I know what happened to Joe's wife." I sat up, then pressed the yellow button on the railing on the side of the bed so it inclined. "Were you ever fearful for Stella?"

"No—according to Kek, somehow she fell under my protection."

"Was I some sacrificial item for Kek?" It came out more harshly than I wanted. "Chosen when I was a child?"

Calvin slowly rubbed his eyebrows with his index finger and thumb. "I didn't know about Joe's little plan until after you moved into Leo's apartment in the States, but no, that wasn't it. It was more innocent; the curse was based on love, and Leo is smitten with you. It seemed as if it was breaking down his curse—he was regaining the senses that he lost from the curse, but only with you."

Oddly, Nick freaking out when I accidentally drooled on him flashed through my mind. Although Leon's reaction to the same situation was more understandable now. "Such as when Leon was excited that I drooled on him in my sleep?" Not the most glamorous moment, but it would explain why he was so animated about it.

"Exactly. Up to that point, Leo couldn't feel the sensation of temperatures."

I recalled the first day when Leon rested his cheek against my cheek as he smelled me. "And smells?"

"And taste." Calvin sat on the edge of the bed and nudged my shoulder with his. "I wasn't lying to you that day about your pie. The man was crying on the phone telling me about how good it tasted." He flashed his mile-long smile.

That smile felt like reassurance, but it only opened the door to my insecurities. "Do you—" This was going to be difficult to ask, but if Leon was talking to him about me, he should know the truth. I inhaled swiftly and let it out with my exhale: "do you think that's what Leon fell in love with, or was it me?"

"Leo wasn't looking for a heroine—you caught him off guard. In the middle of the bloody night, he calls me to talk him down. After only a few hours with you, he was head over heels smitten. Only a small part of the conversation had to do with him regaining his senses; everything was about you. His heart was being warmed; however, his mind was racing, fueled by fear. I told him to just let things happen naturally. He wasn't this bitter old man; he was still that twenty-six-year-old man looking to share his warm heart with someone. I prayed that you were being sincere with him. Leo deserves to feel love."

That should have made me feel warm, but I just felt numb with more questions. Leon wasn't the only one that wanted love. "And Kek? How did Kek go from wanting death to wanting me?" Growing up, I was endlessly told I was nothing special, yet I had attracted the attention of a god. There had to be some weird revenge story behind it.

"I'm guessing that Kek saw you never saw Leo's curse. He believed in your heart and wanted it for himself. Ultimately you halted his suicide mission."

"Did he cause the visions?" I could picture in my mind Kek hiding around the corner, pointing his long index finger at me, then casting some Egyptian curse to deter me from Leon.

"No, I think they came with Leo's curse. Almost as a way to dissuade you from falling in love so you couldn't take Kek out. Which didn't happen." Calvin patted my hand. "I don't think you should be questioning Leo's love—his curse was only to be broken by true love. Your love for each other is pure."

I still didn't know how I felt about the motivation behind Leon's love. Leon had all his senses back and still told me every three minutes that he loved me. Despite that, part of me couldn't let the thought go that Leon loved what I brought back to him more than he loved *me*.

Calvin leaned forward, resting his arms on his legs. "Did you know that cat you were being sweet to was, in fact, Kek?"

My eyes widened. "Noooo..."

"Yeah," he tittered, "that's why Leo was having such a difficult evening. You brought Kek right to him."

With that, a new pain rose in my throat. "I swear to you I didn't know. If I did, I would have never brought him over. I thought he was your parents' cat. He was so friendly, and I didn't want to leave him there alone. I wanted to give him some love. I swear, I didn't know." The more I thought about that moment, the more my lip snarled and my nose crinkled. No wonder Kek had fallen for me. I only fueled his ego by calling him the god of all gods, Ra.

The mixture of emotions was going to result in me throwing up on Calvin as my stomach began to turn. "He's gone now, right?"

He nodded. "Even though he was falling in love, you still gave him what he ultimately wanted. He just wanted to be free from this world." His voice rose. "Don't ever think you have blood on your hands—you freed him."

My heart still beat furiously within my chest. "It didn't seem like it in that moment."

CHAPTER 33

Leon sat in the robin-egg-blue vinyl armchair next to the bed with his head hanging. His right arm rested on the bed beside me so he could hold my hand. He wasn't supposed to be staying here tonight. Because of the nature of my attack and my current state, the hospital felt it would be better if everyone gave me some time to rest. I could see their reasoning; the longest that I had stayed awake yesterday was for my conversation with Calvin. Otherwise, I couldn't keep my eyes open. I was in and out of it and hardly spoke to anyone from that point forward. I wasn't trying to be rude—I felt as if I didn't have anything in me. Part of me wanted to run away, and the other part of me didn't want to be alone.

My heart was fighting my mind. My conversation with Calvin and the past few months were all storming within me. When Leon wasn't around, my mind would spiral as I wondered what was the truth. I didn't want to believe I was a pawn. I wanted to believe in everything I felt.

Gently I tugged Leon's arm toward my chest. Yesterday the one thing I wanted most was to be next to him, and I still wanted that comfort now.

Startled, he turned his head in my direction, exposing the redness in his eyes. His head had been lowered because he was crying, not sleeping. Swiftly he turned away from me, wiping his eyes before turning back to me. His chest rose once, then he rested his head against his arm on the bed so he was at my level.

This couldn't have been easy on him; I knew that feeling of watching someone, wondering if they were going to wake up.

"Hi," he whispered, his eyes fixed on mine.

"I don't feel right," I whimpered. "Will you lay with me?"

"I would, but I don't want to make you uncomfortable if you are sore."

Tears stung my eyes, blurring his image. Had seeing what happened to me on Saturday changed his view of me?

I released his arm. "I'm sorry." I rolled over and stared at the blue diamonds on the peach curtains until they became vague circles.

The mattress lowered, drawing me to the middle. I felt Leon beside me, but he didn't move. Leon had to be disgusted with me after that creep contaminated me.

"Nora." Leon spoke softly. "More than anything, I want to take you into my arms to kiss all your pain away, but not all your bruises are visible. I'm timid—I just don't want to make you uncomfortable."

Gently Leon squeezed my right hand, enough to draw my attention toward him. He lay there on his back with only his head turned in my direction. His eyes were like a dark, fiery sun setting on the edge of a lake. A stream ran from his left eye. "I am so sorry for not being there to protect you from him. I am so incredibly sorry for not being there. I don't know how to fix this. I would have killed him, but you were my only focus that night."

I watched as Leon rolled over to his side, his head lowered against his bent elbow. I rolled to my side, too, and scooted closer to Leon until his forehead rested on my chest. I ran my fingers through his thick hair as his subtle babbles of apology moistened my shirt and chest. We were all entitled to react in different ways. I was going to let him have his moment.

His breathing gradually began to slow to a more relaxed pace. His arms tightened around me for a second as he rolled onto his back, then swiftly his arms dropped to his side.

Gingerly, I slid my arms under his head and rested the unbroken side of my face against his. He was never going to hurt me physically; I could trust in that.

The next morning, I woke up to an empty bed. Before Leon left, he had whispered in my ear that he needed to go meet with Forrest to interview new attorneys. This case was not in the realm that Forrest practiced, but he was going to help Leon find someone else. Leon took Pharrell with him. Gordon had left the previous night to get back to Journey. It was opening day for a new hunting season, and he was required to be present. Calvin was going to leave in the afternoon to get back to teach his classes on Wednesday. I didn't think Sean was going to leave until he had Ivan's blood on his hands. Out of all of them, he was the one I could tell was taking it the worst.

I sat with my knees up to my chest with my head resting on my arms as I stared out the window. Calvin's words replayed in my head as he sat in the chair in the corner of the room. Leon loved me, but did he really?

Nick was right—we didn't know each other after six days. Leon had kept so many details of his life away from me. If they believed I was the one who could end the curse, they should have believed in me enough to tell me the truth.

The sound of the curtain being drawn back with force shadowed my thoughts and drew my eyes to Dan entering the room with a rounded back, red glowing throughout his thinning dishwater-sink hair and face.

"How dare you have your mother arrested at the club last night," he growled as he neared the bed.

Both Calvin and Sean shot up, but I gestured for them to stand back. I was interested in how this conversation was going to play out considering I was almost murdered on Saturday.

"Your grandmother was present; she is now having chest pains from being so embarrassed in front of all her friends. In fact, she wants to press charges against the police for police brutality."

"Didn't you only say Susan was arrested?"

"Yes, which should have never happened, either. What the fuck is wrong with you to do that to your own mother? She gave you life, she's given you everything, then you have her arrested."

"How would I have her arrested? I've been in the hospital since Saturday. Up to yesterday, I was unconscious from Ivan drugging me, slamming my face into the pavement, then choking me."

"Lies," Dan sneered. "Mom told me that you had planned all of this out for attention, since Stephanie's wedding is next weekend."

Stephanie was now scheduled to marry Ivan in the States—in Puth, to be exact. Ultimately, my grandmother had put a stop to the wedding happening in Canada. Once she found out the wedding was to take place there, she refused to attend. Something about refusing to travel any further than Puth's city limits. Dan forced Stephanie and Susan to relocate the wedding to a local venue in Puth. With the short notice and the fact that Ivan didn't practice any religion, all the lavish venues were already booked. From what I heard, the wedding was going to take place in Dan's garage and the honeymoon was going to take place in the castle that Dan and Susan had supposedly bought for Ivan and Stephanie as a wedding gift.

"I'm not paying for this." He gestured around the room. "To be personally flown to Balvin and have security present. This is just insane; you deserve to die for a stunt like this. All you have ever done is disgrace the Carter family name."

"I think Susan going to jail for the premeditated murder of her own daughter and your other daughter is to marry the man that did this to me is more of a disgrace to the Carter family name." I shrugged and gave him a devilish grin. "But what do I know? I'm not a Carter."

That only enraged him more. He pointed his trembling index finger at me.

Calvin stood up and moved to tower over Dan.

"Get the fuck away from me," Dan growled. "I will own you."

"Excuse me," Calvin peered down at Dan, "I think not. Say your peace to Nora, then get out of here."

Dan jabbed a finger in Calvin's face as he glared at me. "I'm not paying for your protection. It was all a stunt."

"How?" I sneered. "Tell me how Susan putting a tracker on my vehicle was my fault. Tell me how Ivan attacking me from behind was a stunt."

"Do you think I'm dumb? I've seen you with Ivan, how close you two are when Stephanie is not around."

That knocked the wind out of me for a second. "It was never my choice to be near him. If you had ever paid any form of attention to me, you could see that he makes me uncomfortable."

Dan just ignored me. "And Mom wouldn't have had to put a tracker on your car if you would have come home. Since you decided to run off, Mom has had to pick up your slack, and it has been stressing her to no end. She told me that she went to the hospital for exhaustion and a twisted ankle from cleaning. You should have come home when you got to town. The house is a mess; there are dishes in the sink, the cat boxes are full, laundry to be done, the trash is overflowing, and the bathrooms are gross. This is all your responsibility and you know it. Besides that," his voice rose, "they laughed at her and denied her care because you were messing around with one of the staff members there. And not just any staff member—a fucking laundry boy. A hospital full of doctors, and you pick the lowest of the lowest!"

He was delusional to believe I would just walk back into that life like nothing happened.

Calvin and Sean began to bounce with their snickers; it was too much, and they both started laughing. I couldn't blame them—it was obscene, but this was how Dan thought.

To him and my grandmother, who constantly called him King Dan, he was the greatest of them all. Dan believed his words were the only ones right, even if I had hard evidence to prove him incorrect.

Calvin tried to compose himself before he looked down at Dan. "Are you serious? Your daughter was assaulted, and your main concern is the state of your house?"

"Have children someday and you will understand." Dan gestured toward me. "Especially if they turn out like this one."

With that, I rolled my eyes.

"Roll your eyes one more time at me," Dan moved closer to my IV pole, "and I will choke the life out of you myself with your IV cord."

"Throw out all the threats you want." Just to spite him, I leaned closer to his face. I had no fear of him anymore. "I do not fear you. I will not honor you."

"You will respect me." Dan swung the back of his hand across my face. "I am the best father that ever was—show some respect."

"You will respect Nora." Calvin bear-hugged Dan, dragging him to the back wall. "You have no idea who you are dealing with."

"I will own you," Dan scoffed, "if you do not release me at once."

I leaned forward and pressed the call button four times quickly. No more time needed to be wasted; Dan wasn't going to back down until I apologized for everything and said it was all my fault. Even if it was far from the truth, it was Dan's truth.

"Mark my words, you are going to end up alone and poor someday," Dan snickered, "because no one will ever love you. And don't expect to come crawling back to us, either—you are dead to us for this. I have never been more ashamed than I am right now."

Two hospital security guards rushed into the room. Without

removing his arms, Calvin walked Dan out of the room with the guards and Sean following behind him. One guard and Calvin returned to the room to get my statement while Sean spoke to the other guard.

There was no reason for Dan to be here in the first place. Even if I refused to testify, there was so much video evidence of Ivan talking about Susan that she was going to be convicted. The only way around it was for me to drop all charges against both Ivan and Susan. Dan was only here to instill fear in me so I would bow before him again. It wasn't going to happen this time; I wasn't going to just roll over for him anymore.

"Calvin." I gestured toward the door and lowered my head. "Would you please step out?"

I just wanted to be left alone. I wanted to go back to the beginning of summer and choose my path differently this time.

"No, Nora." Calvin sat on the edge of the bed next to me. "I'm here for you."

"Please, may I have five minutes alone?"

His shoulders rose as he took a deep breath, undoubtedly not comfortable leaving my side. He patted my leg, then stood up. "I will be right outside the door if you need anything."

"Thank you."

When the door closed, drawing my knees to my chest, I flipped my hair forward and rested my head on my knees. Now I was in my own darkness, not one that Ivan, Dan, Kek, or even Susan had created for me. In my own darkness, I needed to rid myself of the Carters. For far too long they had lived in there rent-free. In every possible way over the years and especially in the last few months, they had shown me I had no place in their hearts. With every tear, I endeavored to expel them from my mind and my heart. Even if I had to replace thoughts of them with Kek, I was going to free myself. Let my family talk about how awful I was; I never had a chance in the first place. And if my family couldn't see the truth, they were of no value to me going forward. I would rather be alone and poor than live in their world anymore.

The door creaked and footsteps neared.

"Please leave," I said softly.

"I can't," Leon's hand gently moved up my back. "Twice now I have messed up by leaving your side only for you to get hurt again." His hand glided down my arm, moving all my hair to the left. "Until we are home, I will not leave your side again."

"I don't want to be here anymore," I whimpered.

"I know."

With every movement of his hand, my back tensed up, my heart starting to race. With a huff, I tried to calm myself down. Exhaling, I said, "I'm going to be trapped here with a trial. Something else is going to happen, and I'll never get to leave this place. It consumes me, like it's my curse."

Maybe there was something to it; two vampires had fallen for me, and my own family disliked me. Perhaps Dan was right and I was nothing good. I deserved all this negative karma. My family in Canada only saw what I let them see. My fingers trembled as I felt the warmth seep out of them.

"There are no more curses. I think you should focus on the fact that you are a blessing." His arms tightened around my torso. "*My* blessing." He kissed the side of my head. "Don't be discouraged. Just trust in me."

"Trust in you? Of course, I trust you." I sneered. "Even after you hid your true age and your dietary requirement from me. It turns out you were the one person I was searching for, but I found that out while you were making out with someone else. Why wouldn't I trust you?"

"Nora," his expression dropped, "what are you talking about?"

"What I am talking about is that you never loved me; it was what I brought back to you. You were in love with being able to feel warmth, being able to taste things, and being able to smell." I shifted on the bed. "And it wasn't just you. Joe was only kind to me all these years because he was going to sac-rifice me to Kek. And the Hughes, it was a risk for them to take me in right away. I mean, the odds were stacked against me, but now they get to tell people that their daughter saved Journey and its king."

"No." He shook his head. "None of that is true. My senses were coming back because I loved you, not the other way around."

I wasn't going to listen to him. "Leave," I growled, then hid my face in my knees again.

"Please sit up so we can talk about this."

"No, there's nothing to talk about," I snapped, raising my head so I could glare at him. "Everyone just needs to leave, go home, or whatever. Forget I ever existed because I have never existed. I am just what everyone else wants me to be. You don't need me anymore. I freed you—just go back to Canada!" I ges-tured between us. "This is over, so for the final time, LEAVE!"

My heart raced with the sting of my own words. Part of me couldn't believe myself, and the other part was breaking. I could feel myself leaning away from Leon, then everything went black again.

I was back in the cave with Kek. I watched myself slide Sigrid under my leg without cutting myself. I could see the pleasure in Kek's grin as he relaxed enough to run his fingers and nails down my leg. His eyes were sincere when he told me not to be frightened. He was going to take me as his queen. I belonged to him.

I didn't want this; I didn't want Kek in my head, planting the seed that I was his and should have never killed him. It was wrong.

I didn't want anyone in my life right now. Why couldn't these visions show me the future instead of the past?

CHAPTER 34

Nick ran every test, but there was nothing physically wrong with me, even though the trembling and blackouts were getting worse. Visions played in my mind on a never-ending loop. After the visions of the parking lot, I would come to crying or screaming at Ivan to get off me. Whenever I had a cave vision, I felt paralyzed, trying to study every detail to find answers. My only saving grace was that by the second day of being banned from my room, I no longer heard familiar voices outside my door. Different nurses stopped in to check on me, but otherwise I was alone in the hospital room.

"Dr. Yaman," I heard footsteps rushing down the hall as the door handle clinked, "she is not allowing visitors."

The footsteps stopped outside my door. "I am not a visitor." Her tone was harsh; it almost sounded like Heather from my first day here. "I am a director of this hospital. If I wish to speak to a patient, I will do so."

The curtain swung back. A lady walked in, her hair up in a golden bun, adding two inches to her height. She either had impeccable skin or was younger than I thought she was. Her round, oversized glasses revealed blue eyes exactly like Nick's. Her lips, however, were the opposite of his, serious and straight. It was Nick's mother, Heather. She was clearly here on business, not for a friendly visit.

Heather set down a sky-blue folder filled with paperwork. "I've been told that this was your second assault in less than six months. Is that true?"

"Yeah." I glanced away. "But in the first one's defense, I don't think he was going to intentionally hurt me, unlike this last one."

"Did you know the first attacker?"

"No, but... It wasn't, like, a sexual attack, more like he..." There was no way I could tell her that Kek came from a different time where he was allowed to just take someone as his wife.

She cocked her head. "Please go on."

My shoulders dropped. "His plan was to take me as his wife. The more I learn about him, though, the more I think he was just lonely."

Heather flipped through the folder. "And the other one."

"He has harassed me since I was twelve." I rubbed the back of my neck. "I can't talk or think about that night without fainting. So, let's not talk about him unless you want to be dealing with a fainting goat."

"All right." She turned around and laid the papers on the bed. "These are your discharge papers."

I froze. Now what? I had pushed everyone out of my life. I had no job, nothing to fall back on. I had lost the freedom of confidence I had at the beginning of the summer. Now I was just a fainting goat with no purpose in life except to allow Ivan and Kek to continually haunt my dreams until they became nightmares.

Heather squeezed my hand. "I am going to get you the mental health help you should have been already receiving for your assaults."

"I can't afford to stay here. I was planning on moving, so I resigned from my jobs. On top of that, my father thinks this is all an act, so he's refusing to pay for my medical stay. I have no health insurance without these positions, and I wouldn't put it past him to remove me from his insurance."

"That doesn't matter. You are a victim of a crime; the State will step in." Her head tilted to the side as she studied me. "Leonora, are you suicidal?"

I glanced up at the ceiling, studying the dust strands. "No."

"Look me in the eyes and tell me the truth," she ordered.

Biting my lower lip, I peered back into her eyes. "Am I going to off myself? No. Do I wish to not be here anymore? Only every second of every hour."

That was enough to get me a first-class wheelchair ride up to C4, the psych ward. It was no longer a case of exhaustion; I shouldn't have been passing out like a fainting goat. The only thing saving me from this new humiliation was that no one knew I was discharged and admitted for psychiatric treatment. Heather swore anyone who asked would be informed I was still there for complications from my assaults, and she even blocked Nick's access to my medical file.

CHAPTER 35

The first three weeks were rough; I had to talk about everything. The only joy of my day was waking up to new flowers in my room.

Now it was my last night. Which also meant my last night with Thea. To celebrate the end of my treatment, we snuck down to the cafeteria before it closed to get some ice cream, then sat outside in the green space, enjoying the evening sun with our treats. Thea was my assigned resident psychiatrist, yet she had grown to be more of a friend than anything. We chatted and goofed around, and she always had a good scoop on the hospital gossip, so in the evenings when I was free from formal sessions, we would turn her scoops into telenovelas for our own little enjoyment.

"So, here's the one question that I have never asked." I peeled the wrapper off my waffle cone. "Which department has the cutest residents?"

"Nora," she nudged my shoulder, "are you hunting for a resident to go home with tomorrow once you leave?"

"Oh, gosh, no," I chuckled. "Tomorrow is a chance to restart my life. I'm going to set out to find a new location, a new career, and for sure a new vehicle." No one from this life was ever going to find me again. "That plan doesn't include any men. Besides, I've already lived with a resident in Puth. He's the best; classically handsome and protective—but he's just...meant for someone else."

"Maybe I should transfer up to Puth." She fiddled with a blade of grass. "I was told the cutest resident here plays for the same team. The whispers are that his partner waits for him when he gets off."

"That's so sweet. I bet they're lovely together," I cooed.

Judging by her frown, it was the wrong thing to say. "I mean, maybe he has an even more amazing twin brother." I poked her arm. "You know, even with identical twins, there is always a cuter one."

"My luck would be that he is a twin," Thea mumbled, "and with a twin sister."

"Is he a resident on your floor?"

"No, the neurological department. Because of the way our floor is designed, we have a window between our waiting rooms. I see his partner hanging out there until his shift is over. I think his partner even walks him to work."

I gave her a look. "You aren't going to say his name, are you?"

The left side of her lips curled up and, with the swift wink of her amber eye, I had my answer.

I locked arms with her, trying to heave her up. I was eating again, but the muscle strength I had prior to returning to the States was all gone now. I fell onto my butt with a snort. "Let's go keep him company tonight."

"Nora, are you sure about this? I thought you didn't want to be social right now."

"Maybe they're just workout buddies, in which case," I pushed myself up, "clearly, I need to join them. Besides, would you want to sit by yourself every night waiting? We can go keep him company for the evening. Then you will have your answer one way or another."

Thea stood up, brushing off the back of her scrubs. "My evenings are going to be boring without you." Then, with another sly wink, she said, "Let's do this."

Soon enough, we were in the back set of elevators generally reserved for employees. They were an interesting set of elevators, with doors that opened on both sides. The front set of doors opened to areas where patients and visitors were allowed, while the back set opened to secure employee-only areas.

The back doors opened on the second floor, drawing my attention toward them. My eyes instantly widened as the man approached. I knew him by his build and how every hair on his head lay perfectly.

Just because I was thinking about him earlier didn't mean I wanted to see Nick right now. At this point, I wasn't sure what he was told about my release. There was no way they were going to hide it from him that I was no longer on his grandfather's floor.

He walked right up to me, then immediately turned around without looking up from his phone. His cologne filled my mind with memories of him walking me home each night from the bar.

My heart raced, trying to shadow the memories. I didn't want him to know I was still here; I definitely didn't want him to know *why* I was still here. It wasn't that I wanted him, I just didn't want him to lose his view of me when he found out I was committed. It was already going to be a difficult conversation talking to him about the assault.

Thea tapped me. Pointing to Nick, she mouthed, "That's him."

"Nooo," I mouthed back to her. She had impeccable taste, but she told me earlier that he was gay. As far as I knew, Nick was only interested in women.

Her head bounced along with her dark ponytail. "Yeah," she mouthed again.

There was no way. "No," I mouthed back. The other guy had to be his workout buddy.

I had been gone for a month—things could change. I stared at the back of Nick's neck one more time, unable to convince myself. "Are you sure?"

Her head bounced up and down again.

Perhaps there was some truth to it. "No way," I shrieked, "Nick's gay?"

I instantly sucked in as if I could recover my words. When that didn't work, I pulled the collar of my shirt over my lips as I slid down the back wall of the elevator, pulling Thea's arm so she was somewhat blocking me.

Nick's head rose as he turned around. "Excuse me?"

I hid in my knees, praying he didn't see me.

"Hey," Thea slid down the railing so she was standing in front of me at an angle, "how you doing?" It was comical in a non-comical situation, her voice slightly seductive.

"Did you just say I was gay?" Nick sneered, then grumbled to himself before letting her answer. "This fucking rumor needs to end. Just because I take my profession seriously and am not hitting on every female here does not make me gay."

"Yeah, this place can be a little box of gossip and rumors. But, well, everyone sees you leave with the same guy after all your shifts."

He rubbed his eyebrows. "That doesn't make him my partner. He's here—" His ocean-blue eyes moved from the floor to my eyes.

I was caught.

A little too late, Thea straightened to block me from view. "I'm sorry that you got sucked into the hospital drama. Let's try this again. My name is Theodora; you are welcome to call me Thea."

"Theodora." His voice was stern. "Will you move, please?"

"I can't, I was helping a patient out of bed and hurt my back. Standing like this helps stretch it out."

I could only imagine what she was thinking. My beautiful plan was rapidly shattering before me.

"Move four steps to the left right now," Nick growled.

I tapped Thea's leg so she would move. "Thanks, Thea, for blocking the light." I stood and brushed the back of my black yoga pants off. "I think my earring is lost for good. Oh well." I shrugged, then glanced over to Nick. "Hey, Nick, good to see you again. What have you been up to these days?"

"Wait," Thea stopped me, "you know him?"

"Yep, Nick and I were roommates in Puth."

With that, I was instantly pulled into Nick's hardened chest, one arm tightening around me while the other rested on my head. This wasn't the reaction I was expecting. It was the first time we had interacted since the assault.

"I've missed you," he whispered.

"I wasn't dressed provocatively in any fashion," I mumbled.

"I know."

"No, seriously, I was in my dark boot-legged jeans with a unisex concert T-shirt."

"I know."

"I didn't have a lick of makeup on."

He laughed humorlessly. "Nora, I know."

An assault was his worst fear for me—now it had come true. For whatever reason, I felt like I needed to clarify things for him. "He wasn't a regular customer at the bar. He has harassed me since I was twelve..."

Nick walked me backward out of the elevator, cutting me off before I could say anything.

Thea followed us. "This isn't our floor."

"I know." Nick released me. "I want a moment to talk to Nora. Theodora, you are welcome to head back upstairs. We will join you in a little while."

She crossed her arms against her purple scrubs. "That's not how this works."

Nick rolled his head. "She is being discharged tomorrow. I have already reviewed the paperwork."

My eyes widened. "Umm, you were supposed to be blocked from my file."

The corner of his lips curled up. "I am the hospital."

Just off the elevator, there was a nook with four fluorescent green vinyl armchairs. They were ungodly bright and cheerful for a hospital. Maybe this was foreshadowing our conversation.

"Mr. Hospital," I glanced up at Nick with a sideways grin, "did you pick out the color for these chairs?"

"No." Nick sat beside me. "This is what happens when you let department directors decorate their own floors."

My gaze bounced around, but there was no indication of what floor we were on.

He stretched his arms out on the back of the armchair. "What are your plans for tomorrow after you are released?"

There was a sinking feeling in my chest he wasn't going to like my answer. I turned my attention away from him, acting if I was trying to peek into one of the rooms along the hall. "Trade my car in then get on Highway 83 and head south."

"You mean north, right?"

With my lips pinched, I slowly turned toward him, then just as slowly shook my head.

As expected, his eyes squinted as his brows hooded. This was his lecturing look—his unpleasant lecturing look. All I could hope for was someone else to get off that elevator and distract him.

Nick didn't say a word as he straightened his leg, fussing in his front pants pocket before leaning over the armrest. He held something in his hand as he ran his thumb down my cheek.

"Nora." There was pressure on my head as if he was trying to push something into my bun. When that didn't work, he tried forcing it under my bun.

"Ouch!" I squealed and rubbed my head. "What are you doing?"

Nick reached up. Grasping my bun in his hand, he pulled my hair tie until my curls bounced onto my shoulders. He placed something upon my head. Just by the weight of it, I knew right away what it was. I tilted my head and let the heart agate fall into my lap. All I could do was stare at it; Miss Gemma Ann would have been so disappointed in me.

Nick picked up the heart and held it between us. "You have lost your heart—it's not this one, either." He tucked the agate back into his pocket. "Nora, it doesn't have to be this way. I know that you tried to shut everyone out. After what your parents did to you, I don't blame you there. On the other hand, I watched the life you created in Canada come down here and stand at your side as if you were their own baby." His lips curved into a soft grin. "I see why, after six days, you never gave up... Go home."

It was frustrating to hear those last words leave his lips. Life wasn't that simple; I couldn't snap my fingers and make everything perfect. "Am I just supposed to waltz right up there after being confined for a month? I was sane the first time I went up there, now they are all going to see me as the crazy lady that was locked up for a *month*."

"Nora," Thea grumbled, "not once were you behaving erratically. That's not why you are here; you were thrown into a sand trap and just needed a little help getting out of it. Anyone else in your position would be here too."

Nick's eyes narrowed and moved back and forth as if scanning or calculating something. This was a new look; I had never met scheming Nick before.

"No," he snapped, "I have a better idea for you." Suddenly he drew out his cell phone and began texting.

CHAPTER 36

Nick had some scheme up his sleeve, but he wouldn't share it with Thea or me. Instead, he guided me through the hospital with my eyes closed. Thea wasn't so keen on this at first, but by the time we exited the elevator, I could tell by her softening tone she was coming around.

Judging by the fragrance floating in the air, we were back in my room. There was also the sensation of people moving about the room. All the commotion halted and I sensed someone in front of me. My shoulders rose and tensed. A powerful essence seeped into my nose and down into my heart.

He wasn't supposed to be here—I was never going to get my clean break with him here.

"I told you to leave," I snarled, keeping my eyes closed.

"Maybe this wasn't a good plan," Thea whispered.

"Just give it time," Nick whispered back.

I had never seen this much compassion within Nick. He almost felt like a different person, bringing me back here to make up with Leon.

"No." Leon's tone deepened. "I'm not leaving until you open your eyes."

With the audience, I didn't feel like arguing. I crossed my arms against my chest and shifted my weight to my back leg before opening my eyes. This was my battle stance; I wasn't going to let Leon sway me.

I studied his short, trimmed beard for a second. It was

slightly patchy on the tip of his chin, although filled in nicely up the sides of his cheeks. This was unfair, but almost expected. Every time we were away from each other, he always came back better than before. All I could do was huff with new frustration and glare at him for making this a hundred times harder.

Leon took a step closer to me. "Joe wasn't sacrificing you—he believed in you. More than that, he wanted to give you the life that you deserved. To him, you were born to the wrong family and should have been born to him. But in his heart, he knew you deserved more than him. He wanted you to come home to be part of our family."

That hit a little harder than expected. I folded my lips between my teeth trying to keep the sorrow of how much I missed Journey within.

"Truthfully, I think you should have been born to the Hughes. I swear, you and Ruby are two bubbles from the same bar of soap. I have known her all her life—you are her little clone of cheerfulness, happiness, and love. She loves her boys, but she always wanted a little girl. And by asking her to teach you how to bake, you might as well have signed the adoption papers. This never had to do with curing my illness; it was about family and love."

"And you?" I said, finding my words while using the sternness in my voice shadowing the pain in my throat from my tears loading. "Say your peace, then leave."

Leon took another step closer to me. "I don't know why you're trying to push me away..."

Nick chimed up playfully as if he was on a gameshow. "What is... She's fearful that there is going to be social stigma once the people up there find out she was committed for a month."

I glared at Nick as he sat on the bed, swinging his legs back and forth. "I'm going to regret saying this, but I liked the old you: the one that didn't believe in love. Right now, you are not helping anything. Please leave."

Thea stood up. "She's right; let's give them some privacy."

Nick walked over to Leon and rested his arm against Leon's shoulders. "I will be back for my boyfriend at 9:00 p.m. so he can walk me home." His arm curled, taking Leon with it. Without a beat, he kissed Leon on the cheek. Then he caught up with Thea, putting his arm around her shoulder so he could lean in and whisper into her ear.

Leon's brows moved up, transforming his forehead into abstract art. It was so unexpected all I could do was cover my mouth and try to hold in my giggles.

"I don't know what just happened," Leon said, and the panic could be wrung out of his voice, "but I swear there is nothing going on between Nick and I..."

I held up my hand to mute Leon while I composed myself. "There is a rumor swirling around the hospital that Nick's boyfriend walks him home every day. I guess he..."

I couldn't finish my statement; my thoughts froze everything within me. There was no way Leon could have gotten to my room before we did unless he was already on the floor. It wasn't Nick's boyfriend or workout buddy—Leon had stayed here every day waiting for me. That realization stopped my giggles.

"I could never leave you alone here. I can't go without you either. Journey isn't my home anymore unless you are beside me."

"Leon," I whined, "I'm not the same anymore. I'll always have this cloud over me."

Leon held his hand out to me, and I didn't hesitate in accepting it. He took my other hand, then raised my arms as I took a step toward him. It may have seemed like a dance, but I felt like he was testing to see if I was comfortable next to him.

Leon released my hand and wrapped his arms around my torso. I felt lost and safe all at once; I loved him. I wanted what was best for him. But mostly I wanted this forever.

The silkiness of his bottom lip glided up my neck. "There

is no cloud—you are the sun. Nothing will ever be able to dull your shine." His lips moved to the middle of my neck as he let his teeth sink in gently. "They will have to judge me before they could ever judge you. Let's not forget I was a vampire for the last six hundred six years."

His arms released me, and his hands moved to my cheeks. "Besides, I think they would find you crazier for not seeking out help for the last six months. Our kingdom isn't perfect, but no one holds things like that against anyone. There's also the fact that, as the king, I will not allow such behavior against our queen."

"I am no queen—and I thought the throne was no more. Doesn't Canada still follow one of the European monarchs?"

His chin rose a touch as his head rocked to the side. "Officially, there is no throne anymore; informally we follow the tradition. Which means when we return, there will be a ball so I can formally ask your father for your hand, then ask you in the traditional way."

I placed my hand on his chest, so he wasn't able to move any closer to me. "Tell me the truth."

He knew instantly what I was asking. "The truth is right here, right now. Even in this state, the way you look at me is the same. I wasn't expecting you at all, but for the first time in six hundred six years, I felt like me again. It wasn't because I could feel your warmth or even smell your perfume; it was the way you peered up into my eyes that made me feel rich. You were breathtaking. I was done for. Every second after that just kept getting better because it moved from just being a physical attraction to falling for your dorkiness, your kindness, and your passion. I wasn't trying to keep you around for things that you were bringing back to me. I wanted you for the one thing that I had never felt before."

Leon moved my hand to his pec. "In here."

CHAPTER 37

It was my discharge day—possibly. The paperwork was taking forever. By 11:00 a.m. it still hadn't been completed. I sat staring out the window at the traffic below, slightly disappointed I wasn't one of those people, free to move about. I was confined to my room until my discharge was officially signed off. It wouldn't have been so bad, but this was the first day without any new flowers and Leon wasn't here, either. With the excitement of being discharged, I had hardly slept the night before; this was truly the longest morning of my life to date.

"What is this?" Nick leaned against the doorframe in his navy scrubs, his arms against his chest as he peered into the room. "I thought you would be gone by now."

"Me too." I moved my feet to the floor as I sat up.

Nick walked over to the bed, then laid down as if he was going to take a nap. After pulling up the blankets, he raised the head of the bed. "I got this invite to a ball on Thursday." His head leaned to the side with his eyes widening. "A formal ball, with a dress code."

He may have been surprised by the ball—I, however, was more surprised that Leon had invited him. Perhaps in this last month, Leon and Nick had formed enough of a friendship that they trusted each other.

For this ball, as tradition stated, I was to have the first dance with Leon, then I would have the next dance with Gordon. For the third dance, everyone was welcome to dance with us. At the end of the dance, Gordon would kiss my left hand, then hand it over to Leon. We would dance alone before everyone and, at the end of the dance, I would curtsy. Leon would reply by kneeling before me and placing the ring on my finger. From that point, everyone would join in again and the ball would end around 5:00 a.m. with a breakfast feast for all in attendance. It all sounded magical until after breakfast, at which point Leon and I would be kept apart from each other until coming together at the altar. There was no wedding planning done together; since we were in Leon's kingdom, he was the one to host and plan the wedding events. I was to spend my time interacting with the new kingdom to familiarize myself with its people.

In the olden days, I would have traveled there with my outfits for the event already prepared. Since the people of Journey had been looking forward to this day forever, Wanda—the town seamstress—had made all the dresses required for the festivities. All I had to do was meet up with her for fittings and alterations.

"So, do you know what is going to happen at this ball?"

"Yeah," Nick tittered, "and I understand there is a wedding taking place on Monday. At this point I don't know which one of you is crazier: Leon for wanting all this so soon, or you to be going along with it. And speaking of, are you two really going to have this 1400s-themed engagement and wedding?"

A longer engagement would have made more sense since we had just met over the summer, but the one constant thing I wanted in my life since I had met him was Leon. I wanted him beside me every night and to wake up beside him every morning. The uncertainty of overcoming hardships down the road was far less than the desire to have him in my life as that permanent fixture. It was time to enjoy building our lives together.

"It's their tradition. Honestly, it sounds more magical than the weddings nowadays. I mean, come on, how many balls have you been invited to in your lifetime?"

"Just this one." Nick pulled his cell phone out and flipped his finger against the screen a couple times. "My leave has been approved." He smiled up at me, his upper lip uncovering that dreaded tooth. "My lady needs someone present from her court since I heard you don't intend to invite anyone from the States to these grand events."

This was true; I didn't plan on inviting anyone. I wanted a new life without the baggage of my past following behind me. Puth was one of the larger cities in North Dakota, yet still small enough for word to spread like wildfire. I may have been dead to him, but as soon as Dan heard about it, he would weasel his way into the wedding.

I may have healed myself, but that didn't change the behavior of the people around me. When I crossed that border, I was going to let my American life disappear with Leonora Marigold Carter.

"Well, this is odd." Leon walked into the room in casual jeans and a fitted black sweatshirt. "Did you guys switch roles?"

Nick chuckled. "You had me up all night going on and on about the ball and wedding." He rolled toward Leon, lowering the bed. "I need a nap."

"Hey now, you were the one that kept asking more and more questions."

They began bickering as if they had been friends for years.

With Nick attending the ball, I wondered how much of Leon's past was going to come forward. In their discussions, I wondered if Leon played it off or made subtle hints to Nick so it wouldn't be as big of a blow. I could see this new, playful Nick being more accepting of Leon's history than the old Nick.

Leon engulfed me in his arms, drawing me out of my thoughts. "I'm sorry for no flowers today. We have a long car ride home, and I didn't think you wanted to be fussing with a vase of flowers or worrying about spilling in your new vehicle."

Leon was behind the flowers every morning. They had to be beyond expensive. Nick could roll over; Leon was going to get more than a simple thank-you kiss.

"Please don't be sad." Leon tucked his hands into the back pockets of my jeans. "This weekend you will have all the flowers."

"The flowers were the highlight of my days." Softly I took his bottom lip between my lips, then drew back, releasing it. "Thank you so much."

His hands moved from my pockets down to the backs of my thighs as he leaned over, lifting me up to his chest. I loved being in the strength and warmth of his embrace.

"No," Nick whined, covering his eyes, "babies are born here, not made here. Put her down. I don't need to see this crap in my hospital."

All I could do was chuckle at how much I was enjoying this new Nick.

Leon lowered my legs, his arms shifting to the middle of my back. "I made sure that you will still get flowers each day before the wedding."

"Can I have you instead?"

"Ugh, I wish." Leon tightened his arms around me. "Every time I get you back, I lose you somehow. I'm going to miss you those few days."

"Well," I let my lip graze his, "after this break, I will be your wife."

"My queen," Leon corrected me.

"Oh, god." Nick sat up. "I'm not going to have to listen to this crap for the next six days, am I?"

Leon rocked me so he could turn toward Nick. "No, you'll be staying with Sean at his place. Nora will be staying at Gordon and Ruby's, and I am going to be at our home mostly."

Leon wasn't talking about the apartment above the bar—he was talking about the castle. Even being up there this summer, I hadn't been to the castle. I couldn't imagine what the state of it would be like since Leon lived in his apartment in town. Had Leon abandoned it when he was cursed? That would mean no electricity or running water. That would mean no daily hot showers, heaters, or toilets. Now I was starting to question if a longer engagement would be necessary...or if Leon was testing my commitment to him.

"We're to live at the castle?"

His eyebrows rose and he cocked his head. "Yes, an apartment above the bar is no place for my queen."

"You two need to tone it down." Nick pushed off the bed and walked over to Leon and me. "I will be up later tomorrow," he said, then held out his hand for Leon.

Leon shook Nick's hand and pulled him in for that weird man pat-hug before releasing him. "Sounds good. Have a safe trip."

By 1:39 p.m., we were back on the road to Journey, although now I was officially Miss Leonora Ann Hughes, a birth citizen of Canada and a proud owner of a not-so-plastic SUV recommended by Gordon.

CHAPTER 38

I hugged my pillow to my chest, laying on my side while I admired the pearl tulle glistening with afternoon sunlight: my gown for tonight. It hung off the freestanding mirror to the left of the window.

I had been put down for a nap so I would be well-rested for tonight. Gordon had drawn the curtains and tucked me in for my nap about half an hour ago like I was a little toddler. In fact, the whole house was going to take naps so we would all be rested for the festivities later.

There was no way I was going to sleep, though—my excitement was more powerful than an energy drink. Besides that, there was something magical about the dress that kept drawing me to it. Yesterday I spent the day with the master of the seamstress trade, Wanda. She descended from a line of blacksmiths and seamstresses. Her basement was a showroom of vintage dresses from over the years, spanning back to Leon's original era. It was like stepping into a fashion museum with all the dresses in their own protective glass cases, organized in chronological order.

In addition to a new dress, I got a couple of history lessons from Wanda. When King Leon was to settle on a lady, he was expected to offer her a gift. Back then, fabrics and beads and whatnots were not available as they are now; receiving a dress was like receiving a rare gem bracelet. Being the local seamstresses, Wanda and her ancestors had to be prepared for this day and needed to keep up with the fashion trends. The future queen couldn't be wearing a colonial gown if everyone else was in flappers.

For tonight's ball, the ladies were allowed to wear whatever dress they chose, and that went for this future queen as well. I could have chosen from grand ballgowns with intricate beaded corsets, golden beaded flappers, or modern mermaid dresses. Nonetheless, it was this simple sweetheart A-line dress that I was drawn to. The dress was more enchanting than simple. The tulle was a pearl-white, while the silk under-skirt was a soft pink, adding a level of innocence to the dress. The pearl tulle on the bodice was a thick basket-weave pattern that gave the illusion of a heart. A thin rose-gold belt connected the bodice to the skirt.

The pattern was from Leon's era, though I didn't know that when I selected it.

The bedroom door cracked open; Leon's head popped in and he raised his index finger to his lips as he squeezed through the crack in the door. Turning around, he gently pushed the door closed, holding the handle until it latched silently.

"What are you doing?" I whispered.

Everyone in Journey was holding tight to their traditions, and I had already been warned that I couldn't see Leon until the ball—however, I wasn't going to complain about this visit. Our eight-hour drive back wasn't enough time.

Leon slid into bed, pulling the covers up as he turned toward me. "It's part of the tradition that I get to scope out my potential fiancée prior to the ball." His head bounced once as his expression turned serious. "In fact, I was told firsthand by the prior king that this is allowed." He inched closer to my chest. "We must follow that old king's ways."

Playfully, I leaned away from him, crossing my arms. "Oh, I've been told about that," my brows lowered, "but no one told me that scoping out meant getting into bed with these ladies. King Leon, I think in today's standards, scoping out would be called test-driving. Not acceptable."

"With their knights standing guard, that was hardly the case." He pulled me on top of him. "But the opportunity is here; I was told that my knights are going to take a nap as well."

Sitting up with my knees on either side of him, I crossed my arms against my chest, pushing my breasts up so they appeared fuller. "How does one scope out a potential fiancée in the 1400s?"

Something must have caught his eye; Leon's head cocked to the side. His expression was so soft and pure that I got lost in it for a second before realizing what he was checking out in the corner.

Swiftly, I pulled off my shirt and tossed it at his face to distract him from my gown—he wasn't supposed to see it yet.

Again, I crossed my arms against my chest, this time pushing up the satin pink polka-dotted cups that gave the bra a 50s feel. "Was this what you were hoping to scope out when sneaking a peek at your potential bride?"

Leon tossed the shirt off his face, lips curving, but still tried to peer around me.

I undid the clasp on my bra but left it in place, dropping my hands.

"I wanted to observe their behavior; how they treated their staff, how they treated my staff..." He straightened, his eyes remaining fixed on mine as I moved my hands back up to my bra.

I tossed my bra at him playfully. "What do you need to scope out with me?"

Leon laid the bra over his head, covering his ears with the cups, then tied the straps under his chin. "Nothing. I miss you. Waiting to see you again at the ball was too long of a wait." He held out his arms to me, clapping his fingers as he tried to contain his laughter.

I bit my bottom lip, but with the bra on his head and the look of love in his eyes, I couldn't help it—my chest started to bounce as I tried to suppress my giggles. Even covering my mouth, there was no containing my giggles. It wasn't even giggles at this point; I was convulsively laughing with my eyes watering from trying to hold everything in. The man before me was a king with a pink polka-dotted bra on his head. There was no holding back the laughter from this obscene image.

"Baby," Ruby knocked on the bedroom door, "put away your phone and go to sleep. You need your rest for tonight."

We froze.

"Umm... I'm sorry, Mama," I pinched my lips together to conceal my laughter.

"It's okay." Ruby's tone softened. "Sweet dreams."

The awkward silence was filled with footsteps walking away.

Before laying down on Leon's chest, I removed my bra from his head. "Could you imagine if Ruby caught you in here with a bra on your head? I doubt claiming it was tradition would save you from her right now."

Leon kissed my cheek. "You are worth the risk, especially hearing you laugh again."

Lifting myself just a touch, I slid my hands under his grey T-shirt, letting my nails glide against his skin. "I think I should be scoping you out." I kissed his neck before sitting up so he could pull off his shirt. "Every time you come back into my life, something physically changes on you."

"You—" Leon exhaled ecstasy, "are scandalous."

I tittered warmth into his neck. "Coming from the man that snuck into my room a moment ago."

Leon's hands tucked under my waistband. "If I knew this was how that was going to play out, I would have tried harder to get closer to those princesses."

His words knocked a snort out of me. I moved down his chest. "Ummm...no." I kissed his sternum before moving my lips to his right nipple, warming it up for a second before adding a little pressure with my front teeth.

"Eep!" Leon shrieked—and not a little one, either, but a loud and high-pitched squeal. I slid off him onto the bed. This was the first time I heard him make that noise, not even when Kek...

Oh shit. My heart started racing as I instantly realized my mistake. "I'm so sorry," I apologized, then drew my knees to my chest and hugged my arms around them.

That was one thing I couldn't figure out how to address in counseling, so I had never brought it up. I still struggled with doing anything that could possibly trigger Leon. Never did I want to make him uncomfortable, but it was hard to remember he wasn't just a twenty-six-year-old guy.

Sitting up, Leon studied me for a second before he ran his arm against my shoulders, drawing my ball form to his chest. "It's okay, I wasn't expecting that; you just caught me off guard." With his thumb and index finger he moved my chin up. "Not so hard next time, but for sure there needs to be a next time."

Thumping echoed from the staircase—it sounded as if someone was racing up the stairs. Then my bedroom door flew open, and I was ripped out of Leon's arms. Everything was happening so incredibly fast—I only knew it was Sean by his cologne as he squeezed me tight in his warm, massive arms.

"Sean." Leon spoke calmly. "Please put Nora down."

Sean's brows lowered. "What the...what were you two doing?"

Leon raised his hands. "She's safe, Sean. It wasn't her—"

"Scream of horror." I grinned up at Sean. "We were messing around, and sometimes I can be overly dramatic or playful."

Sean didn't need to know that it was Leon who screamed—I didn't want him ripping on Leon for screaming like that. I also didn't want to have to explain how I made Leon scream in that manner. I wasn't one to kiss and tell, nor was I going to let Leon take the fall.

"Are you sure?" Sean walked me over to the bed, then

dropped me. "It sounded as if you were in trouble."

I glanced over to Leon, biting my bottom lip. He placed his arm in front of my chest while he looked around for my T-shirt, then back to Sean, who was standing there with his arms crossed.

It was time to change the topic.

"I thought you were hanging out with Nick today. You know, showing him around and such."

"Journey is a two-minute tour." Sean's head cocked to the side. "He's with Pharrell getting his outfit for tonight. Why are you shirtless in bed with Mr. Sterling when you were supposed to be resting?"

Oh, I was in trouble. Forget Leon's status—this was big brother rage.

"Sean, Nora is safe; you are excused."

Sean ignored Leon as he scooped up my shirt from the floor and tossed it at me. "Get this on before Ma and Pa get up here and see you like this." He pointed a stern finger at me. "You are getting engaged tonight."

I gestured toward Leon. "To *him*, Sean. I am to be engaged to him."

Leon sighed and shook his head. "Nora, stop." He scooted up to the head of the bed. "Sean, come sit with us."

I put my shirt back on as Sean came over and sat between us.

"Sean, look at Nora—she's safe now. Kek is gone, and there is nothing here that is going to hurt her again. No one in her family knows she is up here; Forrest and Joe are planting the seeds around Puth that she moved to Nepal after her release. Because of the trial, Leonora Marigold Carter still exists, but no one down there except Joe knows that." Leon gestured toward me. "Leonora Ann *Hughes* exists. I know it's in your blood, but those days of standing guard are over. We are all free to live our lives without fear."

CHAPTER 39

After everything was cleared up with Sean, things got back on course. Leon got to stay for a slice of pie, then all the guys were vacated from the house to get ready at Sean's place. This left the house for Ruby and me to get ready. Wanda stopped over for a last-minute fitting, and Peggy stopped over to style our hair.

The evening continued with a few more ladies stopping over to visit or to see if we needed anything. They all told me stories about Leon over the years. The last visitors were ones I wasn't expecting—dressed to the nines, Sean and Trevor arrived on a royal horse carriage pulled by two massive Clydesdales with matching cool grey coats, their manes and tails the darkest shade of black. The feathering on their lower legs was the same shade of black. Without a second thought, I walked over to the first horse and let my hand slide down his massive velvet muzzle.

I couldn't figure out how people didn't instantly fall in love in Journey as I did. The enchantment was heavy in the air. The horses were mythical, the people were warmhearted, and there was a man like no other.

In his cotton Victorian coat with velvet-covered buttons and a matching collar, Trevor jumped down before me. His arm rolled about before him as he knelt. "My lady, are you ready to meet your king?"

I was ready to step back into the 1400s to give Leon the

Great that one night he was robbed of. I was ready for tonight to transform that separation in my mind between my Leon and the king. I was ready to trust my heart.

I nodded to Trevor. "Of course."

I glanced up at Sean, whose eyes glistened as Trevor's did in the porchlight. I nodded and gave Sean a soft smile as well.

Trevor held his hand out to me, then swiftly bounced his eyebrows before patting his left pec. I chuckled as his eyebrows bounced again. Trevor had packed some liquid courage for me and didn't want the other two to know. That would be something if the future queen showed up drunk as a skunk.

Gordon sat beside me, patting my knee, as Sean and Trevor drove us to the castle. I leaned against his shoulder, giving him a warm, close-lipped grin. He seemed more nervous than myself. Perhaps Gordon had written off this day from ever happening in his lifetime.

We arrived at the grand castle that I had fought to save from my family. Never in a million years did I think things would have unfolded in this manner. Ever since that day with Miss Gemma Ann, King Leon had been my symbol of love. I was going to protect his legacy as much as I could because I believed in his heart.

Leon fit the bill for King Leon in my mind. Watching him in my visions was insane enough, but if someone had told me that at the beginning of the summer my main mission was to woo a six-hundred-thirty-two-year-old king to save him, I would have laughed at them and told them how ridiculous they sounded.

The castle wasn't a grand fairy tale palace but more of a fortress. There were no moats or drawbridges, yet there were four watchtowers attached to a massive lord's residence, the wooden roof of which was divided into two by a courtyard with a beautiful garden. The brick of the castle walls matched that of the apartment building above the bar, aged with weather and moss.

We arrived after everyone else so I could make my grand entrance. This wasn't something that I asked for; it was another one of their traditions. Gordon was to walk me down the center of the ballroom floor to the king. This would be the first time the kingdom would be allowed to get a glimpse of their future queen. I was to pay no attention to them but to walk proudly with my eyes on the king. Just as his kingdom, this was the first time he would lay his eyes upon me—that is, if he followed tradition, which he did not.

Yesterday, while sharing the history of the kingdom, Wanda let it slip that this was not, in fact, Leon's first engagement ball. With his father's blessing, he would impersonate the help to get closer to the princesses before the balls. One ball was not enough time for him to see if he wanted to spend a lifetime with this lady. As the story goes, it paid off: he caught one princess in the act with her father's first knight, another already with child, and a few were just downright unbearable to be around.

The string quartet started playing "Can't Help Falling in Love" as Gordon and I walked down the aisle.

The women may have been allowed to wear whatever dress they pleased, but all the men were in black morning suits with grey vests, white collared shirts, ivory ties, and charcoal trousers—except two gentlemen: Gordon and Leon. Gordon was in a black evening suit with a white wing-collared shirt, a black bow tie, and black trousers.

My king sat on his throne on the landing, dressed in what I think would have been classified as a white medieval suit with gold embroidery down the seams of the jacket and a larger knotted pattern just an inch away from the seam. The cuffs of the jacket were also embroidered, though his trousers were plain white.

Gordon stepped before me, blocking my view of Leon. "Your Majesty." He bowed and, as he rose, took a step to the left. "I present to you my daughter, Leonora Ann Hughes."

I felt as if I was on a movie set with actors and actresses that had been practicing their roles forever. Then there was me, with a case of nervous giggles. I felt as if I had just been hired off the street for my role. I wanted to yell "Cut!" so I could take everything in.

"Baby girl," Gordon hissed, "bow."

Startled, I jumped before swiftly lowering my chin, maintaining eye contact with Leon as I held my skirt on either side with my forefingers and thumbs. I placed my right foot behind my left, then slowly bent my knees to lower myself about half a foot. Still maintaining eye contact, I realized this wasn't a dream or a movie set; it was reality. Gracefully I straightened my knee and stood.

Leon's lips puckered, trying to stifle his own giggles.

The string quartet began to play "Cheek to Cheek" as Leon and I descended the stairs to the ballroom floor hand in hand. I was expecting Leon to slowly dance with his cheek pressed up against mine as the dance started, but we moved across the dance floor as if we were Fred and Ginger, mirroring their every move from the original film. It wasn't difficult for me to keep up with Leon; I knew Ginger's moves flawlessly. I had spent many nights with my dance partner in high school practicing this dance for competitions. Never did I imagine that all those nights of practicing were going to prepare me for this moment.

Leon dipped me, slowly drawing me up as we turned. I closed my eyes for a second as he rocked us back toward the wall. I just wanted to stay like this for the rest of the night; my eyes closed next to him, cheek to cheek.

Breathing the moment in, I opened my eyes again. Releasing me, Leon spun away for a second, then returned as I leaned against the doorframe, admiring his moves as my mind drifted back to that first night. The warmth I had felt in my chest as I observed Mr. Bartender watching that young couple out on the dance floor while thinking to myself what it would be like to dance with him had been nothing compared to being in this moment with him now.

Leon leaned in, resting his hand on my cheek as he panted, his lips widening into a Duchenne smile. "That was no fib that you were telling Niles that day in the bar."

I slid a little closer to him, my gaze roving down to his lips. "I have won trophies for my performance of 'Cheek to Cheek.' It's my favorite dance."

We didn't need the string quartet; even during the visions, the depression, and everything else thrown at me, my lips always knew how to dance with his. His fingers softly ran along the underside of my jaw, following it to my chin. With the same softness, his thumb pressed my chin upwards so my eyes would return to those black star sapphires shining from the candlelit chandeliers.

The sound of footsteps down the stairs filled the air, then grew louder as they rushed toward us. It wasn't enough to draw either of us from the moment. He was more enchanting now than ever. There was no curse for me; I was his now and always.

Gordon cleared his throat before Leon could lean in for his reward for our performance.

I had forgotten we had an audience. Calvin held out a napkin for Ruby as she tried to staunch her tears. At another table, Trevor was giving us two thumbs up as Sean silently clapped for us.

"Your Majesty," Gordon bowed before Leon again, "may I have the next dance with my daughter?"

"Right." Leon stood upright. "Of course." He bowed with a sly wink toward me.

This moment was one of the deciding factors for the wedding taking place on Monday. Before this next dance, I was to curtsy and nod to Gordon if I wanted him to give me away to Leon at the end of the dance. If I refused, I would ignore Leon and take Gordon's hand to lead him out to the dance floor.

"Your Majesty." I lowered my chin to Leon, then turned and held out my hand to Gordon. "Papa, I would like this final dance with you."

The string quartet began to play "I'll be Hard to Handle," most notorious from its feature in the film *Roberta*. This night was a dream—I had fancied films from this era because of the dance scenes. That little hopeless romantic within me thought it would be a fitting song for a father/daughter dance. It was a fun, playful tap dance; I could see why Gordon chose it.

"Baby," Gordon led me to the dance floor, "be Ginger one more time for me. I want to tap."

"I don't have my tap shoes on, but I will do my best to keep up with you."

Just as Leon, Gordon danced effortlessly, swinging me out and tapping. We mirrored our movements, and once again, I felt like Ginger, gliding across the dance floor and kicking out my feet.

In the original dance, in the next set of moves I was to pretend-slap Gordon. Even pretending, I didn't want to do it. I knew the fear that a raised hand could deliver. It wasn't appropriate and would set a bad precedence over this surreal, elegant ball. I crossed my arms against my chest, hiding my hands until the sequence of steps was over.

Gordon tapped around me, stopped before me, then engulfed me in his arms. One hand rested on the middle of my back while the other rested on the back of my head.

"Leonora Ann," he whispered. "I am so incredibly proud of you. And that isn't because you are marrying the king but for everything you overcame to become the woman that you are today. You will always be my baby," he chuckled, "even if you have your own babies. I love you so much, and you have made me the proudest papa."

The air left my lungs. I had written off ever hearing those words.

Since the dance was almost over, Gordon gestured for everyone to join us on the dance floor. However, the room remained silent except for one set of steps nearing us. I glanced over my shoulder to see only Leon joining us on the dance floor.

Everyone remained seated as Gordon raised my left hand to Leon. There was a nervousness rising within me that I may have messed up the sequence of events. Leon already misunderstood me once when it came to an informal proposal; this was the last place I wanted that to happen again.

As Leon led me to the middle of the dance floor, I spoke softly. "I thought everyone was to join us. Why is no one getting up?"

Leon swept me around, his hand in the middle of my back. "After six hundred years, it is time to change it up." He winked before turning toward the string quartet. "They'll all join us after this dance."

The string quartet began playing before I could ask any more questions. The song was a newer one—"You Are the Reason." All I could do was follow his lead through the dance. For being only our second dance together, I knew his body as if we had danced for years.

"Do you trust me?" he whispered as he gazed down into my eyes.

The last time he had asked me this question, I had said yes, albeit accompanied by a bunch of snarky, unfair comments. But I was no longer that person; I was me again and knew, even with less than two weeks together, I wholeheartedly trusted him. "I do," I whispered in reply.

He rested his forehead against mine. "Close your eyes."

With my eyes closed, I continued to follow his lead across the dance floor. Soon the air went from warm to cold and crisp, the music not quite as loud anymore. It didn't matter if we were out where the wild things were. I didn't want this dance to end nor was I ready to open my eyes.

Leon dipped me once more. "Okay, open your eyes."

Behind Leon, the stars had come down to watch us dance, yet it was his eyes that were spellbinding.

Slowly he drew me up, squeezing tight for a second, then knelt before me. He took my left hand into his hands with one eyebrow raising and the other dropping, creating that baffled pattern on his forehead. "That night I didn't want to go out to a bonfire with a bunch of people; I just wanted to close the bar so it was just the two of us. I have wanted to dance with you ever since that first night in the bar. I always want to be able to dance with you and not wonder what it would be like. I don't want to wonder anymore where you are at night; I want you to always be beside me, dancing, sleeping, and in my life." He chuckled as his cheek began to glisten in the light of the night. "I feel like I have asked you this a thousand times because all I want from you is to be your husband." He held up a small gold band with a stone in the middle of it. "Become my wife and I shall forever be yours."

I joined him on my knees and threw my arms around his neck, causing him to fall backward onto the ground. Then, remembering the last time he misunderstood my physical response, I squealed, "Yes." I kissed all over his face between my words. "I love you. Forever."

CHAPTER 40

Even with the slight ripples in the lake, I could see my reflection. My hair was up in a formal, flowing bun. My forehead was adorned with a gold headpiece, pearls and diamonds dripping down the sides of my head with a teardrop diamond in the middle. My eyes were golden as well, lined in black with white on the bottom. Pushing myself up, I brushed the sheer black skirt off. Nick and Sean would have a heart attack to see the bodice of this dress: gold chains overlaying a black bralette.

The grass crinkled as someone approached me from behind. "May I have this dance?" His voice was muscular and soothing, slightly familiar.

"Of course." I offered my hand.

He wore a three-piece suit, the jacket slightly off-black with deep red embroidery stitched from the collar to the lapel and down to the hem. Identical embroidery ran parallel to the buttons down his matching black vest. Dangling from the second button from the top was a silver chain with an Egyptian boat pendant. Adorned above his red button-down shirt but below his collar was another silver chain, this one with a frog pendant at its center.

There was something uncomfortable about him as he slowly led me to an outdoor patio that I just couldn't put my finger on.

He drew me closer to him. "Is everything all right?"

I nodded, studying his smoky eyes. "I've danced all night,"

I tittered as I examined his facial features. He was wondrously handsome. "My performance may not be the best right now with my exhaustion."

His right hand moved to my lower back. "We'll take it slow." He grasped my hand and held it up.

The noise of people inside carried outside through the windows, but it was just us on the outdoor dance floor. My eyes remained on his as he carried us around the floor, though from the corner of my eyes I could see the stars hung low as though watching us dance. They were mesmerizing, drawing my attention away from my dance partner.

He spun me out, then twirled me into him, my back against his torso. "I've missed you," he whispered before spinning me out again. "Where have you been?"

I couldn't recall if I had ever met him before. "About a month ago, I was attacked in the parking lot when Leon and I went to pick up my brother Pharrell from the airport. Leon and Nick moved me from Puth to Balvin to receive top-of-the-line care for the complications from that attack."

"What?" He stopped dancing and his hands moved to my cheeks. "My Queen, are you all right?"

"Yep, I'm all fixed up now."

He bowed my head and kissed my forehead. "This Nick, who is he?"

This wasn't the first time someone bowed my head and kissed it tonight, even beyond Leon. It must have been tradition, like kissing the top of the hand.

"Nick Yaman; he's a neurological resident in Balvin and Puth. He's in town this week for the wedding."

"Oh, yes, him. He shall be rewarded for caring for my queen. Now, the other we do not speak of anymore."

I was not a queen without my king—this more than slightly annoyed me. "Hold up." I took a step back out of his grasp. "Without our king, I am no one's queen. Show some respect. Leon is the king. As the future queen, I will not tolerate this type of prejudice against him."

He leaned back, crossing his arms against his chest. He wasn't overly built, but still powerful. "You are not his." His hand lifted and tapped his chest. "You are my queen."

Even in my dreams I hated being called queen. "The last man that called me his queen like that I speared him in the chest," I sneered.

"Yeah, I know," he snapped. "It stung like no other. And did you really need to burn me? Come on, you ended the curse." He placed his hands on his hips with his elbows out. "Do you know it took Osiris forever to bring my body back to its natural form?"

All the air fled my lungs and my eyes moved back to the necklace under his collar—he was Kek. This dream was going to take a sharp turn into a nightmare fast. I needed to wake up.

I walked past Kek, turning to head toward the water. Perhaps the coldness of the water could snap me out of this dream.

Kek grasped my upper arm. "Where are you going?"

Our shoulders were touching. I peered into his eyes. I had never seen him in his true human form, only his cursed form, which is why I couldn't place him earlier. "Time to wake up— this dream needs to end before it gets dark."

"Come with me." His hands moved to my shoulders, drawing me before him. "There will be no more darkness. You are to live in Aaru among the gods as my queen."

"No, even in my dreams I am not yours. I am Leon's." With a step back, I wiggled out of his grasp. "Leon and I are to be wed on Monday. I don't want to live among gods. I want to live with my husband."

"Well, maybe you shouldn't have killed me, then you could have lived in the mortal world, but since you did, we are going to be together forever in the Aaru."

"There's no way." I shook my head back and forth. "There's no way Osiris is going to allow you to take me. I prayed to him to save another man."

"Osiris is the one that pieced me back together. He does not humor himself with mere mortals, just us gods. He's not going to care if I bring you there."

"No, he's a benevolent lord of all." I tapped my chest. "I prayed to him to spare Leon. He listened; Leon lived when everyone said he was going to die. And if it wasn't Osiris that stood by me," my voice rose, "it was Hathor that did. She will stand up for love—my love for Leon."

I walked away from Kek. Even in my dreams, I didn't want to be in his presence. Darkness and evil were no longer allowed in my head, and he was walking darkness. To end this, I was going to walk into the lake.

Before I could reach the shoreline, though, he jerked me back to him.

"Let me go," I growled as I pressed my fists into his chest.

"Relax, take a breath, and I will let you go."

"We can't do this." I wiggled in his arms. "I killed you."

"Yes and no. Again, you didn't need to burn my body, yet you did free me from that treacherous mortal life." His eyes moved to my lips as his head tilted. "So we are even—let's go to Aaru now."

"No, go find someone else. This is never going to work; it will end horribly."

"Once we are in Aaru, you will no longer remember this mortal world."

"How so? You still remember me."

"Just trust me." He opened his arms and I collapsed to the ground.

I would need to be dead to enter Aaru. Was he going to kill me?

I needed him to start talking so I could weave my plan and overpower him again.

His hand gently glided across my back. "It's going to be all right. I promise it will be swift and painless; nothing will happen to your body."

"No." I sat back on my knees. Forget his plan—I wanted out of this. "I don't want to die, and I am not ready to die. For twenty-three years I have been at the misery of my family. I've had enough evil in my life; my own mother ordered my sister's fiancé to attack me. Up here, I have this beautiful, loving family. I know that you know how amazing the Hughes are, or you wouldn't have been hanging around my oldest brother all the time."

He fell back on his butt, resting his arms on his legs. "What are you getting at?"

"You are going to take me as your queen, right?"

He nodded, his eyelids lowering for a moment.

I needed to buy time so I could get to Calvin. He was the only one that could tell me how to defeat Kek again. "Let me have the next month to enjoy my family...please."

"No," he snapped, "that's too long. With the upcoming wedding, you may have a day."

"A day? No. Please, Kek, this next week is supposed to be amazing with the royal wedding activities. I get to meet and hang out with everyone in town. I will be staying with my family the entire time." I knew what would get me at least a few days. "I am not allowed to see Leon until we come together at the church." I pouted, pushing out my bottom lip. "Please, Kek, let me have until the wedding."

He inhaled and rubbed his eyebrows with his thumb and middle finger. I had more pull over this god than I realized. His hand dropped, palm-up. "Give me your arm."

"No." I jumped up and backed away from him. "You want to kill me. I'm not going to let you touch any part of me," I growled.

"If you want your final weekend with your family to say goodbye, you will give me your arm. My Queen," his tone softened, "I swear I never want to hurt you or cause you any harm, outside of taking you to Aaru with me. Again, you should know it's not going to hurt when that happens. Please don't live in fear these next couple days; just enjoy being mortal."

This wasn't a dream anymore. I didn't know what it was, but I needed to agree to his terms. I held up my left fist, flashing my wedding band in his face. His eyes rolled, then he rolled my fist over. He placed his index and middle finger against my pulse. Fearful he was cursing me in some manner, I took a step back.

He peered into my eyes, his arm tightening around my back and pinning me against him while his fingertips burned the skin on my wrist.

It felt as if someone pressed my wrist onto a burner turned to high. My heart started racing. "Lies," I whined as I tried to free myself.

"I'm sorry, My Queen, I needed to do this." His forehead moved against my forehead. "You wear his temporary ring. I am going to show all that you are mine forever. I promise this is the only time I will ever hurt you." He moved my arm up to his lips and kissed the burning sensation away.

Instantly I sat up in bed, feeling like I was falling. The red numbers on the nightstand glowed 11:06 p.m. I drew my knees up to my chest, resting my elbows on my knees.

"It was just a dream," I whispered to myself, "just a dream." It had to be a crazed dream from the lack of sleep; I had stayed up until 7:00 p.m. to try to keep my sleep schedule on track.

Out of habit, I rolled over and tapped my phone. My arm lit up, highlighting the side profile of a sitting frog statue. My heart sank as if my death sentence was being read to me as I stared at the hieroglyph.

CHAPTER 41

Forget tradition—Leon needed to know what was going on. I didn't care who heard me leave; I took off out of the house as if it was on fire. Leon's apartment was about two miles away from the Hughes' house. Fear of death and the chill in the air was a hell of a fuel.

When I got to his door, I leaned against the frame as I knocked. It all felt so fake, but my new tattoo told me it wasn't. All this crap was supposed to be over. I killed Kek and broke the curse. I wanted my fairy tale ending with Leon.

The door creaked open to Leon, his toothbrush dangling from his mouth, in just gym shorts. His eyes lit up with his grin, quirking his toothbrush as he slurred with excitement, "What is this?"

He removed his toothbrush and set it on the entryway table. Without saying a word, I quickly wrapped my arms around his neck, hiding my face in his chest for a moment. I just wanted him to squeeze all the fear out of me and tell me he knew how to fix this. He had to know how to fix this.

"You know," his hands moved to my hips, drawing them closer into his, "that we are not allowed to see each other until Monday, but this has to be the best surprise ever."

He had no idea what he was in store for. "I thought I was having a bad dream."

"The punishment for this is," he joked as his arms tightened around me more and his breath warmed my neck.

Any other time, I would have wanted this and let it go further, but I couldn't now. "Death," I whimpered.

"No." He pushed my shoulders so he could see my face. His eyebrows veered in as his head cocked to the side.

All I could do was stare at him until his image blurred. I couldn't find it in my heart to tell him our forever was going to expire before Monday.

"Nora, what's going on?"

"He's not dead... No, that's not right; he said Osiris put him together. But he told me he couldn't find me, so I don't think he can come here. But he's coming for me on Monday. He promised," I whined as my knees gave out and I began to fall to the floor.

"Nora." Leon caught me just before I collapsed. "Who?"

I held my left wrist above my head for Leon. "He branded me like a piece of livestock."

Leon grabbed my wrist. I could feel him trembling. He fell to his knees, then to his butt, releasing my hand. His hands moved to my sides just as they had at the optical, then he drew me to his chest, so I was straddling his legs. His knees lifted allowing me to be more at an angle against his chest.

"Nora," his hand moved up the back of my neck and the other pressed into my back, "please tell me where this came from."

"I thought it was a dream. I woke up startled and saw the marking on my wrist. I remember at the exact point he gave it to me. I can't explain what it was, but it wasn't a dream if he was dishing out tattoos with just his touch."

"Earlier you said death was your punishment. Is he going to take revenge against you for killing him?"

"No." I wiped my cheeks. "No, he's not mad at me at all about that. It's the opposite—he's infatuated with me. On Monday he's taking me to be his queen to live with him in Aaru. The Egyptian afterlife. He promised my death wouldn't be painful nor would it compromise my body in any way."

Leon's lips rested against the top of my head. His chest rose and dropped with his shallow breaths.

Sitting up, I rested my forehead against his as I ran my fingernails through his hair. "I was able to talk him into allowing me until Monday to stay as a mortal. I couldn't get past Monday because I think he wants me before the wedding can take place."

"I know the answer." Leon's tone was strong and reassuring as if he was trying to convince himself. "But this isn't something you want, right?"

"I don't want to live in the afterlife with a bunch of narcissistic gods or even royals. All Kek has going for him is the god thing, and that's not going to sway my heart. All I want is you—my Adonis."

His bottom lip trembled as his hand moved up to my cheek. "He doesn't deserve you."

With the movement of Leon's thumb across my cheek and his words, horror flushed through me. I hadn't inspected the rest of my body for new markings. I pushed Leon's hand away and covered my cheek. "Please tell me he didn't put a frog on my cheek."

Leon shook his head. "You're painted into someone else. I can't imagine this is your night attire."

I glanced down at my chest to see that it was still adorned in gold chains. My black heels were now covered in red dust. I moved my right hand to my forehead and, sure enough, there was the headpiece. It was the same outfit in which I danced with Kek. I just wanted to rip everything off me; I wanted nothing to do with Kek on my body. Despite that, the heaviness of the clothing was weighing me down, and all I could do was drop my head so my tears might dissolve the dress away.

"Let me help." Leon's fingers ran across the crown until he was able to pull it off my head. He squeezed me into his chest as he stood up. "I'm going to undo everything that he did to you tonight."

And that is what he did.

CHAPTER 42

In the morning, Leon drove me back to the Hughes' house. When we pulled up, Ruby and Pharrell were setting dishes for breakfast on the teak farmhouse-style outdoor table. By the lowering of Ruby's eyebrow, I was going to be in for it for staying with Leon last night.

I headed over to her as she set a pitcher of orange juice down on the table. "Good morn—"

"Baby girl," Ruby interrupted as her snarl appeared, "where are your clothes?"

I didn't have any clothing at Leon's place anymore, so Leon had let me borrow one of his T-shirts and a pair of sweats. We were able to get the drawstring tight enough so they wouldn't fall off my hips. "I—"

"Ruby, not now," Leon snapped. "We need to have a meeting." His tone mellowed. "I want everyone present, including Alba and Idalia."

In his bronze fleece-lined sherpa jacket and jeans, Pharrell walked over to us. He was the thinner version of Calvin and slightly taller than Sean. "Leo." He swung his hand out and shook Leon's lower arm. "Why do the swords need to be at the meeting?"

"Going forward," Leon released Pharrell's arm to grasp my wrist, raising it up to them, "one of my knights will stand guard beside Nora until we can stop him."

I had seen the people-charmer King Leon, but this was

authoritarian King Leon firmly directing his knight. Yet I didn't need knights standing guard; I just needed a sword again. Not any sword—I wanted Sigrid back.

Pharrell's cracked fingertips scraped against my arm as he drew me away from Leon. They must have become that way after spending years in Egypt's dry environment. "Why is Kek's hieroglyphic tattooed on your wrist?"

I stared into his eyes, wishing he was Calvin. Calvin knew about the visions I was having with Leon. He didn't have to that day with my little episode, but he made me feel comfortable. I still didn't know my relationship with Pharrell. He knew of Kek, but was he going to believe that Kek came to me in my dreams to brand me?

I glanced over to Leon for reassurance that I could trust Pharrell. Leon's eyelids lowered with a subtle nod of his head. With a deep breath, I let it out: "Kek is not dead. Osiris pieced him back together." I held up my wrist. "And—surprise—he's going to come for me on Monday so he can take me as his queen."

"No." Ruby clenched her hands into fists. "No, no, no. The curse was broken; he should be dead."

She didn't give us a chance to say anything, hiking up her pants and running into the house, hollering for Calvin and Gordon.

"Aaru is where the gods spend their afterlife. As far as I know, no mortals are allowed there." Pharrell gestured toward me while slapping Leon's chest with the back of his hand. He almost sounded excited. "She will be the first mortal allowed in Aaru."

"How?" I leaned back on my back leg, crossing my arms against my chest as I shot a couple daggers at Pharrell. "How on earth would you know that?"

Pharrell moved his arm across my shoulders as he started to walk us towards the firepit. "Calvin wasn't the only one that befriended Kek."

That wasn't comforting, Calvin told me at most they were social acquaintances. I could feel my shoulders starting to hunch up—with Pharrell's excitement I think he was friends with my future murderer.

"Pharrell, halt." Leon boomed from behind us before moving in front of Pharrell. "Am I able to trust you if you are friends with Kek?"

Pharrell held his right hand out to Leon. "My loyalty has and will always be with you."

When Calvin, Gordon, and Ruby came walking down to the firepit, I instantly held up my wrist for them.

Calvin stopped in his tracks. "Fuck" slipped from his mouth.

Leon and Pharrell both gave each other a wide-eyed stare. I could only imagine Calvin knew this was coming but didn't think it was real with the wedding on the horizon.

"You will explain yourself right now," Leon demanded of Calvin.

Calvin walked up to us and flicked his hand at Leon. "Dude, move, I want to sit next to my baby sister."

"Sit on the other side of her," Leon snarled.

There was no sitting on the other side of me, though. Ruby was there, her hand resting on my leg as if she feared I was going to fly out of my seat at any moment.

Leon slid down the bench, leaving just enough room for Calvin to sit down. Gordon moved into the armchair, remaining noticeably quiet.

"Morning." Calvin leaned in and kissed the top of my head before continuing. "I received a letter last week from Kek."

"Wait." Pharrell spoke up from the other side of Ruby. "You didn't tell me he wrote to you again."

"I thought it was irrelevant." Calvin peered into my eyes. "It was dated the Monday before you broke the curse."

Judging by his eyes, this wasn't going to be good. "What did it say?"

Calvin gestured at me. "You come bouncing to town with

all your bubbliness, rare emerald eyes—you just had to garner the attention of not only an old king but a god as well."

"It wasn't like I was seeking out either of them. And yeah, I know that already," I grumbled, sitting back with my arms crossed. "Kek was trying to proposition me in that cave."

Calvin's eyes widened for a second, then he continued. "Kek sent me a letter detailing his new infatuation with you. He couldn't figure out how you were born a mortal and not a god. And that's the thing—unlike in other mythologies, such as the Greek or Norse, Egyptian gods do not mix with mortals. He intended to make you as he was so he could have you as his own. He added that what he truly wanted was to take you to Aaru with him. Again, he was tired of this mortal world, yet he needed to find a way to lift his curse so he could go back to Aaru and speak with Osiris."

He didn't need to say more. "I lifted his curse..." My chest dropped. "Kek and I argued about what Osiris would and wouldn't allow. He told me that Osiris wasn't concerned about some mortal."

Forget Osiris—I needed another god.

I tugged Calvin's arm. "How do I reach out to Hathor? She is the only one that is going to be able to save me from Kek. She's the goddess of love, and what Kek has for me is far from love. And not to forget—her father is Ra, god of all the Egyptian gods. They are far more powerful than that dark little frog."

"No." Pharrell shook his head slowly. "In all my studies, I have never come across a situation such as this. We can't just pick up the phone to call Egyptian gods; it doesn't work that way. Especially if he is accessing your unconscious mind."

I didn't want Pharrell's advice on this matter; I wanted Calvin's.

I pinched my fingers to my thumb at Pharrell. "Zip it—I would prefer Calvin's advice on this matter."

Pharrell sat back, crossing his arms against his chest. "I see who the favorite brother is."

"Wrong," Gordon tittered. "Wait until Sean gets here and you see the two of them together."

Defeated, I leaned forward with my arms on my legs and my head down. I needed to figure this out before Sunday.

The weight of Calvin's hand slowly moved up and down my back. "Pharrell is right; Kek is the only god that we have ever had access to."

Why couldn't he just be a trooper and tell me what I wanted to hear? My mind drifted back to the cave when Kek told me he would teach me how to shapeshift. I mumbled into my lap, "I should have just let him bite me in the cave—at least then I could visit you all." Raising my head, I gazed at Gordon. "Kek said I wouldn't have memories of this life when I entered Aaru."

Gordon didn't say a word, only crossed himself.

That was it; I shot up. "What hunting season is open right now, and where is there unposted land?" On second thought, that wasn't going to work. I needed to go somewhere where Kek couldn't find me to give me a better chance. I jumped up and clapped my hands together. "I have the perfect scheme to get around Kek." I gestured with my arms out as I walked to the side of the firepit in front of all of them. "Before I disclose my master plan, I want open minds and," I looked Leon in the eyes, "for you all to think about the long-term goal."

Flames flickered orange into his eyes. Even with the sorrow lingering, the love was still present.

I walked over and sat next to Leon, taking his hands into my own. I looked toward the sky, trying to press the lump in my throat down. "We needed to think about the long-term consequences. I know how to get around Kek, but it will come at a cost."

"Please don't worry." Leon rested his head against mine. "Kek will be handled."

I drew back. "How, when he is only accessing me?" My

voice rose a little. "I have a plan that we all need to follow." I just needed to rip off the bandage. "I am going to beat Kek at his own game. He's not going to kill me—I'm going to get myself killed first."

"Baby girl," Gordon grumbled.

"No, listen. When he takes me to Aaru, he is going to wipe my memory. I will lose all of you. But if I can make it to Heaven, Kek will not be able to touch me. That means I need to die before Monday. And since he couldn't find me in the States, it will have to take place down there." I moved my hand up to Leon's cheek. "I am willing to give up my remaining mortal years for our forever together someday."

Leon's chest dropped, his eyes closing. His arms tightened around me as he pulled me onto his lap. That wasn't enough for him; his hand moved up my back into my hair as he pressed his forehead against mine. "I am going to do everything possible," he whispered into my ear, "to ensure that we get our remaining mortal years together. Kek is not going to steal that time away from us, in this life or the next."

"No," Ruby snapped. "I do not stand for that plan. I will not let Kek or anyone else kill you. Calvin and Pharrell, you befriended that demon once before—take your father and hatch a plan that only includes Kek's demise. The rest of us have a wedding to worry about."

Pharrell huffed. "I need to carve out some time for a few dance lessons before the wedding. I was a little rusty at the ball. I happened to see online that my baby sister was the state champion—maybe she would take some time out of her wedding planning to teach her older brother."

Calvin's booming laughter filled the air. "You need lessons, but I would like to practice with her first." He gave me a wink. "Since I am her favorite brother."

When I stood, Calvin picked me up so we were chest to chest and spun me about. From the corner of my eye, I could see that Gordon, Pharrell, and Ruby had moved next to Leon and were talking. Calvin took one glance back at them, then danced me away from the firepit to the back porch. We continued to dance, me pressed up to his chest.

I appreciated him for distracting me, but I didn't know if I had it in me to kill Kek again if all he was going to do was come back and try again. I felt like it was the beginning of a never-ending cycle. I knew I needed help from someone above to get away from Kek. However, Pharrell was right—I couldn't just pick up the phone and call another god.

CHAPTER 43

Calvin's enthusiasm did not carry over as we sat around the table in silence, waiting for Nick and Sean to join us. Ruby couldn't look at me without crying, and Calvin retreated into his own head, trying to figure out a solution to my dilemma. Gordon, Leon, and Pharrell had headed over to the castle. Leon had said it was for wedding planning, but I think it was for something else since Calvin was to join them as soon as Sean arrived.

"Leanora," said a soft, soothing voice.

"Yeah," I replied, rolling my sausage back and forth with my fork, utterly drained.

"Leanora," the voice said again.

"Yes?"

Calvin tapped my shoulder. "Yes what?"

I sat up, frowning. I could have sworn I heard someone talking to me.

"Leonora," the voice urged, "come to me. I'm here to help you. For I am Freyja, the Goddess of Love."

The only goddesses of love I knew of were the Egyptian goddess Hathor and the most famous goddess of love, the Greek goddess Aphrodite.

"Leonora," the voice repeated, "come to me. For I am here to help you. I am Freyja, the Goddess of Love."

"Calvin." I tilted toward him so no one else could hear us. "Tell me about Freyja, please."

He turned with a lowering brow; we were only inches away from each other as I breathed in his orange-juice breath. "Freyja was a Norse goddess that was classified as the goddess of death, fertility, love, and war. Why do you ask about her?"

"Is she a trustworthy goddess?"

The voice spoke once more. "Leonora, I am Freyja, the goddess of love. I will help you defeat Kek."

With that, I didn't need Calvin's answer. Instantly I stood up, knocking my chair back. "I need to use the restroom, please excuse me."

Calvin pushed himself away from the table. "I'll come with you."

"Seriously?" I laughed. "I have to poop. There's no way Kek will try to take me while I'm pooping. The smell alone will stop him from entering the bathroom." That was a lie, but I needed to buy some time—I didn't know how long it was going to take with Freyja. "It might be a while; I am going to dig into the depths of the internet on my phone."

That stopped Calvin in his tracks, and he sat back down.

Quickly I rushed through the house to the front door, only to open it to Nick and Sean standing there.

"Hey there." I flashed a smile as I took a step outside. "Breakfast is set up outside on the patio. Leon and I forgot the champagne for the mimosas. I'll be right back." I leaned up and kissed Sean on the cheek.

"All right," Sean said, "we'll see you in a bit," then he headed inside.

Nick must have been fresh out of the shower; his hairline still wet. "I thought you weren't allowed to see Leon until Monday?"

I ran my hand through my hair. "We decided to blend traditions."

Nick snatched my arm. "When did you get a tattoo? This is awful."

"Geez, Nick." I pulled my arm away and hid it in the front

pocket of my hoodie. "Don't hold back."

A diamond-blue light bounced behind Nick in the trees; that had to be Freyja. "I have to go—just head in the house and out the kitchen door."

I didn't give him a chance to say more. I took off, pretending to head down the road until it curved. Once I knew I was out of Nick's sight, I took off into the trees, following the light until the cliff face that I had blown up was only yards before me.

As I peered down the cliff, the light sunk below the surface, continuing to glow. Perhaps Freyja was showing me where Sigrid was resting. Sigrid had to be my key to defeating Kek again. Without a beat, I pulled my shirt off, then stripped down to my underwear. With a step forward, I dove off the cliff.

The water wasn't cold for it being the first few days of November. Without that freezing panic present, I continued to swim deeper as the light glowed brighter, illuminating Sigrid. She rested beneath a boulder that took nothing to move. Even with Sigrid released, the light continued to glow.

I noticed what looked like a hair pin glowing next to another boulder. It wasn't just any hair pin—even under the water, I could tell the gold matched my wedding band, and the pattern was the same. The pin shined as if it was as sharp as Sigrid. This had to be my weapon to defeat Kek. My battle with Kek was going to become more even with the help of this other god. It wasn't just any Egyptian god—I had the support of a Norse goddess.

Starting to run low on air, I knew I needed to surface soon or I wouldn't be able to haul Sigrid up. I kicked to the surface and let myself hover there, calmly floating on my back in the water as if it was just a relaxing summer day out on the lake. I don't know how to explain it, but the feeling associated with Kek's master plan wasn't present as I watched fluffy white clouds dance across the sky.

A couple of minutes later, the feeling of calm evaporated with the sounds of a leaf blower nearing—no, not a leaf blower. It was Sean's ATV. Another ATV hummed in the background, overshadowing Sean's voice as he yelled something. The sounds grew louder, nearing the cliff.

Instantly I submerged myself so no one would be able to identify me from above. If I was able to stay submerged for the next ten yards, I could get around the bend of the cliff so I could surface without being spotted. I hoped that Sean had just taken Nick out for an early morning ride.

As I descended, the water temperature didn't change; it wasn't cold at all. I intermittently surfaced for air before diving under again. During those moments of surfacing, I could hear my name being called out near the shore. This wasn't going to be good—between Kek and my master plan, they were going to think I was trying to off myself.

I scanned the shoreline, remaining submerged just below my eyes. On either side, the shore was lined with little cliff faces and rocky, jagged edges. Calvin paced the sand, calling out my name. I just needed to find a blind spot where I could slip past him to get back to the house. If Calvin got distracted on the other side of the shoreline, I could rush up to one of the cabins before he heard the water splashing or saw the movement from the corner of his eyes. Then I could sneak back to the house as if nothing happened, pretending I was in the bathroom watching a show on my phone the whole time.

Leon's old pickup tore down the gravel road, a red dust cloud billowing in its wake, stopping just before the cabin I was planning on using as my cover. He was supposed to be working on the wedding—or, more realistically, my funeral. This could only mean one thing: someone called him when they couldn't find me.

With his cell phone clenched in his left hand, Leon yelled out to Calvin. I couldn't make out his words, but I could hear the trepidation in his tone. I didn't want to be the reason for his anguish.

Taking a breath, I thanked Freyja for helping and watching over me. Then I submerged myself again, making my way to the shore until the water became too shallow to continue underwater anymore. There was going to be no way around it—I had to stand up. I needed to come up with an excuse.

"There!" Calvin's voice echoed as I walked up the bank a few yards away. "Nora," he bellowed, "you have some explaining to do!"

All I could think to do was act casual about the whole situation. If I wasn't stressed, perhaps they would mellow out.

"Oh, hey, Calvin," I yelled back at him cheerfully as I squeezed the water from my hair. "You didn't need to come down here; I just remembered where I left something. I may have black hair, but sometimes I can be a blonde. We need it for Monday, and I didn't want to forget it."

"Nora." Nick's arms swiftly wrapped around me. He was not the first one I expected to reach me as I walked to where the snowy sand met the grass. "Oh, shit, Nora, you're not shivering. That's a sign of moderate hypothermia. I need to get you inside." His left arm remained on my back as he made to scoop me up.

"No, Nick!" I shrieked, grabbing at Sigrid. "Stop! I don't want her to slice you."

"What?" He took a step back.

Taking two steps to the side, I brandished Sigrid. "So...this is Sigrid." Trying to distract him, I wiggled my eyebrows as I stabbed her into the sand. "She is so fun to play with."

"That's a sword—I thought Sigrid was a person." He rubbed his eyebrow. "There's something strange going on up here."

"You have no idea," I tittered. "And yes, this sword protected me once."

"Nora!" Leon rushed up, engulfing me in his arms with

such force it knocked the air out of me. He buried his face into my left shoulder.

I cuddled him against me. "There's nothing to worry about," I whispered, "I'm safe."

"You've been missing for the last three hours." He drew his head back. "Sean said they found your clothes on the cliff."

My arms dropped and I took a step back. There was no way; there was no way I had spent hours in the lake swimming to shore. "No, that's not right. I haven't been gone that long." I held up my hand. "See, it's not wrinkly."

Leon's trembling hands moved to my cheeks as he turned my head, examining my neck, then my face. "Was it—" He looked over to Nick, then back to me. "Was it him again?"

"Nope," I tried to sound playful to ease his mind. "My groom's outfit for our wedding on Monday wouldn't be complete without his sword." I gave him a wink. "Let's just say that I remembered where I left her last time."

Before Leon had a chance to squeeze me again, I walked over to Sigrid, drawing her out of the sand. "I found your lady," I pointed her between Leon and Nick, then swung her so Leon would be able to grab the handle.

Leon's breaths became shallow as he rubbed the tip of his chin, holding Sigrid with an outstretched arm. He didn't seem to know how to respond as his trembling hand moved from his face to glide down Sigrid's smooth black leather, then to the carved, knotted metal.

Calvin draped a large coat over my shoulders, then cradled me in his arms. He peered down at me with stress pinching the edges of his eyes. "I'm not upset with you, but what were you thinking, taking off to jump into the lake?"

I felt like a toddler in his arms as I gazed into his eyes until pain in my throat released, blurring his image. His frustration and disappointment were worse than I imagined. But, even worse, I didn't feel like I could tell him the truth. For whatever reason, it didn't feel right telling any of them about the hair pin.

"I'm not mad at you." Calvin lowered his head and whispered, "But you need to be honest with me. Was Freyja speaking to you earlier? Was she the one that told you where Sigrid was?"

"It wasn't as if we had a conversation." I barely moved my jaw as I spoke; I didn't want anyone else hearing me. "She told me she was here to help me with Kek."

"Calvin," Leon held up his right index finger, "remember Kek could never touch you because of that blood pact I made when I was younger?"

"Yeah, what are you getting at?"

Leon flipped Sigrid so her handle rested on the ground between his feet. "If I do it again with Nora, maybe it will protect her from Kek." He tapped the tip of Sigrid's blade, then held up his finger so I could see the red drop of blood. "Tap her quick and it only will sting for a second. Don't worry, I'm fully healed." He gestured to me with a reassuring smile.

"Hold up." Nick walked in front of me, blocking me from Leon and Sigrid. "Nora is not going to touch a sword that has been sitting in the bottom of the lake for months. This is weird and horribly unsafe. What we should be doing is getting her dry and warm."

Sean snuck behind Nick and I. Without speaking, he locked his arm into Nick's and forced Nick out of the way.

"Nora is safe—she'll be all right."

Keeping my focus on Leon, I tapped my left index finger on Sigrid's point.

Nothing—no sting or sharp pain. I felt nothing.

I glanced down to see I hadn't pierced my finger. Again, I tapped the tip, with the same result. I ran my finger up the outer blade, but still nothing. Thinking maybe the skin was callused, I tapped every finger on the tip, then slapped my palm against it.

Holding my hand up to Calvin and Leon, I asked, "What happened? I've been cut before in the past, why doesn't she cut me now?"

Calvin squatted down and examined my leg. "Possibly Freyja put some protection on Sigrid to protect you from getting diced up when you swam back to shore with her. You're warm to the touch—this shouldn't be possible."

"Freyja?" Leon wiped his finger in the grass. "I haven't heard that name spoken since I was a child." His brow lowered, creasing his forehead. "Nora..."

With everyone else gone, I felt comfortable enough to tell him about Freyja. "Yeah, we are talking about the same Freyja. There's not much to tell—she introduced herself and told me to follow her. She never took a human form; all I saw was a blue light bouncing through the forest then below the water." I shrugged my shoulders and held my fist up to my chest, exposing Kek's marking. "I guess, with Kek being real, I believed she was as well, so I jumped."

CHAPTER 44

Leon agreed to let me open the bar for the day. I just wanted to be around people that didn't know about the death cloud hanging over my head. Gordon was starting to keep his distance from me; I tried to brush it off as he was busy with all the traditions that came with the upcoming wedding. Ruby couldn't stop crying if she looked at me, to the point that Leon and Sean made her leave the bar to go with Gordon.

Word spread around town quickly, and the bar filled with people by 2:00 p.m.

With another bottle of whiskey killed for the night, I headed into the back room to grab another one. Arms wrapped around my torso, Leon's essence penetrating me in the best possible way. I breathed him in as my eyes closed. His breath warmed the nape of my neck as his right hand inched up to his favorite resting place. His other arm tightened around my torso, drawing me further back into him. Being surprised like this by far was the best part of the day. It was like hearing your favorite song playing on the radio after not hearing it for years.

"Calvin has an errand to run." His silky lips ran along my outer ear. "Come upstairs with me."

Resting my head against his chest, I closed my eyes. I wanted to say yes—perhaps that was the key to getting rid of Kek. If I gave myself to Leon, I would be his and Kek might lose interest. Or would Kek go after Leon?

In my heart, though, I wanted to give myself to Leon on our wedding night. I didn't want to do it just to avoid being taken by a god who probably didn't care if I was pure or not.

"No." I took a step out of his embrace. "I need to get back up front."

I had forgotten how draining it was to work at a bar all day, and by the end of the evening, I was beat. Sean, Nick, and I decided to light the firepit and hang outside until the temperature dropped too low. The others were either working on wedding stuff or planning my funeral. I was too tired to care.

Something had gone sideways between Leon and me, and now he was keeping his distance. I assumed it was because I had rejected his offer, but the man he was in my heart would have been respectful and not pouty.

"Hey." I let myself fall against Sean's shoulder. "I'm sorry if I drool on you, but there is no way that I am going to stay awake much longer."

"I'm washable." The flames danced in his eyes. "It's fine."

He was far from that man I judged him to be the first time we met. I never imagined that he would have a permanent place in my life. He had truly become my brother and friend, guiding and protecting me. I was more than grateful he was here.

The outdoor sectional soon transformed into a black gondola with a red interior. We were floating down a channel with grassy sides and trees above with dangling branches of flowers. I watched as a petal fell to the water, which glowed fluorescent blue as it alit. Further down the channel, the branches were adorned with lights.

I leaned over the edge of the boat, letting my finger dangle in the water as the boat traveled down the channel. This was magnificent; I had to be dreaming.

"I've missed you." Kek's voice drew my eyes from the water

to the hand he held out to me. "What did you do today?"

I looked up to see Kek was wearing a velvet coat with a leopard pattern. The lapels were matte black, matching the button-up underneath.

"You're not watching me?" I asked. "I thought you could see all in the mortal world."

He drew a black pocket-square out of his breast pocket. "My eyes do not work when you are around the ones protected by that damn sword. I have the power to take over mortals—not to do harm or overpower, just to see through their eyes."

"So," my nose crinkled, "you live in their body like a parasite?"

"No," he tittered. "Let's just say that I'm that little bug on your shoulder."

I watched as another petal danced through the air, then landed upon the water. "Whose shoulder did you hang out on?"

"Your little brain doctor." He scooted forward and grasped my hands. "Only because I wanted to make sure you were safe and give you time to grieve." He sat back and crossed his arms. "The king was supposed to die," he sneered.

"That's oddly human of you," I laughed. This was just getting weirder.

"I'm not fully the monster that I was depicted as. In fact, every morning I was the one to kiss you on the head. I was the one that walked you home every night from the bar."

The same man who had given me the fear of what was in the shadows had walked me home every night to comfort me. The oddest thing about it was never once did I feel uncomfortable around Nick. I was cool with him moving in with me right away. Did that mean I didn't even know who Nick was?

I wanted to see if it was all Kek or if Nick did have a thing for me. "I'm guessing it was you that was territorial over my bar outfits, not Nick."

"Money or no money," Kek snapped his fingers, then

pointed at me, "you should only be wearing such things for me." His eyelids lowered, his gaze fixed on me. "You are far more beautiful through my own eyes," he murmured, "than those of others or even from the shadows."

I snorted. "Thanks for the sweet but slightly creepy comment." This was all too weird. I glanced up at the trees above us. "Where are we?"

"The land before Aaru, Duat." He held out his hand again. "Come with me and we shall go to Aaru now."

I shook my head violently. "No, Kek, I'm not ready yet."

He sat back, crossing his arms against his chest. It wasn't hard to tell he was disappointed. Although...

Sean shifted a touch, just enough to wake me, and I heard voices approaching. Sitting up, I wiped my mouth, then stretched out with my eyes closed. I couldn't imagine I had been out that long.

"Nora," Leon grumbled, "what are you wearing?"

Ugh... This wasn't how I wanted to be woken up. I fell back onto Sean with my head resting on his lap and my face facing his torso. I was going to steal more of his warmth before moving. "Chill out, everyone is entitled to some down time." I was raised to believe wearing sweats or pajamas in public was trashy, but I didn't think wearing them around a fire with my brother and a friend that I had lived with was such a big deal. He had to be bitter about earlier.

"Wait—" Sean's sounded panicked. "She had on a dark grey matching outfit... Pants and a sweatshirt." His arm shifted. "Nick, she's been laying here all night in that outfit, right?"

"I drifted off, but that is not what she was wearing earlier. Dear god, Nora." Nick sneered, sounding like Kek. "Are you not to be married on Monday?"

He had done it again—opening my eyes, I saw I was in a red bralette with black lace. Things that should have been covered up were now visible through the sheer material. Standing up, I covered my chest and looked down. "Damn it." I lowered the sheer red thong to see he had branded me again with his name in hieroglyphics across a region he should have never touched.

"Well, that explains why he kept staring at me the way he was. It had to be when he snapped his fingers—we were talking about my bar outfits."

Calvin unzipped his jacket and handed it to me. "Nora, where were you?"

"Kek said it was the land before Aaru, Duat." As soon as I put the jacket on, I hiked up my shoulders and brought them in, freezing.

"No way." Pharrell pushed Sean aside and pulled me beside him. "What was it like?"

"It was incredible—we were on a gondola, going down a channel with grass embankments. The trees above had branches filled with flowers. When a petal fell, the water glowed."

"Where was Kek?" Leon growled.

"On the other bench. All we did was talk; I'm trying to get as much out of him as I can."

"Are you sure about that? Just talking, with your new outfit and tattoo?"

"Don't go there," Calvin mumbled. "She doesn't have control over what Kek does with her."

"He's respectful with me." I glanced over to Nick and paused, unsure if I should continue. I don't think he knew someone had been living in him for the past couple months. With an inhale, I thought about my words for a moment longer. "Nick and Sean, head home for the night. Calvin and Pharrell, we need to have this conversation in private."

"Nick and Sean, leave," Leon ordered. "The rest of us are going to sit here while you tell us what happened." He sat down on the sectional with his elbows on his knees and his head resting on his closed fist. "I want to hear all about your wonderful date. What was this, the second date? I'm guessing you did more than stare up at flowers while laying on your back, but what do I know?"

"Leo," Calvin sneered, "this is not the time to be covetous."

"Did you not see the placement of the new tattoo?" Leon gestured at me without taking his eyes from Calvin. "Why is she allowing him to touch her?"

"Whoa." I waved my hand in front of my body. "I have no control over this. I was fixated on the environment around us and getting Kek to talk. I need *him* to talk so I can gather information. This isn't like dealing with Ivan; Kek is a god, and at any moment he could just take me to Aaru."

Calvin walked over to the armchair and patted it. "Please sit and tell us what he said to you."

I glanced around to make sure Nick and Sean were no longer around, then I lowered my voice. "In the States, he was living with me through someone else's eyes. When the protection of Sigrid is present, he is unable to access him."

Leon leaned forward, then pinched the bridge of his nose. "He's been using Nick to get close to you this entire time?!"

"From the sound of it, yes. And from the sound of it, he was able to control Nick a little."

"How so?" Calvin asked gently.

"He was the one to walk me home every night."

Leon stood up and began pacing back and forth. "You had no right to be living with a man you knew nothing about. It's not like you had to pay rent—you didn't need a man, for sure one you knew nothing about."

I wasn't going to just sit here while Leon had his little temper tantrum; this was hard enough without having to listen to that crap. "I lived with you and for sure didn't know the truth about you either," I sneered.

"So, we're the same?" Leon stopped pacing. "I'm just some guy, and now you're moving up the line? Going from a bartender to a doctor to a king, then to a god. Next you are going to try to move on to Odin."

"Odin is Norse." Calvin corrected Leon at the wrong time, but nonetheless he continued. "You're looking for Ra, since she's dealing with Egyptian mythology."

Leon looked as if he was ready to blow a fuse, and enough had been said. I wasn't going to listen to anything else that he needed to get out. Without saying a word, I stood up, pulled his ring off my finger, and placed it in his hand. I handed Calvin his coat, then walked over to the fire.

"Put the coat back on," Leon growled, then snapped at the guys. "Show her some respect and cover your eyes."

Leon was the one lacking respect for his awful words.

I started undoing the clasp on the bralette. "Kek is only in my life because of you," I grumbled as I tossed the bralette in the fire. "Nick is only in my life because of you." I moved down to the garter belt, unhooking it from the tights.

"Nora," Calvin stood up, holding out his jacket, "please don't do anything irrational. There are people here that still love you. I have a feeling your original plan isn't going to work out as you hope."

I tossed Calvin's jacket on the bench; I didn't want anything on my body that didn't belong to me. I didn't want to be touched; I didn't even want to hear the words spoken from their mouths. They were going to listen to me for once.

"I wanted Nick's neurological knowledge to help you. No, that's not even right—I went to meet his uncle and ended up with him as the professor instead." I threw the tights to join the bralette in the fire. The way the flames changed from orange to green and purple halted me in my tracks for a second. I glanced over to Calvin for reassurance, but his head was bowed.

"Nora, just stop," Leon ordered.

"No." I growled as I slid the garter belt and thong off, throwing them both in the fire. The flames changing colors wasn't enough of a distraction this time to lower my rage. "You are an asshole to believe all of this is has been for my pleasure or advancement in life. I did the things I did out of love for you—and for my own survival."

"Nora." Now Pharrell held out a jacket. "Please take the coat. It's freezing out here."

"Pharrell," Leon growled, "cover your eyes."

"You are awful—" I accepted the coat, but this time I balled it up and chucked it. It didn't make it far, landing just on the other side of the firepit.

Calvin reached behind him as he whispered to Leon, "It's best that you take back what you said and apologize to her now."

"It's a little fucking late at this point." I wasn't going to listen to him. Inhaling deeply, I pulled my shoulders back and stood up tall as I glared at Leon. "No one has the right to my body or me anymore, and that includes you." I took long steps toward the patio door. I was going to show them who was more powerful and didn't need protection.

"Nora, stop," Leon ordered, rushing to my side. He grasped my upper arm and twirled me into his chest.

I peered into his broken eyes; his words hurt too much to show compassion right now. "No, Leon." I pushed out of his arms. "I did not come here looking for love; I came here to fight for someone else's love. I believed in King Leon's story." I tapped between my breasts. "I wanted to protect it. I was going to stand up for his love against everything that was wrong. I didn't come here for you—none of what happened in the bar or around the fire was planned. I wasn't chasing after a guy to further myself in life."

Leon held out his coat. "Please put this on."

"Fuck that!" I pushed his hand away as my vision blurred with tears, my anger growing. "Let me tell you what did happen; when I am with you, I feel safe, protected, warm, and even before you said it, I felt loved. It was real to me, made up of all those little magical moments, like in the bar when I gave you that mug that resulted in your soft smile; it was there at the bonfire when you kept me close, and it was there when you stayed with me at the hospital. It wasn't because you owned the bar, it wasn't because you were the old king, and it wasn't because you bought me flowers each day." I raised my left hand up, brandishing my ring finger. "It was always because of this one thing that money, power, or status will never influence."

"Nora." Leon took a step closer to me. "Let's go inside to warm up a bit and talk about this." He raised his hand as if to brush my cheek off, but I leaned back.

There was nothing left to talk about, nothing more that needed to be said. I wiped my eyes. "If you see me the same as my mother and my sister, you are not the guy my heart believed in as a child. Go be with Stephanie—she is the prized Carter." I turned around and headed toward the door when I heard Pharrell speak up.

"Why did you have to be an ass to her tonight? Kek isn't going to wait until Monday now—you just handed her over on a platter." Pharrell growled.

"Pharrell, we are going to prevent that. Go trade places with Sean," Calvin ordered. "Out of the three of us, she is the closest to Sean. I don't want Kek getting wind of what just went down, but she is going to need someone."

I wasn't going to need anyone; I had been under twenty-four-hour surveillance since this all started. Kek was going to come for me no matter what; I was the only one who could save me now.

"No," I snapped, stomping my foot onto the frozen cement. "I don't need male protection. I don't need protection from anyone anymore. It does no good—I was sleeping on Sean when Kek took me again. So enough of this; I will not be made a prisoner anymore! I want to be left alone!"

After changing into some of my own clothes, I stood right outside the front door, staring into the darkness. I had no car; we had left it at the mechanic for an oil change and new winter tires. I was stranded; I couldn't leave this place even if I wanted to. With Leon's old pickup parked to the right of the house, I knew he was still here. Even with our disagreement, I didn't think he was going to leave the Hughes' house tonight.

I didn't want to see him. I didn't want to see anyone. I just needed some time with myself to figure out what I was going to do next.

CHAPTER 45

I sat admiring the bottles changing colors with the flickering neon signs above the back wall of the bar. They were the only lights, and there was no reason to turn on more, since the bar was closed. With Leon staying at the Hughes' house, I was free to gather my thoughts on how I was going to move forward.

I lowered my head on my arms resting on the bar. Leon's words didn't feel right—or at least that was what I was trying to tell myself. He had never been that crude toward me.

"Rough night, eh?" said a sweet, heavily accented voice.

Lifting my head, I saw a tall, white ceramic mug. The warmth of tea wafted toward me. "I'm sorry, but the bar is closed for the night."

"Oh yeah, I know, although you seem like you could use a cup of tea and some encouragement."

I looked up to see a woman with golden hair braided down the right side. Her eyes were closer to the bridge of her nose, beautifully bold. Her Cupid's bow was predominantly set over full lips. Her face was strong, but the button tip of her nose made up the softness.

There was no way... I studied her more as she walked around the bar. She hiked up her high-necked, deep green dress with gold embroidery before she took the stool next to me. She looked to be in her mid-forties, and for sure she was not one of the locals, nor was she of this time.

I recognized her only by her resemblance to Leon. I needed

to put what happened at the fire behind me and be polite to her. I took a deep breath. "Please excuse me, for I am an American. Do I bow before you?"

She leaned against the bar and chortled as she twirled her beer mug. "I take it you know who I am."

"Queen Astrid. I see your son in your features."

I couldn't wrap my mind around it; I was having a conversation with Leon's deceased mother. Gods were one thing, but now the dead were coming to me as well. Nonetheless, it felt natural, as if it was Ruby before me.

"Leon is out at the Hughes' house tonight—that would be the white house with the green trim about two miles out of town. Gordon is Bartholomew's descendant, and Ruby is Gavin's. They will welcome you with open arms."

"I haven't come for my son." She slid the mug closer to me. "I've come to speak to you."

"Thank you." I took the mug into my hands. "Forgive me, but I think you should go see Leon. He's having a difficult time and is not himself right now."

The warmth of the mug was overshadowed by the warmth of her hand on mine as she leaned closer to me. "He was wrong for every word that he said, but please, just for tonight, forgive him. Fear makes men muttonheads, and my son is no different. He's scared of losing you."

That was a little too late. "I've already given your ring back." I shrugged my shoulders "He thinks of me in a way that is not true."

I was not chasing these guys for personal gain. That was never what this was about. I wanted to save King Leon's legacy because, growing up, I needed that symbol to believe in. I never wanted to believe what I was taught. I wanted to believe that the bond between two people was strong and unique to only them: that such a bond was magical.

"No, no, no." She set her beer down before even taking a drink. "He didn't mean to push you away. He just doesn't know how to handle these emotions. Please, for tonight, put that argument aside—he loves you."

I studied her as she took a drink of her beer. She could have been with Leon instead of trying to fix things on my end. "Kek is coming for me before Monday, isn't he?" I whispered, fear rising within me that this was going to go down sooner than later.

"Yes." She sat up straight and crossed her arms. "He cannot be trusted. It ends tonight. You will end him before he has a chance to get you tomorrow."

I shook my head. "I'm not ready. I need more time with him—I have nothing planned out. There has been no consistency to where he brings me, I—" My heart started racing and I couldn't bring myself to speak. My hands trembled as my fingertips went numb, the warmth seeping out. I was going to fail.

"My child." Queen Astrid leaned closer to me, placing her hand on my shoulder. "It is going to be okay. The goddesses in Aaru are here to protect you. However, you are the one who must kill Kek again." Her hand slid down my arm to my wrist, and the softness of her hand was replaced by the sleekness of metal.

Glancing down, I saw a thick gold bracelet gracing my wrist. I traced my finger along the rows of teal and red stones, stopping at the center of the bracelet on a depiction of a woman wearing a horned headdress—Hathor.

"Kek should have never regained access to you after you broke the curse. The curse was based on true love... It was fair for Osiris to bring Kek back, but that is where it should have ended. I don't think Ra knows what is going on. Hathor is going to speak with Ra, but regardless of that, you need to prove yourself."

This was just getting more and more complicated. I, the mortal, was going to have to prove myself to Ra and kill another Egyptian god. If he didn't listen to Hathor, how was I to sway him? Hathor was his daughter, and I was just a mortal.

Queen Astrid had to know the answers.

"How? I am no god. How am I going to prove myself to the god of all Egyptian gods?"

"With a decoration." She raised my right hand. "This isn't going to be some massive sword fight. Place this hand on Kek's chest and tell him what you feel in your heart."

"Whoa." I leaned away from Queen Astrid. "Are you sure that will work? I mean, I have told Kek I don't want to go to Aaru a bunch of times, but he still presses the issue. And not to mention it irritates him to no end if I talk about Leon. He's going to lose his temper with me, wipe my mind, then kill me so I can go to Aaru with him."

There had to be more to bringing Kek down than words. The first time around, I had to spear him in the heart, then cut his head off.

"Sometimes the hardest things in life are just being honest with ourselves, *being* ourselves." She pointed to the cup. "Drink."

I wanted to laugh. "When I fail..." I held the cup to my lips, then stopped. The realization was setting in. Kek was going to take my memories, but Leon would still have a lifetime to cope with his memories of our last interaction. "Tell Leon that earlier wasn't the shape of my heart. I am sorry for my words toward him; they were unfair. Please make sure he knows I didn't surrender to Kek willingly. Tell him I love him forever."

"You are not going to fail." She smiled softly. "I believe in you."

I felt warmth rush through me instantly as the liquid hit my tongue. Then I felt the coolness of the bar counter on my cheek, my eyes closing. There was a second where I could feel Queen Astrid grazing her fingernails through my hair, as I did with Leon, and her soft words whispered in my ears. It wasn't a language I knew, but it was comforting as the darkness crept in.

CHAPTER 46

A warm breeze kissed my eyelids, opening them to the blue skies above with white, pillowy clouds. Sitting up on my elbows, I discovered I was on the side of a hill surrounded by tall grass swaying in the breeze like waves kissing the shoreline. Sitting up further, I drew my knees closer to my chest. I was no longer in my jeans and hoodie, but navy shorts and a white tank top knotted above my right hip.

"Your heart is sad." A hand ran across my back. "I can feel it in my own." Kek delicately drew me into his chest. "Why, My Queen?"

My anxiety rose as I closed my eyes. I needed to do as Queen Astrid had told me. It was going to be all right—I could tell Kek wasn't going to hurt me.

I fanned my hand out before him.

"Oh my."

Those two little words carried so much emotion; there was sincere excitement hidden within sorrow. His lips rested against the side of my head, and his arms tightened around me, then he drew me onto his lap.

If I was going to do this dance with him, I needed to follow his lead. Imagining he was Leon, I rested my arms on his shoulders, hiding my face in his neck. I was supposed to speak from my heart, but I needed to get my head and heart on the same page.

Kek's head rested against mine as he softly spoke. "If you

need more time for your heart to heal, I will allow it."

"Pardon?" I drew back until I could see the truth.

His eyes narrowed, though not in an upset manner. "It's not ideal…" He rested his right hand above my left breast. "However, your heart is filled with fear and sorrow. With the wedding off, I will allow a longer courtship so you may become more comfortable with our arrangements."

Queen Astrid's words overlaid my feeling of excitement; she had warned me that he couldn't be trusted. This could just be a ruse to get me to let down my guard, then he would sweep in and kill me without a second thought. It was time, but I needed him vulnerable first.

My hand rested against his cheek, allowing his head to nestle into my palm. "That is very kind of you, Kek. I appreciate it."

His eyes moved to my lips, pressing our foreheads together. This was a horrible idea; I knew that look.

"Kek," my hand lowered to his chest, "please, no."

"Of course." He leaned in closer, his breath kissing my lips. "I am a gentleman."

Was he trying to convince me or himself?

His bottom lip grazed my bottom lip, and instantly I reared back.

"Kek, no." I pressed his chest harder, the fear rising. I just needed to breathe. With an exhale, I said, "I'm sorry, but no. It doesn't matter what world we are in; this isn't right." I tapped my left breast with my left hand, leaving my other hand over his heart. "If it was right, I would return your feelings, but I can't. My head, my heart, and even my body is wrapped up in that old bartender. Why?" I shrugged. "I have no idea. However, I do know that it's not one-sided. He loves me just as much as I love him. Our love broke that vampire curse—that must say something."

His head dropped a touch. "A sword to the chest and cutting my head off ended that curse," he sneered.

I felt like there was no way talking from my heart could save me, but I was going to try. "I never came to Journey looking for love; I was looking to *defend* love from my sinister family. I don't regret it happening, either—I would fight everyone and pray to all the gods to be with him again."

He snorted. "I never came to Journey looking for love either—that was the last step to ending all of this. But the first time I saw you out on that run, your body spoke to me. I just wanted to be in your world, whichever it may be." Kek raised his head. "Let him go. An old king is no match for an Egyptian god."

"Status doesn't matter to me; it's the love in his head and heart that counts."

Kek's eyes widened as he pinched his lips together. "There will be no love."

"Why?"

He glanced to the side, then back to me. "He's dead."

"What?" I shrieked. There was no way—this had to be a ruse.

"The doctor is going to end him tonight." His hand moved up to my cheek, trying to brush my tears away. "It's time to let him go."

"No," I sobbed, "don't kill him. Let him live and you can have me, but please don't kill him. He is my peace...my laughter...my comfort...my heart. Darkness will set in if he dies. I will never be the same."

Kek's jaw dropped as he gasped. His hand moved up my back, into my hair, then he thrust my head against his. "This is pointless," he growled. "Osiris is going to bring me back. And until he does, you will belong to that doctor of yours."

"No." I tried to draw back, but he refused to let me go. "I will never be yours." Glancing down, I saw his shirt was saturated with blood—the bracelet must have stabbed him. "I will stab you a thousand times if I have to, but my heart will never belong to you."

His breathing was getting shallower, his hand subtly releasing me. He moved his other hand up to caress my cheek. "You are my queen," he whispered. "We will be together again."

His eyes turned white, his pupils disappeared, his hand dropped, and he fell back into the grass.

Projecting from the bracelet on my wrist was a dagger.

I had speared him in the heart.

My heart raced. I wasn't in the mortal world—I had killed Kek in Duat. My fingers tingled until they went numb.

Ra was going to punish me when he found out.

Falling to the side, everything went black.

CHAPTER 47

The sound of Leon's voice filled the air.

Someone grasped my hand and gently patted my cheeks.

"Nora," Leon said nervously, "please wake up."

I wasn't ready to open my eyes. They weren't ready to open yet, exhaustion defeating me. Why couldn't this crap go down in the morning? I wasn't meant for this middle-of-the-night drama; I was a morning person.

"Please..."

Arms shifted me, and I recognized the familiarity of Leon's embrace.

It was no longer a matter of exhaustion; I couldn't respond. My head was limp, and my arms moved like noodles as he tugged me closer.

"Please, Nora." His hand glided against my cheek and his lips brushed against my forehead. "I don't know how Kek treats you or what kind of life he is promising, but I know my love for you, and I know your love for me. Even when I'm being ridiculous, I still believe in us—do not trade us for him. I am yours—forever."

There was a disturbance, and I was suddenly dropped, my temple hitting stone floor. The pain promptly opened my eyes to a blurred commotion before me: Nick slammed Leon onto the floor, straddling Leon's waist and pinning him by the upper arms, inhibiting his movement, giving Nick the upper hand to reach for Sigrid on the table beside him. Leon regained his strength and threw a punch. Nick held out his arm, blocking the blow. With a flash, Nick poised Sigrid above Leon's chest.

"NO!" I screamed, pulling myself up with the assistance of a barstool. "NO!"

It was a waste of breath. Nick ignored my outburst and stabbed Sigrid into Leon's chest with such great force that Leon's legs rose, then dropped again. His feet parted, as if it was the final sign it was over.

I dropped to my knees on the floor. Kek had won; Leon was dead. I knew this, but I felt frozen, unable to process what I had just witnessed.

Sigrid clattering against the floor echoed throughout the bar, covering my whimpers.

Nick snarled. "You brought a fake sword to a fight—you truly are lame," he sneered.

Excitement rose within me; Sigrid had refused Nick's command!

Looking up, I watched Nick throw a right hook, his fist successfully connecting with Leon's left eye. Nick leaned forward with his head lowered to Leon, speaking so low it was impossible to hear, especially with the ringing in my ears.

As if I was being controlled by someone else, I pushed myself off my knees and lunged onto Nick's back. The man was a brute—it didn't faze him in the slightest. I drew the pin I had found in the lake from my hair and stabbed it into the nape of his neck. The pin glowed just as it had when Freyja led me to it.

Nick's back caved for a second before he collapsed upon Leon, causing me to roll onto the floor with my hand caught on his back. Nick's shirt was saturated with red just as Kek's shirt had been only minutes ago. Hathor's bracelet had been released again and speared Nick in the back—in his heart.

Drawing my hand back, I watched the golden blade reveal itself, dripping with Nick's blood. My heart raced as my hand trembled, numb again. Standing up, I slowly backed into the bar, startled by it pressing into my back, causing me to drop to my knees again. I had just killed an innocent man.

Calvin weaved his arms through Nick's, pinning him against his chest.

Leon sat up, breathing deeply, resting his arms on his knees with his head lowered. He was alive—Kek had failed again. This new elation was the final drop on the roller coaster of the night. Falling to my side, the cool floor kissed my cheek as I watched Leon for a moment longer. His head rose, and our eyes met as if for the final time. A single tear expelled from his right eye, and I followed it down his cheek until green blocked my view.

With Queen Astrid here to protect me and everything else ended, my eyes blurred and closed.

"No one will have access to her until that atrocious man is out of my view. You there—" Queen Astrid must have been gesturing toward someone as she paused, "make the arrangements to send him back to his homeland. You will not accompany him on his journey; send your father and middle brother. You shall return to be her guard until further notice. Send for your youngest brother at once."

Hands slid underneath me—Leon. More than anything I wanted to wrap my arms around him and hide in his neck, but no part of me was willing to move. It was starting to get frustrating that I kept losing control over my body.

"I'm going to take her upstairs."

"No, Leon." Queen Astrid spoke with authority. "Leave her be until her guard returns."

"I will not leave my queen lying on the floor."

"Your queen?" Queen Astrid repeated, baffled. "She wears no ring—how is she your queen?"

I was almost glad I couldn't be a part of this.

"She was... Until I spoke foolishly to her. I was wrong. I disappointed her in so many ways tonight." I felt him lightly brush my cheek with his hand. "She needs to open her eyes so I can tell her how sorry I truly am." His hand ran down my arm, then again to my cheek. "She's cold to the touch. I'm taking her upstairs."

"No, Leon, she needs to be left—"

Before she could finish her sentence, Leon cut her off. "Is she with him?"

"I don't know, my little prince. I think she may be in shock. Tonight has not been the easiest for her."

No joke. I had stabbed two guys tonight. My normal night count was zero. I literally had blood on my hands of both a god and a human. And the worst part was the night wasn't over—who knew what would happen when Osiris or Ra found Kek dead in Duat?

Leon shifted me and tucked something soft around my arms and upper torso.

"What are you doing?" Queen Astrid's voice echoed with bemusement.

"She's freezing, I'm trying to warm her up." I felt Leon's forehead press against mine as he softly spoke to me. "I know that you are stubborn and determined when it comes to your heart. Listen to your heart—listen to my heart. I love you." Warmth fell onto my cheek. A hand rested on my leg. "This isn't enough. I'm going to run upstairs to get a blanket and see if I can find any clothes she might have left up there."

"Why would she have left clothes at your apartment?" Queen Astrid sounded vexed.

I knew enough about the 1800s to know that even kissing was scandalous. Once more, I was glad I could only listen.

"Because," Leon jostled me, "when I was transitioning, she took it upon herself to care for me day and night. And—" he tittered, "she was concerned that I was going to lose the bar, so she and Sean opened it back up."

"Why would you lose the bar?"

"To her, I was a bartend—"

Queen Astrid cut him off. "She didn't know? That can't be—she had to know. You have been the king for the last—"

"I never told her, and it was forbidden to be spoken about to anyone outside of our kingdom. I wasn't expecting to live much longer; things were changing, and I thought I was dying." His grip on me tightened. "It didn't change anything when she found out the truth, either. Now Kek's meddling is changing things."

My heart began to race. I gasped for air, my body trembling and numbness moving to my hands and up my arms. I had been starting to warm up against Leon, but now I felt as if I was in an ice bath. I heard words being spoken around me but comprehended none of them.

"Open your eyes and sit up," ordered a stern female voice—that wasn't Queen Astrid, or even Ruby.

My eyes finally opened to the familiar sight of Leon's bar. I pushed myself up on the counter where Leon must have settled me. I shifted, preparing to jump down, but stopped when I saw a lady dressed in a white sleeveless dress woven with intricate gold chains from which hung a gold pendant: cow horns against a disk-like sun. She wore the symbol of Hathor. I stared at her straight, shoulder-length onyx hair and nose that almost squared at the tip as mine did. Her eyes were emerald gems.

Slowly I tilted to the side, glancing at myself in the mirror behind the bar, then looked back to her again. The only difference between us was that she was a dark umber, while I was that northern pale.

She glanced back at the mirror, then to me. "We are really uncanny, and this explains why that little amphibian wouldn't leave you alone."

My words juddered as I gazed upon her pendant. "Are you..." Crap, I was drawing a blank on how to properly address her. "Lady Hathor?"

"Only the Goddesses of Love should be the ones to deliver the good news to you." She held her left hand out to me. "Kek is no more. He shall never have access to this world again or to you in the afterlife."

I rested my wrist in her palm, imagining she wanted her bracelet back.

Hathor clasped her other hand over the bracelet. "He's a pain and only wants what he can't have. And since I am tied to Horus, he was trying to take you as an imitation." She glanced up. "A beautiful one, at that. So, if Osiris brings him back, Horus—his son and my husband—has given me his word that he is going to take Kek's eyes as punishment. I have also spoken to my father, Ra, and you have his protection from all other Egyptian gods going forward."

My head cocked to the side as my eyes widened. "Thank you" fell from my lips. I was too shocked to think of anything else; my mind was spinning. Kek had only wanted me because I was the mirror image of Hathor. Thinking back on it, I wondered if that was why he never addressed me by my name, only as his queen.

"Well then." Hathor ran her index finger and thumb down my jawline. "I must be off." Her other hand raised my right hand as she slid warm metal onto my middle finger.

Glancing down immediately, I saw a gold ring with a round red gemstone in the middle of an intricate U shape. It was her symbol.

Before I could say anything, she spoke again. "I am proud of you for the way that you handled Kek. There isn't any other mortal or even god that I am more proud to have wearing my hieroglyph." With a soft grin and a pat on the shoulder, she walked into the back room.

Moments later, a diamond-blue light flickering about drew my attention from the back room door. It was the same light from the forest that led me to the hair pin and Sigrid. It darted from bottle to bottle as if looking for a specific one, finding none of them pleasing.

It dawned on me, and I was almost certain which bottle it was looking for. Promptly I let out a sharp whistle, then leaned to my left, tapping the countertop with my index finger, indicating the cabinet below where Leon kept a spare bottle of his pirate whiskey.

Two glasses appeared as the amber bottle rose from underneath the counter. The glasses filled until they were a quarter full, then the bottle settled next to my agate heart atop the counter.

My amused expression dropped as I stared at the heart, thinking of Nick.

"You're spiraling," said a sweet, soft voice. "When he returns to Balvin, he will have no memory of ever meeting you." She must have been the Norse goddess Freyja—she was breathtaking. Her hair was a soft gold, curled over her ample breasts. Her widow's peak was covered by a knotted gold piece that matched the knotting on Leon's parents' rings and the hair pin I had found in the lake. I was in awe of her beauty.

"How will that be possible with the trial coming up? Forrest already has Nick on the witness list..."

"Kek didn't tell you about your wedding gift?"

"You mean to kill Leon?"

"No," she waved her hand before me. "Kek learned in detail what happened to you in that parking lot." This wasn't going to be good. "He wanted to give you the ultimate wedding gift, so he paid your family a visit by inhabiting one of their cats. Your sister had passed out but had candles burning in her room. Your mother was in the linen closet with Ivan, while your father and grandmother were in the study talking."

"Please, forgive me." After everything, I couldn't piece together what she was saying. "It's been an evening and a half—how is that a wedding gift?"

"Fire," Freyja said with a deep sigh.

No more needed to be said; my mind filled with images.

Kek, the white Persian, tail on fire, ran along the wall of the main hallway. He stopped before the linen closet, then dragged his butt against the carpet, igniting the floor, giggling as he pranced off to the office.

"He ensured that there was no escaping; he wanted it to be the most painful revenge for how they treated you."

Air moved swiftly in and out of my lungs, panic setting in. "Oh my god."

"Hey." She rubbed my shoulder. "Don't think about what Kek did—remember, you are free. Free from Kek, free from everything in the States. There isn't a soul down there that knows who you are now." She lowered herself before me, staring me straight in the eyes. "Your life is going to begin first thing tomorrow." Standing, she held up her drink. "Tonight, you and I drink to celebrate your victories!"

"Are Hathor, Leon, and Queen Astrid going to be joining us?"

"Hathor?" Her chin tucked in. "No. Queen Astrid needed to get back," her lips curled into a mischievous smile, "and we don't need the king here right now. I don't want to sit here listening to him grovel at your feet for being cretinous all night."

"Okay," I tittered.

"We are going to enjoy this, then I am going to give you your rest. Tomorrow is a new day, and you will not wake up with a heavy heart. Today's events should never be forgotten—however, I promise your heart and your mind will be filled with peace."

CHAPTER 48

Leon was dangling off a pastel green, regal-looking sofa with elaborately carved champagne-gold trim and rolled English arms. He couldn't have been comfortable. His blanket was rolled up on the floor.

Quietly I tiptoed over to him, shook out his blanket, and tucked it over his body. His head was still painfully angled, but he slept peacefully. There was no way to correct his head without waking him. Since he seemed at peace, I was going to leave well enough alone.

Resting against the windowsill, all I could do was appreciate how beautiful it was going to be today. The sun was slowly rising, making the snow glisten as if a pixie had sprinkled white and gold glitter about. It must have been close to 8:00 a.m. If my life was normal, I would have gone for a run or made breakfast.

Last night's conversation from the fire played out in my mind, ruining my perfect view. This was going to be a mess when Leon woke up. I don't know why he had brought me to the castle or stayed with me—I had half expected to wake up in my bedroom at the Hughes' house, not here. Even with his little confession after I returned from Duat, I didn't know how to fix the words and accusations we had fired at each other.

"Nora." Panic rose in Leon's voice; he must have seen the bed and assumed I left or was taken. "Nora!" he cried out.

I peeked my head out from the curtain to see Leon clenching his chest, holding his necklace within his shirt. His bottom jaw quivered as his chest rose with deep breaths. His brows made abstract art on his forehead, although this time it wasn't fun.

It felt as if time halted as I rushed to him, falling onto my knees. His hair was damp as I raised his head into my chest. "Leon," I whispered, dragging my nails through his hair, "it's okay." He needed some of that peace Freyja had bestowed upon me. Gently I kissed the top of his head and, without removing my lips, whispered, "I love you."

His jaw still hung as he continued to take deep breaths, the pace of them starting to slow as he peered into my eyes.

I rested my forehead against his, the tips of our noses touching as his breathing leveled out. Once more I ran my hand through his hair, trying to provide him with familiar comfort.

His head turned, trying to examine my wrist. Giving up, with a soft force he grasped my wrist and lowered it before him. "Nora—" His eyes widened and his breathing began to increase again. He grasped my other wrist and held both of them up. "Nora..."

He was looking for Kek's mark, but all signs of Kek had been removed from my body at some point—though at what point, I was unsure. I still wore the symbols of other gods, Hathor's ring on my right hand and Freyja's pin in my hair.

Leon may not have known the meanings behind my ring or hair pin, but he knew there was one more place Kek had branded me. It was the worst possible spot—Kek knew what he was doing when he placed it there. Even after his death, I was anxious to see how my relationship with Leon was going to play out going forward.

Standing up, I drew the hem of the shirt over my head, then tossed it onto the bed.

Leon's lips pinched as he ran the tip of his index finger just below my bikini line.

I drew his chin up with my index finger and thumb, then

spoke sternly. "He's dead…again, but this time Hathor is going to make sure of it. Turns out Hathor disliked Kek from the start and was upset that Osiris even brought him back. Kek will never have access to me again."

Leon's eyes were wider than the disk on Hathor's headpiece. He had just recovered from a panic attack; I was going to send him into another with all of this, but he needed to hear it. Gently I trailed my thumb across his lower lip. "Freyja is also involved—she's the one that gave me the hair pin, used to undo Kek's curse on Nick. She promised me that no other gods would ever have access to me. I am now protected by all Norse gods as well."

"Are you real?" His hand rose to my sternum, then his fingertips danced down to my belly button.

Before I could respond, Leon engulfed me in his arms with his damaged cheek pressed against my breast, listening to hear if my heart still beat.

I let him have his moment, knowing I couldn't rush him when he was clearly in need of comfort.

"It's still in there," I whispered as I ran my fingers through his hair like a comb. Before I could finish my statement that it belonged to him, Leon cocooned me in his arms.

Gently I wiped his cheek. "It's okay; it's over now." Kek was no more; we were free to move forward.

"No," he whined, tears streaming, "please, no… I'm so sorry for everything. I never wanted any of this for you. This is exactly why I never wanted to fall in love. Well, I never thought it would go to this extreme, but I never wanted this for you."

Where did that come from? It almost sounded as if he was pleading with me to stay. "Leon, this wasn't what I…"

"I apologize for my actions and my words." He drew my head down to his. "They were wrong in every form. I was beside myself: a god was threatening you from another world. He was being inappropriate with you. I had no way to access him, no way of protecting you. I couldn't breathe. I felt like I was going to lose you. I was going to lose my sun's warmth, my bird's song, my flower's essence, my heart. I know why Kek wanted you, but just because he was a god didn't mean he deserved you." He gasped. "He may be dead, but he still won."

The only way to fix this was to be clear and direct. I sat back up on his legs. "Sit up," I ordered him sternly, crossing my arms against my chest.

Once he was upright, I reached for the hem of his shirt and pulled it off. I was going to show him that he was wrong, that Kek didn't win. Leaning in, I blocked his view from what I was doing. Swiftly, I undid the clasp of his necklace, sliding the ring off the chain and placing it on my left ring finger.

"Nora," Leon shifted, "what are you doing?"

I could feel the bars of wrinkles appearing on my forehead as I gave Leon a wide-eyed stare. I pressed my right index finger above the scar on his chest as I held my left ring finger up. "Do you love me?"

His chest deflated with relief, the corner of his lips curling up. He reached around my head, drawing my lips to his for a moment before moving to my forehead and gently kissing it with his hands on either side of my face.

I sat back, crossing my arms again. "Well...? I am still waiting for my answer," I snarked, trying to hold in my grin.

Unexpectedly and silently, with his hands on my hips, Leon shifted me closer to him. His torso curved as his lips made a path from my left breast up to my neck. His breath warmed my skin. "I might have to show you."

I liked his way of answering. There was a sense of relief with his playful actions and ravishing moments that things were going to go back to how it was that afternoon before the ball. There had been so much strain on our relationship lately—I wanted to be lazy and forget every awful thing we said to each other and call a truce. Judging by Leon's current actions, it felt as if he wanted the same thing.

"After last night, I didn't think I would ever feel your lips again." Leon rubbed his knuckles up and down my spine.

"I guess with that," I rested my arms on his shoulders, tickling his hairline after he drew me back to his chest, "I am going to have to make up for all the kisses that you missed out on last night and kiss all your injuries." Leaning in, I kissed the little gash below his eye. Nick had done a number on Leon under Kek's curse: his neck, left eye, left pec, and upper arms were all blue and purple.

I trailed kisses down his chest and back up, making my way to his neck. He angled his head, giving me more access to his neck as his breathing deepened. His fingers curled into the lower side of my butt cheeks, grinding me against him.

His injuries seemed to disappear after I kissed them, replacing his pain with desire and pleasure as well.

With his neck cleared, I moved up to his jawline as his hand moved up my back, pulling me flush against him. His dark eyes were still dilated.

I was holding on hope that I could heal his mind as I had his body. I softly turned his head, and, with all my new faith in Freyja, kissed his left temple.

Nothing happened, so I turned his head and kissed his other temple. Nothing.

I bit my lip as I studied Leon. He had to be filled with anxiety and horror; if I could physically cure him, I should be able to mentally as well. My gaze fixed on those four perfect circles on his neck. I felt like that little square was the perfect little box to unlock all his consternation.

With a deep inhale, I rested my lips perfectly in the forbidden target that constantly gave me anxiety during our intimate moments. Leon's knees drew up, pressing into my back as he whimpered as if he was in pain.

"Don't stop," Leon whined. His hand moved to the back of my head, ensuring I couldn't stop.

Something wasn't right. More than anything, I wanted to

stop, even though he had ordered me not to, but there was something preventing me from moving my lips from the once-forbidden square.

A moment later, his legs fell, and his head dropped into my trembling hand. "It's okay."

I drew my hand back and moved from him. "What happened?"

Leon grasped my waist and pulled me back to his lap as if I was a doll. Then his hand moved down my arm until it secured against my hand. "It's all right. You didn't hurt me at all." Gently, he kissed my hand. "I saw every event in my life play out from the night Kek damned me to this morning. A lady was speaking to me, telling me she was giving me peace from the misery that these events caused. She told me that I—no, correction—" Leon tapped my chest with his fingertips, "that *we* were entitled to a beautiful life together for many years to come. She would protect us going forward to the end of our days and beyond. It was odd, because at first glance I thought it was you."

My chest dropped with relief—I knew exactly what had happened. "Egyptian gods are not supposed to be allowed to enter our world in their own form anymore." I was unsure how Hathor had done it in the bar last night, though, granted, her father is the god of all Egyptian gods. "They need a host. Kek was infatuated with me because I am the pale version of Hathor."

"Hathor..." Leon raised my right hand, inspecting the ring on my middle finger.

"Hathor." I leaned a little closer. "You were just kissed by the Egyptian goddess Hathor." I pinched my lips and wrinkled my nose playfully. "What do you have to say for yourself?"

He buried his fingers in my hair, drawing my face closer to his. "That we need to listen to that wise god by enjoying living." His lip grazed my bottom lip. "First, I am going to enjoy more of your breathtaking lips." His lips moved down to my chin and then my jaw. "And every other mesmerizing part of you until they come for us to get ready for our wedding. Our wedding is this afternoon."

"Wait." I frowned. "Today is Sunday." Warm excitement blossomed in my chest and cheeks.

Leon snorted as he raised my left hand. "Since you already put your ring back on," he interlocked his fingers between mine with our hands still raised, "I hope you will say yes to marrying me this afternoon."

I could have tackled him or screamed it from the top of my lungs—instead, my bottom lip trembled, and tears swelled as I nodded mutely.

The sunlight peeking through the window was lighting his eyes like black star sapphires, reminding me of every moment I caught him admiring me. I could never imagine that blank canvas of King Leon drawn in with such a wondrous man as the one before me.

"In your eyes I can see the reflection of the richest man in history." His lips moved up into a soft grin. "There is nothing richer or even more powerful than our love."

ABOUT ATMOSPHERE PRESS

Founded in 2015, Atmosphere Press was built on the principles of Honesty, Transparency, Professionalism, Kindness, and Making Your Book Awesome. As an ethical and author-friendly hybrid press, we stay true to that founding mission today.

If you're a reader, enter our giveaway for a free book here:

SCAN TO ENTER
BOOK GIVEAWAY

If you're a writer, submit your manuscript for consideration here:

SCAN TO SUBMIT
MANUSCRIPT

And always feel free to visit Atmosphere Press and our authors online at atmospherepress.com. See you there soon!

ABOUT THE AUTHOR

EDA SCOTT was once a little girl hiding her love for writing. Today she no longer hides her passion for writing. She enjoys writing romance with a sprinkle of paranormal to add to that fast-paced emotional rollercoaster.

Eda lives in the Midwest, where the weather is unpredictable, with her husband, son, and daughter. During the day Eda is a bookkeeper at a local consulting firm. Her evenings (and weekends) are filled with children's activities and spending time with her family. At night when the children go to bed her passion comes to life. Unless there is a concert, then you will find her there.